The Stone is Turned

THE COMPOUND SERIES: Book Five

LYNN VADNEY

Desert Willow Publishing

Copyright © 2015

THE STONE IS TURNED
The Compound Series: Book Five

By Lynn Vadney

Desert Willow Publishing, PO Box 7719, Abilene, Texas 79608-7719

Printed by Lightning Source, Inc.

Paperback ISBN 978-1-939838-17-9
E-book   ISBN 978-1-939838-18-6

Cover photography by Janet Vadney

The Stone is Turned, book five of the
Compound Series, is dedicated to our tireless
public servants. This series has been about our
nation in crisis. May our leaders, in whatever
capacity, remain fearless and dedicated.

Characters

Major characters

Jack Thorne — U.S. Navy Seal
Lily Jacqueline "Jackie" Schwartz — baroness
Ralph Merrill — Lily's bodyguard
John Thorne — U.S. Navy Seal
Robert Somerton — local commander
Lieutenant Bruce Williams — local officer
Mr. Patterson — regional trader
Lieutenant Curtis Jones — local officer
Reginald "Reggie" Patterson — Mr. Patterson's son
Lawrence Brighton — computer tech at the compound
Martin "Max" Maxton — M.D.
Doug Kasper — baron
Matt Finke — baron
Wayne Brashear — U.S. Marine Brigadier General
Al Porcelain — friend of Lily

Minor characters

Tim March — mechanic and driver
Ryan Sealy — U.S. Navy Seal
Linda Owens — clinic office manager
Joey March — Tim's son, mechanic at clinic
Jupiter Worthington, Jr. — vendor in market
Armando Cuevas — café owner
Ricky — deceased sniper
Brad Kraft — U.S. Navy Seal
Montgomery "Monkey" Preston — master carpenter
Jorge Ramirez — young construction worker
Tyrone "Tyrant" Tyler — deposed commander
Jeff Clark — engineer
Clarence Barton — deceased baron
"Thai" — young teen
Chris Morris — M.D.
Spencer Blakely — deposed commander
Stanley Williamson — head engineer
Mr. Hobbs — provides cell phone service
Marvin Finley — computer tech for the commander

Minor characters (continued)

Frank Smith — attacked Mr. Barton
Darla Smith — Frank's wife
Gertrude "Trudy" Debauch — Frank's mother
Angelica "Angel" Gonzales — Jorge's girlfriend
Walter Schwartz III — Lily's deceased husband
Bob Royal — Lily's oldest brother
Gary Brown — U.S. Navy Seal
Marie Gonzales — Angel's mother
Jill Baker — M.D.
Melissa "Missy" Smith — Frank's mistress
Henry Davis — Frank and Darla's son-in-law
Serena Hermann — James Hermann's wife
James Hermann — engineer
Buster — leader of the scavengers
Eva Johnson — RN, head nurse
Lynnette Thurman — RN
Rene Collier — lab tech
Tommy Walker — counselor
Brett Cockrell — irritating young man
Ed Randolph — M.D.
Tom Royal — Lily's middle brother
Cisco — Mr. Barton's former enforcer
Officer Hayes — deceased officer
Rose Williams — Buster's wife
Jenny Walker — Jeff's girlfriend
Josie Vaughn — teenager
Todd Jenson — U.S. Marine Colonel
Preston "Posse" Posey — elderly man
Gordon O'Neil — owns radio station
Cathy Porcelain — Al's wife
Walt Schwartz IV — Lily's son
Stephanie Thorne — John's wife
Josephine "Jodie" Vaughn — Josie's mother
Randall Laird — Mr. Finke's mechanic
Mindy Merrill — Ralph's wife
Marissa Rae Worthington — Jupiter's wife

Bit players have very minor roles

AUTHOR'S NOTE

All five books of The Compound Series are written as stand alone novels, each complete in itself with any references to events in other books explained. If, however, you are reading the entire series, or even just two books, a chronology may be helpful since the series is not in chronological order.

Books one and two, *Sinking Sand; Grab the Pole* and *NOT the least bit SORRY,* begin two and one-half years after massive terrorists' attacks destroy society. Both begin on Labor Day, the first Monday in September. Book one covers twelve days in the life of U.S. Navy Seal John Thorne. Book two covers three and one-half months, ending in mid-December, and relates the tragic events set in place by Frank Smith.

Book three, *The Full Weight of Their Survival,* is a prequel to books one and two. It begins in February, just under one year after the terrorists' attacks, and covers a year in the life of Lily Schwartz, coming to a conclusion at the end of January, just short of two years after the attacks.

Book four, *Stephanie's Anguish,* is a prequel to books one and two and a sequel to book three. It begins at the end of March, two years after the attacks, and ends in mid-August just before the beginning of books one and two.

Book five, *The Stone is Turned,* wraps up this post-apocalyptic tale. It begins in May a little over three years after the attacks and ends in early December, three years and nine months after the attacks.

Book 3: *The Full Weight of Their Survival*
   One year after the attacks: February to the next January
Book 4: *Stephanie's Anguish*
   Two years after the attacks: March to August
Book 1: *Sinking Sand; Grab the Pole*
   Two and one-half years after the attacks: September
Book 2: *NOT the least bit SORRY*
   Two and one-half years after the attacks: September to December
Book 5: *The Stone is Turned*
   Three years after the attacks: May to December

PROLOGUE

It has been three years since terrorists brought the nations of the world to their knees. On the North American continent, life has been brutal under the slave society which emerged from the chaos as men fought each other for survival. Women and children have no rights. Men have only the rights they gain by force. Alliances constantly shift.

Law and order is gaining a toehold in one small Texas town; it has been a slow process. The first commander was ruthless: ruling by fear and intimidation. A bold and bloody coup by two of his officers was a necessary first step. The new co-commanders outlawed guns, imposed a curfew, and initiated a tax on the local power barons instead of relying solely on bribes and profits from various activities such as the slave trade, commerce, and scavenging.

Hope lies in Commander Robert Somerton's powerful ally, Baroness Lily Jacqueline "Jackie" Schwarz—the exception to the rule that women do not have rights. The capable widow has expanded her operations over the last two years and now controls three major enterprises and is poised to add several more—some very lucrative. He has no regret over his alliance with the strong-willed woman. Last fall, she helped him depose his lawless co-commander, but will they be able to take down the brutal and extremely powerful barons without plunging the area into lawless chaos?

ONE

Former U.S. Navy Seal, Jack Thorne, leans forward. His military haircut reveals his perfectly oval head beneath the short brown stubs. His sun-bronzed skin is approximately the same shade of brown as his hair. "Jackie," he politely states, addressing Baroness Lily Jacquelyn Schwartz.

Seated in the front passenger seat of the fifteen passenger van, Lily swivels around to face him. The baroness is the petite leader of their out-of-town compound. Despite nearing forty, she retains her well-toned, gymnast's body. Her dark hair is cut short in a flattering style which compliments her attractive face. The laugh lines around her eyes are barely visible.

"Where are we authorized to go today?" Jack asks because of their tightly controlled postattack society. If an officer catches them in town without authorization, they will be taken into custody.

The capable widow replies, "The market, clinic, and everywhere in between; that covers most of the business section of town. As long as you're with the commander, you shouldn't have any problems. Call if you need authorization for any other area; I'm limited on the number of areas I can enter, or I would just authorize you for everywhere."

Tim March, their fifty-two-year-old mechanic, pulls to the curb at Guzman's Sidewalk Café. His straw-colored hair is graying at the temples, giving the man who has labored all his life the distinguished appearance of a financier. Ralph Merrell, Lily's six-foot-four and muscular bodyguard, slides open the door of the gray van. Jack steps onto the sidewalk, followed by his younger brother John Thorne, also a former U.S. Navy Seal.

Local authorities, Commander Robert Somerton and Lieutenant Bruce Williams are waiting for the two Seals. They are shaded from the afternoon sun of late May by a dingy umbrella over the patio table. The middle-aged commander is tall and his short-cropped hair has greyed, but brown hair is scattered amidst the now dominate grey. The lieutenant is younger and athletically thin. His recently trimmed coal-black hair reveals that his dark complexion comes from the sun. On the nape of his neck, a thin strip of white skin is visible between his hairline and his tan.

While waiting, they have been sipping iced beverages, a refreshing treat on the warm spring day. The lieutenant sets his glass down and lets his eyes track the stunning Baroness Jackie Schwartz as her driver pulls away from the curb; he is thankful that no one can read his mind, especially the baroness.

Jack walks up and extends his hand. "Commander."

The tall, grey-haired gentleman stands and shakes hands. His stocky build gives the appearance of athleticism, but it is an illusion. The former insurance salesman, turned unwilling officer of the law, has difficulty restraining the bulge in his midriff, especially since he has been reunited with his wife who is an excellent cook. His southern drawl is pleasing to the ear. "You're Jack, aren't you? And I presume this is John?"

John shakes the commander's hand as Jack extends his to the second officer. "That's right. And which Lieutenant is this?"

The lieutenant whips his eyes away from the disappearing grey van and thrusts his hand toward Jack. "Williams."

"Pleased to meet you, Sir."

"Nice to meet you."

"Gus," Commander Somerton calls to the proprietor. "We need two more colas please."

He sits down and turns back to the two tall, strapping, almost identical, young men who are settling into the flimsy plastic chairs. At least, they are young to the middle-aged commander, strapping from anybody's viewpoint. "Let's get down to business; we need your expertise." He lowers his voice to a whisper before speaking of former U.S. Navy Seals, Nolan Graves and Ryan Sealy. "The training Nolan and Ryan are giving the officers is greatly appreciated. You realize, of course, that many policemen were murdered in the lawlessness after the massive terrorists' attacks three years ago. Most of our officers have absolutely no training in law enforcement, including the two of us. I have to admit, though, that Lieutenant Williams has made rapid progress in his training."

The young lieutenant grins with an expression meant to be benign but which clearly conveys to the two well-trained men that he is hiding something.

Adrian "Gus" Guzman walks up, sets iced colas in front of Jack and John, and wipes his hands on the dirty apron covering his protruding belly. He has always been a 'large' man, but since he now sells the pastries whipped up by the capable chef of Baroness Schwartz, he finds himself indulging in sweet pleasure a little too often. "Anything else, Commander?"

"We might need a refill in a few minutes."

"I'll keep an eye on your drinks."

After watching Gus walk away, the commander turns back to his urgent conversation. "We need help on more than Nolan's self-defense tactics and Ryan's firearm training. We need help with strategy. I'm sorry to have to say it, but the criminal element here is quite competent in everything they do. We have officers who quake in their boots at walking their beat, especially at night. I have to send them out in two's and three's which means we can't cover the area adequately. Every time we have an officer killed in the line of duty, it gets worse. And ... quite often, we don't catch the culprit."

The commander looks up as a tractor-trailer rig rumbles down the narrow and congested city street. With a lop-sided scowl, he mutters, "Mr. Patterson's driver should know to stay off the downtown streets. They're supposed to use the route on the outskirts of town."

"Don't look at him!" Jack stridently whispers as he lifts his glass to his lips. He gulps the carbonated cola.

Commander Somerton quickly looks down at his drink. His knuckles turn white as he clinches his fists in anxiety.

"Yeah, we're totally involved in our conversation and drinks," Lieutenant Williams agrees. He lifts his glass to his lips, drains it, then turns his head away from the street and rattles his ice. "Hey Gus! We need refills!"

Since his back is to the street, John sets his glass down and whispers, "Do you have any rifles?"

"In the trunk." Commander Somerton nods toward his unique gold-colored squad car with the maroon racing stripe identifying it as an official vehicle of the formerly nameless town. In his eyes, it is unfortunate that the cell phone company dubbed the town Somerton, although usage has evolved into Somertonville. He forces a smile onto his face as the rig passes.

The commander's expression sobers. He pulls out his phone and quickly taps in the number for the northwest checkpoint. "Just checking; are you guys all right? … Okay, see ya'."

Concentrating on remembering the order which he has not turned in for table two, Gus sets four more glasses on the table and gathers the empties. When he turns away Commander Somerton taps in the number for the northeast checkpoint.

"They're out of sight," Jack whispers.

As the four men leap up from the table, Commander Somerton calls, "Put it on our tab."

Gus turns back. "No problem, Commander." He shakes his head at the sight of the four men leaving their untouched refills on the table. Their haste and the phone to the commander's ear are a dead giveaway that something has happened. Since he hears no gunfire, he merely turns away, trying to recall the almost forgotten order for table two.

Lieutenant Williams opens the trunk and hands rifles to the Thorne brothers. "You two are deputized today, but stay with us so the other officers won't shoot you for being armed. Grab more ammo."

He hands a rifle to Commander Somerton. "Any word on the other checkpoint?"

"Nah, I guess we lost the officers at the northeast checkpoint."

The commander turns to Jack. "You two take the lead. Lieutenant Williams and I will be right behind you, guarding your backs. Don't shoot anyone who looks like he might be one of Mr. Patterson's men being held hostage."

He punches in the number of Lieutenant Curtis Jones as he strides behind the three younger men.

In the busy market of jumbled stalls built with recycled boards on a large parking lot, Lily Schwartz walks up and smiles. "Mr. Patterson, I'm glad your health has improved."

"It took a while to regain my strength, but I feel almost youthful," the elderly baron, one of the most prosperous regional traders, replies.

He looks toward an approaching tractor-trailer rig and pushes his hat to the back of his balding head. Only a fringe of grey hair remains, a tiny strip circling the back of his head. "They're late, but it looks like your commercial dryers are finally here."

"We appreciate everything you do for us."

"I wonder why he's coming through town. All my drivers know to use the route that bypasses busy streets."

The smile deserts Lily's face.

Mr. Patterson walks toward the edge of the open-air market as the semi pulls to a stop. "He should also be coming from the east not the west. This might be one of the new ones. I guess he got lost."

The petite baroness strides after the tall baron and catches up as he nears the passenger side of the cab. She notes the fear in the driver's eyes and steps in front of the elderly gentleman as the man descending from the passenger door raises a rifle. She sees the driver close his eyes and slump over the steering wheel. Mr. Patterson steps to the side. The armed man sneers and aims; Lily reaches back and shoves Mr. Patterson without taking her eyes off the gunman. Mr. Patterson groans as he hits the ground, but the shot ricochets off the pavement behind him. A loud, anguished groan rips through the busy market. Pandemonium ensues as the vendors and their patrons scramble for cover.

Lily leaps toward the gunman with full knowledge of the danger but an overwhelming instinct to save Mr. Patterson. She grabs the barrel of the startled man's rifle before he can get off another shot. With her other arm she fends off blows from his fist. She unleashes a powerful kick on his knee and then his midsection.

Inside the cab, a hijacker sheaths his hunting knife and pushes the dead driver from the cab. He fires his rifle at Ralph who is shoving Tim behind the gray van. The hijacker steps down on the running board and fires a fusillade of shots into the van. A bullet ruptures the gas tank. It explodes. Ralph pushes Tim in front of him as they dash for cover. The gunman fires a shot at the fleeting men. Tim groans as the pain sears his calf muscle. John Thorne's shot fells the gunman. Ralph grabs Tim by the waist and drags the smaller man into the alley.

The rear doors of the trailer open. Jack and Lieutenant Williams take out two armed men who fire at them. The gunmen fall to the ground and the doors are quickly pulled shut.

Lily swings the butt of the rifle at the head of the gunman she has injured and disarmed. He staggers and begins to fall. She grabs his arm and yanks him away from the cab. A gunman who had been in the sleeper section of the cab reaches the door. He fires at Mr. Patterson as the unconscious gunman falls. His unconscious body lurches when the bullet enters his back. Mr. Patterson groans when the battered bullet rips through his flesh.

The stunned gunman quickly recovers from the surprise of shooting his 'partner in crime' and fires a second shot into the market. Lily hears his shot hit its mark; she is familiar with the unique sound of a bullet striking flesh, either human or beast. She steps sideways for a clear shot around the open door. The gunman aims at her but hesitates. Her shot finds its mark in his chest. He teeters then begins to fall. She dashes toward him, grabs the barrel of his rifle, and wrests it from his loosening grip so it won't fire wildly as it hits the ground. His limp body thuds onto the pavement.

A lull in the gunfire ensues. No other gunmen appear to be in the cab. Lily walks around the cab to her burning van and looks for bodies. There are none. She is relieved that Ralph and Tim eluded the raiders. She expected as much. She knows she can count on former policeman Ralph Merrill to protect untrained and aging Tim March.

The lull is broken as a shotgun blast from inside the trailer blows a hole in the thin wall of the trailer. Lily dashes to the front of the cab, taking cover from the gunman inside the trailer who blindly fired through the thin wall. She hides one rifle underneath, laying it beside the large tire. Another blast follows. There is a short pause and then two more blasts. She peers around the fender. Rifle barrels appear in each of the four ragged holes.

Lily looks toward John. He signals: *shoot the gas tank.*

She crouches by the front bumper and takes careful aim. Gas is dripping from several bullet holes; most are old and plugged with screws but one was apparently made during today's hijacking. John and Commander Somerton are in her line of fire. John signals that he will keep the commander out of the line of fire then pulls him behind the corner of the brick building.

Four more holes are blasted in the other side of the trailer, the side facing the market. Lily times her shot to coincide with one of them. It ricochets off the tank and strikes the pavement near John but fails to ignite the fumes. She lies on the ground for a better angle.

A shot is fired from the trailer and strikes the metal trash container in the nearby alley. She looks toward the gunman's target and assumes that Ralph and Tim are hiding in the alley. She can almost hear Tim's voice telling her that he is too old for this sort of thing. She sighs. She hopes he gets the chance to actually say it. She would feel more confident if she could give her unarmed bodyguard the extra rifle to ensure the survival of the two men.

She looks up at the four rifles protruding from the holes in the side of the trailer then back at the gas tank. She slithers backward and crawls underneath the front bumper. After a moment's consideration, she backs out and rolls out away from the cab, watching the four rifle barrels. None point in her direction. She takes aim. Her shot strikes a jury-rigged connection on the tank and a tiny stream of gas spews from the miniscule piercing. Immediately she fires again, striking the tank beside the volatile stream, producing a burst of sparks. The tank explodes. As she rolls back to cover, a bullet fired from the rifle protruding from the nearest hole in the side of the trailer strikes the pavement beside her.

Anguished cries and a frantic clamor emanate from the trailer. John, Jack, and Lieutenant Williams take aim at the doors. When the fire begins to engulf the front of the trailer, both rear doors fly open. Accurate shots from the Seals and the lieutenant mow down six men who jump from the burning trailer, firing wildly. One injured gunman, lying prostrate on the pavement, lifts his head and aims. Jack and Lieutenant Williams pump two more bullets into his body. His head slumps to the ground. His grip on his gun loosens.

A rifle is tossed out the back of the trailer. It clatters on the ground. Two more rifles and a shotgun quickly follow. After a moment of silence, except for the ominous crackling of the spreading flames, three very young men, mere teenagers, slowly approach the open doors with their hands on their heads. Black smoke swirls around them and orange flames leap behind them as the springtime wind whips the angry fire.

Despite her anguish, Lily calmly phones the clinic office manager, Miss Owens as many of the patients call her. "Linda, I guess you heard the shots. ... We have several injured. Send a medical team to the market near Mr. Patterson's stall. I'll authorize everyone on duty then see who you send and make any necessary changes. Be sure to send Joey. We lost our gray van and will need to scavenge another one. He can help his dad with that after they shuttle the injured to the clinic." Tim's son, Joey March, is a mechanic who serves as the clinic driver and all-around handyman.

She slips her phone onto the waistband of her jeans and pulls her web-link device from its position on the other side of her waist. She switches on the power and begins tapping. Commander Somerton walks up. She keeps her eyes focused on the tiny screen. "Commander, who's injured? Are there any dead, other than the driver and these pirates?"

Impressed with the speed at which the trained men gathered information and assessed the situation then issued orders to Lieutenant Williams and three other officers who quickly reached the scene, the commander cannot keep a smile of confidence off his face. "Your driver has a through and through on his leg, but Ralph applied a tourniquet."

Tears moisten her eyes.

"A stray bullet hit Jupiter in the arm."

"Jupiter! Oh no! He's such a good man." At the thought of the amiable vendor being injured, a tear rolls down her cheek. She wipes it off on her shoulder without a pause in her rapid-fire entries.

"We lost one officer in the market."

Jack steps over. "He didn't take cover as he rushed toward the firefight."

"Okay, that's one thing I want your guys to teach my men and also how we can better protect our checkpoints," Commander Somerton requests. "We lost three officers at our northeast checkpoint. How's Mr. Patterson?"

Jack replies, "His hip appears to be broken—"

"Sorry," Lily calls in remorse, with her attention focused on her authorization entries.

Mr. Patterson rasps out in obvious distress, "That's quite all right, better than the alternative."

Jack grins at the upbeat attitude of the resilient old man. "And he was nicked by the bullet which went through the gunman."

"That's nothing," the elderly man asserts.

Lily completes her entries, puts up her device, and steps over to Mr. Patterson.

As John renders first aid, she kneels by the elderly baron. "We'll take good care of you, don't you worry. Where's your son?"

"He's on a run to the port. He should be back some time today."

18

"We'll notify him as soon as we can and see that everything is taken care of until he arrives," Lily assures the benevolent trader who has helped them from the beginning.

"Sorry about your dryers."

"That's okay. I'm actually the one who set them on fire," Lily admits.

"Actually," Commander Somerton interjects, "the trailer appears to be empty."

Mr. Patterson smiles despite his pain. "I guess your dryers are still out there. I'll send another truck for them. If this truck was hijacked before picking them up, we should have them within a week or at least by June first. If not, they've been dumped and we may never find them, and it took us so long to get these."

She stands. "Where's my injured driver?"

Commander Somerton sighs. "Still in the alley."

She stares at the smoldering carcass of the gray van –their best van— as she walks past. Flames lick up the last of the combustible upholstery.

TWO

It is late in the evening, but Lily and her three guards have remained in town despite the dusk to dawn curfew imposed by the commander and his former co-commander for the safety of all residents in the still-volatile Texas town. They think of themselves as living in Texas despite the lack of any remnant of state government since the chaos following the terrorists' attacks. After all, you have to have a name for things.

They are sitting around the table in the break room of the medical clinic. It is a simply furnished room in poor repair. The white paint on the cabinets, covering half of the outside wall, is pealing. Neither has the door to the alley been maintained. A small refrigerator sits beside a supply cabinet which is beside the door to the clinic hallway. The other two walls have been repainted in a nondescript light green. An assortment of straight-backed chairs lines one wall.

Lily, Ralph, John, and Jack are devouring a late supper of Sophia Cuevas' delicious burritos. She and her husband Armando Cuevas toil in a small café in an isolated part of town. In addition, he collects Bibles which are scavenged from abandoned homes by the homeless in exchange for food and sells them to Lily for a tidy profit. She is delighted to be able to obtain any scarce item via what might be called the black market, but as far as she knows, it is not an illegal activity for the homeless. Why Armando hides the Bibles under the counter, she does not know; she just accepted his decision, partially because it was conveyed to her in whispered tones.

Between bites, John asks, "Are we still going to be able to get beef? Wasn't Mr. Patterson the only trader who brought in cattle?"

"His son should be able to take care if it," Lily replies. "If not, then at least one of the other regional traders would be more than happy to step in and take over the cattle trade. In fact, I'm not sure why Mr. Patterson has a monopoly on it."

"His cattle ranch is fifteen miles to the south."

Complete surprise flashes across Lily's face. "What? He's getting them on one of his northern routes. He doesn't have a ranch."

"We saw a cattle ranch when we were tracking Ricky through the hills." John is speaking of a dangerous but now deceased sniper they were trying to apprehend eight months ago.

"Do you mean about fifteen miles south along the river?"

He nods. "I guess we should have said something. Ricky obviously hadn't gone that far, so we turned around. We wanted to get back before dark."

Lily inquires, "Did you see any people?"

"No. The house was on the far side of the pasture, and we probably couldn't have seen anyone. Our binoculars weren't strong enough to get a good view at that distance."

"Don't we have a stronger pair?"

"The other team had them," John states, referring to the three Seals who went north along the river searching for Ricky.

"Were there any major roads near the ranch?"

Jack shakes his head. "Not on the north side where we were. It's in the hills in a wide valley that's much larger than ours." He is speaking of the abandoned farm, where Lily settled with the women and children under her capable care when she migrated to the area almost three years before. The next February, they discovered that a brutal slave trade had developed in the nearby town and began rescuing family and friends out of that cruel system. As soon as they began their lucrative business of providing medical care to other residents of the area, they had no lack of funds limiting their rescue efforts and have steadily added to the number of residents at the farm, building plain, utilitarian dorms and cottages as rapidly as possible. Their out-of-town haven now resembles a small town nestled in the hills.

"Jack, why don't you talk with Brad about investigating the ranch," Lily instructs, speaking of Brad Kraft, the highest-ranked former U.S. Navy Seal on their compound. He is in charge of the military men on their security force. "My guess is that nobody knows about the ranch. It could have been abandoned like the farm we're on. If it's occupied, see if you can make contact without getting shot and barter a trade agreement. If it's abandoned, evaluate the possibility of putting in a road along the river so we won't have to go into town and around the hills to it."

"There're roads all through those hills," Jack replies. "They are just two-rut hunting roads, but we could easily string them together by clearing and leveling short stretches between them. A small truck would be able to get through."

A loud rapping on the back door startles them. As Lily washes down her bite with a swig of water, Ralph lays his half-eaten burrito on his plate, walks to the door, and opens it. "Mr. Patterson, come in."

"How's my dad?" Reginald "Reggie" Patterson curtly demands as he strides toward the table.

Lily replies, "He's still in surgery. I suppose they told you what happened."

The scruffy young man replies, "Briefly; they said you saved his life."

"I tried but our new doctor says a broken hip in a man his age is very serous, especially since we don't have everything we need for the surgery. They have to use older techniques instead of the advances introduced shortly before the terrorists' attacks. Sorry about pushing him down."

Reggie runs his hands through his blondish hair, pushing it away from his eyes and managing to partially reestablish his usual pompadour. "They also said your new doc is a bone guy."

"Yes."

"When can I see him?"

"We're waiting for them to tell us he's out of surgery. Why don't you sit down and have a burrito."

"Don't feel like eating." He plops in Ralph's chair, pushes the plate aside and props his elbows on the table.

Ralph walks over to the wall, brings another chair to the table, and returns to his burrito. Lily studies Reginald; he doesn't look particularly anguished. She signals John to get a bottle of water for their guest and turns her attention back to her food. Ralph picks up his bottle and slyly looks at Reginald while gulping the water. As a former policeman, he is not used to casually sitting beside a man on the opposite side of the law. John sets a bottle of cold water in front of Reginald.

Dr. Joseph Swindler, the orthopedic surgeon, enters from the clinic hallway. He wears blood splattered scrubs. Snippets of grey hair protrude from beneath his green cap. His round face tops a muscular but chubby body.

Reginald jumps out of his chair. "Doc, how's my dad?"

Looking over the top of his reading glasses, Dr. Swindler replies, "He survived the surgery. We'll have to wait and see how his recovery progresses. Surgery's quite an ordeal for an elderly person, especially under the primitive conditions we have here. And I'd call the gunshot wound minor in a younger person, but with an elderly person, it can be very serious."

"When can I see him?"

"He's awake. I made sure of that before I left him. Let me give Mrs. Schwartz a report before I take you to recovery."

Lily interjects, "That's okay, Dr. Swindler. You can talk to me later. Let's take care of family first."

She glances at Jack as he covertly signals a vague warning about Reggie. "John, please accompany Mr. Patterson and see that there're no snags. I'm not sure the new personnel would know him by sight."

John grabs his plate and bottle of water and follows Reggie and Dr. Swindler. They will pass through the darkened clinic then enter a long corridor to the recently reopened hospital next door.

After their footsteps recede, Lily turns to Jack. "What's the problem?"

"We saw how you two looked at him."

"I didn't know we were that obvious."

"John picks up on subtle clues. He'd seen the guy before and gave me a heads up to watch him closely."

"Ralph, I'll let you go first since you're the one who shot him."

Jack's eyes widen.

Ralph lays down the last bite of his burrito. "He almost killed three of our men. Monkey had gone in with the flatbed truck for supplies." He turns to Lily. "Who was with him?"

"I think it was Jorge and Joey was driving. It's been a long time." Jorge Ramirez is one of the young construction workers who, for the past two years, has been working with master carpenter Montgomery "Monkey" Preston as they rapidly expanded the abandoned farm into a primitive but sufficient haven of safety for over a thousand residents.

"Yeah, that first summer we were here. Lily and I were guarding the men who were building the guardhouse by the gate. We didn't want them to get surprised by the sniper who was giving us problems at the time. Our truck came flying over the next ridge—"

Jack interrupts, "Was the road as potholed as it is now?"

24

Ralph nods. "They weren't going all that fast, just too fast for the road conditions. They were followed by one of Mr. Patterson's smaller trucks. Young Patterson was hanging out the window, firing at them. He blew out a tire and our truck flipped. I hit him in the shoulder and then killed his replacement before he could get off a shot at our stranded men. They backed over the ridge and fled."

Jack asks, "How were Monkey and his crew?"

"Not injured, fortunately."

"I'm surprised your relationship with the elder Mr. Patterson is so amiable."

Ralph flashes one of his rare grins onto his usually impassive face. "Lily, I'll let you answer that one."

"We hid it from him, guessing that his men wouldn't report it. We figured they'd lie and say they were attacked in another town, and they did. At the time, we didn't know Reginald was one of the gunmen. We didn't meet him until later. We were negotiating for deliveries to the compound and didn't want to damage our relationship with Mr. Patterson. Our population at the compound was getting too large for us to haul enough food out there in just two vans. We really needed the deliveries."

"Why didn't you report it to Commander Somerton?" Jack asks. "He seems like an honest man."

"At that time, he was merely an abashed officer and Commander Tyler ruled with an iron fist. It was more likely we'd be attacked than spur Commander 'Tyrant' toward decreeing justice. As lawless as it is now, it was much worse then."

Jack laughs at their nickname for the prior commander, a fitting moniker for many of the brutal commanders—or usurpers as he thinks of them—that he has encountered since the nation was thrust into lawless chaos.

Jack's expression sobers. "While we're on this subject, let me ask another question. When we were at the café, it seemed like Lieutenant Williams was hiding something. Do you have any idea what?"

Lily shakes her head and looks at Ralph. He shrugs. She turns back. "What was the context, what were you talking about at the time?"

"We were talking about training the officers."

"See if you can get to know him better while you train them."

"Okay, but I'd be leery of him, if I were you."

She looks at Ralph then back to Jack. "We'll remember that, and keep me posted if you find out anything. We want to make sure our relationship with Commander Somerton remains amiable too. It hasn't always been, so I'd like to know what's going on with one of his most trusted lieutenants. I'd want to know immediately, if it looks like he's plotting a coup. That'd mean he isn't as honest as our current commander, and it'd set us back to have a dishonest commander—again!

"You know Commander Somerton has absolutely no training in law enforcement, and even though I trust him as a man, I'm not sure I trust his decisions as commander due to his lack of training. He is well aware of his shortcomings as an insurance agent turned peace officer but sometimes … well …." She throws her hands up. "I'm glad he's agreed to us training his men. It should help."

Ralph adds, "I think I know Lieutenant Williams from somewhere but can't place him."

"Let me know if you remember," Jack requests, "especially if it's from a wanted poster."

"It's been two years and I haven't placed him yet, just like I can't place Ricky."

"He looked familiar too?" Jack guesses.

Ralph nods.

A gentle rap on the outside door interrupts them. Ralph walks over and opens it. "Commander, come in."

"Hello, Ralph. Hello, Mrs. Schwartz." The Southern gentleman nods at the baroness.

"Hello, Commander."

He looks at Jack. "You're John?"

"Jack."

"I'm sorry. I'm getting bad at remembering names, especially since you two look so much alike."

Jack grins. "We're brothers. What do you expect?"

"You even look a lot like Jeff, especially since he's gained some weight."

"He's our cousin, and it's not fat. He's been working out in our guard training program. It's the first time I've ever seen muscles on my skinny little nerdy cousin." Their intellectually gifted cousin, Jeff Clark is an engineer. Physical prowess is a new pursuit for the young man who always considered chess his sport.

Ralph offers, "Have a seat, Commander."

As he sits down, the commander glances at the wall and his thoughts turn to the prior year's major crisis. He is glad they repaired the hole someone kicked in the wall in anger, but even the neatly repaired and repainted wall reminds him of the kidnapping and how ineffective he was in dealing with the lawlessness of the recently deceased Mr. Barton and Ricky. Mr. Barton was one of their most powerful local barons. He and his henchman, Ricky, were responsible for several murders.

Commander Somerton stifles his wondering thoughts and turns to Lily. "How's Mr. Patterson?"

"He's out of surgery and awake."

Using her official name as a baroness, he states, "Jackie, let me get right to it. We've grilled those three boys who surrendered. They were on a kidnapping raid. They were after a woman named Lily Gibbons. Apparently they expected to just grab her and take off."

She rolls her eyes and thinks *that's all I need right now: another problem to add to everything we're dealing with already.*

He continues, "I don't know why they expected to find her in the market. I can't find anyone by that name on any of our slave registries. Do you know who she is? Is she one of your illegal residents?"

She decides to avoid the painful topic, for a few minutes anyway. "I thought you knew that my illegal residents were rescued from Mr. Barton. They're legit now."

"There's still one—"

A startled look appears on her face. "Oh, that's right. There's one who didn't come from Mr. Barton's."

A look of disgust clouds the commander's face. "Actually … she did."

"Really?"

"When Mr. Barton and his entourage drove into town, he was a 'nobody'. They were merely another group of immigrants escaping the chaos up north and weren't well received. He lined up his girls and let Tyrone have his pick." He is speaking of former Commander Tyrone "Tyrant" Tyler. "He chose Thai. Then somehow Mr. Barton took over the electric company and—"

With a disapproving scowl, she interrupts, "He traded Dr. Morris for it," speaking of Dr. Chris Morris, an obstetrician she has recently redeemed from the brutal slave culture.

He looks at her with surprise, knowing that the event happened before she migrated to the area.

"Jeff told me."

"That explains a lot." The commander rubs his chin.

Lily shrugs. "Anyway, with Commander Tyler deposed and Spencer in prison, I thought we could consider her a legitimate resident of our compound too." Prisoner Spencer Blakely is Commander Somerton's former co-commander whom he deposed, with her assistance, because of his rampant lawlessness while running the slave trade from the local prison.

The commander returns to his inquiry about Thai. "What I was going to say is that I've noticed that you don't have her listed on your registry."

"We don't know her name. We're sure Thai is a nickname and she insists her last name is Tyler, since they were … 'married'." Lily makes quote marks with her fingers.

The commander rolls his eyes at the thought of the young girl being married—especially to the brutal commander he deposed. "Back to the raiders: you don't have a Lily Gibbons?"

She tilts her head and looks at the commander with sadness. "That's my maiden name."

Jack interjects, "That's why those two hesitated instead of firing at you immediately."

"I'd be dead if they didn't want me alive," Lily admits. "I was right there with no cover, especially since my first instinct was to save Mr. Patterson."

Commander Somerton pulls a photo from his shirt pocket and stares at it with a furrowed brow. "Your name's Lily?"

"Lily Jacqueline Gibbons Schwartz."

"Now that I think about it, I've heard people call you Lily. I guess this does look like you." He hands her the photo.

The quality is poor. It was taken from a distance and probably with a cell phone. Her youngest son is beside her as they leave their home. She wipes a tear from her eye as she recalls his death at the hands of Mr. Barton's sons. It was the first instance of lawlessness that she endured after the attacks. The reign of terror that ensued lasted for several months. She looks up. "This was taken shortly before the terrorists' attacks."

The commander states, "I guess they knew you'd be waiting for your dryers. Do you have any idea who might want to kidnap you? After all,

Mr. Barton is dead and we've accounted for all his slaves, not that any of them—other than Ricky—would do something like that."

She shakes her head. "I don't know anybody else it might be. This was obviously taken when he first began stalking me, so it might be someone who didn't migrate with him. We'll have John investigate. He can talk to those who migrated with Mr. Barton and see if they know of anybody he left behind. I don't see why anyone would've stayed behind; after all, the utilities had failed. We didn't even have water."

"I've heard he had some brothers," the commander states.

"He had three older brothers, but I barely knew them. I never even saw any of them after they left for college. I have no idea where they ended up."

"One of them could have come back and settled in your hometown," the commander suggests.

With an amused grin, Lily states, "Our hometown was in the state of Washington."

The commander arches his eyebrows. "I didn't know you weren't a native Texan."

She laughs.

"You've kind of picked up a twang."

"I didn't realize it. I guess that's because I've been here so long. My husband moved me down here the summer after my freshman year in college."

"You got married that young?"

"We married a few months after we came down. He encouraged me to transfer to get away from my brothers. He was just a friend at the time. Actually it was his dad who suggested the transfer."

The commander inquires, "Could it be your brothers who're after you now?"

"I'm sure they stayed in Washington and ran Granddad's dairy farm. They never went to college and were all still there when I left. Let me add that my brothers and Mr. Barton's brothers are now between the ages of forty-two and fifty-six. I don't even remember seeing the oldest Barton brother, only photos. He left for college thirty-eight years ago when I was a toddler, and it's been twenty years since I've seen my brothers."

Commander Somerton sighs. "I guess that's pretty much a dead end then. I can't see anyone traveling halfway across the continent for a kidnapping. Travel has been much too dangerous since the attacks."

Jack surmises, "It's obviously someone who knew Jackie before she married."

"Or someone who only knows me through association with Mr. Barton," Lily suggests.

Commander Somerton heaves a sigh of exasperation. "We'll see if we can get more information out of the boys, but they insist they never met the man who hired them. Only their ringleader met with him."

"Which one was the ringleader?"

"One of those in the cab."

Jack mutters, "Well, we're not going to get anything out of a dead man."

The commander turns to another area of concern. "How're you doing with Mr. Barton's engineers?"

She hides her frustration. "They're impatient. It's been more than six months since he died. They want the electric co-op set up instead of being listed as slaves of his estate." Speaking of her informally adopted son, who is a computer whiz, Lily continues, "Lawrence says he's ready with the changes to the registry program. All he'd have to do is put it on the online computer, and it'd show up on our web-link devices. It's really a simple change; very similar to the setup for the vendors on the financial program. How're you doing with the negotiations with the other barons?"

He exhales sharply. "Only Mr. Patterson and a couple of others have agreed to the co-op. All of the others want to retain the slave culture completely, including some who tentatively agreed the first time I talked to them. I don't know why they've retracted their agreement. They weren't forthcoming with an explanation. A few even want me to replace you as executrix of Mr. Barton's estate, but I'm not going to do that. There's nobody else I'd trust in that position, and I'd be totally at sea taking care of the business end."

Referring to Stanley Williamson the chief engineer of the local, in limbo, electric facility, she inquires, "I assume all the barons would object if we let Stanley act as the executor?"

"Yeah. He's a slave. That would really rile them."

"I guess we're at a standstill on this too." She sighs with resignation.

"Even lowering the rate you're charging for electricity didn't change anyone's mind," the commander grumbles.

"That was Stanley's idea. Now that the wind turbines have been repaired, we're selling to surrounding areas instead of buying so we

THE STONE IS TURNED

can afford to lower the rate locally. Sorry it didn't change any minds immediately. They're probably thinking that we'd raise the rate again as soon as the co-op is a done deal."

He smiles with optimism. "You're thinking it may win them over in the long run?"

"It's more like: that's what they'd do. They'd renege on a deal as soon as they got what they wanted so expect us to do the same."

His optimism vanquished, he drums his fingers on the table. "We have some real nasty barons around here."

She changes the subject. "How're Spencer and the other errant officers doing on the work detail? Have they gotten the hang of patching potholes yet?"

"They're pretty miffed. I guess they expected to sit around in prison instead of exerting themselves. Thanks for loaning us the engineers to supervise them. They're doing a great job, especially Jeff."

"That's why Jeff's been training as a guard. He felt he needed it to work with the prisoners."

"Two more are claiming that their participation in the crimes was from coercion and have asked for leniency. I'd like you to talk with them," the commander requests. "You have a real gift for sizing up a stranger on a first meeting. See if you think we can trust them to be law-abiding citizens. We might commute their sentence and find a place for them, but I think we're past reinstating any more as officers. I think we've ferreted out all those that I'd trust in that position."

"I'll go to the prison early on Monday and spend a few minutes with them." Monday is the day the local barons pick up newly purchased slaves at the prison five miles north of the town of Somertonville. However Lily and her fellow revisionists, the thousand or so residents of their compound, think of the slave trading not as purchasing but as redeeming.

Though the town was originally named Somerton, after the expansion of communications over a wide area, there were two towns named Somerton. The other town had used the name since the eighteen hundreds, so they changed their town to Somertonville. The town had merely received the moniker of Somerton courtesy of the mobile phone company since Mr. Hobbs needed an official name for each town where he provides service. Without asking permission, he took the liberty of naming each town after the local commander. Robert Somerton was not thrilled about his name being chosen by strangers for the honor but did not object. He would have been less thrilled if it had been dubbed Blakely, who was his co-commander at the time. And Tyler would have been an objectionable name for everyone, except perhaps Thai. She is probably the only person with fond memories of the tyrant. She luxuriated within the confines of a mansion Tyrone had commandeered in the most exclusive—that is formerly exclusive—section of town, with every whim satisfied, that is, if Tyrone could procure it and commanders can procure almost anything. She considered herself the youngest queen in the history of the world; however since she was young when the terrorists struck, she was uneducated and ignorant of world history.

The commander looks down with a sorrowful expression. Lily knows she will have to ask. He will not voluntarily confide his concerns unless he has already thought of a solution and is requesting assistance with implementing it. She sighs. "What's on your mind?"

"All the problems we have. We've tried to make it as safe as possible, but we still have problems with the road bandits like these today as well as all the local criminals who can easily work around our system of authorizations."

Lily asks, "How're they getting around the authorizations?"

"My officers don't know everyone by sight. A baron might authorize one of his men to go to the market. Another man will also go to the market. If the unauthorized man is stopped, he claims to be the one with authorization. My officers have no way to check anyone's real identity, and the criminals can get away with anything. It's the daily reports Nolan suggested a few days ago that have alerted us to what's going on. We have people being reported in two or even three places at the same time, but by then, it's too late to do anything about it. It looks like my men are stopping anyone who looks suspicious but don't have enough to take them into custody. We tried having the officers phone Marvin, thinking he could alert the second officer who calls on the same man, but it's too time consuming. This is why we're asking for help. It's apparent there are better ways to do things."

Jack inserts, "Mr. Patterson's driver alerted the commander by driving on a restricted street. That's why we were in the market right behind them."

Commander Somerton runs his fingers over his graying hair. "If they'd been able to disburse in the market, we'd have lost a lot of people today. Please tell Mr. Patterson that his driver died a hero. That's the least we can do for the poor fellow, and they said the rest of the crew was killed and their bodies dumped in the hills."

Lily suggests, "Let's see what Lawrence and Marvin can come up with for a more reliable identification system." She is speaking of their respective computer personnel, Lawrence Brighton of the Schwartz compound and Marvin Finley a vital member of the local authorities.

"Let's go to a similar problem. We need a standing authorization for an emergency medical team so they can be quickly sent out whenever and wherever needed," she requests.

The commander shrugs. "They came quickly today."

"That's because I was there. If I'd been somewhere else, someone would have had to call me then I'd call the clinic and then I'd start entering the authorizations. Today I had to authorize everybody on duty, since I didn't know who they'd send. I didn't want to delay getting a team over there. All I need is your okay for Lawrence to add another standard authorization. Every day, Dr. Maxton can assign an emergency team and you or one of your officers can call the clinic. We could even dedicate a phone kept by each shift's emergency team leader, so the number can always be the same. It could be entered in all your phones for quick dialing. Imagine what would have happened if I'd been injured today."

"Or not happened," the beleaguered commander mutters. "You have my authorization for the change, and see if Mr. Hobbs can provide a phone with an easy to remember number. I'll tell Marvin and see if we can find an ambulance."

"Any van would do, even a hearse."

The commander inquires, "How're your guys doing on that helicopter on top of the hospital?"

"They lack a few essential parts," she replies. "The regional traders are on the lookout for them. I understand one of the officers killed at the checkpoint would've survived if he could've been quickly transported."

"Yeah, he died in the car as Lieutenant Jones rushed him to the hospital. Have you tried searching for the parts on the web?"

"They haven't had any success yet, but we do have a couple more cameras coming for your patrol cars."

"Great," he replies. "Having those cameras has two advantages. It's cut down on crime. The criminals around here are leery of getting caught on video." He furrows his brow. "Or maybe they're just getting better at hiding from the officers. Anyway, we've used the videos to our advantage when confronting the barons about the activities of their slaves. I suppose it's enlightened the barons about their rogue slaves. ...   Or maybe, it's just made the barons chastise them for getting caught. I don't know. Maybe, it's cut down on crime." He tries to run his fingers through his hair, forgetting momentarily, despite the fact that it was his decree, that military-style haircuts are now required for all officers. "Anyway, the cameras have at least helped keep the officers in line. They can't cut their own deals with the criminals if it's going to be recorded."

"Or maybe they cut their deals off camera?" Jack glumly suggests.

Commander Somerton frowns. "I guess. Forgive me for rambling. I think the cameras have cut down on crime by both the criminals and the officers. Too bad we just started keeping crime stats."

"We could use the videos in training the officers. Show them what they could have done differently," Jack suggests.

A smile brightens the commander's face. "Okay, so there's a third advantage. I'm sure this one will actually work."

"Maybe it will even increase the effectiveness of the first two."

"Jack, I'm going to enjoy working with you."

Commander Somerton turns back to Lily. "When's the wedding?" There is no doubt as to whose upcoming nuptials are on his mind.

"I think Linda has settled on next month. I'll have to check on the exact day. How's Lieutenant Jones doing?"

"Nervous. He has the prenuptial jitters but a real big grin most of the time."

She laughs. "I think they'll make a nice couple."

The commander decides to ask about her engineer who absconded after he attacked brutal Mr. Barton. Frank was rescuing his daughter, but it was still an illegal act. "Let me ask about Frank before I leave. Is he still sending you slaves he's rescued from brutal masters in other areas? Or did he just eliminate the one who abused his wife before you redeemed her?"

She looks at the southern gentleman with sadness. "It's hard not to redeem slaves who've been abused, but I don't want to be an enabler and abet his activities as a rebel. After talking with the women he sent from Mr. Compton's, it's obvious that he's operating outside of the law. He may be destabilizing the towns. I want to work within the law. I can't encourage him by taking the slaves he frees. It tears me up but I can't do it, not even though I know the barons he deposes are as lawless as they come. It'd undermine our efforts to bring law and order to our own community. I'd be seen as someone who condones working outside the law."

The commander mumbles, more to himself than the others, "I guess after hastening Mr. Barton's demise to rescue his daughter, he thinks he has nothing to lose."

THREE

Sitting beside the tranquil pond near the farmhouse, Lily has her feet in the water and her elbows propped on her knees. A large river runs through their compound just west of the city of Somertonville, and it was the river that drew Lily and her entourage to the abandoned farm. A reliable source of water was essential after the utilities failed. The farm was isolated from the dangers of the nearby, mostly abandoned, city and a much safer place to set up residence. During the next two years their presence changed the farm dramatically. As she began redeeming friends and family at the slave market in town, the number of residents quickly outgrew the facilities. Fortunately one of her first redemptions was a master carpenter who began their continuous building project. Another early redemption was engineer Frank Smith who set up a reliable water and sewer system. Without the skills of numerous people, the safe compound would not have been a feasible endeavor.

"Hi, Lily."

With a glum expression, she looks up as Darla Smith slips off her sandals. The tall blonde sits beside Lily.

"Hi, Darla."

Darla plunges her feet into the river and immediately yanks them out. "That's cold."

Lily swishes her feet in the shallow water at the river's rocky edge. "You get used to it after a minute or so."

The usually slender, pregnant woman eases her feet back into the water. "It does feel good on my swollen feet. It was just the shock. With it this warm, I expected warmer water."

"It'll feel a little less cold next month."

Darla laughs. "June is only a week away. I wouldn't expect it to warm up much by then."

"It gets hot here, pretty quickly. I'm surprised it isn't hotter already. Last year, May was pretty hot. How're you feeling?"

With amusement lightening her tone, forty-nine-year-old Darla retorts, "Pretty good for an old pregnant woman. This one is a lot easier than the first; at least, I'm healthy this time instead of still reeling from chemo."

Lily welcomes the distraction of idle chatter with the intelligent and patient wife of Frank Smith. She has been idling away a Saturday morning, thinking about the unfortunate events of the day before. It pains her to have injured Mr. Patterson so severely. She knows she saved his life and that there was no better scenario other than foreknowledge of the raid which she, of course, did not have.

She pushes Mr. Patterson from her mind and asks, "How'd a gal like you end up with a guy like Frank?"

An expression of—perhaps wistful—amusement settles over Darla's face. "I almost didn't. He asked me out about two dozen times before I said yes."

Lily's eyes widen. "I've of been mad at him for stalking, for being that persistent."

"It was over three years, so it wasn't bothersome. He only asked about once every two months, so maybe it was only eighteen times or so."

"That's still persistent even if it wasn't stalking. What made you finally give in?"

"That's a long story."

"This is Saturday. I have the rest of the day."

With an amused smile at the memory of her courtship with her husband of twenty-eight years, Darla begins, "It started my first week at college. We were all sitting around someone's dorm room getting to know each other, and of course, the subject turned to boys. Within minutes, Frank was the topic. General consensus was that he was the best looking, best personality, smartest, brightest future, and from a wealthy family. He was considered the best catch by all the vain, social climbers, and I was getting bored. But anyway, to go on: the most forward of them had flirted with him and even though he flirted back, to her chagrin, he didn't ask her out. The mousey girls were pining that they didn't have a chance when one of the most demure girls spoke up. We were surprised to learn that she had a date with him."

"What was he looking for: putty in his hands?"

"That's what we thought when a girl—sorry, but I've forgotten all their names now—anyway, one who went to high school with him enlightened us. She told us about his reputation. According to her, all the girls wanted to date him. He was choosey and a girl who caught his eye considered herself privileged. Then she turned to the girl with the date and told her that if she valued her virginity, she'd pretend to get sick and cancel the date."

"Did she?"

"She grinned and said he sounded like the perfect guy to lose it to."

"What happened?"

Darla emphatically states, "Nothing."

"Nothing?"

"That's right. He didn't even kiss her. In fact, he brought her back early when she got ... ah ... shall we say, boldly flirtatious."

"What was going on? Did he not like her or something?"

Darla shrugs. "It happened with every date he had. Flirts couldn't get a date, good girls wouldn't date him, and nothing happened when he did take a girl out. We begin betting on who'd be first. Well, I never participated in that, but those who did contributed a dollar each time he had a date, and the pot was going to the 'lucky' girl. I didn't consider her lucky, but that's what she was called. It spread to other dorms and soon we—I mean—they had two treasurers and a growing bank account."

With a wide-eyed expression, Lily states, "I cannot imagine what was going on."

Darla leans back on her hands. "I found out."

Lily waits for her explanation.

Darla sits up straight and leans toward Lily. "I, personally, wasn't interested in Frank or such boy-crazy girls. I found other friends with whom I had more in common. That's why I don't remember those girls' names. We didn't socialize, at least not much. I was putting what I considered a minor and uninteresting event behind me, but he was friendly and kept asking me out. None of the other guys I dated had panned out into a lasting relationship, so I finally went out with him. After three years, I decided it was safe to date him since no one had won the pot, and my curiosity was beginning to get the better of me. I told him I knew about his high school days and asked him point-blank what he was doing. He told me that he'd realized he didn't want to marry that kind of girl so decided he shouldn't be that kind of guy."

"That tells me how he got a first date, but how'd you end up marrying him?" Lily asks.

"I had fun and he was very considerate and kept asking me out and I kept having fun with such a really nice guy and I eventually gave in and let him kiss me, on about the tenth date, and it appeared that the tiger had changed his spots."

Lily politely hides her amusement at Darla's slip of the tongue.

"Or that his high school classmate—whom he hadn't dated—had exaggerated his reputation, so how could I turn down the most romantic proposal ever with a guy that I was fighting not to fall in love with."

"What in the world did he do?"

"He took a rain check on a date and—"

"A rain check?"

"Yeah, a rain check; he said he already had the tickets but he was sick and he'd asked one of his buddies to take me to the game—as just friends—and he was a really nice, trustworthy guy so I went with him. I was kind of hoping that maybe his friend would pan out to be more than just a friend, and I'd leave Frank behind. But you know how they play those games between innings."

"Oh, baseball not football," Lily mutters with sudden understanding.

"Yeah, it was the spring of our senior year. They announced that the fan with a sticker under their seat was going to walk out to the mound, blindfolded and on red carpet, for a surprise. My date reached under my seat and came up with the sticker. I was afraid of some prank so told him to go, but he insisted that I go. So he escorted me to the field, the red carpet was laid, the teams were lined up beside the carpet, and my date escorted me to the mound so I knew me stumbling down the carpet wasn't the gag. He let go, and I heard Frank's voice over the loud speaker asking me to marry him. I ripped off the blindfold. He was on one knee, in a tuxedo, microphone in one hand and ring in the other."

"That is romantic but embarrassingly public."

"Yeah," Darla agrees. "I know my face was bright red. I could feel the flush."

"You obviously said yes."

"Before I could even give it a second thought," Darla admits. "I gave it plenty of second thoughts afterward, but Frank stayed the gentleman. He's always the charming gentleman."

"What'd the girls do with the money? I'm assuming there was no lucky girl."

"Gave it to me at our wedding; it was embarrassing because they told the whole story. I don't remember inviting those girls to our wedding, but the core group was all there. So anyway, we had one whale of a honeymoon. We'd had simple plans since Frank's wealthy family was his step-dad and he and Trudy were divorced." She is speaking of Gertrude "Trudy" Debauch, Frank's multimarried and divorced mother.

"I guess Frank managed to get the kind of girl he wanted?" Lily observes.

"Yeah, but he didn't stay my kind of guy."

"I know."

Darla inquires, "How long have you known?"

"I suspected when I was working for him that he wasn't very moral," Lily admits. "That may have contributed to me leaving, but it was a subconscious contribution. It's hard to get evidence of his misdeeds."

"He's one wily dude. He's actually a great husband except for his … ah … you know … straying."

Darla smiles and turns to a related subject. "How'd you get together with your husband?"

"If you'll believe it: I turned him down too."

"How many times?"

"Once," Lily replies.

"So the second time was a charm?"

"Nah. I pursued another guy and got engaged."

They hear footsteps behind them and turn to look. Angel Gonzales and Jorge Ramirez are slowly strolling toward the river with their eyes riveted on each other. They look up and stop in their tracks. Jorge points downstream and they turn.

Lily calls, "Jorge!"

They stop and look back. Lily points up the hill toward the houses. With reluctance Jorge guides Angel away from the river; privacy is not an option for them.

Darla whispers, "She's underage, isn't she?"

Lily shakes her head. "That's not the problem. Even if she was still underage, Jorge's very responsible and trustworthy. That's why he's received Marie's blessing to court her daughter. The problem is that several couples have already gone that way."

41

"That's becoming a problem, isn't it?"

"Yeah," Lily replies. "We're going to have to deal with those whose public behavior is a bit lewd. Those who seek privacy ... we'll just have to tolerate them."

They sit quietly for a few minutes then Darla asks, "Walter Schwartz was your husband, wasn't he?"

"Yeah, did you know him?"

"I was always interviewing him for some story for the paper," the former journalist states. "I thought he was a real nice guy from the first time I met him. What didn't you like about him?"

"He was a big man like my three mean brothers. My dad was small and the nicest guy on earth. So ... I was naïve and only dated small guys."

"Okay, so high school," Darla guesses.

"No. College freshman, just like you."

Darla turns down one corner of her mouth in a grimace.

"You don't think I should've still been so naïve when I went to college?"

"Not a smart gal like you."

Lily reveals, "When you have three mean brothers, it really colors your prospective until you are boldly confronted with irrefutable evidence that your premise is totally wrong."

"So was your little fiancé mean?" Darla guesses.

"No, he was one of the sweetest little atheist nerds there ever was."

"So you didn't like his atheism?"

Lily admits, "At the time, I didn't care. I didn't see any difference between adherents of any belief system. The preacher's son that I dated in high school only behaved when his parents were around, otherwise I could talk him into anything. Religion looked like a big hoax to me. Just hide your transgressions and pretend you are good. Later I understood that he was naïve, and it grieves me to think about me leading him astray. He was only fourteen. Well ... so was I, but I was a little more worldly wise. Well more like hedonistic."

"Like Susie."

Shock courses through Lily. Susie Morrow is their master chef and a tart-tongued, petite firebrand of Asian parentage who has confessed, privately, that she is carrying Frank's child. "You know about Susie? She wasn't going to say anything. She didn't want to hurt you."

Darla's expression is glum. "The wife always knows. I knew from the first moment I met her. When Frank plays dumb, that's a dead giveaway. There's no way he really thought an Asian woman was Hispanic, and he kept putting in other little hints in the conversation like saying, to Susie not to me, that he didn't really know her. Then she said she was an All-American party girl. The wife always knows. It's those attempts to hide it that are the dead giveaway."

"But you're never quite sure?"

"It's more like you're hoping—hoping that it's only your own suspicious nature and that nothing happened. You try to pretend that you don't know and ignore all those little clues, hoping it isn't true. Eventually you have to admit to yourself that you've known all along."

Darla sighs then inquires, "What happened with your little atheist?"

"He was murdered in a burglary."

"Sorry, I didn't mean to bring up such things."

"That's all right. It was a long time ago, and I'm glad I married a Christian and that I finally let him teach me the truth."

Thinking that she is turning the conversation away from the painful topic of murder, Darla asks, "How'd you finally get together with Walter?"

"He was always so nice. Steve was murdered just as spring break started and—"

"Sorry, here I go again, making you talk about his murder."

"That's all right. It was more than twenty years ago. The pain does diminish over time. So anyway, when his body was discovered, all my friends had already left for spring break. Walter was the only one in my circle of friends still in town. I didn't consider him a friend. He was just a friend of my friends and I'd been avoiding him as much as possible, but he came to my aid. I accepted it because I had nowhere else to turn."

"What about your parents?" Darla inquires.

"Dead."

"Sorry. I keep dredging up bad memories for you."

Lily reveals, "That's about all I have about growing up, but at least my parents died of natural causes. Mom died of emphysema when I was twelve and Daddy had a heart attack when I was a senior. I left my grandparents' home under less than ideal circumstances, in fact, under the supervision of the sheriff."

"Okay, skip on back to Walter helping you," Darla requests.

"I had nowhere to go. I couldn't stay in the dorm—it was closed for the holiday—and Steve's apartment had crime scene tape on the door. I didn't have enough cash to pay for a hotel for a week. I'd let my checking account get down to almost nothing, and it always took at least a week to get a transfer from my trust fund. I'm sure that's because my oldest brother, Bob, was executor of Dad's estate. Walter offered—"

Darla interrupts, "No credit card?"

A quick look of frustration flashes across Lily's face. "My brother wouldn't let me have one, so I only had a debit card. Anyway, Walter offered to take me to his parents' house. Even though I didn't trust big guys, I accepted since Walter had always been so nice to everyone and I rationalized that we'd be with his parents."

Lily's problems with her brothers tempt Darla to be thankful that she had no siblings. She turns her attention back to Lily's story. "And it turned out really well?"

"Eventually, but I was extremely leery when he drove to the airport. He stopped and called his mother and I talked to her a while and then consented and he bought me a ticket and we flew to Houston. Turns out his dad's an attorney and Walter told him about the problems I was having with my brothers and he had all kinds of good suggestions for things like restraining orders, getting a new license plate for my car, and painting it something other than fire engine red. He suggested transferring to a new school after the term and helped me set up my finances with an attorney in Chicago so my brothers couldn't find out where I was."

"Wow, my life's been a cake walk compared to yours."

"Marriage to Walter was pretty much a cake walk until our oldest son had some behavior problems and started hanging around with the wrong crowd. His new best friend was called Gyp. I have no idea what his name really is, but he was a real bad influence. Things went downhill fast. Other than that our marriage pretty much mimicked what I observed at his parents' house during spring break. I didn't know people could live with so little stress in their lives."

"Is that what got you?" Darla solicits.

"Everybody in his family was super nice, and Walter stuck with me and was always there to help."

"Was he really romantic?"

"Not in the least, more like practical."

Darla raises her eyebrows.

"After we transferred to Texas—well, that's when he entered law school; I transferred for my sophomore year—we did things together but never dated until we were engaged. We didn't even hold hands."

"How in the world did you ever get engaged?"

"I was being hard to convince, and he understood since he knew about my brothers. His pursuing me would've turned me off and he knew it so he just stuck with me as a friend, even when I dated other guys."

"I still don't see how in the world you ever got engaged."

"Family gathering at his grandparents' house; the whole clan was there for Thanksgiving. His parents weren't unique. None of them was perfect, but they all dealt with whatever life threw at them. They had family they could turn to for help and support, mostly emotional because that's what you need most to deal with life and that's what I didn't have much of in my family. And all of them were big. There wasn't a scrawny guy in the bunch. I said something to Walter about the happy marriages in his family. He said that's the kind of marriage he wanted. He asked if that's what I'd like. I said yes. He said: how about we try it together. I said okay and we were married in a couple of weeks."

Darla admits, "I am in awe. I guess those of us who had it easy take risks, like I did with Frank, and those who have it rough are more cautious."

FOUR

Lily leans against the shady side of her van. It is not her usual Monday activity. It fills her with anxiety that the prison transport bus is a day late, but all she can do is patiently wait. She has already talked to the two prisoners, the former officers, to assess their commitment to becoming law-abiding citizens. One appeared remorseful, but the other seemed to be trying to work the haphazard system of local law which lacks a judicial branch.

While waiting, she watches one of the local barons out of the corner of her eye and lets her thoughts ramble. She wonders if he is one of the few with them or one of the many against the co-op for deceased Mr. Barton's electric company. Judging by the baron's openly sour expression, she hazards a guess that he is against it but not vehemently so. Perhaps he is like many in the unstable culture who always side with the majority, no matter what. At the present time, the majority is against the co-op and almost anyone is a potential enemy. Perhaps it is too early in the recovery from terrorism and criminal chaos to be moving for such a big change in the local baron-slave culture.

Stanley Williamson and the other engineers are pushing for an immediate change in their status from slaves to having ownership. Lily cannot blame them. They see Mr. Barton's death as their opportunity for freedom. She wishes she could give it to them legally instead of just practically. They operate as if they were a co-op except for the authorizations she has to enter on the web-link device. She is thankful that Lawrence has set up the system so that she can authorize everything they request with just one tap.

It occurs to her that she should ask Lawrence to set up the medical authorizations the same way. After all, whatever the medical director, Dr. Martin "Max" Maxton asks for, she authorizes. And now that she thinks about it, there are several other areas where that would work and save her beaucoups of time. Any time that she can save on the tedious authorizations can be well spent with her multitude of other tasks, which continually grow as the size of their safe haven expands.

The prison transport bus turns off the deteriorating highway. She walks around her van and waits beside the open sliding door. Lieutenant Rambler and six officers walk out the prison door and down the sidewalk. All are spiffily dressed in identical uniforms including caps covering their identical buzz cuts. The term that pops into Lily's head is clones, but at least they look more professional than they did under the prior, very lenient dress code.

The officers unlock the gate and wait outside. The bus pulls to a halt. The door opens and a guard steps down. "Sorry, Lieutenant, but we blew a tire."

"That's all right." Lieutenant Rambler steps onto the bus to address the slaves. "Listen up. Since your bus was late, two of the barons are waiting. We'll direct you as you step off the bus. Don't try anything. Do you see those guards in the towers? And see that scrubby little brush all around? You won't get far so just don't give us a hard time. Okay?"

He steps down, stands beside the door of the prison bus, and pulls out his web-link device.

"I'm Doug Kasper," a voice behind Lily says.

Startled she turns. The other baron has walked up behind her. He is a small man with short, light brown hair and a nondescript face. She extends her hand and replies, "Jackie Schwartz. Glad to make your acquaintance."

He keeps his hands in his pockets and scowls. She leans against the van, puts her hands in her pockets, and crosses her left ankle over her right. Despite her apprehension due to his unfriendly demeanor, she keeps a smile on her face as she studies the bland countenance of the ordinary-looking man and patiently waits for him to speak.

"I can't say as I'm pleased to meet you. You have too much power in my opinion. Where do you get off getting so cozy with the commander?"

She flippantly replies, "You know what they say: *if you can't beat 'em, join 'em*. Why don't Commander Somerton and I meet with you sometime? We could always use another ally."

"What in the world are you trying to do? Push us all out?"

She gently shakes her head. "We're just trying to make it safe around here. There's still too much danger. Last Friday, we had four officers killed and three men injured by criminals from out of town. A baron was one of the injured. He's in serious condition. If we all band together, we can face the dangers together and hopefully do something about them."

"You're just going to destroy us like you did Mr. Barton," he angrily asserts.

"I didn't have anything to do with that and neither did Commander Somerton."

"I heard it was one of your slaves who killed him."

Lily admits, "He went rogue because Mr. Barton had his daughter and she was in danger."

"But he had a cultural center over there. He was providing his slaves with activities such as ballet and opera. That was a real high-class joint. I sent a couple of girls over there. They wanted to be ballerinas."

"You're naïve. The officer who went through the videos Mr. Barton made told me that what he saw made him sick. We've destroyed them all otherwise I'd show you what your girls were really taught."

An anguished look clouds his face. "Oh?"

"You shouldn't listen to gossip. You should check it out with a reliable source."

"But I thought the officers were reliable sources."

"Not when Mr. Barton hides his illegal activities. And remember, some of those officers you thought were so reliable are now in prison. Commander Somerton would've been willing to raid the Grande Hotel and take Mr. Barton into custody, if he had been able to determine what was really going on there." She inwardly sighs. She knows that he would not have been able to, just that he would have been willing. She longs for a more civilized society and actual power for the authorities.

"I guess I could … ah … talk with you and Commander Somerton."

A soft smile lights up her face. "I'll set it up with the commander, and we won't be pushy about it. All we'll do is talk and try to convince you there's a better way to do business around here."

John Thorne walks over to the van. Two officers follow, escorting a line of shackled prisoners. One officer kneels to unshackle the ankles of the first, a Hispanic youth. He appears to be about fifteen but has a hardened expression on his young face. Three years of brutal slavery can hardened almost anyone. The officer stands and removes the shackles from the boy's wrists. He turns toward the next in line. The boy drops his hands to his side. John waves toward the open van door.

The youth lunges toward Lily, considering the petite baroness an easy target. He is mistaken. John checks his trained reaction and merely watches her subdue the youth and push him to the ground. Doug Kasper backs away. The officers keep watch on the shackled slaves to make sure none join the fray. Lily pulls a hand-sharpened object from the boy's hand.

Lieutenant Rambler walks over. He plants his fists on his hips and amusement lights up his face. "A shank! Sorry about that. We'll talk to the officers who transport the slaves."

"Thanks." She hands over the crude weapon.

He touches his forehead in a semisalute, turns, and walks away.

She turns to look at Mr. Kasper. He has walked back to his own vehicle. She intended to ask him the names of the two girls he gave to Mr. Barton. She makes a mental note to do that when she and the commander meet with him.

She turns back to the boy she is pinning to the ground. "Ernesto Ibarra."

He remains defiantly silent.

"You have a sister named Esther."

He looks up at her. Now she has his attention. Briefly! He looks around at the tall, muscular guards surrounding her two white vans. They are watching but none have made a move to help the petite but strong woman who is firmly holding him down. He has no leverage at all.

"Would you like to talk to her?"

He looks back at her. Holding him securely with her knee and one hand, she pulls out her phone and punches in the Cuevas' number. Esther is Armando's teenage niece. "Hello, Armando. Esther's there, isn't she? … I know she's anxious, but the bus broke down so we're running late. I'd like to let Ernesto talk to her. … Hello, Esther. Here's Ernesto."

She hands him the phone. "Just get on the van, okay?"

He takes her phone. "Hello."

She watches him. His attention is riveted on his whispered conversation with the sister he has not seen in three years. He selects the seat behind the driver.

Lily turns to John who is unobtrusively listening to one side of the Spanish conversation. "Change of plan. You drive this van and let Joey take the other one."

He nods and signals Joey—who is far from fluent in Spanish, though he is making progress. Spanish classes are a new requirement for everyone at the Schwartz compound who deals with the public in town. Some grumble more than progress. Others, like Joey, diligently study. Even Lily is taking the required class, however her gripe is that she hasn't time to study sufficiently.

After all the 'rescued slaves' are seated, Lily strides to the lead van and steps on the running board under the sliding door. She looks at the disheveled men and women filling the van and smiles. "We have a safe place here. Well, as safe as we can make it. You're no longer in danger. We call this redeeming our loved ones instead of purchasing slaves. Most of you have relatives or friends waiting for you when we get to the compound. We'll tell you more after you've had a chance to clean up and eat. You should heed Lieutenant Rambler's admonition to not try anything but for a different reason than the one he gave. We have some rules for safety so listen to what you're told, and we'll make sure you understand the reasons later. Okay, Joey, let's roll."

She steps down. A guard, former U.S. Navy Seal Gary Brown, climbs in and slides the door shut. Joey starts the van and turns toward the paved road.

Ralph opens the passenger door of the second van. Lily climbs in and turns toward the back. Ralph shuts her door, climbs into the back, and slides the door shut. John shifts into first and follows Joey.

"Bye, Esther. I'll see you later." Ernesto hands the phone back to Lily.

"Ernesto, you'll be going to *Tio* Armando and *Tia* Sophia, but we'll have to give you sufficient training as a guard first. They have a café in town, and it's not as safe as our compound out of town. We provide them with a couple of guards, but Armando thought it'd be best if you were trained too. Esther and *primo* Teresa—"

He snickers, despite his best attempt to hide it.

"Oops, I mean Esther and *prima* Teresa come out for schooling a couple of days a week, so we'll set that up for you too. We're planning to move the school into town, but it'll be a while since we're still working on moving the medical personnel and engineers into the town. It's taking a while to repair abandoned homes for all of them and build a security fence to make it easier to guard. We like to keep everyone safe. Are you going to be okay?"

Ernesto nods. "Esther told me all about it, that you can be trusted, that you're her savior."

"I wouldn't put it that way. We do our best and wish we could do more."

She turns to the rest of the disheveled and abused people in the van and repeats the short speech she gave in the other van, ending with, "I can go ahead and answer some of your questions now."

An older man queries, "You seem to own quite a bit, the hospital and the school. How'd a petite little lady like you get so powerful?"

"We discovered a need for services that we provide for ourselves, so provide them for others. Well, we haven't opened the school to others yet. We won't do that until we move it to town. But back to your question: it seems the slave masters—by the way they're called barons here—have no interest in sharing any advantage they have and that leaves a vacuum which we're more than happy to fill. Income from our medical services provides us with sufficient resources to redeem our families and friends. We also actively search for people who can fill the gaps in our services and take in any stranger we come across."

"What I really meant was how'd a little lady like you get to be a baron? I guess you're a baroness, or are you just helping your husband who's the real baron? I saw what you did when Ernesto jumped you, but still."

"I have a brown belt, and I'm an expert marksman. Those skills came in handy after my husband was killed in the violence after the terrorists' attacks," she replies, finally able after three years to openly speak of the tragedy in her own life without intense emotions overwhelming her. "And I'm one of those really strong-willed people. Sometimes I grate on people, but it's kept us safe. I should add that guns are now illegal. The only ones allowed to carry firearms are the officers. That's one of the things our commander has done to bring safety to the town."

"What all do you own?" the man asks.

Even though she would like to correct his assumption that she personally owns anything, she refrains from mentioning that the compound is run democratically since—for reasons of safety—they cannot let that information become common knowledge in town. The recalcitrant power barons they are trying to convince to accept an electric co-op would rally in opposition to the sorely needed progress toward civilizing the local society if they knew how progressive the Schwartz's operations really are. Only after the newly redeemed former slaves are assimilated into the community, will they be told the secrets of the compound.

Lily replies to the man's question, "We're on a large farm and sell many products, most of which are seasonal. You'll see our large farming operation south of the buildings. We have a hospital that we recently reopened, but the outpatient clinic has been operating for about two years. Recently, the owner of the electrical utility died and I was appointed executrix of his estate, but I just let the engineers run that. It's out of my area of expertise."

She pauses. John whispers, "One other thing."

She looks at him in surprise for a brief moment. "Oh ... we have a large number of Navy Seals and one Marine, so we have well-trained guards and will be training every one of you men who're able bodied."

With a skeptically raised eyebrow, a younger man blurts in surprise, "You train us? What if we overthrow you?"

"By the time you've received that level of training, you won't want to. You can ask John here." She taps his arm with her fist. "He was determined to leave and find freedom but eventually learned that we're trying to create freedom here. Some of the women have asked to be trained in self-defense, so we start a beginners' class for women about every three months. You're as safe here as you could possibly be in this chaotic, uncivilized culture. We've also started training the local authorities. Hopefully better trained officers will be able to decrease the crime rate in town and make it safer for moving the school.

"And we'd like to add a news broadcast to our local radio station's music-only format. We're particularly interested in putting together some kind of weather reporting network, but that'll take cooperation with surrounding towns and we're not sure about the state of surrounding towns as far as safety, etcetera. Accomplishing that may be pretty far in the future."

The older man smiles as he remarks, "Sounds like civilization is coming back."

"As soon as we can accomplish it, but there is strong opposition from those in power."

"Nobody ever wants to lose their advantage," the younger man states.

Lily replies, "You got that right."

Another man asks, "How many people are on your compound?"

Lily furrows her brows. "I lost track a long time ago. Including the medical personnel and engineers in town, I'm sure it's well over a thousand, maybe fifteen hundred."

"How do you have room for all of us?" a woman asks. "I noticed that you filled two vans today. Do you do that every Monday?"

"Since we've moved the medical and engineering personnel into town, we have vacant cottages that we built during the first two years. We also have large dorms in the main building that we can use for any overflow. We're willing to accommodate anybody even if we have to fill all available floor space with cots. We don't want to turn down anyone who needs refuge so make sure that having space for them isn't the limiting factor. We might also train some of you in construction. We always have something going on in that area. Right now it's repairing rundown homes.

"The number of people I pick up each Monday varies. I actively search for relatives first then for friends and acquaintances. It depends upon how many I find. Occasionally I only need one van. I'd gladly make two trips, if I needed to, but haven't ever found that many in just one week." She stops herself before she blithely reveals that they had three vans until last Friday. She does not want to mention the recent raid and the multiple fatalities.

Thinking of vans, she looks at John. Since Tim was injured by the gunman, John and Jack went with Joey to scavenge another abandoned fifteen-passenger van but found that most had been cannibalized for spare parts or vandalized. None had a full set of tires. Instead, they brought back a gas-guzzling SUV which reminds her of a tank. It elated all the Seals and most of the men at the compound. Her major gripe is that it does not hold fifteen passengers. They left it at the clinic today, so they could use the clinic van for the trip to the prison.

A woman asks, "What's the name of this town?"

She turns her wondering attention back to the passengers. "The phone company named it Somerton after our commander, but we had to change it to Somertonville."

"That means you don't have any idea where we are, doesn't it? This is just like everywhere else. They destroyed all signs and every shred of identifying evidence to confound those foreign invaders who never appeared and everybody moved around trying to find food and water. I don't suppose any of the original residents are still here, are they?"

Lily does not allow the woman's irate tone to influence her own soft and patient tone. "Not that we've found."

"What happened to the people here? Do you know?"

"We can only guess. There was obviously a tornado which destroyed the northern part of the city. The graves indicate an epidemic swept through. We have no way of knowing if it killed everyone or if some left to escape the epidemic or riots or whatever was happening here."

The older man asks, "Could there have been an attack with that poison?"

Lily shrugs. "That would be consistent with some of what we found."

He guesses, "Deserted and nobody took anything because they ran when the first few fell and someone yelled poison."

Lily replies, "You realize, don't you, that it'd only take one person falling for any reason, such as a stroke, and someone yelling poison and everyone would panic?"

She changes the topic to avoid the wild and unsubstantiated speculation that has occurred with prior groups of new residents. "I suppose you'd like to know something about our location?"

They all nod.

"We're somewhere in Texas, fairly near the gulf coast. That's all I can tell you."

FIVE

The two vans pull up in front of the main building on the isolated Schwartz compound. A covered porch spans the length of the long, plainly built building. To the left is a three-vehicle carport separated from the main building by a windowless wall. To the right is the wing housing the massive dining hall and adjoining kitchen. The van doors slide open, courtesy of the attentive guards seated beside them, and the timid new residents pour from the vans and are ushered inside.

Lily watches as one van is driven into the carport. The clinic van heads back into town with a full compliment of guards. Soon they will return with the SUV which they have dubbed 'the tank'.

She then turns and follows Ralph across the porch. He opens the front door of the main building, and she steps inside. Most of the twenty-one dirty and famished men and women are eagerly gulping ice water and munching on the pastries, fruit, and other snack foods laid out buffet style on the homemade tables in the west end of the large main room.

A few are still waiting to wash their hands at basins of soapy water manned by Angelica "Angel" Gonzales. Dirty towels are piled at the feet of the beautiful Hispanic teenager with lustrous, black hair, hanging in loose curls to her shoulders. A bar of soap slips from the grasp of a young woman, bounces off the edge of the table, and slides across the floor.

"Let me get that for you." Ernesto Ibarra sets his food on a vacant table, chases the slippery soap across the floor, and pushes it against a table leg. He picks it up with both hands and brings it back, holding it carefully lest it slip from his grasp.

Angel points toward a soap dish beside the basin and smiles. "Thanks."

He dips his hands in the dirty, soapy water and rubs the soap from his hands. Angel hands him a towel. He smiles his thanks, dries off, and drops the towel on the pile at Angel's feet.

The abashed young woman who dropped the soap dries her hands, walks over, and picks up a glass of ice water. She raises the glass to her lips and turns toward Lily. Their eyes lock. After a refreshing gulp, she walks over. "May I speak with you?"

"Sure. Go in my office over there in the corner." Lily points to a door in the far southeastern corner of the large main room. "I'll be there as soon as I get a glass of water. Do you want anything to eat?"

"No thanks. I'm fine."

Lily watches the woman stride across the room, winding between the haphazard arrangement of the motley collection of sofas, overstuffed chairs, and other scavenged furniture which fills the east end of the main room.

Lily turns and takes a step then suddenly teeters to a stop. "Sorry. I almost didn't see you."

Marie Gonzales, Angel's mother and a carbon copy of her daughter but twenty years older and slightly heavier, hands Lily a glass.

"Thanks."

"Do you want any food?"

"No, it's getting very close to lunch since the bus was late. I'll just wait."

Marie offers, "Do you want me to bring a tray to your office?"

"No, I'll try to cut off the interviews during lunch and come to the dining hall."

"The dryers arrived today."

"Good. They found them quickly."

Marie grimaces.

"Damaged?" Lily asks.

"No. Lizzie did a victory dance. They couldn't calm her down." Marie is speaking of a teenager with Down's syndrome. She is short and heavy set with thick, medium-brown hair curling about her face in angelic fashion. Her pleasant disposition endears her to everyone, young and old alike.

"Did you take her to Max?"

"No, we took Max to her," Marie exclaims. "He said we need a psychiatrist."

Lily arches her eyebrows. "We need a psychiatrist to deal with a retarded child?"

Marie shrugs. "I guess it'd help. He gave her a shot of something, and she's still asleep. Marcus and Rebecca are staying with her. Hopefully they can keep her calm when she wakes up, but if not, a couple of guards are nearby."

"I'll check on her later."

Marie nods and turns toward the crowd. She strides over to a woman who has finished her food and is downing the last of her ice water. "Do you want more water? Or would you like to clean up? We have clean clothes for you in the ladies' shower."

Lily walks across the room, enters her office, and closes the door. She smiles as she walks to her desk and sits down. "You're the pediatrician aren't you?"

"Yes, ma'am, I'm Jill Baker."

Lily sets her ice water on the desk. "You can call me Jackie."

"Okay." The young doctor sets her moist glass on the wooden desk.

"It's unusual for someone to apply for a job here."

Jill replies, "I realize that, but I wasn't being utilized there. The other pediatrician saw all the children since I finished my residency just before the terrorists' attacks and was low man on the totem pole, so to speak. I had to do all the things the other doctors didn't want to do, including emergency surgery. We'd heard of the hospital being opened here, so I asked if there was some way I could transfer."

"How many doctors did you have?"

"There were three of us. The other one is trained in Family Practice."

"Did you have a hospital?"

Jill shakes her head. "Only a clinic. Since you opened the hospital, a lot of the patients started coming here, especially if they needed a specialist. The town is so small now that we haven't been staying very busy, otherwise they wouldn't have let me leave."

Lily inquires, "What's the name of the town?"

"I think they call it Perkins after our commander."

Lily opens a desk drawer and pulls out a mobile phone brochure, the closest thing they have to a map. "I see it, two towns to the north. I knew people were coming from other towns but didn't realize they were coming that far."

"You have quite a reputation for good medical care," Jill compliments.

"How'd you get started with the clinic there?"

"We were providing emergency care during those riots after the terrorists' attacks when a band of rebels attacked us. Commander Perkins came to our rescue and has been protecting us ever since. A few of our doctors and nurses have disappeared over the years. We're not sure if they were killed, captured, or just fled."

"So you haven't been subjected to the abusive slave culture?"

"We've certainly seen the results of the abuse!" Jill exclaims, not hiding the disgust she feels. "But no, none of us who managed to stay have been abused. Commander Perkins is a good protector and for safety, I never left the clinic. Our houses had been ransacked. There was nothing left, so we lived in the clinic building."

"How did you fare going through the prison system? Were there any problems along the way?"

"Commander Perkins is using some of the money you paid for me to assure my safe passage, maybe most of it. He gave an advance to the prison officer who accompanied me all the way, and I saw things change hands every time I changed buses. He didn't want me spending the night in prison, so I was picked up early this morning. That's why the bus was late. There was no flat. They just had to wait on me as I transferred from bus to bus. Apparently their scheduling isn't very standardized."

"That's for security," Lily informs her. "They don't want the criminal element to know when the buses are running."

"I need to instant message Commander Perkins and tell him I got here safely, so he can honor the rest of his agreement."

"After a few more questions, we'll go see Lawrence. He's our computer expert."

"Thank you. I believe he's the one I talked with on that instant messaging system."

Lily leans forward, props her elbows on her desk, and folds her arms. With anxiety, she gently squeezes her arms, pushing her thumbs into the soft flesh inside her elbows. "You know we have no way to check your resume, and none of our doctors or nurses recalls meeting you. Dr. Maxton will put you on probation until he can determine that you really are a doctor."

"I understand."

Lily relaxes. "We give everyone a week to rest and recuperate from the abuses of slavery, or more if they need it. You don't appear stressed, but you'll still get a week's rest. We may have you man a clinic here before assigning you to the hospital. We have a large population of children and they haven't seen a pediatrician in years, but Max will make that decision."

"Is Max, Dr. Maxton?"

Lily laughs. "Yes, Dr. Martin Maxton. You'll find that we're very informal around here. We started as just a group of friends. In the hospital and all places in town, you'll have to be very formal and call our medical director: Dr. Maxton and me: Mrs. Schwartz and our commander: Commander Somerton, etcetera. But out here, when there are no outsiders visiting, you can call us Max, Jackie, and Robert."

"You're close friends with the commander?"

"We've become close, once we learned we could trust each other. Jill, do you have any questions?"

"Will I be able to see only pediatric patients, or is that a question for Max?"

"Max will decide the specifics, but I can assure you that you'll have to help cover the specialties for which we have no coverage."

"What specialties do you have?"

"Max is an internist. We also have a cardiologist, an obstetrician, and an orthopedist. We assign one doctor to come out here every Monday to see the new residents and take care of the other residents at the same time. I'm sure they'll schedule all routine visits for the appropriate doctor but when it's your turn, you'll have to see everyone who comes to the Monday clinic, no matter what their problem. If something comes up that you can't handle, you can call the clinic or we can take them into town. It's only a thirty minute drive and after the road is repaired, it should take only fifteen minutes or so."

"I noticed the road."

"Are the roads like that all the way to Perkins?" Lily asks.

Jill nods. "They're bad all over. I didn't ride on a single good road today. I assume from your statement that someone is repairing them here?"

"Yes, we have many engineers. They're training some prisoners to do road work."

A grimace appears on Jill's face. "Is that what you make the slaves do while they're in prison?"

"Not the slaves," Lily replies. "Most of them come in over the weekend and are picked up by the barons on Monday. But we have some criminals that we keep confined. We've put them to work. Do you have any more questions?"

Jill shakes her head.

Lily stands. Jill picks up her glass and stands. As they walk toward the door, Lily assures the young doctor, "You can always come see me if you have more questions, or call me; we'll be assigning you a phone. After you leave your message with Lawrence, you can clean up and then see Max in the clinic. He's here today since he needs to talk with you about your credentials."

"Sorry I'm so dirty, but we thought I should look like all the other slaves being transported."

"I assumed that."

Lily opens the door, and Jill follows her into the main room.

Marie turns, walks toward them, and calls, "Lily."

As she nears Lily, Marie says, "Missy wants to see you."

Lily nods then requests, "Jill needs to see Lawrence so she can instant message Commander Perkins about her safe arrival. Will you show her the way?"

"Okay."

Lily turns. Middle-aged and pregnant Melissa Smith is seated on a sofa near the door of her office. Lily motions with her hand. "Come on in."

Missy slowly pushes her ballooning body up from the low sofa, her long, blonde curls hanging limply about her face until she finally stands erect. Despite the fact that she is only five months along, the extremely thin woman is having difficulty adapting to her changing shape. They walk into the office. Sadness clouds every aspect of Missy's features from her facial expression to her plodding walk. She apologizes as they enter the door. "I hope I'm not interrupting your interviews."

"I don't think so. Most of them want to clean up first. What's on your mind?"

Missy waits for her to close the door. "I've been seeing one of the counselors, and he says I need to talk to you."

Lily holds a chair for the awkward pregnant woman. "I've noticed you're still as sad as when you came."

Missy plants her palms on the edge of the desk and slowly lowers herself onto the straight-backed chair. "Marcus thinks you might be able to do something about it."

"We'll give it a shot." Lily sits down and forces a smile onto her face. "What's the problem?"

"I miss my son."

"I'm sorry that I haven't found him yet. What do you know about his situation, anything?"

"I saw him a week before Frank came and rescued us from Mr. Compton. He's pretty safe where he's living. He has a fairly decent master, and his job isn't so bad."

"I could make an offer. What's the name of his master?"

Missy shakes her head. "I don't know."

Lily leans back in her chair. "I'll get him as soon as I can."

Missy shakes her head. "He isn't on your list."

Lily opens a drawer, pulls out a form, and slides it and a pen across the desk. "Let's get him on the list."

Missy makes no move to pick up the pen. "I can't."

With a puzzled expression, Lily gently prods, "Why not?"

"Frank's wife enters the names into the computer. He's Frank's son. I named him Cecil Franklin Smith, Jr."

"I see. … I can search for him independently instead of having Darla enter him. Go ahead and fill out the form."

Missy picks up the pen and resolutely enters the necessary information. She slides the completed form across the desk. "Darla's not going to know about this, is she?"

"I'll take care of it separately. Now, tell me—I noticed your name is Smith—you weren't married to Frank too, were you?"

Missy shakes her head. "I was his mistress, and my maiden name is Smith. I always thought that was convenient."

"I gather you're not worried about Darla seeing Cecil after he's here?"

"He isn't a carbon copy of Frank; he looks more like me. Smith is such a common name, and anybody could've named their son Cecil. It's just that it'd be a dead giveaway for her to have to enter Cecil Franklin Smith, even if I left off the junior. That's a rather unusual name. And she knows that I was the receptionist where Frank worked just after college. That's when I got pregnant with Cecil. I'm afraid she'd be able to put it all together."

"I understand. I gather she doesn't know about you and Frank and Cecil?"

"No, we were very careful. She did get suspicious when Cecil was eight, but Frank moved us to Dallas. He rented me an apartment and helped me find a job there. He said that helped and Darla started believing him when he denied stepping out on her."

Lily steels her courage and asks a personal question. "Is Frank the father of this child too?"

Missy smiles broadly and nods.

Lily is relieved that the sadness clouding Missy's features seems to be fading. Just the idea that they will look for her son has begun to lift her depression. Even if they don't manage to redeem him, Missy will at least know she has tried.

A serious expression replaces Missy's smile. "I'm glad Frank came and rescued all of us from Mr. Compton. I know he didn't come to rescue me; he didn't know I was there and was surprised to see me and might not have come if he'd known."

Missy bows her head and heaves a melancholy sigh then looks up at Lily. "I really don't want Darla to know. I never meant to hurt her, and I know Frank didn't. He loves her. He never loved me."

Uncomfortable hearing Missy's confession, Lily folds the paper, puts it in her pocket, and stands. "I'm glad you're feeling better."

"My counselor told me that he couldn't help me, that I had to come to you, and he was right. I'll tell him that his advice was right on."

"I'm going to lunch now. Are you headed that way?" Lily asks.

"Yeah! I actually feel like eating, first time since the morning sickness."

"You're way too thin. Is Dr. Morris calling this a high-risk pregnancy?"

"Yeah, for more reasons than one; he calls my age advanced. I guess I am as far as pregnancy is concerned, but I don't like the sound of it. It makes it sound like I'm seventy or something. He's a very plain-spoken man."

After lunch, Lily walks into the kitchen and looks at Marie Gonzales. She smiles at the memory of Marie's amazing father Antonio Juarez. He was in charge of their farming operations until he died nine months ago. It is a comfort that his death was from natural causes.

Lily turns and walks over to Susie Morrow, their very pregnant head chef and another of Frank's mistresses. "Getting anxious?"

She sighs deeply. "Yeah, all the women tell me the last month is the worst, especially in hot weather, and I can tell you that they're right! My back is killing me. I'll be so glad when the little guy gets here. He must weigh twenty pounds. At least, that's what it feels like to me."

"You've trained enough chefs. You could take some time off," Lily suggests.

"Keeping busy keeps me from dwelling on the way I feel: the aching back, the swollen ankles, the teensy bladder."

"Find some sit-down jobs to do instead of staying on your feet all the time."

"I try." A chime sounds. Susie awkwardly dashes toward the ovens.

Assured that Missy won't see her, Lily walks over to Gertrude Debauch, Frank's mother. "How're you, Trudy?"

"Fine, Lily, just fine. How're you today?"

"Okay," Lily replies then lowers her voice to a whisper. "What's Frank's full name?"

"Frank Leroy Smith. Have you been talking to Missy?"

With surprise, Lily queries, "Do you know about it?"

"We all do, but Missy doesn't know that. She thinks we're all in the dark. And Frank thinks Darla doesn't know. But Alex doesn't know so it's really a complicated web, keeping track of who knows what. Anyway, Frank told Missy that his name was Cecil Franklin and that he went by Frank because the boys called him Sissy when he entered school as Cecil. He had a good idea that she'd name the baby after him, especially since her last name's also Smith. He never did like her. She chased him all through high school. He'd come home complaining about her. My husband finally told him to just give her what she wanted and maybe she'd leave him alone. But it didn't work. It just fueled her confidence when he came back after getting his degree."

Trudy leaps to another topic, her current favorite. "I'm going to enjoy that great-grandchild of mine when she arrives in September; they're going to name her Daryl Ann. Alex and Henry are going to be the best parents. Oh, I sound just like a doting grandma, don't I? Well, I really enjoyed spoiling Alex when she was growing up. She was my only grandchild ... well, not really; I just never got to see Cecil. Anyway, I spoiled her rotten. In fact, I pretty much spoiled Frank when he was growing up. And ... Darla tells me she's going to have a son; so, I can spoil a Frank

Leroy Junior too. I hope that's what she's going to name him, but I'm not interfering. It's her decision. I haven't even hinted."

Lily walks into Lawrence's cluttered lair. "Hey, Lawrence."

"Hi, Lily."

She sits down in the chair beside him. "Thanks for working late."

"That's quite all right. You brought in quite a group today, and I understand the need to speak with the new people as soon as possible. I was glad you enlightened me as soon as I walked in the door."

She laughs; her memories of her first tenuous venture into the local slave trade remain vivid even two years and three months afterwards. She knew not how the slave market worked, but she knew she must rescue two dear friends. "Denise was quite surprised when you tried to enlighten her."

Embarrassed, twenty-four-year-old Lawrence Brighton turns away and mutters, "I hope you didn't tell Charles that I winked at his wife." He had immediately repented of his rash action on his first day of freedom; Denise Anderson has children his age! He was just trying to convey to her that everything was going to be okay.

"I didn't but Denise might have."

"Oh, don't tell me that," Lawrence pleads.

She turns to the reason for her visit to the computer center. "What've we got?"

They both turn toward the computer monitor. She pages down the list of bids on the slave auction. "Whew, we already have ten bids out. Next Monday will probably be another big group. I really like this automatic bidding program you wrote. I'd already be behind if I had to enter all the bids by hand."

"Do you like the random stall feature?" Lawrence asks.

"That stalls my rebid when someone outbids me, doesn't it?"

"Yeah."

"Does it seem to keep us out of bidding wars?"

"Yeah, and we're winning the bids in the end too."

"Okay, that's good. Keep fine tuning it."

"I'll have to. We're dealing with people on the other end, not a static machine."

"I have an exception we need to deal with." Lily pulls the piece of paper from her pocket. "Frank's mistress is here and—"

"I know."

"You know?" Lily asks in surprise.

"Darla told me. Missy didn't give us any information on her son, but Darla entered what she knew. She knew Missy would like to see her son but wasn't going to spill the beans."

"I have the accurate info so let's check it out."

Lawrence's fingers fly across the keyboard. When Cecil Smith's database entry fills the screen, Lily quickly scans it. "Darla missed the year of birth by five years. He's twenty-four instead of nineteen. That might be one reason why we haven't found him. Here's his full name and birthday."

His fingers again fly across the keys.

"Thanks, Lawrence, and don't tell Missy," Lily warns. "She thinks Darla's completely in the dark, but you'd better tell her that we updated Cecil's info. But Alex and Henry don't know."

He rolls his eyes at the complicated web of lies surrounding sweet and virtuous Darla and her anything-but-virtuous husband.

"How're the bids averaging out?" she asks, turning the conversation away from the deceitful Smiths.

He keys back to the bidding program. "It's still rising. I'm afraid we're going to have problems with inflation."

Lily replies, "Keep an eye on it. If the inflation slows even though it's still rising, I think we'll be all right."

Lawrence informs her, "I set a minimum lag of two minutes between individual bids."

"If I were bidding by hand would I be able to do one every two minutes?"

"Maybe."

"Lengthen the lag," Lily instructs. "You could also bid on some who aren't on our list and 'lose' them and see how that affects inflation."

"What if we win them?"

"That's never bothered us before. The only reason we aren't bidding on strangers is that with so many people here now, we expect to fill to capacity with just family and close friends of our residents. The occasional stranger won't hurt. How's our average bid this time?"

His fingers fly. "It's about the same as last Monday night at eight p.m. The initial jump seems to have leveled out."

"Good, so maybe the bids will average about six thousand again. Maybe we've put some brakes on inflation. I was afraid that the automatic bidding system would cause it to skyrocket. I've also told Linda to back off on the fees we charge patients. I suspect the cost of medical services has a great deal to do with the price of everything."

"That's probably very influential on the local inflation, but how's the clinic doing? Will we use up our surplus and have to fuel the inflation to continuing redeeming as many as possible?"

"Clinic usage has increased, so we're still building up our surplus," Lily informs him. "I'd lower prices more but don't want to overwork our medical personnel. They're already working long days."

"That new doctor's going to help. I told Melody, and she's delighted to have a pediatrician and wants to know when she can get the kids seen."

"Max said they'll schedule visits for all the children very soon."

"Thanks. I could separate out the medical personnel and have a higher ceiling on them."

"Weight it pretty heavily toward the military personnel too. If the system collapses, we'll lose our surplus. It doesn't pay to be wealthy in such an unstable environment. We could lose all advantage and be back to square one, so let's strengthen our position as much as possible. Keep up the good work, Lawrence."

Without pausing, Lily asks, "How's the system of IDs going?"

"Marvin and I should have a presentation ready for the commander in a couple of weeks."

"Is that when you expect the equipment to come in?"

"I'm basing it on how long the camera's take, so this is just an estimate."

He turns away from the monitor and looks at her. "I have another request."

"Okay."

"Melody's birthday is coming up, and I'd like to get her a very special gift."

"What do you have in mind?"

His fingers fly over the keyboard. He pulls up a web site offering jewelry for sale and selects a diamond necklace. "I got her one like this just after we got married. It's the only extravagant thing I ever bought. I used my first paycheck at the bank to buy it and she adored it, never took it off. It was stolen, and I'd like to surprise her and replace it. I'll do whatever I have to do to purchase something so expensive for a personal reason. I know we don't indulge ourselves. Our goal is the redemption of slaves above all else but it'd mean a lot to me, to be able to give this to her."

Lily requests, "Can you enlarge the photo?"

"Sure. There it is."

"Did she say Mr. Barton stole it when they were with him during the migration?"

He looks at her with surprise. "Yes."

She shakes her index finger at the image on the screen. "I have that necklace. He sent Serena to the clinic with it to pay for the visit back when we were bartering for everything. We didn't know whether she stole it or what, so we just put it away so she'd never be found out." She is speaking of Serena Hermann, wife of engineer James Hermann. Both were formerly enslaved by Mr. Barton.

"Do you still have it?"

"Of course."

"I mean, you're sure it's not lost or stolen? I mean, Thai might if she saw it."

"Lawrence, I check it each time I get out Thai's baubles. She never looks at it. It's in a separate box, and I just checked it yesterday when I put hers back. When do you want me to get it out?"

"Her birthday's next month. I was asking in advance because it takes two to three weeks for those cameras to come in. I was expecting to have to order it and who knows if this site is legit, anyway. Can I see it now?"

"Sure."

SIX

On the roof, Lily steps across the ridge and sits beside Max. "What're you doing on the roof?"

He opens his eyes and sits up. "Just waiting on you; I knew you'd be up here sooner or later. I don't get much chance to talk to you now that we've moved into town."

"Do you want me to stop by the clinic more often?"

A smile brightens his expression. "That'd be nice."

Though her strong-willed personality grated on him at first, he has gained respect for her over the last several months. She is a capable and adaptive administrator and manager. He is not sure which title would better suit her role on the compound, but she has earned his respect for the apparent ease with which she runs the large and complex operation. Her personal life is another matter, but nobody is perfect. Because of his own failings, he must give her the benefit of doubt.

"What about Lizzie?" Lily asks. "Does she need medication or something?"

He shrugs. "I really don't know. Did you go see her?"

"Yeah, she was awake and calm but kept asking for the nice man."

"She means Frank, doesn't she?"

"Yeah, he was real nice to her. That's the only way she can express her gratitude to him for bringing her out here. I had a hard time explaining that he's gone for good." She sighs. "He was a very patient man with the girls."

Max rolls his eyes.

Lily asks, "What do you think of Jill Baker? Is she really a doctor?"

"Yeah, I grilled her. If she's not a doctor, she'd have to be a nurse with about twenty years of experience."

Lily laughs. "She looks barely twenty."

"She's closer to thirty."

"Thirty-one." Lily lays her head on her bent knees. "Is there anything specific you want talk about?"

"We'd like to start a nursing school."

"That's within your purview as medical director. Use your discretion and tell me what I need to authorize, and I'll talk to Robert about some kind of official licensing for the graduates."

"I hadn't heard nursing school mentioned so wasn't sure how the idea would be received."

Amused, she smiles. "Don't you remember me saying, when you first arrived, that we'd let you open a medical school."

"I thought you were joking."

"If society's going to return to normal, somebody's going to have to do it sooner or later." She jokingly adds, "Otherwise we'd work all our doctors to death and enter the dark ages again. Someday we really do expect to open a medical school."

He smiles for lack of a suitable retort.

She states, "Nursing school will be a good start. I'll inform the security committee at our next meeting, and then we'll bring it up at the monthly council meeting. Oh that's tomorrow night. I'd better ask the security committee to meet tomorrow. I think that'd be better than waiting a full month. Let me ask this: what timetable were you thinking about?"

"We hadn't really discussed it, but it's obvious that we need to do it. We just about work all our nurses to death, but most of the aides we've trained would make great nurses. We'd like to be able to utilize them in more responsible roles and recognize them for their excellent work since we can't give them a raise. It's kind of a disadvantage to not be paying anyone a salary."

"I guess we can wait a month. Do you remember the discussion about moving the school to town? It was all about safety for the children, the logistics of schooling children who lived in two locations, and diplomas for the graduates. The idea that this is the direction we need to take was a given. Not opening a school wasn't even mentioned, not even by any of our rabble-rousers who always present the opposing view. With the nursing school, I expect that we'll have a lively discussion about the timing or inquiring about who'll be teaching them and maybe even how we'll license them but it's almost certain that it'll be easily accepted."

He nods.

72

"Max, do you have your suggestions ready for how we'll reorganize the council now that we've moved the medical branch into town?"

"I followed your example and set up a committee. Lou's been elected chairman, so I think they'll do a fine job." He is speaking of Lou Piedmont, a former fireman who has been trained as a physician's assistant.

Max segues into a related topic. "I've been talking to the engineers about ventilation in the hospital. It's going to get hot soon and the hospital is designed for air conditioning. They said there's not enough Freon or anything of that nature available at this time to run such a large system. They may have to make some major structural changes in the building to keep the inside from feeling like an oven in the summer heat."

"And you're asking my opinion on that?"

"I don't know anything about engineering either. I guess we'll just have to trust the engineers on this."

"Yeah," she replies. "We have a good bunch here. Does it sound like it's going to be costly?"

"Maybe or just time consuming."

"We're still building a surplus even with lowering the rates for medical care, so money won't be a problem. We have plenty of engineers, so I don't think we'll be limited by a lack of expertise or workers either. And surely they can scavenge what they need from vacant buildings if it isn't available on the open market. Buster and his cadre of scavengers must know every inch of town. He can find what they need." She is speaking of the leader of the homeless men who trade scavenged items for food.

"You're always the optimist, aren't you?"

She laughs. "Sometimes it's hard with all the setbacks we have around here, but I've learned we can depend on our people. That greatly eases my burden."

"Yeah. I learned today, that I can depend upon your advice."

With an amused smile, she teases, "Max! You just learned that today. You've been here over a year."

He leans toward her. "It was just that one bit of advice you gave me that I didn't want to follow. I've trusted you on everything except my relationship with my daughter."

"Did you talk to her today?"

"After supper I spent some time with her and the grandkids. Lawrence was still working, so I talked to her while Larry played and she fed Brittany. I confessed a brief account of the sins of my youth and how I've changed my life since learning that God is real but there are still consequences to be faced. I think she understands now why my marriage to her mother soured. We ended up on the floor with the kids crawling all over me. That's much better than sitting in silence and letting Larry tweak my nose because we couldn't talk. I'm glad I finally took your advice. When Lawrence came in, we were all laughing and having a great time. I left it to her to tell him."

"That's great," Lily states.

"What's up with you?" Max asks. "With it still this cool at night, you're not up here to sleep. Is something bothering you?"

"And you were up here waiting for me. You already knew something's bothering me."

"I can see it in your face, ever since that raid the other day."

"You got the timing right." She looks up at the stars.

"Is it the raid that's bothering you?"

She lowers her voice to a mere whisper. "Actually, it's the fact that killing that raider doesn't bother me. It's always bothered me when I had to shoot someone or even just physically subdued them. I'd shake and come up here alone and cry—"

"Or ask me to give you a sleeping pill."

"Yeah, but not this time. I'm getting hardened."

"Could it have something to do with them killing four officers and shooting Mr. Patterson and Tim? You know they'd have killed many more, if they'd gotten away."

"Everyone I've killed has killed someone or been about to and it still bothered me. It even bothered me when I had to merely threaten. So no, that shouldn't make any difference."

"You're crying now," Max states.

"But I'm crying over not reacting to what I've done."

He puts his arm around her and pulls her close. Tears escape from her closed eyes and trickle down her cheeks.

"Do you mind if I give you some advice?"

She sniffs. "Not at all."

"It might help to talk to Ralph about this. Since he's a policeman, he might have some insight into how police officers deal with issues such as this. I know how doctors deal with having a patient die, but at least we're not trying to kill them. That's a whole different issue than what I experience. He'd be better at addressing it."

"Ralph's so reserved, I'm not sure I'd feel comfortable confiding in him. I'm not sure Ralph would feel comfortable with me confiding in him, and I'd be uncomfortable because he was uncomfortable. I definitely wouldn't be comfortable crying on his shoulder."

"Hasn't he been your bodyguard for three years? Hasn't that put some dent in his reserve?"

"It's only been about two years and it has put some dent in his reserve but not much."

Max cautiously states, "A woman being in charge is a blow to a man's ego."

"Ralph doesn't have an ego problem. He was just as reserved when he was teaching that gun safety class years ago, and he's always been real easy to work with … just like you."

"Just because he and I aren't like Frank, doesn't mean we don't have egos. A reserved man like Ralph just wouldn't ever show it."

"But you don't let it interfere in your decisions. You're rational and practical not egotistical and reckless," she asserts.

They look toward the west as someone climbs the ladder by the back door of the dining hall. A slender man walks across the dining hall roof to the main hall and continues toward them. Max puts his arm down. She sits erect and wipes away her tears. Lawrence walks up and squats beside Max. He seems ill at ease.

Max begins the awkward conversation. "Did Melody talk with you?"

"Yeah, after she put the kids to bed. You really thought you might be my father?"

"Yes. Sorry," Max contritely apologizes.

"Thanks for being concerned enough to try to do something about it before the wedding. I really wouldn't want to marry my half-sister."

Max exhales in relief.

Lawrence awkwardly explains, "Since I didn't know who my father was and with my mother being a single mom with bunches of kids and a hard time keeping a job and sometimes hooking to make ends meet, I was concerned that any girl might be my half-sister or maybe a half-sister to one of my half-sisters. I asked Melody a lot of questions when we first started dating. She assured me that you'd never done anything like that."

"That's not something you tell your daughter," Max replies.

Lawrence laughs. "I can see that, but she said your parents were pillars of the community."

"Yeah but they weren't Christians in any sense of the word so I didn't grow up with a good sense of right and wrong, just a don't-get-caught attitude."

"Do you mind if I ask how you ended up with Paula?" Lawrence tentatively inquires, hoping he doesn't irritate his father-in-law and destroy the relationship he is trying so hard to establish.

"I was impressed with her character. She was different from all the other girls. I tried to find some way to get into the good graces of such a nice girl. When I found out she was a Christian, I decided to become one too but I thought religion was just the traditions of men and didn't pay any attention to the teachings. I learned what I had to recite, so they'd accept me. So basically," Max sighs, "I was faking it. … That is, until I learned the truth and actually changed my behavior."

"I'm glad we're finally able to get this out in the open," Lawrence states.

Max mutters, "Not too much in the open, I hope."

"I just meant among family and you do realize Lily is like family to me. She and Walter took me under their wings when I was fourteen and then became my legal guardians when my mom died three years later."

"Lily told me. She was assuring me that you'd understand my past because of yours."

"Yeah, I'd be a criminal if Walter hadn't been assigned to be my court-appointed attorney for breaking and entering. Although, I didn't actually break in since the doors were left open." Lawrence softly chuckles. "I did almost break myself when I slipped on the wet floor.

"Do you mind if I ask another question?" Lawrence politely inquires.

"I'm hoping our new relationship will always allow that," Max states, hiding his uneasiness. He is hoping for a good relationship with his son-in-law but opening up to a man who is a stranger, despite having been a relative for four years, fills Max with anxiety.

"I was just wondering if you knew what Paula had. It'd mean a great deal to Melody to know what took her mother's life."

Max shakes his head with sadness. "We don't have sufficient lab tests. For many things, we just have to guess based on symptoms."

"At least you and Melody got to see her again before she died, and she got to see her grandchildren. She was really looking forward to Larry's birth then Melody got kidnapped, and we didn't know what happened to her."

Max remains sorrowfully silent.

Lawrence says, "At least you know what happened to Paula instead of being in the dark like so many of the people around here."

"You're right there, Lawrence. It pained me to watch her die and to know that she hadn't forgiven me for my deceit, but at least, I know she's not still suffering at the hands of some brutal master. She had a peaceful two weeks in a comfortable setting, thanks to Lily."

"Max, do you know about Lily's promise to the nurses?" Lawrence is speaking of a promise Lily made to Eva soon after she and Lynnette began providing their services to others. To treat an abused woman then have to send her back to her abuser was causing the two nurses great distress. In tears, Eva pleaded for Lily to do something about it.

Max replies, "Yes."

"Are we making any progress?" Lawrence inquires.

"We still see a lot of abused women and girls in the clinic, but it does seem to be lessening."

"I'd think it'd be a lot less with Mr. Barton gone and all his people with us."

With a satisfied smile, Lily adds, "And don't forget that Commander Somerton cleaned up his force and the errant officers are in prison instead of abusing prisoners."

"So keep 'getting political', Lily," Lawrence states, using their euphemism for her plan of attack. Or maybe it is merely a description substituted for a lack of a plan, since from the beginning they have been at a loss as to how to change society in such a drastic way.

Lawrence stands. "I'll see you two later."

Lily says, "Good night, Lawrence."

"Bye, Lawrence," Max states.

Lawrence turns and takes a step. He stops and turns back. "Why didn't you just ask me about my father?"

Max beckons for him to come closer. He steps back and squats.

"I was hiding my shameful past from my family."

"I could have kept a confidence. I wouldn't have told Melody, if you asked me not to."

Max leans toward his son-in-law and uses a soft but stern tone. "You must never let anything—especially secrets—come between you and your wife lest you ruin your relationship like I did."

"You have a point. I'll keep that in mind."

"Lawrence, I want you to know that I'm glad to have you for a son-in-law, and I know you'll take good care of my little girl and her two precious babies."

Lawrence nods. "Three."

"Oh? Another is on the way; congratulations."

"Thanks. See you two later." Lawrence stands and walks away.

Max turns to Lily. "How're you doing otherwise?"

"Okay."

"How's the pain in your belly?"

"I guess its better. I hadn't noticed it much lately, but it hadn't really occurred to me that it wasn't there." She smiles. "I guess I just don't miss it."

"That's an indication that it's probably stress related."

She laughs. "I guess the stress is down. I haven't been worrying about snipers, ambushes, and eavesdropping bugs. That raid last week was an anomaly. Lately, I've just been worrying about things like forming a co-op against political resistance, Mr. Wong wanting to open a restaurant in town, and Susie wanting to open a bakery and catering business."

Mr. Wong and his family ran a Chinese restaurant before the disruption of society. He and his remaining family stumbled upon the farm while hiding in the nearby hills. Only when a medical emergency forced them to accept help, did they learn that the compound is a safe haven.

Susie Morrow, their chief chef, sought out Lily and migrated with her. Susie and her husband owned a bakery, and Lily was a customer who became a trusted friend.

To turn Lily's thoughts away from the recent raid, Max jokingly inquires, "Are you going to let her do it?"

"Of course. We're promising freedom to everyone when we bring them out here and that includes the freedom to leave. I just informed her that it's probably not safe yet, and that it'd stretch our guards too thin to take on another location in town at this time. And her baby's due next month, so she should wait at least a few months before taking on a major move. But you're probably going to see a number of enterprises in town that started out here. I think we'll be able to put her and Mr. Wong near Armando's. There're some abandoned buildings there and that'd make it easier to guard all three."

"Are you finding more military men to add to our cadre of guards?"

"Yes, and they each add more names to our search list. I've been picking up one or two each Monday, and we already have three we're bidding on for next Monday. And some of the nonmilitary men that they're training will make excellent guards too."

To keep her focused on a nonthreatening issue, he returns to his teasing inquiry. "What're you going to do without Susie out here?"

"How're you doing without Susie moving to town with you?" she counters.

"The cooks she trained are very good. We still have to worry about our waistlines enlarging, especially with that big shipment of pastries you send in every day."

"Yeah, she trained plenty of cooks." Lily lowers her voice and jokes, "Or maybe we should call them chefs instead of cooks. After all, women can have egos too and many of her trainees are men."

With amusement, he nods in agreement.

"Enjoying food is something we've never had to worry about out here … except the times when we almost ran out of food like that siege the winter before you came." She wipes her hands across her face.

"Yeah," Max replies. "You had almost nothing that first night, but it was still delicious.

"Oh, I almost forgot. I'm supposed to tell you that Mr. Patterson would like to have Judge Hahn come see him."

She inquires, "Why does he want to see Roger?"

Max shrugs.

They look over as someone raises the emergency exit of the safe room hidden between Lily's room and the office. Ralph's head appears. "Lily, Rene is hiding in the shower. Even Tommy can't calm her."

Max sighs; he hopes Lily can calm their only lab tech Rene Collier. She is obviously having a stress related crisis due to the abuse she suffered before arriving at their compound. If their most competent counselor cannot calm her, something is seriously wrong. As a counselor, Lily is quite competent in her own right. Perhaps he won't be called on to sedate Rene; it is an unethical practice that he would like to avoid.

Lily kneels beside the terrified young woman. Her dark brown, shoulder-length hair is damp. Without makeup a smattering of freckles dot her cheeks. Her arms are crossed and she squeezes her upper arms to prevent her hands from shaking.

Lily asks, "Rene, what happened?"

Rene mutters, "I heard his voice."

"Whose voice?"

"Reggie's friend, you know, the one who was with him." She bursts into tears; she can't bear to speak of the abuse she suffered at the hands of Reginald Patterson.

Lily warps her arms around Rene and pulls her close. "Who is he?"

Rene shakes her head. "I heard his voice in the hall, so I stayed in here."

Lily offers, "I'll see if Lawrence can identify who we have who came from Mr. Patterson."

With fear permeating her voice, Rene croaks, "What're you going to do with him?"

"First you'll have you identify him by his voice. We don't want to accuse the wrong man."

Rene pleads, "I don't want to face him! That scares me to death."

"We'll put you and a couple of guards behind one of the dividers in the main room and find an excuse to talk with him on the other side. He won't even know you're there."

"I think I can do that." Rene heaves a deep sigh. "So after that, then what?"

"We'll take it to the security committee and go from there, just like we have with Brett." Lily is speaking of a very suave young man with slicked-back, black hair who initially impresses but soon repulses with his crass behavior and incessant pursuit of every woman on the compound.

"He's still pestering several of the girls, and the committee hasn't done anything to Brett," Rene counters.

Lily replies, "He hasn't crossed the line like Reggie and his friend."

Rene wipes tears from her face. "I'm glad Mr. Patterson gave me to you. I feel safe here. Well ... I felt safe here until I heard his voice."

"We'll keep you safe. Until we've identified him, we'll provide you with guards. You've never heard him at the clinic, have you?"

Rene shakes her head. "I'm sure he's not one of the men who work at the clinic, so I'll only need guards here."

"Okay, we'll get this resolved as soon as possible. We don't want him to hurt anyone else." Distressed, Lily thinks, *how can we keep people safe when we have men like Brett and Rene's attacker on the compound? We have to find this man!*

SEVEN

John pulls 'the tank' to a stop behind the clinic. Gary Brown opens the door and jumps to the ground. Judge Roger Hahn slides across the seat of the oversized SUV. As Gary reaches up to assist the elderly gentleman, Roger teasingly grumbles, "Lily ... whoops, I mean Mrs. Schwartz, I don't see why you got this behemoth of a vehicle."

With a grin on her face, she swivels around to face the dignified former judge with a bald dome, a circle of neatly trimmed grey hair, and a droll wit. "I guess I shouldn't have sent the Seals to select a replacement."

"It reminds us of a tank," John jokes as he leans forward and lays his arms across the top of the steering wheel.

"That's for sure," Roger replies as his feet finally reach the pavement. With the assistance of muscular Gary, the debilitated judge did not fall on his face while descending the equivalent of a steep cliff. He admits to himself that it was easier to slide out than climb in; it just seemed more perilous to look down than up. Both times, however, Gary had lifted him as easily as if he had been a small child.

Lily states, "Roger, Gary will take good care of you while you're at the hospital. If we take too long before we come back for you, just have them make you comfortable. And Gary, make sure they know if you're still here at lunch. They're not used to feeding extra mouths on a Tuesday, and I wouldn't want you two starving while the staff is feasting in the break room."

"We'll be sure to do that," Gary assures her then teases, "and since I like Sophia's burritos so much, I'd be delighted if you'd delay until after lunch."

Ralph slides over and closes the door.

John shifts into first. "Where to?"

"Electric utility, which shouldn't take too long, then we'll go to Mr. Kasper's. I'm to call the commander as we head that way so he can meet us there and maybe we'll have one more baron allied with us although I'm not too sure of his commitment either way. He appears to be a waffler." The joking forgotten, she grimaces. "A lot of them appear to be wafflers."

When Stanley Williamson opens the door, Lily cheerfully greets him. "Good morning."

A glum expression clouds the engineer's face. "Come in, Mrs. Schwartz. Let's go in my office."

He ignores Ralph and turns away. They walk in silence through the cavernous building, a warehouse near the electrical substation which Mr. Barton commandeered and turned into a work and storage facility for his engineers, every one of whom is wearing the same glum expression.

Stanley opens his office door. "Ralph, grab any chair."

Ralph moves the closest chair over beside the door. Stanley closes the door and offers Lily a seat.

She assumes that the early morning death of fellow engineer James Hermann, who leaves a young widow Serena and two children, is contributing to their despondency. "Stanley, I guess you've heard about James?"

He plops down in his chair. "Yes, Dr. Randolph had someone call. We'll have the funeral tomorrow. I think he'd like to be buried out at the compound, if that's okay."

"That's fine. Serena already called. They're digging the grave this afternoon."

"He's too young to have a heart attack," Stanley mutters.

"I think so too, but you know he had a stressful life under Mr. Barton."

"We all did!" Stanley angrily exclaims.

Lily stifles her sigh of frustration. She tried to comfort Stanley; instead she irritated him. "I'm sorry about James. As I walked in, I noticed that all of you were sad."

"It's not just James. He was a good man, a great engineer, and we'll miss him but ...."

She waits for him to complete his sentence. He doesn't. "What's wrong?" she urges. "Is it the long wait?"

"No. They do blame me for not pushing you hard enough, but there are other things too."

"Like what?"

He pulls on his earlobe. "It's kind of hard to put it into words. They're grumping about most everything."

Lily inquires, "How did you become head engineer? Were you the head engineer under Mr. Barton? Or is it something new?"

"Mr. Barton was head engineer, even though he never came out here. The rest of us were mere peons. He made all the decisions and whoever he sent, knew he'd better carry them out or have every single engineer agree to back up his change. That was the only way we could defy Mr. Barton, to be one hundred percent in opposition with a list of objective arguments ready. Jeff was usually the one who spearheaded our opposition. He was young but unwilling to just roll over. With no family to protect, he didn't fear Mr. Barton as much as the rest of us. When we learned Mr. Barton was seriously injured, I was the one with the cool head who spoke up and calmed things down. With Jeff missing, I became head by default. We all thought Jeff must have been the one who attacked Mr. Barton and that's why he fled."

"Why don't I send an intervention team over? I have some experienced negotiators and counselors who can probably help sort out the problems and find solutions."

"At this point, I'd be willing to try anything. Mary's the only reason I haven't given up altogether. She's been my voice of reason the last few months. If I were single, I'd have taken off and taken my chances elsewhere."

"I'll set that up tomorrow," Lily promises. "Can you hold out until then?"

He nods.

"Let's go on to other things. The officers have almost finished their scrutiny of the Grande Hotel and the remains of the old motel beside it. Plans are to raze the entire structure to be sure the hidden cameras are all destroyed. Is there anything you want out of there?" She is speaking of the former residence of the engineers and their families, their abode while enslaved under Mr. Barton.

He slowly shakes his head. "I'd like to forget about that entire era in my life. I'm sure the others feel the same. It'd be better for there to be no reminders."

"You'll need to ask the others, out of courtesy," she gently remonstrates with a knowing smile.

"I guess you're right. I've been taking shortcuts lately since it's so tense around here."

"That just makes it tenser."

He wipes his hand over his face. "I'm just so tired."

"You can hold out until tomorrow or you can call a meeting to make a list of the problems that need addressed, the decisions that need to be made, etcetera. I could even wait a day to schedule the team, if you need more time for your meeting."

"You're right, of course. You know, I already feel relieved. Just a little bit anyway." Stanley smiles. "I'll cut down to a skeleton crew at all locations and have a think tank, this afternoon.

"While I'm thinking of it, we'd better wait a day on the team. The funeral is tomorrow. James was a great man, calm and serene and kind to everyone, despite the difficulties we endured under Mr. Barton. I'm sure everyone wants to go. That is, everybody we can spare; we may have to draw straws to see who goes and who has to work."

"Of course," she readily agrees.

"Did the cut in the rates help?"

"Not yet," she replies. "We're guessing that no one believes the rates will stay down once we've installed the co-op. We could cut the rates even more since we're still building a surplus, just not as rapidly. It helps that we're getting paid for the engineers to supervise the prison road crew, and of course, Commander Somerton is taxing all the barons for the improved roads."

"That's one all the barons agree on, isn't it?"

"Yes, they all jumped at the chance. They think they're getting a good deal because the prisoners are doing the labor."

Stanley laughs. "They don't realize that we all have to pay for housing the prisoners—even if they don't work—do they?"

"It appears that most of them don't. At least we are getting something out of it instead of just paying for the room and board of idle men. We'll be using the advantages the barons are reaping out of arrangements like this to help convince them to agree to the co-op. They certainly never received any advantages with Mr. Barton in control of the electricity."

"Except for the extremely low rates he charged," he corrects.

"If you factor in the inflation we've had, the rates we're charging now are about the same as his low rates."

"About that surplus, is it in danger of evaporating?" Stanley asks with concern for the long-term stability of the future co-op.

"It would if the monetary system broke down, but I don't see that happening anytime soon. The rate of inflation seems to be slowing."

"Monkey and his crew are doing a great job of fixing up those houses for our families. Could we spend more of the surplus on our homes? I think that'd be a real morale booster for everyone."

"He can only make them as nice as what's available in the market. It looks like you're going to have to forget about air conditioning for the time being. How're you doing on getting the washers and dryers to work?"

"They've been sitting in the vacant homes for three years and some of the motors are frozen. We've managed to get some of them to work. Our wives are more than happy to share until we can provide working ones in each home. Speaking of our wives, let me say, they are very happy with our situation. They feel like they're in heaven with our living situation returning to something that resembles normality."

"That's good," Lily replies.

"You know ... I suppose their wives are a calming factor for the other men too and that's why things haven't blown up around here, maybe the only reason it hasn't blown up."

"At the meeting, be sure you poll the others on spending some of the surplus to make your homes more lavish instead of just assuming and remind them that you have the freedom to run this like a co-op. The only holdover is that it's entered as Mr. Barton's estate on the official registry, but that's a mere formality. My only requirement is that you keep me informed on what you're doing. I learned a long time ago that I can't be blindsided by the other barons. I can't let them know that I don't have full control of what's officially called my operations."

He laughs. "I heard about Frank's escapades and Commander Tyler grilling you on his whereabouts."

Concern creases her forehead. "That's not getting to outsiders, is it?"

"No, everyone knows we have to keep things like that inside our operations.

"Ah … in our discussions, this afternoon, we may consider cutting the rates again."

Lily leans back in her chair. "That's your decision to make. I'll do whatever you ask, okay? I'll let you know if I think something you want to do is not wise, but it'll still be your decision and it does need to be a group decision."

"Another thing: could we have the entire surplus available to us instead of just authorizing small amounts each time?"

"Don't you want to have control over the surplus instead of having it available every time anyone goes to market? It could disappear quickly."

"Are you saying someone here is dishonest and would spend it on themselves?"

She warns, "I don't think you want to lose it all to find out. I am sure some of the merchants are dishonest and would overcharge if they could. If you want more for anything, I'll authorize it without question but let's don't be reckless."

"I see your point. It's all available to us, but not to others so it won't get pilfered away. We just have to go through the formality of releasing it for each purchase."

He returns to his greatest concern, "Have any of the barons softened their opposition to us?"

Since he has turned the conversation away from the internal problems, she relaxes. "Commander Somerton and I are meeting with Mr. Kasper today. We'll see how that turns out."

"You know his slaves are all illegal immigrants who swarmed over the border after the terrorists' attacks destroyed border control. I don't think any of them speak English except for his sole supervisor."

"Thanks. That could be useful information."

"What's your plan for convincing him to ally with us?"

"I'll look for any advantage to him. I've already found out that he was totally in the dark about Mr. Barton's activities. He even sent a couple of girls over there because they wanted to be ballerinas. You wouldn't know which ones they were, would you?"

He shakes his head.

"I'll also see if he's open to suggestions on how to increase the efficiency of his operation or profitability, etcetera. Sometimes even the smallest thing can make a difference in negotiations."

"We've definitely profited from employing your suggestions," Stanley admits. "Engineers can have quite an ego and resisted implementing your suggestions but after the first one worked so well, we've tried almost every one. I know you don't know anything about engineering, but you certainly have expertise in managing a large operation. That's why I've so readily agreed to your suggestions today. I'm learning to trust your judgment. What'd you do before? Did you run your husband's business or something?"

"My husband was an attorney, so no, I didn't run his office, his small office," she emphasizes. "My last job, which I really liked, was head of the personnel department at Fairchild-Bridles Production, Inc."

"I remember that company. There was quite a write-up about them in one of our trade journals. I don't remember you being mentioned in the article. Maybe it's just my memory and the fact that I didn't know you back then, but we implemented some of the ideas in our personnel department."

"I remember being interviewed for that. They never bothered to send me a copy, so I didn't get to read the finished article. I just assumed the vice president was taking all the credit for my work and that my name wasn't in it."

"Say, I remember Mr. Barton's extreme interest in that article," Stanley reveals. "It was several months old when he was hired and he insisted that our boss look into it. He'd dismissed it when one of the guys brought it up before, but somehow Mr. Barton got him to take it seriously. Perhaps it was because he was a little higher in the bureaucratic hierarchy and obviously a brilliant engineer, a really persistent, brilliant engineer. He advanced quickly due to his successes. We were surprised when the new guy was promoted when Mr. Stovall died so suddenly, but we respected Mr. Barton for all the improvements he implemented in just a few short months.

"Tillie was so impressed that she married him. Tillie's ex was the only one leery of him, but that's to be expected." Stanley sighs and stares at the floor. "Poor guy; he had a carbon monoxide leak in his apartment and the batteries were dead in his detector. Maybe we should've listened to him, but we just thought he was jealous. He wanted to get back together with her."

"I didn't know Mr. Barton was married," Lily states.

"She disappeared soon after the attacks." Stanley grimaces and looks up at Lily. "Our respect for Mr. Barton was our undoing when the chaos struck and our boss disappeared. Well, all the bosses above Mr. Barton disappeared."

Lily inquires, "When was he hired, just a few months before the attacks?"

"That's right. I heard he was stalking you then."

She nods. "I'd just turned him in but nothing came of it before law and order broke down. I didn't even know who the stalker was until he got angry last fall and let the cat out of the bag."

"Mrs. Schwartz, you look like you're lost in thought."

She shakes her index finger in the air. "I'd been wondering how he tracked me down. I guess it could have been that article."

"I guess your name was in the article and it was online, so it would've popped up if he searched for you."

"I guess. Or maybe there was a photo since he wouldn't have known my married name. That photographer took a lot of photos. Most of them were candid shots, so I was hoping that if my photo was used that he'd pick a flattering one."

"I also heard that he had a thing for you since childhood," Stanley remarks, still speaking of deceased Mr. Barton.

She laughs. "Yeah, but I hadn't seen him since he left for college. I still think of him as two different people: Clarence of my childhood and Mr. Barton of the post-terrorist world. The athletic and popular football star I knew is a sharp contrast to the morbidly obese and ruthless baron I met during the migration down here. The only thing they had in common was the swagger."

"We do the same thing except that Clarence the respected supervisor is overshadowed by Mr. Barton the brutal, tyrannical master, and the only physical difference is about seventy-five pounds."

With a glint of mischief in his eye, Stanley politely asks, "Do you mind if I ask if you had a thing for the football star?"

She laughs. "He was five years older than me. I considered him a pestiferous friend of my brother Tom and ignored him as much as possible. In fact, he was banned from our house when I was four. I hid from him by sneaking up on the roof, and they didn't find me until they brought in a search-and-rescue helicopter."

"I bet that caused a stir." His lopsided grin clearly displays his amusement.

Relieved that Stanley is relaxing, Lily continues with the topic he seems to enjoy. "There's even more. When Clarence turned eighteen, my dad told me that he talked to the sheriff and if Clarence even looked at me, I was to call the sheriff."

"That may be why you never saw him after he went to college."

"You're probably right. I'm sure he came home from college, but I never saw him."

"This is enlightening," Stanley admits, obviously more comfortable talking to the formidable baroness. "We learned he was a pervert soon after the chaos started, but it's obvious that he's always been that way. He was after a thirteen year old when he turned eighteen! Ha!"

Out of curiosity, she turns to a serious topic. "I know he used brutal enforcers to keep you and your families in line, but why didn't you band together and usurp control?"

"We never knew who among us he was using as an informant—a coerced informant—and he'd planted those listening devices all over. After a couple of the guys were tortured and killed by Cisco, we were all leery. And he killed the guy who put the system in, so there'd be no source of information for us to use to disable them; although we did manage to disable a few."

"Cisco; I haven't heard that name in a while. I heard he's gone," Lily states.

"Yeah, he's the one who disappeared while on stakeout out at your place."

"I didn't know that was him. You know we don't know what happened to him? We didn't kill him."

"Frank told Jeff that he'd seen tracks of a large panther or something about that time."

She opens her eyes wide.

"You never heard about that?"

She shakes her head. "No one ever reported seeing evidence of a panther."

"So that means Frank was lying."

"Maybe, maybe not, you know Frank."

He nods.

"Okay, anything else?" Lily asks.

"It just occurred to me. In our meeting this afternoon, I could use some info on that surplus."

She pulls out her web-link device and begins tapping.

He grabs a pad of paper and searches his cluttered desk for a pen. "Okay, I'm ready."

"Here's the surplus." She points at the bottom line.

He jots down the figure.

She taps a couple of times. "This is last week's income."

"Have all the barons paid?"

"Yes, except for me. I've been marking our bill against Mr. Barton's medical bill."

"Let me see his medical bill."

She taps several times.

"That wipes out our surplus!" Stanley exclaims.

"If I end up writing it off, it won't bother me."

"Why don't you go ahead and do that?"

"I need it for bargaining," Lily asserts. "If the other barons will agree to the co-op, only if a baron has a large stake in it, then I have that stake. If they don't want me to have any part of the co-op then I can write it off as my concession in the negotiations. They'd feel obligated to concede something if I offered such a huge concession."

He morosely stares at the petite baroness with the reputation as the toughest bargainer.

"Hey, you know I'm not going to use it against you," she argues.

He frowns in disgust. "Why's it so large?"

"I was trying to take Mr. Barton to the cleaners. If he survived, I wanted all of you. I wasn't going to leave him any slaves."

"We appreciate that, but now we'd like that to disappear." He taps his forefinger on the desk.

"We need it for bargaining purposes whenever one of the barons makes an offer to buy you."

"When, not if?" Stanley mutters with wide eyes.

"That's right."

"They've made offers to outright purchase us?"

She nods. "When they see this and I insist that it be paid, they back off. It appears to be large enough that no one can afford to pay it."

"So this is keeping us from going back into slavery with one of the other barons?" he asks to confirm his assumption.

"Yes. Well, let me ask this: is there one of the other barons that you'd trust to take over?"

"Absolutely not, and on this I definitely don't need to ask. We've discussed it, and we're all in full agreement."

"Okay, let me use this to keep you out of their hands," Lily pleads.

"Okay. You're sure you'll write it off? You'll promise us that?"

"Let me reword the promise. I'll use it to your advantage and write it off only after it ceases to have any value to you. But … you can't tell anybody."

"I understand. It can't get around to the other barons," Stanley says to communicate his understanding of her tactics.

"It would totally destroy our leverage in the negotiations."

"I see that there's a reason you've done so well," Stanley admits. His admiration of the strong-willed baroness is increasing.

"Yes, rule number one: hold onto any advantage."

"Okay, we'll keep our egos out of this," he concedes, "but we don't have a surplus after all."

"Yes, you do," she says with great emphasis. "This medical bill isn't part of operations. It's a personal bill of the estate. The operation of the utility is making a profit even with the lowered rate."

He nods with a resigned expression on his face.

"Maybe I should also remind you that you're paying for my men to repair the houses for you."

"So we'll own them?" he guesses.

"I guess. Property ownership isn't too well defined yet. It's mostly just … what's that called?"

"Homesteading?"

"No, it's … oh, I can't think of the term," Lily mutters. "It's where someone just occupies it and the legal owner with the deed loses if they don't protest."

"I know what you're talking about."

She taps her handheld device. "Back to this: here's the amount you've been paid for working on the roads."

"That's for one week?"

"Yes. All of the income and expense are last week's totals," she confirms.

"What's the operating cost?"

"Not much. It's mostly expenses such as food unless you need supplies or parts or something and, of course, the tax."

"I guess the repairs on the homes are personal or could it be considered our salaries?"

"We could consider it an operational expense. Without an income tax, it doesn't particularly matter. However it varies; most of the charges for repairs were at the beginning, but now your engineers are doing most of the work. There's also the charge for the guards we provide. That'll be a continuing expense, and it shouldn't vary."

"We appreciate you setting us up in the same area with the medical staff. I know that's for efficiency in protecting us, but it's also great to have neighbors. It's like a close-knit community over there. It makes our wives happy."

Lily agrees, "Yeah, it's looking more like a normal society around here except for that tall security fence."

"By the way, Jack has been seeing a lot of Lynnette."

She smiles at her mental picture of Jack Thorne and Lynnette Thurman strolling hand in hand. "I was wondering why he wanted to be assigned guard duty there so often."

"When are we going to be able to keep the kids in town with us?"

"That'll be when we think it's safe. The raid last week is a setback and the co-op must be a done deal or we might be endangering the children by opening the school under unstable conditions. Your wives have agreed to homeschool after they get their homes all set up. They'll be safe inside the fenced and guarded complex, and we'll have the kids come out one or two days a week and get their assignments from the teachers. That should help until we open the school."

"I didn't realize our wives were working on that."

"You've probably just been too stressed to listen to Mary," she suggests.

"More like too busy. If someone isn't over griping to me in the evenings then I'm working on one of our appliances."

"Let me assure you of one thing. We're going to get the electric company set up with autonomy even if we don't manage to make it a co-op. I know there'll be resistance, but if all else fails, I'll take over for Mr. Barton's medical bill and set it, the medical facility, and the school up as autonomous entities. Slavery is not in your future. In fact, it's not even your present. It's merely the name on this system."

"You're right. There'd be resistance, but there might be a continuing filibuster from the other barons for a long time."

"That's right, but I'm going to do as I please with 'my operations'." She makes quote marks with her fingers. "I always have. The other barons don't have any control over this. I'm just trying to bring them along the same civilized path I'm treading. I figure that'll bring the most stability to the area and be better in the long run."

"But Commander Somerton has to agree, doesn't he? And he's not going to agree as long as there's opposition from the barons, is he?"

She furrows her brow. "I think that can be overcome. With a better-trained and larger force, it won't matter if some recalcitrant barons are in opposition. It's going to take time to put that in place, but it's progressing nicely. If we have to run roughshod over opposition, I want to do it when it can be sustained."

He nods. "I see, I see. Okay. I understand very well now. And I suppose I have to keep this promise quiet—this promise that freedom is assured, somehow, someway, no matter what?"

"Yeah, it can't get to the barons. It'd ruin our bargaining position too."

"Let me ask a perhaps painful question. Ah … what would happen if something happened to you?"

Lily replies, "I'm working on that. I wouldn't want anyone to think they can stop the movement toward civilization around here by merely getting rid of me."

"Good. I'm starting to see you as a protector instead of someone I need to do battle with."

She is immensely thankful that she has broken through his resistance. Her hope now is that he can persuade the other engineers that she is a friend and ally instead of the enemy. "Is there anything else?"

"Nah, I'll see you out."

EIGHT

Lily walks into the clinic hallway. "Max, are you busy?"

"Of course, but I'll make time for you." He turns toward head nurse Eva Johnson. "I'm taking five. Mrs. Schwartz and I'll be in the break room."

The short, plump nurse with her blonde hair regally styled in a French twist nods to indicate that she heard.

He holds open the door.

As Lily walks in, she asks, "Where's Roger?"

"He's still up in Mr. Patterson's room. I heard they're having a great time reminiscing about the old days. I don't think either of them is old enough to remember horse and buggies, but a lot has changed in their lifetimes."

He pulls out a chair.

"Thanks." She sits down and looks up, momentarily startled that he is walking away.

He opens the refrigerator. "Water?"

"Yes, thanks."

He sits down and hands her a bottle.

She takes a gulp of the cold water and recaps the bottle. "How're the plans going for a nursing school?"

Max sets his bottle on the table. "Lou's called a meeting for tonight to discuss it. We gave both topics to the committee: the nursing school and our suggestions for the council changes.

"How'd your meeting with Mr. Kasper go?"

She replies, "We've set up a meeting tomorrow to tour his facility and discuss ideas for improving his efficiency and profitability."

"Is he with us on the co-op?"

"I didn't press for an endorsement. I didn't even mention the co-op. That never worked with any of the other barons. I'm trying to build a relationship, and we'll see where it takes us."

An expression of indecision furrows his brow.

She smiles as encouragement. "Go ahead. Ask anything."

He clears his throat. "Are there plans to set up the medical operation as a separate entity like the electric co-op?"

She whispers, "I haven't even mentioned it to the security committee. We can't push for change too fast. The barons have to see the advantages. They'd really balk if they knew this was just the beginning of radical changes being planned so the next change isn't in the planning stage … yet. Progress has to be slow or at least appear to be slow."

His grin is apologetic. "So you wanted to be able to say there were no plans, and now I've ruined that for you."

"I'll still be able to rebuff inquiries without mentioning discussing it with you."

He smiles at the twinkle in her eye then looks down with a frown.

"What's wrong?"

He looks up. "We haven't talked much in the last several months. Is that because you … ah … well … is it that I'm integrated into the community now and you were only talking to me because I was having problems adjusting?"

She folds her arms on the table and leans toward him. "You know it's my job to do that, but you should also know that I consider you a friend. I told you that before the terrorists' attacks I was looking forward to getting to know you and Paula after Lawrence and Melody got married, that the two families would become friends instead of just acquaintances. After Paula died, you seemed like you wanted to be alone for a while and I knew you had to grieve and I definitely couldn't help you with that. Nobody could have helped me grieve for Walter. I thought that if you wanted to talk, you'd seek me out and you did." She grins with a teasing twinkle in her eye. "I'm here now because you 'griped' about not seeing me very much, and I'm happy to be here."

His facial expression relaxes. "I guess it's going to take planning to get together now that I live in town. I would ask for you to set aside time for me when I'm out there on Mondays, but that's when you're busiest with your interviews of the new people."

"That does put a crimp in my time. I suppose I could schedule the interviews just until supper and finish on Tuesday morning. With five doctors here now, how often are you coming out: every fifth Monday?"

"That's the plan as soon as Dr. Baker gets the hang of things. Not very often is it?"

"Could we have a doctor's clinic twice a week?"

"Once a week is sufficient for routine care, but if you greatly increase the population then two clinics a week would make sense. For now, it'd put us short in town to staff two out there."

"Is there any particular reason you want to talk or is it just that you enjoy our conversations?"

He crosses his arms and leans toward her. "I enjoyed our conversations—at least parts of them—and have been missing them. It surprised me that I miss them since I was so uncomfortable with all the prying into … ah … extremely personal things, but I do."

"I wouldn't have done all that prying if it wasn't my job to integrate everyone into the community. That's what my apology was for. It was for the prying. I enjoy talking to you and would have gladly done without the prying."

He smiles then frowns.

"What's wrong?"

"I don't want to pry."

"Go ahead. I won't mind. After all your confessions, you might as well pry into my life," she offers.

"Even more than I've already done?"

"Sure."

"I did as much as you did, tit for tat," Max admits.

"Go ahead."

"This is difficult."

She waits a moment then urges, "Well go ahead. Just blurt it out."

He clears his throat. "I've been hearing comments, mostly from some of the officers we see in the clinic."

Ruing Frank's lies about their relationship, his implying that they were lovers, she states, "I can guess what that's about."

Max states, "It seems to come from more than just Frank's lie to Commander Somerton when you didn't want to admit that you two were casing Mr. Barton's place." He is speaking of their attempt to rescue the infant Mr. Barton kidnapped which is the only one Max knows about.

Lily's expression is lopsided with consternation and a touch of embarrassment. "Frank lied to Commander Tyler too."

"That was the commander they deposed when I first arrived, wasn't it?"

Lily nods. "Commander Tyler caught Frank in town before the authorization system was set up. Of course we had no idea that I had to accompany everyone who came into town to scavenge supplies, but Commander Tyrant was probably making that rule up on the fly anyway. It didn't appear to apply to the other barons. Frank and the men with him were all good guards and armed, so I wasn't worried about them any more than if I'd been with them. So Frank lied, but that's probably better than shooting their way out of it. Of course, I scraped Commander Tyler over the coals as much as I could when he came out to report my 'insubordinate' slave. I certainly didn't admit any of his lies were true, but I couldn't outright deny any without admitting that I wasn't in control. That would've damaged my standing as a baroness and impaired the safety of all of us. I had a really precarious hold on my position as baroness and our autonomy at the time. The best I could do was to tell him it was none of his business."

She expects his frown to disappear. It doesn't. "Something's still wrong, isn't it?"

"I saw the way you and Frank were scraping that time you forced him to come to the clinic for his injuries and you had several bruises. I thought maybe there was something behind his lie. I even considered that the story about the reconnaissance trip into town was a cover-up for you defending yourself. Then I found you down at the river crying soon afterwards. You spent a lot of time with him so he'd had opportunity, and I knew there was no one you could report it to."

She asserts, "There is someone to report it to. If he had tried anything, I would've brought Ralph and the security committee in to deal with the problem. Let me assure you that he wouldn't have succeeded; I subdued him a couple of times for other reasons. Early on we had trouble with some of the teenage boys threatening the others, so we've always had a system for dealing with problems. We've made extensive use of it with Brett. You remember him, don't you?"

Max nods. Everyone is aware of Brett Cockrell; they have all been warned about his propensity to irritate every adult without a Y chromosome.

Lily smiles and defends Frank. "By the way, Frank's not a complete scoundrel. I'm sure he'd have risked his life to protect me. He actually did protect me in our little reconnaissance escapade. He was a very good guard and never backed down to save himself if anyone else was in danger, and he would have especially put his life on the line for Henry."

He leans back. "Do you mind if I ask you something else?"

"Of course not."

"Remember when we talked about your childhood boyfriends? Why didn't you mention Mr. Barton?"

"I didn't consider him a boyfriend … or even a friend. He was five years older than me, and I spent my childhood trying to avoid him. If he liked me it was definitely a one-sided relationship, but I really don't think he liked me. He was just mean from my viewpoint."

She looks into his eyes, trying to decipher his motives. Since he remains silent, she asks, "Why all the questions?"

He shrugs. "Just curious about things I don't understand, I guess."

"Are you wondering, perhaps, if I'm like you used to be?"

He scowls.

"If, perhaps, you are wondering if I'm a Christian in name only and just hide my secret sins?"

He shakes his head. "It's pretty clear that you're a true Christian. It's more that I was wondering if you hid your hurts. You have such a tough girl attitude that I thought maybe you would suffer abuse in silence and not seek help."

She looks down at her hands with her brow creased in thought. After a few moments, she looks up. "As a Christian, I'm not going to retaliate or hold grudges. Criminal behavior, however, is a different matter. I would never, let me repeat: never, let that continue. Sometimes, like in our deplorable society here, it takes a while to do something about it, but I will doggedly pursue a solution without wavering. You know, of course, about my promise to the nurses. I made that promise to Eva soon after we started the nurses' clinic. It really grieved them that they just had to patch people up and send them back to their brutal masters, and it grieves us that it is taking so long for me to find a solution. I will work on this as long as it takes, even to my dying day, if necessary."

"Knock, knock." Eva Johnson opens the door. They both turn toward the plump blonde with the smiling, cherubic face. "Sorry to interrupt, but your five minutes has been about fifteen."

LYNN VADNEY

Lily says, "Max."
He looks back at her.
She smiles. "Thanks for caring enough to ask the hard questions."

NINE

Mr. Kasper leans back in the chair behind his desk. A pleased smile cuts across his face. "Mrs. Schwartz, I like your suggestions. I've always felt that we just muddled along with this chicken and egg farm. We certainly have the equipment here to process the chickens instead of selling live ones. If you'll be lenient with me on paying for your engineers' services to get it into running order, I'll be more than happy to enlarge my operations."

She is delighted to be sitting in his air-conditioned office on an unusually warm Wednesday morning at the end of the almost summer-like month of May. "I think you'll find that your profits will increase rapidly once you begin selling processed chicken. Until you're able to pay for their time, I'll just net our orders for chickens and eggs against my fees."

He leans on his desk, clasps his hands, and furrows his brow. "Are the engineers coming from Mr. Barton's estate? I noticed that you called them your engineers. Does that mean that you've taken over his slaves instead of forming the co-op?"

"I had several engineers before I became executrix of his estate. Basically the engineers operate as a unit, but of course, I have to separate them on the monetary system. It complicates matters that the estate still owes me for Mr. Barton's medical care. He was in ICU for a very long time before he died. If any of his engineers work on your equipment, I'll net their time against his bill and you'll owe me, not the estate. That'll keep the transactions streamlined for you."

"I'd also like to take you up on the offer to loan me the funds to increase my stock. I've tried to increase, but something always seems to use up my profits and I only get to order a small number of breeders and layers. I barely keep up with the demand around here. I'll also need to purchase a few more slaves to enlarge my operations. I appreciate that your offer of financial assistance includes that also."

She hides her automatic wince at his use of the abominable term slaves and forces a smile. "I'm sure that your increased profitability will enable you to repay the loan quickly. I wouldn't want you feeling indebted to me."

"I realize from talking to you that you're not out to undermine me and take over my operations. The fact that you're wanting to set Mr. Barton's estate up as a separate entity instead of taking it over for his medical bill is encouraging. Even though I'm not in favor of it being a co-op that doesn't diminish the fact that you're not taking advantage of the situation."

"Mr. Kasper, I've been getting reports from my new"—she hides her disgust and blithely utters the term she hates—"slaves about the situation in other areas of the country. Some areas are beginning to abandon the slavery system. Some are doing it peacefully and others are enduring great civil unrest in the process. I'm afraid the day is coming when we're going to have to make a choice between a peaceful transition and a violent one."

"What are you suggesting? Is someone from outside going to disrupt our peace?" he asks with concern.

"There are bands of raiders roaming around. Some are criminals, but others are trying to overthrow the slave owners. I don't agree with their method of using violence, but it's something we're going to have to deal with sooner or later. At the present time, it appears to be just small bands but eventually they may band together for strength in numbers."

"I've heard that you have some military men. Are you planning to build an army here?"

Lily replies, "I do plan to use them to protect our peace, but I think we'll still have to abandon the slave system."

He frowns. "That could be very disruptive."

"Not necessarily."

He leans back. "What do you suggest?"

"We will have to protect ourselves from outside rebel bands, both the criminal and those who are politically motivated. A well-trained, strong force of officers will be necessary especially if the rebel forces gain strength, but we won't be able to avoid the issue no matter how strong a force we have. My suggestion is that we preempt those who are antislavery and reorganize our operations here."

"So that's why you're for this co-op. Are you suggesting that we all organize as co-ops?"

"That's not our only option. I would suggest setting up our operations on this system," she pulls out her web-link device, "as corporations. I realize that, without a state government, we'll have to set up some kind of legal authorization for corporations or some kind of equivalent and that'll have to include convincing the local barons to sign onto it. But I think that's the way we need to go. It's really not much more than a mere legality, just the name we put on the system. We become businessmen instead of slave masters."

"I see." He rubs his chin in thought.

Lily continues her argument, "If you want a large, profitable operation, you'll need to find a way to govern without merely decreeing your decisions. If you utilize all the abilities of your slaves, they'll follow your leadership instead of resenting your domination. How do you think I run the hospital? I don't go around and supervise everything. I don't know anything about medicine. I pick capable supervisors and let them do their job and reward them for their success. It's the only way to succeed in business. Otherwise your operation will stay small, and you'll just scrape by."

"I think I see your point. I can't do everything all the time," Mr. Kasper admits.

"I think if we add the option for other types of entities on the registry, we'll perhaps unite most of our former country under one monetary system and that'll strengthen our entire economic system. There may be many enterprises not on the system because they oppose slavery and that would open up more commerce to them. It'll open up opportunities for all of us to get everyone on the same monetary system. The stability that will bring will give us a better chance at making a peaceful transition, not just in this town but in other areas too." Lily asserts, "That'll be the only way to thwart the antislavery thugs."

"That system Commander Tyler set up to replace the awkward bartering system has really taken off, hasn't it? We'd still be in the dark ages, haggling in the marketplace without it. I guess that's one good thing that came out of Commander Tyrant's reign."

"I agree with you on that but if we hadn't thought of it, someone somewhere else would have, but then we wouldn't have the option to make changes in it. I think it's a great advantage to have control of the computer program. But you also realize that if we're not in sync with the rest of the country, our program could be supplanted and we'd lose all control and could neither add nor prevent other types of entities. It would be out of our hands altogether," Lily counters.

Uneasy with the politically volatile topic, he returns to their discussion of business. "Would you assist me with a meeting with my slaves? I might need some clarifications on some of the points."

"I'd be happy to do so. When do you want me here? Tomorrow?"

Mr. Kasper concedes, "We could wait until tomorrow, but I was hoping for right now."

"That's fine. I was assuming that it'd take you some time to set it up," Lily replies with a disarming smile.

"Not at all. Yesterday I was too busy for anything but a short conversation with you and Commander Somerton. It was one of those days when I was running around like a chicken with my head cut off, taking care of a mountain of minutiae, so I'll definitely give your ideas some serious thought." He pulls out his phone. "I'll just call Roberto and he can have everyone gathered in the chow hall in just a few minutes."

"Is Roberto your supervisor?"

"Yes," he replies.

"Even small things can help, like giving your supervisors the dignity of being called by their last names," Lily suggests.

"Ah ... okay," he reluctantly agrees.

"I understand he's the only one who can speak English."

"Unfortunately, but he's a good man. I can depend upon him to make sure everyone does their job. I don't have any problems with any of my slaves. I have one very capable supervisor. He deserves the dignity."

Mr. Kasper puts his phone to his ear. "Mr. Diaz, gather everyone in the chow hall. ... Now. ... Okay."

He puts away his phone and stands up.

She stands and smiles. "Mr. Kasper—"

"Doug, please. And may I call you Jackie in private, not in disrespect but because of our close business relationship?"

"That will be just fine, Doug. I'd like to ask you about those two girls you sent to Mr. Barton's, you know, to become ballerinas?"

"Sure."

Not being able to bear the thought of the girls being apart from their family, she asks, "I'd like to know if you want them back. Since he conned you out of them, I'd be willing to do that as executrix of his estate. Were they your daughters or daughters of one of your slaves?"

"They belonged to a cook who died in that little epidemic we had a couple of years ago. I don't know who their father is. Say, Mr. Barton didn't pay for them. I just gave them to him to get them off my hands. I knew I could've sold them, but I thought I was giving them a chance in life." He raises his eyebrows. "Since he conned me perhaps we could work out something to compensate me for their loss?"

She realizes it might be expensive but could turn out to be a pivotal move in turning hapless Mr. Kasper into an ally. "That sounds reasonable. I'll consider it a claim against the estate."

"And you'll put it against Mr. Barton's medical bill?"

She makes no mention of the error in his statement to avoid irritating him with a correction. "We can just net it against the engineers' time. How old were they?"

"I don't know. They were young, too young to work. That's one reason I let them go. They were pretty useless to me. So ... would you pay perhaps half the price of an adult for each?"

She is taken aback by his quick admission of their lack of value to him and his unusually low offer for the children. He is definitely not a hard bargainer and that is perhaps one reason he has not been able to expand his operations. It would not be prudent for her to offer more so she goes with his low bid, thinking that maybe later she can somehow repay him with a favor of some sort. "That sounds fair. I've been paying an average of six thousand. Will you accept six thousand for the two?"

"Deal."

"I'd still like to talk to them. What are their names?"

"I don't recall." He opens the door and waves for her to precede him. She steps out of his office and smiles at Ralph, seated near the office door, and John, seated on the opposite side of the large sitting room. They rise from their chairs. John dashes into the entryway and opens the front door.

Doug watches Lily as he follows her. His thoughts begin to roam. He concludes that she is a successful entrepreneur because she is very smart and extremely personable. He wonders if he could consolidate his power in the business community by combining their operations. It would be quite a coup for such a lackluster fellow as he unfortunately happens to be.

His eyes migrate to her jeans-clad, swaying hips. One corner of his mouth tilts up. He immediately chastises himself for his lustful thoughts and takes a deep breath, not that lust, in itself, bothers him. Surely, there is no way such a beauty will have an ordinary-looking man such as himself.

Frank was good looking and charming. Doug wonders who is replacing him as her lover. He glances at her two bodyguards, both of whom are fit and handsome, a good catch for any woman. He postulates that she would do better to choose someone with more power than just one of her slaves. It can't be happily married Commander Somerton, although the commander would be the logical one for consolidating her power. Perhaps one of the doctors is her new lover or maybe someone in charge of the school she plans to open or one of Mr. Barton's engineers. That would be one way to continue her control over the estate without the appearance of holding onto the reins. With a hidden sigh, he considers his attributes or lack of attributes. He is such a wimp at business and such a klutz personally that there is no way she would consider him.

A sudden thought springs to his mind. Perhaps she is consolidating with everyone on the sly. Letting Mr. Barton's operations be turned into a co-op could be a ruse to hide her under-the-table control through the head engineer and all of this talk of a co-op is merely bunk. If that is the case, he realizes that he wouldn't be consolidating his power by pursuing the baroness. He would be consolidating her power by giving over the reins to his operations. And she does have a very large operation; it dwarfs his. He resolves to be leery of the arrangement between them, especially if she makes any overtures toward him. He has now convinced himself that their business arrangement is a ruse and not a good idea at all.

He stops to inhale deeply then opens the door and walks over to Roberto Diaz. Lily and her two bodyguards stop just inside the door, allowing Mr. Kasper to address the assembly without the intimidating presence of an outsider standing beside him, especially an outsider with a reputation as a tough and extremely successful bargainer. Lily does take note of the smirk Roberto Diaz is trying to hide from Mr. Kasper. She wonders if he is just surprised that Mr. Kasper called him Mr. Diaz, or if there is a more sinister reason.

Mr. Kasper states, "Mr. Diaz, to increase our profitability Mrs. Schwartz is going to help us expand our operations."

The two men turn to face the solemn crowd gathered at the tables. Roberto speaks in Spanish. Frowns indicate that the message is not well received. An undertone of quiet muttering flows through the crowd.

Mr. Kasper frowns and holds up his hands to quell the unrest. "I'll buy more slaves to take on the extra work."

After Roberto's translation, John interrupts, speaking in Spanish. The startled crowd looks at John then back to Roberto, who menacingly scowls at John as he realizes that his illicit fiefdom is slipping from his grasp.

Mr. Kasper opens his mouth. Lily quickly holds up her index finger to indicate that she will speak to her impertinent bodyguard. She turns to John. "What's the problem?"

"His translation isn't accurate. In fact, it pretty much picks out the downside and runs with it."

She turns to the abashed baron. "I suggest that we use an independent translator. Would you agree to that?"

Mr. Kasper looks at Roberto. "I think that would be a good idea."

Lily requests, "Would you mind if my bodyguard explains that?"

"Not at all, and Roberto," he says with stress on the informal first name, "won't mind either!"

As John starts the engine, Lily swivels to look at Armando Cuevas. "Thank you for coming over to translate."

The stocky, middle aged Hispanic man replies, "Glad to be of assistance. I've been wishing Mr. Kasper would slaughter the chickens he sells. I knew he had the equipment. It sure takes a lot of our time to have to do it. We don't have anybody working for us, and I don't want to have to work Teresa and Esther so hard. I'd rather they spend their time on their school work. How's Ernesto doing on his training?"

Lily replies, "He's still on his week of rest. We usually begin the new classes on Saturday."

"So he'll start in three days?" Armando guesses.

"Actually, I've seen him on the mats with the other young men. He's trying to get a head start, and I encouraged him to work out on the weights to strengthen his muscles before he starts. He's very diligent about his routine, even to the point of heeding my warning not to overdo it and end up with muscles so sore that he won't be able to start with this Saturday's class."

"He's a very smart young man."

Lily looks at John. He glances at her as he stops at the corner. "John, you were worth your weight in gold, to pick up on the mistranslation."

A car passes. He pulls into the intersection and turns left onto the main thoroughfare. "It was easy. His translation was so far off that it was clear he was manipulating his master. If he'd been more subtle, I might not have picked up on the nuances. I overheard your suggestion to Mr. Kasper that he purchase another bilingual. I think that's a step in the right direction along with language classes for everyone."

She laughs. "I don't think anyone there will trust Roberto, ever again. Mr. Kasper's going to need a new supervisor, a trustworthy one. Judging from what you overheard among the conversations in Spanish, do either of you think Roberto is going to cause problems?"

John replies, "Several of the men appear to be natural leaders, and I think they'll keep him in check and make sure the work is done properly until a new supervisor is found. Mr. Kasper is actually pretty good at communicating with his thumbs-up, thumbs-down method and just a few mutually understood words will greatly increase the effectiveness."

Armando adds, "John, your Spanish is pretty good. I think that's an accurate observation. I know several of them pretty well. I thought Mr. Kasper was one of our cruelest barons but it turns out Roberto was the cruel one, manipulating everyone. So Mrs. Schwartz, I'm glad you got caught up in the middle of this."

She admits, "It's not the worse thing I've been in the middle of, and I'm glad to know you two don't think we've ignited a powder keg that's just waiting to go off."

"It'll be a small one," Armando assures. "Roberto doesn't have any allies anymore. If he goes berserk, it'll be a minor incident."

"Say, I'm sorry to hear about one of your men."

Lily confirms, "You mean James?"

Armando nods. "Isn't he the one who had the heart attack while working out at one of the wind turbines?"

"Yes."

"I know you're wishing they'd hurry up and get that helicopter working. Would he have had a chance if they could've gotten him to the hospital faster?"

"Dr. Randolph said it wouldn't have mattered. The engineers did a good job with CPR, but he didn't have a pulse and never regained it. The heart attack was just too massive."

John pulls to a stop in front of Armando's café.

Lily states, "We're having his funeral out at the compound and need to let you off so we can get out there in time."

"Okay, I'll see you later. Buster brought a couple more Bibles this morning. I'll send them out when Teresa and Esther go pick up their assignments."

Armando opens the door and slides out. He looks up with a creased brow. "Now that I've thought about it, I think that shifty-eyed man in the back may speak at least a little English. He appeared intimidated and isolated but seemed to be following the English conversations. Perhaps Roberto … ah, forced him to hide his ability."

"Thanks. I'll check it out," Lily promises.

TEN

Commander Somerton cringes. The close range gunshot echoes in the small room. He chastises himself for allowing himself to be manipulated into a trap—a fatal trap. He swallows to pop his ears and maybe reduce the ringing. It does not help. He opens his eyes and glares at Mr. Finke, whose name is distressingly accurate in his opinion—a newly revised opinion formed since the gunshot five seconds ago.

Mr. Finke turns his gaze toward the body of the officer sprawled on the floor. The commander sadly turns his eyes toward Officer Hayes. Mr. Finke clears his throat. Commander Somerton looks up.

"There'll be no co-op! Do you understand?"

He steels his resolve to defy Mr. Finke's tyranny as much as possible. He takes a page from Lily's style of dealing with opponents and keeps his tone soft and evenly modulated. "I can't control Mrs. Schwartz, no matter how many of my men you murder."

"Find some way to dissuade her."

"I can withhold my permission to proceed."

"And you can quit going around to the barons and lobbying for her changes."

"I'll cease that immediately."

"And you'll replace her as executrix of Mr. Barton's estate."

Commander Somerton states, "We'd all end up without electricity. Do you want that?"

"She'd do that?"

"No, the engineers would. It'd be utter chaos to mess with that strong group of men who're requesting the co-op. It wasn't her idea. It was theirs. She'd have probably been happy to take over the utility for Mr. Barton's medical bill."

LYNN VADNEY

Mr. Finke sneers. "Someone, I'll not say who, could take one of them out. That'd convince them!"

"That'd only steel their resolve. After all, they were Mr. Barton's slaves. They're hardened," the commander asserts.

"We'll take out several, one after another until they capitulate!" Mr. Finke exclaims, not realizing that he has admitted that he, himself, is that nameless 'someone' who will resort to violence, not that the commander was the least bit blindsided by his oblique statement anyway.

"Who'd run the wind turbines?"

Mr. Finke remains thoughtfully silent.

Encouraged by the lack of a quick retort from the ruthless baron, Commander Somerton continues his argument. "Then we'd be without electricity, and the other barons would be irate."

Mr. Finke has no offensive argument so resorts to a defensive tactic. "I'll buy more engineers, or we can just buy it from another area."

"We'd need engineers even if we bought it from another area, and who says we can find more engineers. Besides, it'd be costly to purchase it from others."

With arrogant confidence, Mr. Finke counters, "It wasn't under Mr. Barton."

"You don't know how he paid for it, do you?"

"We paid for it!" Mr. Finke irately yells.

"No we didn't. Mr. Barton paid for it with … ah … 'other enterprises'," Commander Somerton states, not willing to elaborate about the videos of all kinds of reprehensible activities which the brutal baron sold, perhaps nationwide, to support his lavish lifestyle and underpriced legal enterprise.

Mr. Finke is again thoughtfully silent, since he understands other enterprises. He has a few of his own, which he meticulously hides from the crusading commander.

Commander Somerton continues his tactic of softly stated reasoning. "If the other barons found out who did it, they'd find some way to take you out. I can't control the other barons any more than I can control Mrs. Schwartz."

Mr. Finke smirks. "Do what you can."

"I'll cease all efforts at pursuing a co-op, withdraw my authorization for it, and try to dissuade Mrs. Schwartz and the engineers."

"Very well."

Commander Somerton congratulates himself for standing up to the murderous baron.

"And I'll take care of Mrs. Schwartz! None of the other barons would be upset about that!"

The commander's face falls. He gulps. Mr. Finke sneers. Commander Somerton considers saying: *that'll be your downfall, she has an army.* Instead, he merely mutters in derision, "Good luck," not that he wishes the evil baron any luck, and not that as a Christian he believes in any kind of haphazard luck. Divine blessing, yes; paranormal luck, no.

Commander Somerton uses the shovel to tamp down the mound of fresh dirt over the inexperienced officer's grave. After completing the task he rams the spade into the soft dirt, leans on the handle, and turns his gaze toward the setting sun. A dazzling orange glow streams across the western sky above the low hills. He thinks of Mrs. Schwartz's compound nestled in the wide valley between the ridges. It is a beautiful, idyllic setting, perfect for a refuge from the brutal world of slavery.

Tears form. He closes his eyes to stem their flow as he recalls all the Sundays he has spent at her compound. Several churches meet in various halls and rooms. He and his wife Ann attend the worship service in the dining hall. Along with Lieutenant Jones, they are the only outsiders who know about the religious freedom enjoyed by the slaves Mrs. Schwartz has redeemed. There are now a couple of groups which, for convenience, meet in two of the homes near the hospital, but he and his wife still prefer to drive out to the compound. Lieutenant Jones, of course, attends one of the house churches with Linda Owens, office manager at the clinic.

With sorrow, the bereaved commander begins a prayer:

> *Lord, forgive me. I feel responsible for the death of Officer Hayes. I feel responsible for the deaths of all the officers who've been killed in the line of duty since I became commander. Forgive me for taking on a job for which I have no training. Please Lord, let the training the Seals are giving the officers protect them from harm. I know it sounds trite, but I pray for peace and not for just peace here but for world peace. Protect Jackie and*

all the engineers from Mr. Finke's threat. Give me guidance in dealing with him. Show me how we can protect everyone from such a ruthless baron. There are many ways he could carry out his threat. How do we guard against his threats?

Sorrow fills his soul as he thinks of his delicate wife.

Lord, protect Ann. What would she do if something happened to me? That abusive baron almost killed her with his lack of human decency. I don't want her to go through that again.

The sudden disruption of his ringing phone causes him to jump. He ends his prayer and pulls out his phone. "Hello, Jackie."

"How are you, Robert?"

"Just fine." He grimaces as he rues the unintentional lie. He is far from fine. "What's up?"

"The equipment Lawrence and Marvin ordered came in this afternoon. Could we have the meeting about the new identification system tomorrow?"

"Morning or afternoon?"

"Afternoon; Lawrence wants to test it before the meeting," Lily states.

"Okay. Let me ask you something."

"Okay."

He clears his throat. "If something happens to me, please take care of Ann."

She promises, "I will. Anything else?"

"Ah … I've hit a snag with the barons. The co-op isn't going over. I'm not going to spend my time talking to them about it."

With a soft voice, she acquiesces, "Oh? Okay."

He is silent as he considers his options.

"Robert, is there anything else?"

"I can't authorize a co-op as a valid entity."

"Okay. Anything else?" she probes.

"You're going to have to find some solution other than a co-op."

"That's not going to go over well with the engineers," she counters.

"I know, but you're going to have to convince them."

"Okay. Do we need to bring Ann out here to protect her?"

"She'd throw a fit. Officers protect her and the officers' wives around the clock. I think she'll be all right at home."

"Okay. Do I have your permission to pursue nonslavery options for the engineers?"

The commander softly replies, "No."

"Oh," she intones.

"But I know that won't do any good."

"Oh? … Okay."

ELEVEN

Off-duty Lieutenant Curtis Jones climbs into the back seat of Lily's SUV and runs his hand over the leather seat. "I like this."

Irony fills her voice. "I'm glad you do."

"But you're not. What's wrong with it … other than it being a gas guzzler?" He grins. "I know that's a problem with the high cost of gas these days."

She swivels toward him. "It doesn't hold fifteen people."

He laughs. "Is your bus ready?"

"My mechanics say it should be ready by Monday."

John settles into the driver's seat. "Where're we going?"

Lily inquires, "Curtis, do you know where Commander Somerton buried those four officers?" She is speaking of the three officers killed at the outpost and the one killed in the market by the raiders who commandeered Mr. Patterson's truck.

"Sure. John, go east on the main road."

With a painfully sharp memory of the moving ceremony at the recent burial for the officers killed in the line of duty, Curtis stands before the four graves, says, "Here they are," removes his hat, and places it over his heart.

Ralph Merrell, Jack Thorne, and John Thorne walk off in three different directions.

Curtis asks, "Where're they going?"

Lily replies, "They're looking for another fresh grave."

She watches him walk off, glances around at her three guards and chooses a fifth direction. They walk in silence for a few minutes.

"Over here," Jack yells.

Lily turns and sprints toward Jack. The other men follow her lead and dash around headstones and leap over graves while wondering about her haste. She stops before the fresh grave. The name is not familiar, but the date of death is the day before.

She turns to Curtis. "Do you recognize the name?"

"Yes. I didn't know Officer Hayes was dead. I saw him yesterday. Robert took him when he went to talk to one of the barons."

Jack observes, "The boot prints in the soft dirt are consistent with Commander Somerton's."

Lily asks, "Which baron was he going to see?"

"I don't know." Curtis steps over to two adjacent graves. "These two are officers too. I haven't seen them for about a year."

Jack walks over and kneels beside one crude marker. He dusts off the date of death and looks up at his brother with sorrow in his eyes. "Sorry, John, but I have to mention this."

"That's all right, bro."

Jack steals himself to mention the kidnapping of his nephew. "Jeff told me that Mr. Barton killed an officer last July and that Commander Somerton quit coming around to talk about returning Lucas."

Curtis reaches down and dusts off the date on the second marker. "This one is the same day. I bet he killed two officers. Do you think Robert has been threatened again?"

"I'm sure of it," Lily replies with sadness.

What're we going to do about it?" Curtis inquires, trusting the judgment of the capable baroness.

"We need to know which baron. If you guys can make subtle inquiries and at least narrow down the list, that'll be our first step."

"Very subtle inquiries," Jack adds.

Curtis nods. "How'd you figure this out anyway?"

Lily replies, "Just guessing; just from the way he said something, not particularly what he said but the tone of the whole conversation."

Marvin Finley and Commander Somerton sit down in the chairs they are offered in Lawrence Brighton's cramped and cluttered workroom. Ralph Merrell and Lieutenant Williams lean against the frame on either side of the closed door. The lieutenant's eyes track Lily Schwartz as she pushes a large box toward the wall and sits on the table behind the two chairs.

Lawrence holds up a plastic card and, without preamble, plunges into his presentation. "Inside this nametag is a chip based on the technology used for those speed-pass cards we used to have. We'll use this equipment here," he places his hand on a gray, metal box with a camera lens near the top of the otherwise blank side facing his audience, "to take a photo of each person. Then we enter the identifying information. Basic information is printed on the nametag but all the information is embedded on the chip and stored on the hard drive."

He holds up a small box. "We'll add these chips to your officers' web-link devices. It'll enable them to scan the nametags of anyone nearby and pull up their identifications. They can check anybody's identification and authorization without the person even knowing it."

Lieutenant Williams asks, "How'll we know they haven't just swapped ID tags? It looks like we'd have to ask to see it so we can look at their photo?"

"Their photo will pop up on the officer's screen. You'll even be able to detect if someone has tried to alter a stolen nametag by putting their own photo on it. The real photo will be on the screen."

"I know the speed passes had limited range. How close do we have to be?"

"Within fifty feet."

Lieutenant Williams keeps his whistle soft in the confines of the small room. "How'll we know whose nametag we're picking up in a crowd?"

"There's GPS technology embedded in the chips. Marvin and I will have to set up the program on each device so you can select from all those in range. We're not sure, yet, just exactly how that'll work. We didn't get to test everything this morning."

"Real Orwellian."

"Yeah," Lawrence replies with a furrowed brow. "It appears other places are having the same kind of problems we are. There're several different technologies available. This one looked like it'd fit our situation the best. Let me tell you about the other features. The chip in the card is read only. No one can reprogram it once we've imprinted it. Nor can they make their own, since it wouldn't match the data stored on the hard drive in these machines and—"

Lieutenant Williams interrupts. "How many machines did you buy?"

"Two. We'll have one, and Marvin will have one. If we find that we need more, we'll order another."

Lieutenant Williams suggests, "I think we'll need more to do everybody in town within a reasonable time. Who runs them?"

"We can train clerks. It's simple data input and the camera is point and click. It's just minutes per person and the cameras can be taken around instead of having the barons bring all their people to a central location."

"I can see security problems with that."

Lawrence flashes Lieutenant Williams a knowing smile. "It requires a fingerprint scan, a password, a key, and authorization can be timed, so we can easily control access."

The lieutenant's look of concern turns into a grin. "Store it in a locked room and track the inventory of the blank cards, and it should be as secure as Fort Knox."

Lawrence continues his presentation. "One important feature is the database which the officers will be able to access. Marvin and I will both have copies and we'll both keep grandfathered backups offline, so we shouldn't ever have our database corrupted to the point that the system becomes unusable. Access to our databases is already very restricted. In addition, that box behind Lily contains some of the fifty cameras we ordered. We can add more if needed. They can be installed in public areas. The control center will use facial recognition software to compare the person with their card and our database. If there's a mismatch or someone without a card or without authorization, nearby officers can be notified."

"I like that feature," the lieutenant states. "That'll make it easier than having to check every person in a crowd by hand, but what if people vandalize the cameras?"

"If the vandals are caught on camera just before the deed or in the act by a nearby camera, you'll be able to save the video, and if they've been photographed—which they should have been—you'll be able to identify them."

"That's if their face is visible on the video."

Lawrence nods. "You will have the data from any ID card carried by the vandal—but it could be stolen. That's the drawback of using only the ID card in a case like that. The cameras can be used for any kind of surveillance, just like those in your patrol cars, except these transmit the feed to the control center. I may be able to find transmitters to add to the cameras in your cars, but I haven't looked into it yet."

Lawrence turns to Commander Somerton. "Since the data embedded on the chip in the card can't be changed, we'll have to decide upon what data we want to use before we start. I've printed a form based on Lily's suggestions and if you can go over that with her, we can rework the form and start making the cards. We can be working on the programs and everything else while that's being done."

"We can go ahead and use the ID cards for physical checks before the system is fully operational." Lieutenant Williams suggests.

"Sure, and one of Lily's suggestions is that we combine it with the monetary system and replace all the scavenged credit cards we've been using."

"So the cards have the magnetic strip?" the lieutenant asks to verify his assumption.

Lawrence turns the card over and displays the strip.

Lieutenant Williams looks at Commander Somerton. "Is there any reason to tell the other barons all the features of this system?"

"I guess not," the commander somberly drawls. "We can tout it as a replacement for the old cards. Buster hasn't been able to scavenge any more from the abandoned homes, so we're running short anyway."

Lily states, "But something's bothering you, isn't it?"

"Yeah," the commander admits. "I guess it's just the Draconian nature of the system. I think we need to do something about the crime problems, but I can see this getting out of hand and abetting crime."

"We can tightly control it so it doesn't get misused," Lieutenant Williams suggests.

"I guess we have to."

"Robert, that's what we have to discuss today," Lily asserts. "Lawrence says the security features can be tightly set."

She looks at Lawrence. "Why don't you briefly discuss those?"

"There has to be an administrator with privileges for all features, but all other users of the system will have limited privileges. Clerks will only be able to make the cards and at preset times. We can set the machines to automatically shut down at night and over the weekend, so even an authorized user can't sneak in and make a fake ID. Passwords can be changed frequently and the key could be kept by someone without a password, meaning two people would have to work together to turn the machine on."

"Or even three," Marvin suggests. "One for the fingerprint scan, one with the password, and one with the key. Maybe during the initial rush to get everyone on the system we wouldn't want to be so meticulous but later we could tighten up. We can also flag a signal as fake so the officers will be able to confiscate the card and question the person carrying it. We can even use the GPS feature to actively track the signal. The bottom line, Commander, is that this is only as secure and reliable as the people running it. Right now, the only people who know about this are the six of us in this room."

Speaking of his capable, young assistant, Lawrence adds, "Wes helped me test it this morning, but he knows everything we do is confidential."

"I suggest we keep its features under wraps and tell the clerks and officers only what they need to know to carry out their duties and the barons and merchants that this replaces the scavenged credit cards." Marvin scowls. "I didn't like working for Commander Tyrant, and I can imagine what he'd do with a system like this."

"Or Mr. Barton," Lawrence suggests with obvious disgust for the fallen baron.

"Robert, if there aren't any other technical questions," Lily states, "why don't we discuss the data and parameters you want to set."

"I think I do have one more question," he states. "It's more of a procedural question. What about the traders from other areas? If they don't have the IDs, how're we going to screen out the raiders like we had last week?"

"I guess we'll have to issue IDs to all traders who regularly come through. Lawrence estimated that it'd take about a month for them to get everything all set up. Traders could be notified that they'll need to stop by and get an ID made. Lawrence, knowing the technical aspects of the system, do you have any suggestions?"

"Sure. Guest IDs could be handed out at the checkpoints and that'd put a GPS chip in the hands of all visitors which would flag them for the officers to watch even though we won't have a photo or any data."

"What if somebody skips with them?"

"We can track it and stop them if they come back. But if they don't," he shrugs, "the cards are inexpensive."

"All right, I guess I'm satisfied now. Lieutenant Williams, do you have any more questions?"

"No, Commander. I'm ready to roll with this. Oh well, maybe not. Will all the authorizations be on the unchangeable chip?"

Lily replies, "My suggestion is that we include some broad authorizations like each person's home, the hospital for all medical people, the substation and wind turbines for the engineers, the market for all traders etcetera and that be imbedded on the chips, but the main database will continue to include the current system of authorizations entered by the barons."

Lieutenant Williams states, "So pretty much, business as usual except for the features to be used by the officers and—"

The lieutenant answers his ringing phone. "Williams. ... Sorry. I can be there in about thirty minutes. ... Bye."

Lieutenant Williams slides his phone into his pocket. "Commander, I need to take some personal leave. Do you mind if I take the car?"

"Mrs. Schwartz, are all your vehicles in use or would you be able to take us into town after we settle everything?"

She grins. "We do have ... the tank ... available."

"All right!" Marvin exclaims. "The SUV will be much better for carrying all the equipment than the tiny trunk of our car. After all, we get the control center."

Lieutenant Williams opens the door and quickly departs.

Commander Somerton smiles at Lily. "We may never have to charge you tax again with all you're buying for us."

"Safety's my major concern. Don't worry about it. Besides the larger my operations get, the greater our share of the tax will be, and we'll also owe more than the others for the road work since we live so far out."

Lily's phone rings. "Excuse me a moment."

"Hello, Linda. ... Of course not. We'd never charge Buster. Whatever treatment Rose needs, see that she gets it. Is it very serious? ... I see. I'll be coming into town in an hour or two. I'll stop by and check on them. ... Oh? Give Buster a clean set of clothing and have him wash up. Tell him we have rules about cleanliness in the hospital and that he has to abide by them. He wouldn't want to add an infection to Rose's problems, would he? ... Okay. Bye."

With a furrowed brow, Commander Somerton inquires, "Has something happened to Rose?"

"She's severely ill. They plan to put her in ICU after they stabilize her. Let's take a look at the form then load up Marvin's share of the equipment."

Lily stands by the nurses' station for a moment and gazes in amazement at the elderly gentleman patiently sitting in a chair outside the glass-enclosed intensive care cubicle. Two doctors and a troupe of nurses perform their ballet of medical care around the emaciated form on the bed.

Lily picks up a nearby chair and moves it over beside the concerned man. "Buster," she gently says.

He turns to look at her.

"I wouldn't have recognized you. You've cleaned up well."

"Thank you, Mrs. Schwartz." He looks down at the floor. "They said I had to clean up, or I couldn't stay here with Rose."

"What've they told you?"

"It's very serious." He turns his gaze toward Rose. "This room is too small for me to stay with her, but they'll fix up a bed in the next room for me. They have to take care of her right now. They'll do that later. I need to take care of her, you know. She's always taken good care of me."

"After she's better, we can put her in a larger room and you can stay with her," Lily offers.

"Thank you. I'd like that."

"What about after she's well; do you have any place to go?"

"We have a safe place. We'll go back there."

Lily gently reminds the elderly man, "Didn't Charley die recently?"

"Yeah, someone killed him. They killed him in his own place."

"You know, Rose may need more care than you can give her."

"We'll be all right. We always have," Buster insists.

"Do you have any family? Is there someone you could stay with who could help you?"

He slowly shakes his head. "Rose and I didn't ever have kids. We have some nephews and a couple of nieces but we lost track of most of them years ago."

"How long have you been married?"

"It'll be sixty-five years this month," he replies with a broad smile.

"You must be about eight-five?"

"I'm eighty-three and Rose is eighty-two." He turns toward Lily and grins. "She's a spring chicken."

She smiles at his joke. "You've done a lot for us. We have a nice, safe compound out in a beautiful valley. When Rose is well enough, you can come out and stay with us. We'll have some of the ladies help you take care of Rose. It can be sort of a retirement for you."

"We'd prefer to stay by ourselves. We always have."

"We have cottages. You and Rose can have one. You'll have your privacy and independence and help will still be nearby. We can even put in a call button, like we have in the hospital. If you need help you can push it."

Buster shakes his head. "I wouldn't want to be any bother."

"No bother. You helped us a lot. We really appreciate all the Bibles and other books you scavenged for us. We couldn't have entrusted anyone else with that task. And you know you're going to have to take care of Rose's needs. You don't need to be having to defend yourself from some murdering thug lurking around your neighborhood. Our guards will keep you safe."

"I'll see what Rose wants to do when she's better."

"Okay. I'll check on you every time I come into town and see how she's doing." Lily stands up.

"Bruce took care of him."

She sits back down. "Who?"

"The nut job who murdered Charley."

"I figured that's who you meant, but I was wondering who's Bruce."

"Lieutenant Williams. He just left. I assumed you met him in the hall on your way in."

Lily stops at the end of the hall and looks through the floor-to-ceiling windows at the fenced-off homes south of the hospital. Montgomery Preston is repairing the roof of the home he shares with his wife Kelly, who is one of the nurses tenderly caring for Rose. Within a few minutes, she is climbing the ladder which leans against the Preston home.

"Hey, monkey," he teases with a grin.

"Hello, Monkey," she greets using the nickname which rightfully belongs to him. She sits nearby and wraps her arms around her knees. "I miss helping with the roofing."

"I only have one hammer up here, otherwise I'd put you to work right now."

"I'd be willing to run down and get one, but I have to go over and see how Charles and his intervention team did with the engineers. It seems like all I ever do is run around and talk to people. This is the fourth day this week, and it's only Thursday. At least I don't have anywhere to go tomorrow, so it'll be like having a three day weekend to just stay at the compound and ... work."

"We have a much larger enterprise now than back when we were doing all that construction."

"You know I like the physical stuff much better than all this political stuff," Lily admits.

Monkey asks, "You're still teaching some of the training classes, aren't you?"

"Just the women's and children's classes."

"You're teaching the children self-defense?"

"The older ones; I was talking about the younger teenagers when I said children. We let them start at age twelve. I also manage to find time to work out with some of the Seals to keep up my skills."

He laughs. "I hear you really get some of the new men."

"Those guys can be real jokesters. They let the new guys think I'm just there for them to practice their moves. They take it real easy on me and—"

He completes her sentence. "And you act passive like that first time Ricky tangled with you."

"Of course,"

"You're a jokester too," Monkey teasingly exclaims.

"Not entirely. We're trying to teach them not to make assumptions. That's the only reason I was able to take down Ricky. He made an assumption. After the kidnapping, there were five of us and we almost didn't take him down."

A mischievous grin lights up Monkey's face. "Say, you can do a handstand on the ridge like you did on your grandfather's barn when you were ten."

She laughs. "I learned my lesson. I won't ever be so brazen as to pull a stunt like that again."

He grins knowingly and guides their conversation to a topic of his choosing. "Did you know Jeff is seeing Jenny?"

"Is that why he likes to live at the compound despite working with the road crew?"

"Yeah, I hear it's getting serious," Monkey states.

"There's a lot of pairing off going on around here now."

"Yeah, besides Linda and Curtis there's Jack and Lynnette and Angel and Jorge and no telling who all else."

"That's a sign that people are feeling safer now," Lily asserts. "Are you getting all the gossip from Kelly?"

"Of course. Who but my wife would keep tabs on all that's going on?"

"Probably several other women," Lily states, inwardly amused that one of their current worries is gossip. But that is a great improvement over snipers. "At least, they've been discretely keeping the important secrets of our operations."

"Even Kelly can keep quiet if it endangers anyone. When she first came, it really got to her that she almost caused a young mother to be found out and executed for accidentally killing her abusive master." He is speaking of a young mother whom Lily redeemed early on. Her husband confessed to the 'murder' and was executed.

Without a pause, he segues into the query he had in mind, hoping to satisfy his curiosity and possibly do a little matchmaking. "Are you and Max seeing each other?"

"I've been stopping in to see him whenever I'm in town. Except today we didn't get to talk. He was too busy with Rose."

Monkey rhetorically asks, "Rose is sick?"

"Yeah, I assume Kelly will tell you all about it when she gets off tonight."

"Nah, she's always been good about keeping patient confidences. She almost got kicked out of nursing school on her first rotation. She got repeated reprimands for breaching confidentiality. When she was told one more and you're history, she took it to heart."

"Yeah, she told me she really can keep her 'trap' shut if she has to." Lily stops herself before mentioning the context of that discussion with Kelly: their missing son, Monty, whom she has not been able to find.

"So … is a wedding in your future too?"

With genuine surprise, Lily asks, "Why would a wedding be in my future?"

"You and Max."

"We're just friends."

Monkey inquires, "Are you sure?"

"We talked about it, and we're just friends."

"You'd make a nice couple."

His subtle matchmaking makes her uncomfortable. She does not like being manipulated, not even by a close and trusted friend. She turns to her reason for dropping by. "I have a message for you and Kelly."

"From who?"

"Liz."

Jubilant that his daughter is still alive, he puts down his hammer and waits for her to elaborate.

"She, her husband, and their children are all safe."

He waits for her to continue. When she remains silent, he inquires, "Is that all?"

"Yeah. Lawrence says that instant messaging may not be secure. He's not sure how many servers the messages might go through and there's a real possibility that without law, people are eavesdropping at will. Liz just sent a terse, vague message, so he replied that you and Kelly are well."

"I was hoping that maybe she'd seen some of her sisters."

"I guess not. Did they live near each other?"

"Nah, our daughters were scattered all over Kansas, Missouri, Tennessee, and Georgia. Just before the terrorists' strikes, Hannah was talking about moving to Illinois. Her husband had a new job offer. I don't know whether they moved or not."

As soon as Stanley opens the door, Lily apologizes, "Sorry I'm so late."

She steps into the warehouse at the electric substation and remarks, "That's quite a smile on your face."

"Yeah, your intervention team went over well. We're reorganizing and are going to govern by committee and elect the committee and our supervisors." With a huge grin, he boasts, "I may not have this tough job much longer. It also helped for them to reassure us that you keep your promises and really are altruistic. And it helps that some of the families have started going to those house churches your medical personnel set up. Some of us hadn't heard about them. We didn't know there was religious freedom anywhere. One of our guys is going to set up another one since he and his wife don't like either of those. They have doctrinal disagreements."

Lily offers, "Is there anything else that I can help you with?"

"Nah. I think you've helped plenty, and we're just going to run with it. We'll be patient as you try to convince the other barons to accept civilization. We understand that you're not the bottleneck on this. We've heard about some who initially agreed then changed their mind and sided with the majority."

"Okay, well I'll be going. See you later."

"Bye … and thanks. Thanks a lot."

TWELVE

Lieutenant Williams stands near the outer door of the prison and watches the transport officers escort forty-five slaves up the sidewalk. June has arrived with almost unbearable heat. A relatively cool breeze intermittently gusts through the door, moderating the stifling heat inside. Each degraded slave is unshackled just inside the door then escorted into the large holding room with instructions to sit down. They obediently comply without any remnant of self-serving human dignity; they are mere pawns in a brutal culture. Pain and sorrow are etched on each bruised and grimy face.

After walking back to the gate with the transport officers, the lieutenant returns to the prison and walks into the crowded holding room. The armed officers guarding them are replaced by unarmed guards.

As the last armed guard exits, Lieutenant Williams shuts and locks the door then turns to face the disheveled and fearful men and women. "We won't hurt you here. There's no reason to be afraid. You'll only spend the night. Monday morning each of you will be picked up by one of the barons. We're going to divide you up according to which baron you'll be going to. Officer Turner, call those going to Cell Block A."

"Burke, Cannon, Lange, and Thornton."

"You four go with Officer Turner," Lieutenant Williams orders. Four men rise. Officer Turner unlocks the door and steps into the corridor. The four disheveled men trudge after him. Two officers follow.

"Officer Ward. Who's going to Cell Block B?"

"Pearson."

A young woman rises.

"Ma'am, you go with Officer Ward."

With downcast eyes, the young woman resigns herself to her fate and accompanies the stocky female officer.

After the door is closed, Lieutenant Williams waits a few moments before turning back to the remaining forty slaves. "The rest of you will be going to Mrs. Schwartz. That's like hitting the lottery. You'll be safe. No one will ever abuse you again."

He pauses and scans the faces of his captive audience. They do not seem the least bit convinced. His eyes come to rest on one beautiful young woman who sits with her head down. She glances up then quickly returns her gaze to the floor.

He looks in the direction of her glance. "Officer! Put your eyeballs back in their sockets! You are dismissed! Go wait in the office! Now, get out of here!"

"Yes, Sir." The officer quickly leaves the room and closes the door behind him. He is careful not to slam the door, despite his anger.

Lieutenant Williams turns back to his skeptical audience. "Let me reassure you that you won't be abused by my officers. No one will be visiting you in your cells tonight. There is nothing to fear. Mrs. Schwartz sent clothing and supplies for you. After the men go to Cell Block C and the women to Cell Block D, you'll be allowed to clean up. The evening meal will be served beginning at five o'clock."

He pauses and looks at their glum faces, which clearly display their disbelief. Three years of danger and abuse cannot be overcome by a few sentences of assurance from a man who wears the same uniform as many of the lying abusers they have encountered.

He steps over to the tearful young woman and leans toward her. Frustrated, he soothingly says, "Honey, you're going to be okay here. Nobody, I repeat, nobody is going to force you or coerce you."

He turns to the guard by the door. "Officer Perry, escort the men now."

He turns back to the group. "As soon as Officer Ward gets back, we'll escort the women."

A knock on the door startles Lieutenant Williams. He takes his feet off the table and sets his beer down. Disgusted that his rest has been disrupted, he reluctantly stands then steps over and opens the door. Officer Ward and the young woman look up at him.

"Lieutenant, she wanted to see you."

"Very well, come in. Thanks, Officer."

The abashed woman stands just inside the door and looks around. The room is barely big enough for the cot, small table, two folding chairs and a mini refrigerator which doubles as a nightstand.

The Lieutenant points to a chair. "Please have a seat."

She sits down. He adjusts an oscillating fan so that it blows on her. Without air conditioning, the ventilation in the secure prison building is inadequate for the warm spring and will be almost intolerable in the hot summer.

"Would you like a beer?"

"Sure."

He opens the small refrigerator and pulls out an amber bottle. Turning back to the table, he uncaps it and hands it to her. She takes a sip and begins coughing. He takes the bottle. "You don't have to drink it, if you don't like it. I have something else you can drink."

He pulls another amber bottle out of the refrigerator and opens it.

She reads the label. "Cheeky Cola. What's that?"

"Cola of some kind."

She sips and smiles. "It's kind of good."

He sits down and looks at her. "I bet you've had it rough, haven't you?"

She nods.

"What happened?"

She bows her head. Tears glisten in her eyes.

"What'd my officers do?"

Startled, she looks up. "Nothing. Nothing's happened here."

"Why are you here?"

She smiles flirtatiously. "I just wanted to see you."

"Oh?" He looks at her for a moment then lowers his voice. "What's your name?"

"Josie Vaughn."

"How old were you when the terrorists struck?"

"Sixteen."

He is momentarily taken aback that she is so young. "Did you finish school?"

She shakes her head.

"Mrs. Schwartz has a school. You can finish your schooling."

"Just high school or does she have a college?"

"I'm not sure what happens after high school. They're going to open a nursing school soon, but that's all I've heard about."

"Ugh!"

"Blood's not your thing huh?"

She shakes her head. After another sip of cola, she gathers her courage and dares to ask a question. "Are you married?"

"My wife was killed."

"Sorry. Any children?"

"No."

He watches her take another sip of cola. "Do you like it?"

"Yeah, it's good. It's nice to have a treat, especially a cold one. What do I have to do in return? The usual?"

He smiles, puts his elbow on the table, and rests his chin in his palm. "Absolutely nothing; it's just my treat for a pretty girl."

She swirls the remaining cola in the bottom of the bottle. "The only thing that would improve it would be to pour it over crushed ice."

He laughs. "No crushed ice around here, but they do have ice in the cafes."

She flirtatiously looks up at him with her head bowed.

He takes note of her flirtation. "I was serious when I said you wouldn't be abused."

She drains the bottle and sets it on the table, wondering when the roofie is going to kick in.

"Why don't I escort you back now?"

She stands, surprised that she feels fine. She follows him to the door. He reaches for the knob. She still feels fine and thinks, *maybe he hasn't drugged me.* She decides that she has misjudged the lieutenant and maybe—just maybe—she could have a protector if she plays her cards right. She puts her hand against the door. He pauses. She quickly slips her arms around his waist, stands on her tiptoes, and attempts to kiss him. He turns his face away, grabs her wrists, extracts himself from her embrace, and sighs as he opens the door. She looks up at him with a puzzled look furrowing her brow.

"I'm serious. No one expects it," he assures her.

"I find that hard to believe."

"In fact, Mrs. Schwartz will be very irate if anyone touches you. We discipline officers who even appear to be thinking about it."

"Like that young officer?"

He nods. "I guess I shouldn't have allowed you in here without a chaperone. Please forgive me."

"I hope you'll forgive me for being so forward. It's just that where I've been their were ... ah ... expectations."

She looks down at the floor. "Where is that officer now?"

"We have him confined on death row."

Her eyes snap up. "Death row!"

"Oh sorry. We only have four vacant cell blocks which we're using for all the slaves today, so there's nowhere else to put him. And just like all of you, he's not locked in a cell. He has the run of the section. We'll merely confine him for a few days and assign him other tasks on a probationary basis. He won't be coming back to work in the prison, ever again."

He tries to keep his smile subdued as he gazes at the beautiful young woman. "Would you mind if I come see you in a couple of weeks. I'll treat you to an iced cola."

"Okay." She smiles with assurance that she can manipulate the kind and gentle man.

THIRTEEN

As they turn onto the main road, two miles from the prison, an ominous knocking suddenly originates from the back of the bus. Tim March pulls to the side of the road and switches off the motor. He turns to Lily.

She raises her eyebrows. "How serious is it?"

"I don't know. I'll check it out and then call Joey to bring the parts we need or ask him to bring the vans."

She nods. He opens the door, letting in a gust of warm morning air. They feel fortunate to have scavenged a bus with a working air conditioner; however without the motor running, they won't be able to utilize it to thwart the June heat which will be upon them within an hour or so. Tim limps down the steps with a tight handhold on the railings and a grimace of pain on his face with each movement of his injured leg. He is followed by two guards.

Lily stands up and turns to face the forty redeemed slaves. "Can everyone hear me?" Many in the front nod but several in the back sport confused looks. She picks up the microphone and pushes the button. "Now …." She checks the button. "I guess it doesn't work with the motor off," she mutters as she puts up the mike.

John reaches under the seat and pulls out a small megaphone.

She takes it. "Can you hear me now?"

"Yeah," someone in the back yells.

"Okay. Our mechanics will either fix the problem or call for vans. I'll go ahead and take questions now since we may be here a while."

Someone asks, "You said mechanics, but I only see one guy working out there. The others look like they're guards."

"Yes, they're guards. The mechanic will call the other mechanic to bring parts or the vans after he's determined the problem. I might add that this is our first trip with the bus and it took them several days to get it to run so this problem isn't surprising at all."

"Earlier, you said many of us have family here; could you tell us who?"

"Since there's so many of you and some of you will prefer privacy, I'll leave the specifics for later. Instead let me address the reason that some of you don't have family here. To redeem as many as possible, we actively search for people with the skills we need in our profit-making enterprises. Our main purpose is to reunite families; we need sufficient profits to be able to do that. When we redeem someone without family here, we don't feel that we're pulling them away from their family since their master was selling them anyway. We'll just actively look for that person's family, so even if you don't already have family here, maybe you will soon. And remember: I said family or friends. It could have been a friend who added your name to our list."

"What are your moneymakers?"

Lily replies, "We have a medical clinic, hospital, and emergency service. Soon we'll have a nursing school. We hope to open our school for children to the public, so we need to expand our teaching staff. And I've recently begun negotiations with the baron who runs our radio station. We see a great need for weather forecasting, so we've searched for anyone who might be able to assist in putting together a newscast."

With amusement, a slender middle-aged man with grey hair and a soothing baritone voice, rhetorically queries, "I get to be the weatherman?"

She laughs and jokingly apologizes. "I hope you don't consider radio beneath you?"

A grin divides Ted Winslow's face. "That's a whole lot better than what I've been doing the last three years."

"Maybe someday we can set up a TV station and let you be the news anchor, but seriously, it's the ham radio operator whom we expect to be the weatherman. We're not sure if hams are active, but we're hoping to establish secure communications with the surrounding areas using Morse code to keep information from falling into the wrong hands. We'd like to at least get a heads up when storms are approaching; we're looking for rather rudimentary weather forecasting at the present time. Anything will be better than being surprised by sudden storms and cold fronts."

An older man speaks with obvious authority in his voice. "Do you have a military?"

Lily is surprised that Wayne Brashear has waited so long to voice his question. Despite three years of slavery, his perfectly erect posture clearly conveys that the former Brigadier General is used to wielding authority. She did not expect patience to be one of his virtues. She promptly replies, "We have a large number of Navy Seals, several other naval officers, and a Marine. They're training all of our guards and the officers. This is a fairly safe area, but we're hoping to improve upon that with better training for all our peacekeepers. We still have occasional raids and a fairly high crime rate in the town. One way we're hoping to improve safety is with photo ID cards. All of you will be issued a card, and you'll be required to carry it when you go into town. Since we haven't had any problems at our compound with intruders for some time now, you won't have to carry it when you're there."

Another man asks, "I'm an engineer. Will I be able to work in my field?"

"Yes. We have engineers working in several areas and ...." She pauses and watches an official white and maroon car pull off the road.

Lieutenant Williams gets out and walks to the bus. He grins as he steps inside. "New bus not working, I see."

"It died," Lily replies. "Are you off duty?"

"Yeah, I have a little free time. I can stay here and help guard you until you can get everyone to the safety of your compound." With a wide grin, he looks at John, lounging in the seat behind the driver's, then winks at Lily. "It looks like John's not doing a bang-up job right now."

John grins. "I'm doing my job. I have your ulterior motive all figured out."

"Lieutenant, I thought you knew John's area of expertise is intelligence," Lily teases. "He doesn't have to 'look' like he's doing his job."

Lily places her hands on her hips and grins mischievously as she stares up into the lieutenant's eyes. "So, John ... what's his ulterior motive?"

"He's interested in that young lady."

Bruce Williams' face clearly conveys his horror at being found out. John enjoys the lieutenant's moment of embarrassment. Lily, however, has concerns of a more serious nature. She wonders if what he has been hiding concerns unlawful activities of an abhorrent nature. She appreciates John's expertise, again thinking that he is worth his weight in gold.

Very softly, she whispers, "Bruce."

He clears his throat and looks over her head, glaring at John with skepticism. "What makes you think that?"

"I noticed the way your gaze always returns to her, even though you never let it linger on her."

"Bruce," Lily softly whispers. "Let's go outside."

"Yes, ma'am."

They walk over and stand by his car.

He lifts both hands up, palms toward her. "I didn't do anything; I swear. She's a looker. The eyes of any red-blooded man would gravitate toward her."

She lowers her head while keeping her eyes locked on his. "I noticed her bowed head when you got on the bus, so explain 'not anything' to me."

He puts his hands in his pockets, momentarily visualizes the petite baroness in alluring attire—an exciting but unattainable prospect he has been craving since the day he first saw the jeans-clad beauty in the town square. Greatly embarrassed to be under her chastisement, he clears his throat and reluctantly submits to her interrogation. "She ... ah ... expected the usual so thought she could seduce me."

"What'd you say?"

"All I said was that no one was going to abuse them here. Actually," he admits with a shrug, "none of them appeared to believe me."

"I appreciate you trying to help, but maybe you should leave that to me. Not that you're not a capable officer, but that just may not be a way to reach people who've probably been abused by their local authorities."

"I don't think I want to work in the prison anymore. Commander Somerton wants to rotate all the lieutenants out there to keep anyone from abusing their power like Commander Blakely did, but ... I just think it'd be better if I didn't do it anymore."

"What happened?"

He asks, "How do you know something happened?"

"I'm good at reading people," she asserts.

"I knew that. I guess I just didn't expect you to catch me."

"What've I caught you at?"

"Well," he stalls. "I had to discipline one of the officers for staring at her. He won't be allowed to work at the prison anymore, so I shouldn't either."

"What'd you do?"

"Man, you're good."

After a moment of silence, she quietly repeats her request. "What happened?"

He looks at the sky. "Ah … she tried to kiss me. I turned away real quick."

Lily inquires, "Where was this?"

"In my quarters," he whispers.

"Your quarters!" Lily exclaims. She rarely raises her voice, but she is appalled at the lieutenant's blunder with the young woman.

"Sorry. She had Officer Ward bring her."

"Maybe Officer Ward should be disciplined too."

"I don't think so," the lieutenant counters.

"Why not?"

"She hadn't been told not to bring anyone to me. We've never had that request before."

"Maybe it should be a rule."

"Okay, I'll discuss it with Commander Somerton. It sounds like you're right on that one."

"Why'd you let her in?" Lily demands.

"In hindsight I shouldn't have, but I thought maybe one of the officers had crossed the line and I needed to look into it. Officer Ward is our only female officer and she can't look after all the women by herself so I thought maybe one of the men did more than just look."

"What else did you do?"

"I gave her a cola and we talked."

"What'd you talk about?"

"I ascertained that she had no complaints of the guards, assured her she was safe then escorted her out."

Lily stares at Lieutenant Williams.

Uneasy under her stare, he fills the silence. "Let me add that I was showing her out when she made her move. Nothing was going to happen as far as I was concerned. I was just concerned about her. I wanted to head off any problems with the officers no matter how minor."

"Okay. I'll let you bring it up with the commander."

"I appreciate you letting me have the dignity of reporting my own breach and making it right. There is one more thing." He clears his throat. "I told her, I'd come see her in a couple of weeks and treat her to an iced cola."

Lily grimaces as she looks up at the tall officer.

"If you don't think I should then give her my apology for not keeping my word."

"I'll talk to her and let you know."

Hope flickers across his face. "Do you think she might be interested in me?"

"Maybe she just thinks a good-looking, young lieutenant could protect her from other abusers."

His face falls.

Wayne Brashear holds his back ramrod straight as he walks into Lily's office. His slacks are sharply creased, his shirt tightly tucked, his shoes freshly shined, and his hair cropped short, military style. In short order, he has found not only the shower but the barber and the laundry and made sure his appearance would pass the strictest inspection of the most demanding superior officer. He is obviously a man used to wielding authority, at least before the terrorists' attacks, and he clearly recognizes the opportunity to regain that authority in their laid-back community. She wonders if she will be able to appease him without ruffling anybody else's feathers. She is quite sure that she will ruffle his.

As Lily closes the door, he grabs her arm. She allows him to push her against the door and calmly looks up at his grim expression. She sports a subdued but confident smile; however her thoughts are focused on defusing his confrontation. It may not be possible, but she will give it her best efforts.

He arrogantly states, "You are no longer in charge here. I am taking over!"

"No you're not, General," she softly replies.

"You have no choice!"

Resigned to the fact that he has given her no options, she pins him to the floor with a few swift moves. "You may now consider yourself a retired general. You're no longer in the military. We'll decide your fate through our legal system here within a couple of months."

"You have a lot of military men here. They will support me in my takeover."

"No they won't. They know what we're doing here and are in full agreement. May I let you up now?"

"Sure."

"You'd better mean that, otherwise I'll have you on the floor again. You're too old to use force. Your skills have deteriorated."

"Bring in some of your military men!"

"Okay." She releases him and pulls out her phone. "Brad, please come to my office and bring Todd."

She puts up her phone and stares at the obstinate man standing beside her desk. He is fastidiously straightening his rumbled clothing. She still wonders if he is going to be useful or if they will have to actually 'retire' him. He looks up.

Exercising patience, she uses a calm tone. "Our two highest ranked men will be here shortly. Please have a seat and maybe I should remind you that most of our military men are Navy officers. You're only our second Marine."

He sits down and defiantly crosses his arms. "You should not call them by their first names!"

"We follow the local customs which were established in the area before we came. You will be addressed as Wayne by everyone." She pulls her chair away from her desk and sits down, leaving ample room between her and the desk.

He glares at her. "That is not right!"

She shrugs and leans back.

"What am I required to call you?"

"Around here, you may call me Jackie. In town, you'll be required to address me as Mrs. Schwartz. No exceptions," she stresses. "You'll also hear people call me Lily and if you want to use Lily that will be fine, but all the military men use Jackie. You may also hear someone call me Mistress, but if you don't want to call me by my first name, I'd prefer that you use Mrs. Schwartz instead of that detestable term."

"Everyone follows this custom?" he inquires with obvious disbelief.

"No," she admits. "Some people with whom I had a business relationship before will continue to address me as Mrs. Schwartz since they've been doing it for many years. I won't ever convince them to call me by my first name, but it doesn't matter if someone doesn't address me informally here. What matters is that we follow local customs with all outsiders."

"I would rather be called General Brashear, but what is wrong with me being addressed as Mr. Brashear? That is more respectful than Wayne!"

She does not hesitate but instead emphatically calls him a slave; she is gunning for the arrogant man's ego. "I'm afraid you're listed on the official registry as a slave. Slaves are generally addressed informally, so when outsiders are present you must be addressed by your first name. We also don't want to slip when we're with outsiders, so stay with the customs at all times even though we could be formal around here."

He leans forward and crosses his arms on her desk. "What are the exceptions to slaves being addressed informally?"

"You're astute to pick up on that."

He leans back in the straight-backed chair and defiantly crosses his arms, an air of arrogance continuing to infuse his every word and gesture. "It pays to be astute in the military."

"The exceptions are those in supervisory positions such as the doctors."

"I do not—"

He is interrupted by a knock. She rises, walks to the door, and opens it. Brad and Todd enter.

After the men are seated around her desk, she states, "This is Captain Brad Kraft, formerly a U.S. Navy Seal and Colonel Todd Jenson, formerly a U.S. Marine. Gentlemen, this is Brigadier General Wayne Brashear, who is now retired from the military. I'm afraid we're not going to be able to use him to bring peace to the area. There will be no more use of military titles, and we'll use first names only. Would you please explain this to ... Wayne."

Brad smiles. "Gen ... ah ... Wayne, we have a chance to bring civilization to the town near here and possibly extend our influence into the surrounding areas. To do that, we mustn't antagonize any of the barons whom we're hoping to influence. We must follow the local customs. Jackie was working on this long before any of us arrived. She's established a network of working relationships which we'll utilize in this effort. Even though she doesn't rule out here, her influence in town is based on the assumption that she does. Any questions, Gen ... Wayne?" Brad shakes his head. "It sure is hard to change old habits."

The former general demands, "What do you mean she does not rule out here?"

"It's democratic. The population is divided into groups who elect a delegate to a council which makes all major decisions and—"

146

"That's a republic?"

"Yes, Gen ... Wayne, you're correct. And from among the delegates a security committee is elected. Jackie, Todd, Ralph, and I report to that committee on security matters."

"Who is Ralph?"

"He's a former policeman who's in charge of the nonmilitary guards, and he's Jackie's bodyguard. He's that big man who was sitting beside her on the bus today."

Wayne sits quietly with a thoughtful expression on his face.

After a moment, Brad inquires, "May I ask about your breach?"

Wayne phrases his reply to retain as much dignity as possible. "I just thought a general would be a better leader, but Jackie let me know that she disagreed."

"We all disagree. This isn't a military regiment commanded by a colonel. Neither is it going to become a brigade commanded by a brigadier general. It's a civilian community." Brad smiles. "The small military unit within the civilian system is controlled by the elected council's decisions."

"What did she mean that your legal system here will decide my fate?"

Lily interrupts, "I'm sorry. Perhaps fate was the wrong word to use."

"Apology accepted."

Brad explains. "We'll discuss your situation with the security committee, and they'll take their recommendation to the general council. After the delegates have consulted with their constituents, the council will vote on a resolution ... whichever one they come up with. And we'll abide by it."

Todd leans forward. "I'm familiar with your abilities and sorry that the last three years have eroded your judgment. I'm hoping we'll be able to use you here, but you're going to have to accept that Jackie's the boss— the head of security in this civilian community. You can just consider her the civilian equivalent of a five-star general."

With disdain, Wayne inquires, "Colonel, why have you been sitting so quietly while the Navy Captain takes charge?"

"I haven't been here very long. I'm still learning the ropes. Brad's been here several months. I defer to the man with more information, and we both defer to Ralph. He's been here over two years. And you must call us Brad and Todd," he emphasizes.

Brad smiles. "Let me tell you about my first day here. I suppose she's told you that everyone gets a week of rest, but she apologized that

147

we were only going to get one day before we needed to start working on a dangerous situation left by a ruthless baron who'd been incapacitated by some unknown assailant. But in fact, they had to come get us out of the shower before we'd even had a chance to clean up. We spent the night looking for land mines around the wind turbines on the southern mesas. We finally found them at dawn and began diffusing them. We were really in a quandary when we got to the bomb rigging the door, but we were saved by Jackie's expertise. It wasn't some unknown equivalent of C 4. It was children's modeling clay. We were then able to quickly rescue the computer geeks who'd been held captive in the hidden lair and stranded without food and water since the only men who knew their location were either dead or in a coma."

Wayne grins and shakes his head. "Okay, you guys have convinced me. Do you have any more stories like that?"

"Not many. It's usually pretty mundane around here. Two of the men were with the commander a couple of weeks ago when raiders struck, but I'll let them tell you about that firefight." Brad grins. "And I'm sure you'll be both amused and enlightened to know that Jackie took out two of the armed raiders in hand-to-hand combat."

Wayne looks at Lily with a skeptical expression then glances at Todd who reacts with an affirming nod.

Two hours later, Todd escorts Wayne to the dining hall. Lily looks at Brad. "What's your recommendation?"

"He's a good general when he has all the information, but he's a take-charge guy and unfortunately runs pell-mell into a situation when he knows he doesn't have all the information. He's quick to admit his error but puts the blame on subordinates for not briefing him thoroughly. That's one reason he's only a brigadier general. He's brilliant enough that he should've made it to four stars, if he'd only kept his foot out of his mouth. He prefers quick action over careful assessment. Ah ... don't let him know, but we called him General Brash."

She grins in amusement. "Do you think we can use him instead of retiring him?"

"I'm sure we can find a place for him here. If we could give him some title, like Director of ... whatever, then he'll be a great asset. Todd would know his areas of expertise and would be able to make the recommendation."

She props her elbows on the desk and puts her fingertips together. "Ah ... we need to stroke his ego, and he'll do all right."

"I guess that's a good assessment."

"I noticed he's quite a story teller."

"He's got a ton of war stories. He must've been in every war during his long career. I don't think he ever sat one out in an administrative post of some kind."

"He loves to listen too. Do you think all his stories are actually his own?" Lily asks.

"I hadn't ever thought about that. He always tells them in the first person. I've sat in many audiences while he charmed the crowd with vivid accounts of valor."

She grins mischievously. "With the vividness greatly enhanced, I'd guess?"

He laughs. "Probably."

"I'll let you guys take care of his ego and find a place for him, and we'll make that our recommendation to the committee."

"Another thing: he should know the names of several in Special Forces."

She nods and starts to get up but notices his sudden look of sadness. "What is it?"

"I'm sorry, but I almost forget to tell you. When you called, we'd just been asked to help the nurses with that old man who used to do the preaching in the dining hall."

"Posse?" she asks, speaking of Preston "Posse" Posey.

"I guess that's his name, the one that Lawrence recorded all his Bible lessons. I was impressed that he was still going strong even when his body wasn't and he had to sit down instead of stand. It was obvious that he thought he should be standing in all the recordings. Well anyway, he went to take a nap and didn't get up for lunch. Someone went to check on him, and he was dead. They told us to tell you, and they called someone else to help them. When I saw who you had in here, I knew it'd be better to wait until he was gone to tell you. Sorry, but I knew you'd probably want to go right away and I wanted you in here while we talked to ... Wayne. Oh, it's still hard to call him by his first name. And … ah … you know … ah … I assume that his … ah … watered down explanation of his breach was slanted in his favor?"

She smiles. "Shall we say: severely censored."

FOURTEEN

Carl Marshall, a former U.S. Navy Seal, looks at the blazing sun above the box canyon south of town. He fingers the binoculars hanging around his neck. "Gets kind of warm here."

Ryan Sealy laughs at the obvious joke; it is approaching one hundred degrees. As he glances over at Commander Somerton who is parking nearby, Ryan quips, "What do you expect? It's summer, we're in the South and not near any large bodies of water."

"Rotten place for a bunch of Seals to be."

"We have a job to do here."

"I know," Carl replies. "I'm glad to finally be in a situation where my skills are useful. Speaking of our job, look at that officer's stance."

"Well, go correct it, 'new assistant'."

Carl laughs and walks over to the inexperienced officer.

Commander Somerton wipes the sweat off his brow and steps up beside Ryan. He scans the twelve men on the firing line. It is the usual Tuesday lineup. Five are new officers, five are veteran officers brushing up on their infrequently used skills, and two are Mrs. Schwartz's guards. "How's the training going?"

"It appears a few of your officers have never fired a gun before."

"That's not surprising. We have to randomly select young men to train as officers. Some of them probably have criminal records."

"What do you do about that?" Ryan asks.

"We give them a little pep talk and tell them that this is a chance for a new life, a law-abiding life."

"Only one officer in this group can hit the bull's-eye."

"Yeah," the commander agrees. "Lieutenant Williams has a steady hand. He's a native Texan. He probably grew up hunting with his dad or something."

Ryan turns his attention back to the officers on the firing range. "One hasn't even hit the target."

Carl steps back to watch the stance of the neophyte as he takes another shot. His assigned target is the nearest hay bale; it remains unscathed despite twenty minutes practice. Carl puts the binoculars to his eyes. "Missed; try again, Officer North. Hold your hand very steady as you slowly pull the trigger. Forget about the bull's eye. Just try to put one in the hay bale."

"Carl!" Ryan calls. "Come meet the commander."

He strides back, faces the commander, and holds out his hand. "Glad to meet you. I'm Carl Marshall, new assistant firearms instructor. I just started today. I arrived a week ago, yesterday."

"Commander Robert Somerton; pleased to meet you."

Carl steps over to stand beside the commander as they watch the ten officers. "Well—" A bullet silences Carl.

"Cover!" Ryan yells. Every man on the firing range hits the dirt. With relief, Ryan thinks, *well, we got that idea across; that's one lesson down, ten thousand to go!*

While brothers Jack and John Thorne scan the low hills, Ryan looks around. Carl is sprawled nearby with blood gushing from his chest.

"That was meant for me!" the terrified commander rasps between hyperventilating gasps of air.

"I know." Ryan looks toward John.

"He stepped beside me, just as the sniper got off his shot!"

"I know. Calm down."

"Okay, whatever you say. I'll try. I'll try." Commander Somerton rubs both hands over his face. He feels the gritty soil transfer from his sweaty palms to his sweaty face. He attempts to brush off the grime. He focuses on the task to take his mind away from the horror of their dilemma, pinned down on the rifle range without cover. The cars are parked several yards behind them, too far for a quick dash for cover. In front of them is the expanse of the rifle range with twelve paper targets centered on twelve round bales of hay, placed at varying distances from the firing line, accommodating everything from side arms to rifles. For practice with a sniper rifle, they retreat to the hills behind them and aim into the canyon. The box canyon is nestled among the mesas south of town that are covered with a array of precisely placed wind turbines with lazily turning blades.

Today's sniper is not here to practice; he is hidden among rocks along the canyon wall.

Ryan reports, "John has signaled that they've spotted him."

A shot echoes through the hills.

Ryan exchanges a series of brief signals with John then turns toward Commander Somerton. "Jack got him. He appears to be the only one, but we're going to take this opportunity to teach your officers pursuit methods. Each of us will take three of your officers in tow and approach the sniper from three different directions. We're going to assume that he's merely wounded and that he has accomplices, which we should do anyway. That leaves one officer to stay with you. I don't think you could handle the exercise at this time."

"I think you're right there," the commander admits.

"Which officer would you like to stay with you?"

"Lieutenant Williams. No, wait! He's my best Lieutenant. I'd like him to learn the skills you're teaching. Just leave me the most scared neophyte."

"Are you sure?"

Commander Somerton replies, "Yes, we'll be fine."

"I volunteer!" Officer Donald North, the neophyte who cannot hit the hay bale, yells.

"Okay, crawl over here." Ryan watches the young man try to scramble across the dirt. "Stay down. … Turn sideways and roll. … Okay, quickly. Watch the gun in your hand."

Seconds later, the dust-covered officer takes a deep breath as he lies nearby.

Ryan hides his dismay at the officer's trembling hands. "Officer North, you and the commander take cover beside that car over there. Stay on the side away from the direction of the shot."

"Yes, Sir. Which way was the shot?"

Ryan points to the north. Commander Somerton draws his gun, rolls over beside the car, sits up, leans against the door, and holsters his gun. He turns his gaze away from the dead Seal and watches Officer North roll over and sit up beside him. Ryan barks orders. Within seconds the two men are alone.

The commander's eyes wonder toward the dead man. He forces his gaze to Officer North. "You're terrified, aren't you?"

"Sorry, Sir. I should have said something on the first day, but this just isn't my thing. Guns and I are complete strangers. It's been that way ever since I was eight, and some kid brought one to school."

"Did he shoot anybody?"

"No. Turns out it wasn't even loaded, but we sure had a big scare before they discovered that."

"Didn't they get everybody out within a few minutes?"

"Everybody but us. We just cowered under our desks for hours as he ranted and raved and swung that gun around."

"I can understand how that would strike fear into anybody. How're you at things such as computers?"

"They're strangers to me too. I'm what they politely call academically challenged. In fact, my nickname was Stump."

"Do you think you could learn data entry?"

"Sir, I don't even know what that is."

"It's supposed to be simple. Let's give it a shot. Marvin will teach you."

Officer North quickly agrees. "Okay, I'll try it. That's much better than being out here."

"Okay, you're our new clerk," the commander declares.

"What if I can't hack it?"

"We'll look for something else for you."

"What else have you got?" the officer inquires, hoping for some assignment that isn't above his limited abilities.

"I don't have much, but I could trade you to Mrs. Schwartz. She has lots of different enterprises. I think she could find something for you."

"I'd like to live out at her compound. I hear it's nice."

"We're going to try you as clerk first. Marvin needs the help, and I really don't care if you have to use the two-finger, hunt-and-peck method."

"That's fine, Sir, and I'll do my best at the clerking. Marvin seems to have it pretty easy, staying in his workshop all the time. ... Well, most of the time. He doesn't have to go out and patrol the streets, and he says he really likes your wife's cooking."

Despite his terror, a slight smile relaxes the commander's face as he thinks of his wife. "Yeah. She's a good cook, all right."

Commander Somerton wipes the sweat from his brow and listens to the rumble of voices as the three Seals and his nine officers return. Four of the officers carry the dead sniper. With relief, they drop the body beside Carl Marshall and wipe the sweat from their faces. The commander stands. Officer North jumps up and follows him to the sniper.

Jack steps up beside the commander. "Do you know this man?"

He shakes his head and looks at his officers. They shake their heads. "I suppose he wasn't carrying his new ID card, was he?"

"No, Commander."

He pulls out his phone. "Marvin fixed me up with this camera phone. I can just click, and then maybe I can figure out how to send it to him. If this man has one of the new cards, we'll be able to identify him."

In less than a minute, Commander Somerton says, "Thanks, Marvin," puts up his phone, and looks up.

Jack remarks, "That was quick."

"Yeah. I like this new system. When everybody has a card, then we won't have problems identifying anybody."

"Do we have an ID?"

"This is William Blunt who's registered with Gordon O'Neil."

"We have a problem." Everyone turns toward John. "Mrs. Schwartz has been negotiating with Mr. O'Neil to broadcast weather reports over the radio. About three weeks ago, we got a news anchorman and a ham radio operator to assist with that. This morning we dropped them and Darla off at the radio station, and Darla's seven months pregnant."

"What's that got to do with anything?" a novice officer asks.

"They may be dead or being held captive," Commander Somerton grumbles. "Did Mrs. Schwartz and some guards stay with them?"

"She left one guard with them, but she went over to Mr. Kasper's after dropping us off," John reports.

"Is he a Seal?"

"Yes, but you know he's unarmed," Jack reminds the commander. "This man has obviously been fighting. He has several injuries, the kind of injuries you'd get if you tangled with a Seal ... and won."

"What do you men suggest?" the commander solicits.

"Well, Commander," Ryan states, "this is an opportunity to teach your officers how to rescue hostages."

A puzzled look appears on Officer North's face.

"What's the problem, Officer?" Ryan gently inquires.

"What if they're dead? There wouldn't be any hostages to rescue."
Lieutenant Williams grins. "We still get the practice."

Jack Thorne cuts through the security fence on the east side of the isolated broadcast station. He slips through followed by Lieutenant Williams and two officers. John Thorne cuts through on the north side, followed by Lieutenant Jones and two officers. Brad Kraft does the same on the west side. Stacked behind him are Lieutenant Rambler and two officers. Commander Somerton nervously follows Todd Jenson on the south side. Two officers closely tail the beleaguered commander.

Four officers and two military men wait behind a building two miles down the road. Popular tunes from four years ago softly spill from a radio. Tim March parks their SUV behind the line of official vehicles. Ralph hops out and opens the passenger door. Sporting a frown of displeasure Lily slides out and walks over to Wayne and his 'aide', U.S. Navy Seal Trevor Nichols. Wayne quickly delves into an account of the day's events and plans. With patience, Lily listens to his rehash, despite full knowledge of every detail and her chagrin that she was left out of the planning stage. The raid was authorized by Commander Somerton, but her men were only authorized to train the officers, not lead them on a raid. She is ruing the possible political fallout of a military-style raid.

The four armed teams slowly work their way around the square, nondescript building housing the radio station. They check each window and each door. The fifth and sixth teams slip through the breaches in the fence and scout the residential building. Within minutes the first four teams select entrances. Carefully coached officers take their places and relay signals. Two doors and two windows are breached simultaneously. As a synchronous unit, the four teams rush inside and methodically clear the rooms with the uniformed officers following the well-trained military men. Startled workers quickly surrender. Officers are left to guard the men kneeling by the wall with their hands on their heads.

Jack and John stop on either side of the closed office door. Ryan and Todd are stacked behind them. All four check their pistols. Four officers watch from positions of safety. John reaches down and slowly turns the knob. Jack places his hand on the hinged side of the door and pushes it open. "Who's there?" a male voice familiar to everyone calls from inside the room.

The Thorne brothers charge through the doorway. "Don't move! Put it down!"

Three shots are fired. Ryan and Todd quickly recover from their automatic recoil at the bullet passing between them and peer inside the room. Mr. O'Neil slumps in his chair. On his chest, two circles of blood enlarge. Gravity takes effect and the stains droop downward into irregular and elongating ovals. Jack steps around the desk and takes the pistol dangling from Mr. O'Neil's limp hand.

Ryan and Todd dash to the next closed door, stand on either side, and signal two officers to stack behind them. They check the readiness of the two officers then Ryan slowly turns the knob. Todd pushes the door open—silence. Ryan and Todd charge through the door. Darla excitedly mumbles through the gag in her mouth. Todd holsters his pistol and rushes to untie her while Ryan signals the two officers to enter and untie the three men.

"Can I go to the restroom?" Darla anxiously whispers. "Is it safe?"

Todd replies, "We've cleared everything except the control room."

"Just send one of their men in to inform him. They'll have no problems with a change in command here." She waddles out the door as rapidly as possible.

Todd strides out and finds the nearest worker. "She says you'll have no problem with a change in command?"

"That's correct, Sir."

"Okay, stand up. You can take your hands down. We've cleared every room except your control room. We don't want to disrupt the program, but we want him to know what's going on." Todd turns to Ted Winslow who is rubbing his wrists and flexing his legs after his long captivity tied to a chair. "Do you know how to run a radio station?"

Ted replies, "Yes." The former TV news anchor's grey hair is now ash blond with graying temples. He lacks only the double chin to resemble his former on-air appearance, but with the excellent meals in the dining hall, he has gained five pounds in his two weeks at the compound.

Todd instructs, "Go with this man and keep the music playing while we talk to everyone."

Todd turns to Jack. "Take everyone into that conference room over there. Darla says none of them are going to cause any problems."

Jack nods. He walks into the next room and begins barking orders to the officers and their captives.

Ryan puts his phone away and walks over to Todd and Brad. "House is cleared, and they're bringing everyone over here."

Nolan Graves walks up to the three men. He is rubbing his wrists which clearly show signs of struggling against tight bonds. "Sorry, Sirs. Mr. O'Neil put a gun to my head. I knew I couldn't protect the others with a bullet swimming around in my brain."

Brad smiles. "You made the right decision. Good work."

Commander Somerton leans against the wall of the large room. His stomach is churning. Inwardly, he is anything but calm. "Okay, men. Let's go over the situation for Mrs. Schwartz."

He nods at Lieutenant Williams, who promptly steps forward. "Briefly, Mr. O'Neil took your people hostage and sent William Blunt to assassinate the commander. Carl Marshall was shot in the chest and killed. Jack killed the sniper. We stormed the station and residence. Mr. O'Neil drew a weapon and fired. He was shot and killed. All hostages were freed, unharmed. Mr. O'Neil's people surrendered and have no objections to a change in command. In fact, I've been told they welcome it."

Commander Somerton looks around. "Any suggestions?"

Lieutenant Williams promptly suggests, "Mrs. Schwartz could be appointed executrix of Mr. O'Neil's estate."

Lily's soft voice clearly rings out, commanding attention. "What about political fallout?"

The men look at Lily; her creased brow displays her displeasure with the turn of events. "I've been assuring the barons that I'm not interested in taking over other barons' enterprises. It'll set back negotiations on the electric co-op for me to be seen as interested in expanding my position, especially after a military-style raid."

"I agree with that argument," Commander Somerton states with sorrowful resignation that the solution is not going to be easy.

Todd scratches his head. "Mrs. Schwartz, what do you suggest?"

"I need to talk to Commander Somerton." She walks into another room. He plods morosely after her.

158

She looks up at the distressed commander. "Is this the baron who killed Officer Hayes?"

"You know about that?" he exclaims in alarm.

"We figured it out. So ... was it Mr. O'Neil?"

"No," he replies.

"Who was it?"

He merely shakes his head.

"Why won't you tell me?"

"Trust me. We need to slow down on these changes around here," he cautions.

"Somebody pretty powerful, huh?"

He nods. She turns and strides into the outer room. He steps to the door and leans against the frame. Everyone turns their attention toward the baroness.

She is not happy but hopes she can contain the situation. She forces a smile. "My suggestion is that we hide the events of today. Since there was no interruption of the radio broadcast and this station is in an isolated spot, we should be able to do that. Later, when other forms of enterprises are accepted, we can organize the radio as an autonomous entity. What does everyone think about that?"

One of Mr. O'Neil's men timidly raises his hand. She nods.

"I like the concept, but don't see how we can accomplish that."

"What're the snags that you see?"

"That authorization thing for one."

"That's easy. My computer guy will take care of it. Do you know where his web-link device is?"

He nods.

Lily inquires, "Any other problems?"

He looks at his fellow workers. They all nod. He turns back. "We're all for it. And we think you should know that Mr. O'Neil planned to kill you when you returned for your team ... and ... ah ... it was to be after watching your team being tortured and killed ... especially the pregnant woman, and we're not sure why. He seemed delighted with the offer of a joint effort to set up weather forecasting then the next day, after he came back from the market, he was dead set against it."

A phrase automatically pops into Lily's head. *The baron who killed Officer Hayes threatened Mr. O'Neil too!*

"That settles it as far as I'm concerned," Commander Somerton states with finality and an overwhelming urge to leave the stress of the day's events behind. "We'll leave you to sort out the details. Lieutenant Jones, you stay with Mrs. Schwartz and report to me later."

"What's our plan if anybody comments about seeing this raid?" Lieutenant Williams asks.

Jack replies, "Training exercise. That's what we said this was from the beginning."

Lieutenant Williams speaks with a loud voice. "Did everyone hear that?"

People nod.

"We've had several training exercises recently and will have more in the coming weeks. This was just one of them. Mr. O'Neil agreed to assist us since he wants to be sure his station remains safe and secure. Is everybody on the same page?" Lieutenant Williams looks around. People nod. He nods at the commander and strides toward the door.

As Commander Somerton walks toward the door, Lily steps over, touches him lightly on the arm and whispers, "Robert." He leans over to confidentially position his head near hers. She whispers, "Leave a couple of officers at the roadblock with Wayne and Trevor."

"I don't think we need a roadblock anymore."

"Wayne needs the important job, and we don't want him in here during the delicate negotiations."

"Oh? I bet the guard with him isn't really his assistant but more of a babysitter?"

She winces at the derogatory term. "He's on ah … probation at this time."

"I could tell, by the way he took charge at the roadblock, that he's a bull in a china shop."

As the officers leave, Lily turns toward John. He has a huge grin on his face. It is obvious that he likes active duty as do the other military men. She smiles and playfully taps his arm with her clinched fist as she walks past. She stops and looks up at the spokesman for the radio personnel.

He asks, "What do we need to do?"

Lily replies, "The first step is for all of you to elect a leader. While you're doing that, my men will repair the fences and broken windows and bury Mr. O'Neil's body."

FIFTEEN

As Lily escorts him from her office, words surge forth from Dr. Gregory Cole, "Thank you very much, Mrs. Schwartz. I really appreciate what you're trying to do here. I wish they'd been doing that, where I was. Now, I'm so happy that I ticked off Mr. Carrasco. I thought I was a goner and was ecstatic when he merely sold me instead of killing me. I really thought he was going to kill me, but I guess I'm worth more dead than alive. Oops, I mean more alive than dead. Got stuck on an old cliché there. Do you mind if I ask how much you paid for me? Oh never mind. I don't know anything about the monetary system. I hear it's totally different from dollars. I'm absolutely delighted to be able to work in a hospital again even if it doesn't have AC. I'm not going to complain about the heat. It may be hot with July almost here but it's not going to bother me, not one iota. It sounds like your engineers are doing a bang-up job of ventilating the hospital. After all, what did people do before AC anyway? I'm not going to complain about that or anything else. I have a whole new perspective on what's important. So thank you, thank you very much. A million thank you's."

With a smile, she opens the door, anxious to usher the verbose doctor out. If every newly redeemed person was so irritating, she would dread the Monday afternoon interviews instead of enjoying the discussions— at least she enjoys most of them. "Our doctors are looking forward to working with you. We're delighted to have an anesthesiologist on our staff now, and we have a very good nurse anesthetist who's been begging for help. I'm sure you'll find her a delight to work with." But Lily is not sure any of the medical personnel are going to be delighted to work with him or that he'll keep his promise not to complain. She has been told he is a good anesthesiologist but has discovered the grating personality that everyone failed to mention.

He grabs her right hand with both of his and pumps it up and down. "I'm sure I will. Thank you so very much, and I'll get in the names of my wife and children and all our close relatives immediately and every doctor, nurse, aide, and lab tech that I know. Where do I go for that?"

"They've set up a table right over there," Lily replies. "Fill out a form for each one. If you don't know someone's exact birthday or something, put down your best guess and mark it as a guess."

"Okay. Thank you, thank you!"

"Okay, Dr. Cole."

"Okay." He reluctantly releases her hand and strides toward the table manned by Serena Hermann.

Lily looks at Serena. The widow cannot hide her sadness. It was a great shock for James to die so suddenly and at such a young age. With the severe shortage of women at their compound, there are many single men who are almost fighting over the young and extremely good looking widow. They are daft for rushing her. It has only been four weeks; Serena has not had time to grieve.

Lily turns her gaze to the men and women waiting for their interview then at George Lemont, who is sitting beside the office door. He indicates the morose man who is next. Al Porclain sits with his lean frame hunched over, his hands clasped between his knees. His brown hair is cropped short, revealing the beginning of male-pattern baldness on the crown of his head.

She smiles pleasantly. "Al."

He looks up with sorrow filling his grey eyes. He stands and walks into her office, head bowed. Lily shuts the door and follows Al to her desk. She sits down and looks up. His grimace furrows his brow.

"Hello, Al. How are you?"

"I'm okay, Lily. How're you?"

"I'm fine. How's Cathy?" she asks, speaking of his wife and her best friend.

He bows his head. "She died."

She now understands his lack of cheerfulness. Despite his obvious sorrow, she would like to know what happened to her best friend and it might help him to talk about his pain. "Sorry. Please tell me what happened?"

"We were vacationing at our place in Colorado when the terrorists struck. It was rather isolated so we stayed up there and lived off the land.

She'd only brought one packet of pills so she got pregnant. Without medical help she died in childbirth. I did save the baby." He sniffs and wipes the back of his hand across his face. "It's been two years, but it's still so painful."

His brief statement has eased her mind about Cathy. Lily is thankful that Cathy was never subjected to the brutal slave culture. "Sorry. We'll look for your children."

"I don't think they want to see me. They blame me for her death. The next time Rick and I came back from hunting, the other children were gone and two men were waiting for us. I haven't seen any of them since."

"We have a large operation here. We can easily keep them separate from you and provide them with counseling and school, etcetera. Bringing them here is the only way to know they're safe."

"I understand," he assures her.

"Do you know anything about your parents or sisters?"

"No."

Lily promises, "We can search for them too."

"How about Cathy's Dad?" Al inquires.

"I found him about a year later, and he died a natural death three weeks ago."

"That's good. Well, I don't mean that he died. I mean that—"

"I know," she interrupts. "Are you going to be all right?"

He shrugs. "The worst part is alienating my children."

Despite his anguish, he attempts to smile, managing only a thin-lipped half smile. "Have you found any of Cathy's brothers and sisters?"

She shakes her head.

"So you don't know whether they're dead or alive?"

"No."

He inquires, "Is the whole country in utter chaos?"

"It seems to be changing. I talk to everyone about where they've been. Lately, I've been getting a few reports that the brutal system of slavery is lessening in some areas. Sometimes it's a peaceful transition from within, but sometimes it comes from a brutal attack by an antislavery gang. One brings stability, the other brings chaos."

"I can guess which one is which," he remarks with pointed sarcasm.

"I do have one report, just one, of a group of people being protected by their local commander."

"There're probably more."

"Probably but they most likely do just what we're doing and hide it from everyone to avoid raids. And ... they're probably not prone to selling those whom they're protecting, just like us."

Al asks, "How large is your operation?"

With an amused smile, Lily says, "I've lost count. It's well over a thousand and growing rapidly."

He lowers his head and stares at the floor.

"Do you have any questions?"

"I guess not. ... Well, maybe so." He looks up. "After my week of rest, what job will I be assigned?"

"You'll help Lawrence and Wes. We can always use another computer geek."

He smiles weakly. "I'm glad your family is here."

"It's Wes Young who helps Lawrence, not my son Wes."

"Oh."

She lowers her eyes. "My two youngest and Walter were killed."

"So you still have Walt?"

She shakes her head and fights her tears over the memory of her eldest Walter "Walt" Schwartz IV. "He was having troubles and ran away shortly before the attacks. The police didn't manage to find him before the chaos struck. I don't know where he is. The only family I have here is the son of my cousin. His name is Branson Parker. He's fifteen."

"What about that young man that you and Walter took in when his mother died?"

"That's Lawrence."

A smile finally displaces the sorrow on his face. "I'll be very happy to work with him. What's he doing?"

"He and Marvin Finley, who works for the local commander, have several projects they're working on. They set up the system on that web-link device and—"

His smile vanishes; surprise widens his eyes. "You mean that monetary system all the masters use?"

"Yes, it started here," Lily affirms.

"Wow!"

"We're also installing an ID system for the commander. That's just getting under way."

164

Al inquires, "Did they set up the web?"

"It was either set up by someone else or never completely destroyed. We don't know which. We just added to it. At first all the sites were pornography."

A derisive chortle escapes from his mouth. "I guess we could expect that."

"Later we began finding trading sites. So far, the ones we've ordered from have been legitimate. You'll have to talk to Lawrence about it. You know I'm definitely not a computer person; I just learned the basics necessary for my job. If you don't have more questions, I need to see a few others before supper."

"Can I meet you for supper?"

"I guess. If you come up with questions, you can catch me anytime. Well, maybe not anytime. I seem to do a lot of running around in town now, but anytime I'm here, I try to make as much time as possible for the new people."

They walk to the door. She is relieved that even though he is not smiling; his expression is relaxed. She thinks of Cathy, and a tear forms. She wipes her eye. She knows Al would have liked to see his father-in-law. He could have gently told the elderly father about the last days of his youngest and favorite daughter. Maybe they will find some of Al's six children soon. She suddenly realizes that she forgot to ask where he has been. She resolves to ask later, perhaps during supper.

Lily steps into the main room. She looks toward the nearby sofas and is surprised to find only two people waiting for interviews. She looks over at George with a questioning expression.

"Thought you and Al might talk a long time, so suggested that all but the next two sign up for interviews after supper. Have the list here." He holds up one of the blank forms. On the back is a column of signatures.

"Good thinking, George. Maybe one of these will be talkative. Either that, or I'll get off early."

Al calls, "Lily, thanks for having supper with me."

They meet in the center of the main room and walk toward the dining hall.

His grin is wide and his eyes shine with delight. "I've been looking over the compound while you finished those two interviews. It's quite a place you have here, and they tell me there're almost as many people in the compound in town as there are out here."

"That's right. We just moved all the medical and engineering families and support personnel into town to be near their work. Did you go see Lawrence?"

"Nah, I'll wait until next week. I'm looking forward to that week of rest you promised. I haven't had a vacation in over three years. It was really hard work to live off the land. My boys were a great help with the hunting and stuff and the girls helped Cathy with everything she had to do around the cabin. It certainly gives me great respect for the pioneers. Then after I was captured, there was no telling what those brutal slave drivers expected of me. I've done everything from garbage detail to washing dishes to tacking on shingles. If I walked into Lawrence's setup, I might never get up. That'll almost be like a vacation to sit down at a computer again."

"We're early for supper so let me introduce you to a few people."

She pushes open the door to the dining hall and strides across the empty room to the bustling kitchen. "Hey, Susie. I see you're sitting down."

"Yeah," the small Asian woman replies. "I don't know what labor feels like, but I think it might be starting."

Lily turns to Al. "Susie's going to be a first-time mother. She's our head chef and everyone complains about her cooking." She pauses for comic timing. "It's really bad on your waistline."

They laugh then Susie groans. "I think Jude's going to come tonight. They told me it's a boy, so I'm naming him after my husband."

Lily looks around as middle-aged George, an extremely kind and gentle man, walks up.

He grins as he takes Susie's hand. "Come on, I'll take you to the clinic. Dr. Morris was assigned here today just in case Jude decided that today was his birth day."

"Yeah, I had an appointment this morning. He said everything was fine. What does it mean to be dilated?"

Lily watches with a mixture of concern and amusement as they walk across the dining hall. She wonders if George, a mild-mannered father of five, is explaining childbirth to Susie. Unlikely.

166

She turns back to Al. "Let's go meet Marie. She's in charge of supplies."

She leads Al over to an Hispanic woman. "Marie this is Al, Posse's son-in-law. Marie was my neighbor when we moved to that new development out of town."

"Glad to meet you, Al."

"Glad to meet you, Marie."

Lily turns toward an older woman seated on a stool, pushing carrots through a salad shredder. "And this is Trudy."

"Hello, Trudy."

"Hellooo, gooood looooking!" Trudy looks at Lily and loudly whispers, "Is he single?"

Lily laughs. "Trudy's looking for a husband."

"I figure number seven ought to be the one," Trudy exclaims.

"The line is forming, Al. Why don't we go get in line?" Lily suggests.

Trudy requests, "Lily, would you take this bowl over and put it on the salad bar on your way, and I'll just start on the next bowl of carrots."

"Sure, Trudy."

Al quickly picks up the large bowl, and Lily directs him to its usual place on the salad bar.

Lily pushes her tray toward the center of the table. "It's been nice talking about old times."

Al replies, "Yeah, I had fun that semester we were dating."

"So did I, but now I have to go back to work. Thanks for telling me what you know about where you've been. I know it's painful to talk about, but this is the only way we get any news about other areas." She stands and reaches for her tray.

"Here let me take the trays." He stacks his dishes on hers, picks up her tray and puts it on his empty one. "Where do I take them?"

She points and watches him walk away before heading toward the main room. As she nears the end of the row of tables, Serena Hermann leaps up, leaving most of her food uneaten. Brett Cockrell also rises. Lily steps over, stabs her index finger at his chest, and sternly demands, "Leave her alone."

Brett lowers himself back into his chair with a look of animosity souring his face. Lily stares into his eyes. She feels sorry for him. He is desperate. She is sorry she had to manhandle him when he made a play for her, but he is very abrasive and definitely cannot be considered charming. He does not have a chance—not with any woman.

Serena strides toward the back door. Gary Brown holds the door and follows her outside. He catches up with her as she hurries down the path toward her cottage. She looks up with anger. It quickly subsides. "Oh, Gary."

"Hello, Serena. Has he been bothering you?"

She almost growls, "Him and a whole lot of others."

"Sorry. It's only been a month. They shouldn't be such vultures." He reaches in his pocket and hands her a handkerchief.

"Thanks." She wipes the tears from her face and blows her nose.

After walking a few more steps, she says, "I never did thank you."

"For what?"

"For faking it." She is speaking of a time when both she and Gary belonged to brutal Mr. Barton and she was required to 'entertain' on camera.

He grins. "I was pretty peeved at Mr. Barton for pushing a woman on me, when all I asked for was a cigar."

She laughs.

"It's good to hear you laugh."

She smiles and looks up at the man whom her former master tried to make into an assassin. Her eyes glisten with tears; any thought which brings Mr. Barton to mind brings tears to her eyes.

"Maybe I can help you with the vultures," Gary offers.

"How could you do that?"

Softly, he suggests, "We could 'fake it' again."

She looks down. "There're no cameras here. What good would that do?"

"I meant we could stroll together in the evenings and eat together, and I could tell those vultures to stay away from my woman. Then later, when you're ready to actually date one of the nice men around here, we could break up and you'd be free to seek out a man of your own choosing."

"I bet they'd stay away from me if a Navy Seal was my guy," Serena mutters with a pensive expression.

"That's what I was thinking."

"Here's my cottage."

"Ah … if you have time why don't we stroll down to the river? I don't think anybody's seen us yet."

She looks up at the tall, muscular man.

He raises his eyebrows. "Are you saying no?"

"I was still thinking."

"Okay. If you decide to accept my help, just let me know. Goodnight, Serena." He turns and walks away.

"Gary."

He turns back.

"Yes. … Why don't we stroll down to the river?"

He smiles and holds out his elbow. She smiles, hurries over, and slips her arm around his.

Sitting on a flat rock at the river's edge, Serena swishes her feet in the cool water and looks at the placid pool and the slow moving current on the far side. She and Gary have spent the last two hours talking and the moonlight now dances on the rippling surface of the water. For the first time since her husband died, she feels relaxed. Startled, she looks around. She leans toward Gary and whispers, "Someone's coming."

"I know."

"There you are, Serena. I've been looking for you."

At the sound of Brett's too-familiar voice, Serena leans against Gary's side. He slips his arm around her waist, tilts his face toward the petite woman's head, and nuzzles her hair. She tilts her face up and seeks his lips.

"Oh? … Sorry to disturb you," Brett apologizes. It is an unusual reaction for the abrasively confrontational man.

They listen to his footsteps as he walks back across the rocks and away from the river.

When he is gone, Serena breaks off the kiss and states, "That was the worst offender."

Gary laughs. "I think we got the message across."

"Maybe," she mutters. She has no confidence that anyone can rein in Brett, at least, not without bodily harm.

"He's on our watch list. You're not the only woman he's made a play for."

"I know. All the women have been told to be leery of him and assured that he's not going to be trained as a guard."

Serena looks up at Gary's face and turns to a more pleasant topic. "Do you ever get assigned to town, or do you stay out here?"

"I can withdraw my request to transfer into town and stay out here."

"You don't have to do that for me, if you'd rather work in town."

"That's all right. It was just the excitement they had a while back." Now ill at ease due to her kiss, he rambles, "Guard duty around here gets pretty boring. Teaching the classes is fun, though. I'd be glad to stay out here. I doubt if they'll have any more excitement anyway. You're not going to move to town?"

She bows her head in sorrow. "We'd moved to town but when James died, I moved back for the kids' schooling. I'd rather just stay here. It's good for the kids and they gave me my old job back and it's a very rewarding job since I get to help people find their loves ones."

"It'll be a pleasure to take on a second job of guarding you."

She flirtatiously looks up at him. "Did you enjoy that kiss?"

He nervously laughs.

"That's all right." She looks down.

"I don't want to take advantage of my guard duty," Gary states. "I don't want to be the same kind of troll that I'm guarding you against."

"You'd never be that kind of man."

With hesitation in her voice, she inquires, "Were you married?"

"Yes, but I'm sure my wife is dead. I was on board a plane when the terrorists struck. After six months, I made it back and found our home destroyed. There were human bones in the rubble, so John and I buried them and put my wife's name on the marker."

"Sorry. Any children?"

"No, we hadn't been married very long," Gary replies.

"Did you put your wife on the list, just in case those weren't her bones?"

"Yes, Jackie thought we should cover all bases."

"Thanks for helping me tonight. I'd better go check on the children now." Serena lifts her feet out of the water and grabs her shoes.

"Okay, milady. Let me escort you to your door, and would you like me to escort you to breakfast tomorrow morning?"

"I'd be delighted, my good man. And if anybody is hanging around nearby, I'd be delighted if you'd give me a long, lingering goodnight kiss."

They stand and she slips her arm around his elbow. "Was a cigar all you asked for?"

"Yeah."

"That doesn't seem much for an assassination," Serena remarks.

"I never intended to carry out any assassinations. I was going to take the opportunity to skip with a backpack full of supplies, but then he went back to his stack of photos and pulled out one of John's wife. He said Frank had treated her very shamefully after getting her pregnant, and I wanted to come check it out and see how Stephanie was. She looked near death in the photo."

"And you found out that it was Mr. Barton who beat Stephanie, well … not actually Mr. Barton, but he ordered Cisco to do it and then killed Mike Clark for taking her to the clinic and Frank had nothing to do with it."

"Yeah. I may be opposed to murder, but I'm glad Frank did Mr. Barton in. The commander really should have been the one to do it, but I'm afraid that man is in the dark most of the time."

SIXTEEN

Max sets his bottle of cola on the coffee table in the doctor's lounge. "I have something to ask you."

Lily looks over at him. She has been dropping by at least once a week for the last six weeks, ever since his request near the end of May. She varies the day, depending upon her busy schedule. Other meetings have brought her into town this Tuesday. She always schedules Max first just in case he is busy, so she will have a second or third chance to catch him at a good time.

An expression of disgust flits across his face. He pulls out his phone. "Rose coded." He dashes from the room.

She finishes her cola and puts both bottles in the cardboard box beside the small refrigerator. She will come back later—at least she plans to come back later. She never knows what the day holds in store for her.

Lily steps from the ladder onto the roof. "Whose house is this?"

Monkey looks up. "Linda and Curtis. They noticed a leak when it rained."

She sits near him and wraps her arms around her knees. "Why'd you want to see me?"

He ceases his work on the newlyweds' home. "The engineers are getting new carpet in their houses, and of course, everyone else wants new carpet too."

"Is tile and wood flooring available?"

"I don't know."

"If it is, why don't you give everyone their choice?"

With arched eyebrows, Monkey rhetorically asks, "So that's a yes?"

"I suppose," Lily replies. "Our surplus continues to grow, so we might as well use it. It's impossible to use it on redemptions fast enough even though I'm now averaging thirty-five a week instead of twelve."

"You don't think we need to run it by the council?"

"Even though this is expensive, it's within my purview as financial officer to make the decision. I think we should merely report it especially since everyone, absolutely everyone, has been absolutely delighted with our other extravagant purchases lately. It's nice to be ahead of the game instead of scrimping on everything."

"Yeah, we really like coffee and beef and—"

"The beef's no longer expensive."

Surprised, he blurts, "Mr. Patterson lowered his price?"

"No. The Seals found an abandoned cattle ranch. We moved workers and guards over there. For now, we're just slaughtering for ourselves but once they've assessed the situation and settled people on the ranch, we may be able to sell beef. It's not set up as a dairy farm, but they're also working on that so we can have cows' milk instead of goats' milk."

Monkey returns to his unfinished sentence. "The other thing I was going to mention was the fish. Now that Mr. Patterson has a truck to transport frozen food, he's bringing it in from the gulf. I know some people don't like fish, but I think it's great even though it's rather expensive because of the truck. He says the truck was very expensive to purchase and also expensive to run and he wants to get a second one, so I guess the price is going to stay high for quite a while."

She turns the conversation back to their original topic. "My only concern about the new carpet is that you'll be bombarded with requests so keep required maintenance as a priority."

"The carpets in these abandoned houses are in real bad shape. They've all been broken into and seen lots of traffic in the last three years along with getting soaked with rain because the doors and windows were open or broken."

"That settles it," Lily declares, "new flooring is required maintenance. Do you have enough help?"

"A lot of the men have been transferred to Ralph for security around here, but if we're not in a hurry, then I guess I do. It's taken a while for the carpet for the engineers to come in. In fact, it's not all here yet. We aren't even to the halfway point, so I expect we'll have to wait on everything we order."

Lily instructs, "Safety is important so only pull some away from guard duty if you have to. It takes a lot more guards in town than out at the compound, but Ralph is very pleased that there've only been minor incidents."

"We are too. All the women have been commenting on how safe they feel. I hope that continues."

Lily adds, "I think the new ID cards and surveillance cameras are helping. Brad and Todd have reported that the officers have picked up a large number of curfew violators and it's cutting down on people wondering around without authorization."

"So they're cutting them off at the pass?"

"It appears that way," she says.

"I got picked up today."

Her eyebrows arch with concern. "Really?"

"Yeah. I left my card in my pocket last night and tossed it in the laundry basket. Just after lunch, I ran down to Jupiter's to pick up an order of nails. Fortunately, it was Lieutenant Jones who picked me up and the roofing nails were for his house, so he just drove me back and gave me a warning. Tell me, how'd he know I didn't have it? I don't think he overheard me making arrangements with Jupiter to come back and pay later."

"Shh."

He whispers, "There's something special about the cards, isn't there?"

"Don't tell anyone that there're GPS chips in them. Let's just let everyone think the officers are doing a great job."

"I bet this is cutting down on crime, isn't it?"

"It's helping catch the criminals, usually after the fact, but it's a deterrent for them to be collecting charges on their rap sheet. Anyone with a long rap sheet is watched closely, so maybe we'll see a drop in the crime rate soon."

"Do I have a rap sheet now?"

"I don't know. They might not be putting down mere warnings although I hear they're giving lots of warnings since the system is new."

He lowers his voice to a mere whisper, "Especially when it's Lieutenant Jones catching one of us."

She laughs. "It's amazing how you refer to him as Lieutenant Jones in his official capacity and Curtis when you're talking about him and Linda."

"You know, I can't ever get used to hearing you called Jackie."

"That started when I got my first supervisory position. People didn't pay attention to a boss named Lily. It sounds way too dainty. I started using Jackie, but it didn't go over very well; they knew me as Lily. When I got a new job, I just started as Jackie."

"They listened to you then?" he guesses.

"It went much better. I'd better get back to the clinic. Do you have anything else."

"Nah. With most things the phone is sufficient, but I wanted to talk to you face to face about something so expensive. I wanted to watch your expression."

"Just consider that we've redefined extravagant and spend whatever is necessary on housing for everyone. Well … the engineers should set their own budget, not me."

He smiles and grabs another roofing nail.

Lily unlocks the back door to the clinic and steps into the break room. Ralph looks at her with surprise. She keeps her grin of mischief suppressed. She knows that later, in private, he will get onto her for going outside without him, but she was within the fenced perimeter of their residential area except when she crossed the alley.

She locks the door. "Josie, are you all finished?"

"No, they haven't called me in yet. They have some kind of emergency over in the hospital."

Lily replies, "Someone coded. I think that's something pretty serious since Max flew out the door. I'm going to visit with Buster for a little while."

"Have you called Lieutenant Williams?"

"I'll call him after your test, so he doesn't have to wait. We don't want to pull him away from his official duties or tie up his off time," Lily replies.

"Thanks for arranging for me to see him. I know you don't think I should, but I really want to see him."

Buster is leaning forward in his chair in the hospital corridor. He has his elbows on his knees and his chin cupped in his hands. Lieutenant Williams sits beside him with his elbows on his knees and his hands clasped. A look of concern is on his face as he stares at Buster. Lily pulls a chair over.

Lieutenant Williams looks at her and softly whispers, "She died."

"Sorry, Buster," Lily consoles.

Buster looks at her. "I guess we won't be going out to your place." Sorrow is evident in his raspy voice and his eyes glisten with tears.

"You can still come. Is there somewhere special that Rose would like to be buried?"

He shakes his head.

"We can bury her out there, if you like."

"Is your cemetery smaller that all of those in town?"

"Yes, and we can give you the cottage closest to the graveyard and bury her in the plot closest to the cottage. You'll be able to walk over and see her anytime," Lily promises.

He wipes his tears and sighs. "Bruce was encouraging me to stay with you, but I didn't know if the offer was still on without Rose."

"Of course it's still on; anything for the man who helped us so much."

"Buster." He turns toward the lieutenant. "I'll help you pack up and take you out there. I have three boxes of things that I packed up at your place. I'll stop by the officers' quarters and pick them up on my way out."

"What about Rose?"

Knowing that Buster doesn't want to leave his beloved wife of sixty-five years, Lily says, "I'll call Ralph to help. We're in the tank, and we can take both of you out there. I only have one more, no, two more things to do in town and we can be on our way."

She looks up at Lieutenant Williams. "When you get them into the SUV, let Ralph stay with Buster and come into the clinic break room. Josie wants to see you."

He soberly nods. With the precarious situation he plunged into because of her beauty, he sincerely hopes the young girl, who is barely of age, does not want to pursue a relationship with him.

Lieutenant Williams and Lily are sitting at the table in the break room, waiting on Josie. She apologizes, "Sorry about the wait, Bruce."

"That's all right. I'm more concerned about Buster. He's been rambling ever since Rose got sick. I'm afraid he's getting senile."

She assures him, "I'm sure he's all right with Ralph, and he's with his beloved Rose."

"That's a nice casket that Ralph picked up."

"He called and asked if I wanted the expensive one with carved roses. I thought it'd delight Buster, but he didn't seem to notice."

Lieutenant Williams says, "All he has on his mind right now is Rose. I'm sure he'll eventually notice and be delighted. I'll give you my thanks for being so considerate."

She nods.

He asks, "Are you sure you're not leaving someplace unguarded by pulling so many guards over to keep watch on them?"

"Ralph wouldn't allow that. He always includes a bit of redundancy in his staffing. We're never sure what's going to happen. That raid two months ago was a wake-up call. We'd gotten lax. He's kicking himself for not having more guards with us in the market."

"I'm afraid they'd have just been more unarmed targets for those guys," the lieutenant mutters.

"While we wait, tell me a little about yourself."

Ill at ease, he laughs. "What do you want to know?"

"I'd like to know why you take care of Buster."

"And why do you take care of him?"

"Because he was so good to us," Lily replies.

He remains silent.

"Do you know his name?"

"Jeremiah Williams."

"Williams, huh. I know he's not your father or grandfather."

The lieutenant replies, "He's my uncle ... ah ... my great-uncle."

"I guess you're one of the nephews he hasn't lost contact with."

"Yeah; the other was my brother, Jeremy. I haven't told Buster that he died."

"Don't you think you ought to?"

He shakes his head. "It'd tear him up too much. They were namesakes and really close."

"How'd he die?"

"In one of those riots, three years ago."

Lily asks, "I don't suppose he was one of the rioters, was he?"

"Of course not."

"Was he just in the wrong place at the wrong time?" she guesses.

"He was in law enforcement and trying to quell the violence."

"Were you in law enforcement too?"

Eva opens the door. Josie and her mother walk in. Lieutenant Williams looks up at the stunningly beautiful teenager, a young copy of her still youthful mother. When she smiles, a huge smile overtakes his face. "Sorry I didn't bring you an iced cola, but I've been at the hospital all day."

She walks over and sits beside him. "Don't take my smile wrong."

"Okay." A tentative resonance makes his voice sound hollow.

"Your mom and I will leave," Lily politely offers.

"No need." Josie sighs. "This isn't going to be personal."

Lieutenant Williams is relieved that he has been extracted from a sticky situation, but his face clearly displays his disappointment.

Josie grimaces. "Sorry."

"That's all right. I guess I shouldn't have gotten my hopes up that I could snag such a pretty young lady." He rues the bungled apology which tumbled out of his mouth. He did not intend for it to sound lustful and hopes she takes it as a compliment.

"I have a favor to ask, if that's all right?"

"Anything," he offers. He is hoping for redemption.

She bows her head and looks up at him with raised eyebrows. "I'm not going to have to do anything in return?"

"Of course not; this is just like the cola. I'll do anything I can for you and your mother, just out of kindness. You deserve some kindness after what you've been through. If I can't honor your request, I'll be politely frank and say so." He is hoping to salvage some dignity.

"All right. Well ... I'm asking this because you're the only man in the last three years who's been nice to me. Well, that is until I went to Mrs. Schwartz's place. Everybody is nice out there. So I guess I'll always look on you as special because you were the first to be nice to me."

"I'm glad I made a good impression. I was afraid, I didn't." His smile of relief is genuine.

She takes a deep breath and lowers her eyes. "Well, here goes. My high school boyfriend is here. He wanted to be a doctor, but of course, he didn't get to finish high school. Now he has his high school work all done, and he's going to be in the first class at the nursing school here. He's hoping they'll continue to train him and he can at least be a physician's assistant and—"

"And you're telling me all this to say that you two have reconnected?"

"Yeah, we've reconnected." She looks up at his face. He doesn't seem angry. She heaves a sigh of relief.

"Thanks for telling me."

"Well, I haven't gotten to the favor yet."

"Okay," the lieutenant replies.

"We're going to get married, maybe next month, in August. We might wait until September or maybe even October. Now, Miss Lily's looking for my dad—"

"Who's Miss Lily?"

"Oops." She clasps her hand over her mouth. "I wasn't supposed to say that. I mean Mrs. Schwartz is looking for my dad."

"Oh?"

"Yeah, and if she doesn't find him … then … ah … I … ah …."

He smiles. "Just say it. You're not going to make me mad. You can't make me mad." She cannot make him mad because the big blunder at the prison was too much his fault and he has made multiple blunders since then. He realizes that he has been conflicted about her from the beginning. He was drawn to her from the moment he saw her step off the prison transport bus, but he knew all along that he must do the right thing and avoid any entanglements with the stunning beauty.

She takes a deep breath. "Would you be willing to give the bride away? I know you're not old enough to be my dad but—"

"I'm probably closer than you think."

"Okay." She heaves a sigh. "If my dad doesn't show up, I'd like you to give me away."

"I'd be delighted to have the honor, and I wish you a long and happy marriage."

"I'm sure glad there're no hard feelings."

"Of course there're no hard feelings. I wish you the best. I'll just consider you my niece, if you don't mind."

"Thank you, Lieutenant Williams."

"Uncle Bruce."

She smiles. "Okay, Uncle Bruce."

"I have the prettiest niece in the world and if you or your mom needs anything, just call." He pulls out a note pad and scribbles. He tears out the page. "Here's my number. Don't hesitate to call."

She takes the note. "Thanks."

"And one other thing," he says. Surprise flashes on her face. "If your dad shows up, it won't insult me if he gives you away. Just be sure to invite me to the wedding."

Her face relaxes into a broad smile. "Okay, Uncle Bruce."

"Now, let me introduce you to Uncle Buster."

"Who's Uncle Buster?"

He stands up and takes her hand. "He's my uncle, and he's moving out to Mrs. Schwartz's compound today. Auntie Rose died, so I guess I have a favor to ask of you. Please go to her funeral. They're planning it for tomorrow."

She smiles as she rises from her chair and slides her hand around his elbow. "Okay, Uncle Bruce."

"If it's okay with Uncle Buster and the others, maybe we can stop and get that iced cola on the way." Lieutenant Williams chides himself. What is he doing? He should not be establishing a close relationship. He is delighted that the young girl has a beau and views him as more of a paternal figure. It has resolved his conflicting emotions, but his role as 'uncle' should be limited. He is certain that a close relationship will not end well. He needs a graceful, face-saving exit strategy, but for some reason, he keeps getting himself in deeper and deeper.

Josie's mother Josephine Vaughn and Lily stand up and follow them outside. Lily sighs as she remembers Max. She did not get back to see what he wanted. Since emergencies always put all the medical staff behind, she will come back some other day and see what he wants that cannot be discussed over the phone.

SEVENTEEN

John follows Lily into her office.

"Well, what're you all fired up about?" Lily plants her fists on her hips and glances around at the grins of delight on the faces of the men in her office. "Yep, fired up is a good description of you guys, all right."

John takes her by the elbow and escorts her to the desk. "Our chief analyst here," he nods to indicate Wayne Brashear, "has taken all the information we've amassed and determined the identity of—"

"Most likely suspect," Wayne interrupts with unbridled excitement. "Step right over here and let me run through this chart with you."

She looks at the intricate diagram on the large sheet of butcher paper spread over her desk.

Wayne continues, "They assigned that new guy Al to help me. He pulled the names of all the local barons from the computer system, and we've charted them. There are a few whom we can eliminate as the baron who murdered Officer Hayes. Let us start with Jackie Schwartz." He uncaps a black marker and marks over the penciled X on her name.

"We can also eliminate the estate of Mr. Barton." He hands the marker to John who obediently marks out the estate.

"We can also eliminate Mr. O'Neil, obviously, along with Mr. Kasper and Mr. Patterson."

"But not Reginald Patterson," Lily interjects.

"Huh?" Wayne looks at her in surprise.

"Mr. Patterson's son hides things from his dad."

"He works with his dad, I assume?"

She nods.

"Pencil him in and we will eliminate him with the next group." He waits while John adds a box for Reggie beside his dad.

"The next group that we will eliminate is all of the regional traders."

Lily asks, "What's the reasoning here?"

"Competition; no one with so much competition could have this much power over the commander. Then we will eliminate all the vendors in the market and the small business owners like Mr. Guzman, Mr. Hobbs, and Mr. Cuevas. None of the petite bourgeoisie could strike fear in anybody. He would just get squashed like a bug, if he tried."

"I see that doesn't leave very many possibilities," Lily observes.

"That is correct. Now, we look at what each one controls. Take the city sewer system for instance. What would he be capable of—other than murdering officers—that would strike so much fear into the commander? Let the sewer back up? That could cause some problems but not enough to panic anyone. He and his assassin could easily be taken out by snipers and that would be the end of that."

Lily prompts, "Who is our most likely suspect?"

"Let me give you a clue." Wayne reaches over, grabs a water bottle, and sets it in the center of the diagram.

Puzzled, she merely looks at it. Wayne looks at her. She furrows her brow.

"I see you're puzzled. Where do we get the water?"

"From the river," she replies. "We purify it then it's piped in, and we fill the bottles from the faucet."

"I did not realize that. I guess I made an incorrect assumption that made my demonstration worthless. Tell me this: where did you get the bottles?"

"We scavenged them in the early days. Oh? I see," Lily says. "One of the barons began selling bottled water. We do buy some bottled water."

"Yes, the one who runs the water utility in town is very powerful. He could do any number of things with disastrous results. He could easily hide the act, and it would be impossible for your hospital to check for all possible contaminants."

"That's true, but it would also be nearly impossible for him to target specific people and totally unreasonable to eliminate large numbers of his customers. He's a pretty unreasonable man but seems to have good business sense," Lily contends.

"But he could target specific small groups by adding the contaminant just past their junction on the water main and it would not have to kill anyone, just making them sick would cause great panic."

"We need to see if we can track his workers," Lily states.

"Already done."

She looks at Wayne in surprise.

He explains, "Al tapped into the satellites to track the GPS signals of all his employees. He's basically set up a second command center out here. There has been no suspicious activity so far."

"That's a start. Does the commander know about this?"

"Not yet. We assumed you should be the one to confront him. We do not want to waste time with a red herring. This is just a deduction, and I could be wrong about this baron. No telling what is going on behind the scenes that we have no way of knowing. If you will find out from the commander whether this is the guy who is making him act like a spineless coward that will guide our next step."

Lily inquires, "Are there any other likely suspects?"

"Not really. Not that we know, anyway. The baron, who runs the cannery—"

"What cannery?" she interrupts.

"It is pretty far out of town but we are the closest town so he is considered as residing in Somertonville. He is pretty powerful, but he could not target specific groups with tainted products since it all goes through traders before reaching individual barons; same for a few others."

She states, "We'll focus on Mr. Finke as the most likely suspect, but we'll need to take some precautions in the meantime. We can take drinking water to our compound in town without raising suspicions. We can hide it among the other food supplies we take to them. I'm sure it'll require quite a bit of effort to bottle purified water in sterilized bottles out here, but nobody will see that."

"How soon can you get the commander out here?"

She whips out her phone.

Lily strides across the main room to greet the commander at the door. "Good afternoon, Robert. Thank you for coming immediately."

"Good afternoon, Jackie. What's so important?" Commander Somerton asks.

"Let's wait until we're in my office." They walk in silence across the main room and into her office. She shuts the door and walks to her desk.

As he sits down, he eyes the two water bottles on her desk. Anxiety is suddenly evident in his facial expression. His breathing becomes slightly erratic.

She sits down and smiles. "Would you like some water?" She holds a bottle toward him.

His face falls; his eyelids droop, hooding his downcast eyes. He shakes his head.

She swings the water bottle like a pendulum. "Mr. Finke murdered Officer Hayes, didn't he?"

His eyes widen, showing bloodshot whites around each iris. "How do you know that?"

She sets the bottle aside and folds her hands. "Our bull in a china shop makes a very good analyst. Couple that with your reaction to being offered bottled water and I'm right, aren't I?"

He nods.

He remains morosely silent, so she inquires, "Any ideas?"

"I have my clerk tracking him and his assassin. Could your Seals take them out? They'd be easy to find and Jack took out Mr. O'Neil's assassin with one shot, from quite a distance I might add."

Lily counters, "That could spook all the other barons in town. We'll need to consider the political ramifications of using a sniper. My men have suggested staging an accidental death, but my question is whether he might have left instructions for his men to extract revenge on the entire population if something happened to him."

"That's possible. I have my wife boiling all our drinking water."

"That won't help. There are many ways to contaminate the water other than bacteria. In fact, he'd be more likely to use a poison."

"Oh?" He rubs his hands over his face. "What do you suggest?"

"The best solution my men have come up with is to get some proof of his threat. I don't suppose you have any proof that he murdered Officer Hayes?"

The commander shakes his head. "It'd be my word against his."

"I've been meeting with the other barons one by one. I suggest that I continue to do that and eventually get to Mr. Finke. That way he won't be suspicious that we're on to him."

"What're you going to do? Wear a wire?"

She nods.

A loud knock startles them. Marie Gonzales opens the door. Excitement shows in her eyes. "Lily, turn on the radio. The first news broadcast is about to start."

She turns to the radio on the credenza behind her desk. Music fills the room. She turns back, leans toward Commander Somerton, and whispers, "They've been using recordings of Mr. O'Neil to allay the suspicions of people who haven't seen him around lately, so he's going to introduce the broadcast."

Several people walk in, carrying chairs. Soon the room is full. They can hear a radio playing in the dining hall. The music stops.

> *Good afternoon, everyone. This is Gordon O'Neil. I have a new feature and a new DJ to introduce today. This is—*

Mr. O'Neil voice is replaced by a group: *Ted Winslow.*

A pleasant baritone emanates from the radio:

> *Good afternoon, everyone. Before I begin our long-awaited news broadcast, I'd like to explain our method of compiling news reports. There is no way to confirm or deny any of the information we come across, especially on the internet. To make sure we aren't passing along rumors, we will not report on a story until we have six independent reports on the event, at least some of which must be eyewitness reports.*
>
> *We'll begin our broadcast with a weather report for our area. This is a rather rudimentary report. We hope to build a more extensive weather reporting network. The skies are clear and the weather is very warm. The temperature is ninety-five degrees in Somertonville, ninety-four in Perkins and ninety-one in Crutchfield. For those of you unfamiliar with the surrounding towns, Perkins is about forty miles to the north of Somertonville and Crutchfield is about fifty miles south. We hope to add reports from more of the neighboring towns as we make contact with residents with working thermometers. The forecast is continuing clear skies, cooling to about seventy to seventy-five degrees tonight. No rain is in the forecast, merely because there are no clouds in the sky.*

National news, if you consider that we still have a nation here in North America, is limited to three brief stories. A severe earthquake struck Southern California two days ago. Damage is extensive and casualties are numerous. If you have access to a computer, there are photos on the internet. One site which appears reliable is www.capostings.net.

Our second report concerns the former breadbasket of America. Due to our former reliance on hybrid crops, a famine started one year after the terrorists' attacks when the lack of viable seeds caused a food shortage. Costal areas have been able to rely on imports, but without reliable transportation, the interior suffered. Imported food is now able to reach further into the affected area, confining the famine to only the most isolated areas.

I'd like to begin the third story with a disclaimer. Absolutely no reports have been received of a mushroom cloud anywhere. I repeat: there are no reports of atomic blasts anywhere. There are multiple reports of an illness sweeping a large area of the northeast. We consulted with our local experts and the symptoms of the illness are consistent with radiation poisoning; however there could be another explanation. Best guess is an accidental release of radiation at a nuclear power plant, perhaps at an abandoned one. But I repeat: this is a guess.

On the international scene: in Africa, leaders of the Yoruba nation-state and Hausa nation-state are meeting today for a conference on peace negotiations. Other than tribal warfare, their main topic is the epidemics, which have taken more lives than the tribal clashes. Without western medicines and aid, they have seen a resurgence of many diseases including AIDS, Ebola, malaria, cholera, tuberculosis, and polio. They ask that the surrounding nation-states join forces with them to bring peace and stability to the area. A second conference, which will include leaders from any African nation-state or tribe willing to join in the effort, will be held as soon as feasible to discuss solutions to these pressing problems. Tentative date of the conference is August fifteenth.

Our correspondents have made contact with Australia. Their isolation appears to have protected them from the worst of the terrorists' attacks, although they did sustain extensive damage in the larger cities at the beginning of the crisis. As with Africa, the interrupted international trade caused them severe problems the first year, but the resilient Aussies met the crisis head on and have become self-sufficient. They've become proficient in harnessing wind power and solar power.

This is our brief report. We haven't been able to make sufficient contacts in other areas, such as Europe, to develop a story. We'll repeat our broadcast at five o'clock and ten o'clock tonight. We are working on several other stories for tomorrow. Thank you. This is Ted Winslow signing off.

Music begins to play. Lily turns off the radio and watches the crowd leave the room. She is content with the progress they have made and confident that they will eventually succeed in their quest for a civilized society. She sorrowfully counts the cost in lives and hopes more will not be lost.

Samuel Acquah walks over with a small book in his hand and a big grin on his face. The short, stocky African's graduate studies were interrupted by the terrorists' attacks and ensuing chaos, leaving him isolated in the U.S. "Lily, I found this on the shelf back there."

"Do you know what it is?"

"It is a hymn book," Sammy replies.

"In your native tongue?"

"Yes. Where did you get it?"

She replies, "A vendor in the market gave it to me."

"May I have it?"

"Of course."

"Thank you very much. Let me ask a question."

She nods.

"I heard the reports from Africa. Is there a way to find out if my family is alive?"

With sorrow, she shakes her head. "The reports from Africa are gleaned from the internet and reports of hearing radio broadcasts from Africa. They have not found any ham radio operators in Africa and phone service between the continents has not been reestablished, so there is no personal contact."

"What is a ham radio operator?"

"It is someone with a different kind of radio who uses a code to talk to other ham radio operators. They have talked to several in Australia, a few in Europe and some in various parts of North America."

"But communication is getting better, so maybe someday we will get word of my family and I can tell them I am all right."

"I hope so."

"Thank you for the hymn book." Sammy looks at the group of men who have not left the room. "I will go."

She watches him walk out. Ralph closes the door. Todd, Wayne, and ten former Seals gather around her desk.

"Before we start, let me ask a question," Wayne requests. "Do we have any reports of terrorists invading and taking over after their massive attacks?"

Lily shakes her head.

Wayne is relieved. Despite the world-wide terrorists' attacks, there were apparently no invading armies conquering vast tracts of land. Militarily, he would consider that a total failure. It elates him that the enemies of America were so incompetent. *We will rise again,* he thinks then turns his thoughts back to the task at hand.

Wayne tilts his head toward Commander Somerton.

Lily nods to indicate that Commander Somerton confirmed their suspicion that Mr. Finke murdered Officer Hayes, exerting great pressure on the commander.

"Okay, what is the plan?" Wayne asks.

Lily picks up a pen and twirls it in her fingers. "We didn't have time to reach an agreement."

Commander Somerton inquires, "After you gather proof, what do you suggest?"

She stops twirling the pen. "Imprison him and provide the other barons with proof of his ruthlessness. We could take over his enterprise as a public utility and run it like the electric co-op. Perhaps the other barons will relent since water is such an important necessity."

With anxiety, Commander Somerton inquires, "You won't just let the Seals take them out?"

She shakes her head. "Not if we don't have to ... and ... we are assuming that most of the barons will be relieved instead of objecting to our audacity at dislodging a baron willing to kill indiscriminately."

"What about his slaves?"

Lily replies, "They'll have to be vetted before they can return to work. I have sufficient engineers to take over the water facility, and we'll stockpile the required chemicals instead of using anything already on their premises."

"Sounds like you've thought this out thoroughly."

She tries to keep smugness out of her smile. "That's the beauty of a team effort. It might not be the best plan, but we've voted it most likely to produce the desired result."

"I'd like to deputize your team and let you run with this. Who's your head guy?" the commander asks.

Several of the men look at Wayne Brashear. Commander Somerton's face falls as he realizes his blunder.

Lily quickly states, "Mr. Brashear is our chief analyst, and we'd like to keep him in that important position. We need someone of his stature and experience in that position. Our two senior field agents are Todd and Brad. Step forward guys."

Commander Somerton stands. "Ralph, I want you over here too. Jackie, come stand beside them. I'm making you four lieutenants in this branch of local authorities and—"

Muted, but derisive, hoots and catcalls emanate from a couple of the younger men.

Mr. Brashear stands and issues an ear-splitting order, "Silence!" He looks around the room. The chastised reprobates sober.

Mr. Brashear turns to the local official. "Commander, despite their impertinence, I agree with the young soldie … men. It has been a long time since these men have been mere lieutenants."

"Mr. Brashear!" Lily sternly yells as she glares at him with unhidden disapproval. She softens her voice and facial expression. "We have to consider the political ramifications. Our local authorities have only three ranks. It is not wise, politically, for any of us to have the same rank as the commander or outrank him. Neither is it wise for us to outrank his lieutenants. The only other designation is officer. For this temporary assignment, we will accept the rank of lieutenant for the four chosen by Commander Somerton and all other deputized men will be referred to as officers."

She looks at the young reprobates. "This is serious. No joking allowed."

EIGHTEEN

Lily stands at the open front door of the main building and watches Commander Somerton get into his car. Brad looks at Stephanie Thorne who is accompanied by three children and motions for them to wait. She ushers the children to a nearby table.

For confidentially, Brad leans toward petite Lily and speaks softly. "Didn't I tell you Wayne was brilliant?"

"Yes, Mr. Brashear's brilliant but he'll take over if we allow him to and he won't abide by the decisions of the council."

"I know. That was a good save you made to keep him from being deputized," Brad compliments.

"Thanks. You didn't get any indication that he was insulted, did you?"

"No, he's proud of his job as chief analyst."

"For good reason." With her eyes open wide, she looks up at the tall man. "He's saved us months of pussyfooting around trying to pry the information out of Commander Somerton. We'll now call him Mr. Brashear as a sign of respect for him and his position as chief analyst."

"Good idea. I'll quietly let everyone know. Do you think the commander feels insulted by what we've done?"

"No, his feelings seem to be more along the line of relief. He's been discouraged for quite some time, but I think we've given him hope that there's actually a viable solution."

Brad inquires, "How'd such a weak man get to be commander?"

"He partnered with a ruthless officer to topple our brutal commander. They became co-commanders. Later, when we had evidence of his co-commander's crimes, we helped him dislodge Commander Blakely and his loyal officers. They're now being held in the prison."

"Is that the prisoners I've seen working on the demolition of that old hotel?"

"Yes. I think Commander Somerton would be a good leader during peaceful times, but things seem to be deteriorating with him as the sole commander. This is the second time a baron has threatened him by killing officers."

"I've heard that. When do you plan to tape Mr. Finke?"

"I'm not sure. I don't want to appear anxious to talk to him. I must treat him like all of the others and come to him in turn. It's also quite possible that he won't ever agree to talk to me, and we'll have to come up with Plan B. I've known him for over two years, and I don't recall ever talking to him. On rare occasions, I got a terse, grudging greeting from him."

He nods, knowingly. "We're increasing guards at the hospital compound."

"Not obviously, I hope?"

"Nah, our guys will keep in the shadows and quietly subdue any intruders. It might even look like we're being lax."

A pleased smile takes over her face. "That's great."

"Ralph said he'd take care of talking to Marie and the nurses about supplying those in town with water."

"I hope this gets resolved pretty quick. It could get burdensome to bottle water since we don't have any automated equipment for that."

He chuckles.

"What's so funny?"

"I was thinking about you calling us senior field agents."

She grins. "I was kind of working on the fly there. Somehow I had to differentiate between Mr. Brashear and the rest of you guys. That just popped out."

"I'll see you later."

"One more thing before you leave," Lily quickly states, "it was a great idea to put a man whose weak point is acting without sufficient data in charge of collecting sufficient data."

He grins. "That was Todd's brilliant idea. He said Way ... ah ... Mr. Brashear's strong point is interpreting the data and this way it's his responsibility to see that it's collected. You know ... I just got used to calling him Wayne. It was just about to start rolling off my tongue and now here you go and change things. But don't take it wrong. It's a good idea, and I'll be sure everybody knows."

He turns away then stops and leans toward her. "John's wife wants to talk to you."

She turns. "Sorry. I didn't know you were waiting."

"That's all right," Stephanie Thorne says as she leads the three children over. She looks down at her oldest son, nine-year-old Johnny.

He steps forward. The two girls step up on either side of him. He clears his throat. "We have been elected to bring you a message from all the children. Brianna, Kiowa, and I will take turns."

He again clears his throat. "Thank you for the news on the radio."

Brianna Pruett holds her head high. "It is good to hear what is happening in other places."

Kiowa Steele grins, happy that she was chosen for the coveted assignment. "We are sorry there is sickness and famine and earthquakes."

Lily looks from child to child as they speak. "In our science class, we will be helping with the weather report." "In our geography class, we will learn about the places on the news." "In our history class, we will learn about ... about ... ah ... we will learn about their ... history." "Thank you, Miss Lily."

"I'm very proud of you children. You're doing a very good job in school."

"Miss Lily!" Kiowa grins and swishes from side to side. "Do I still think like you?"

"You most certainly do."

"Will I grow up to be a leader like you?"

Lily laughs and puts her hands on her hips. "I hope you don't have to encounter all the troubles I have. I hope we'll have peace pretty soon."

"Do you think my name means strong or is it more like taking stuff?"

"Steele means strong like metal. Stealing, like taking stuff, has an 'a' in it and no 'e' on the end," Lily explains.

"Good. I'll tell the ones teasing me that they don't know how to spell."

"Come along children." Stephanie lightly touches each child on the shoulder. "I'm sure Miss Lily has many things she needs to be doing."

"Bye, Miss Lily," all three children chime in unison.

"Bye."

Johnny turns back. "Miss Lily, I never did thank you for bringing Lucas back."

"Johnny, I'm afraid I don't get to take credit for that."

"Who brought him back?"

"Frank did."

"I'd like to thank him. Is he out at the water tank?"

"No, he's gone."

"Gone? Why'd you let him leave?"

"Johnny, that's what freedom means. It means you can leave anytime you want," Lily explains.

With wide eyes, he rhetorically asks, "So if we're free, we can leave anytime we want?"

Lily nervously laughs, realizing that she has unintentionally opened a can of worms. "Well," she intones, drawing out the *ell* sound to give herself time to think. "Johnny, we try to convince everyone that it's not a good idea but sometimes they leave anyway and we have to let them go. Now, you realize we are talking about adults here? Children need to stay with their parents, so they'll be safe. They can't run off by themselves."

"We weren't safe," Brianna exclaims with a scowl on her young face. "We were at Mr. Barton's without our parents!"

"That's right, but you're here now and you've been assigned foster parents to keep you safe. George and Regina take good care of you, don't they?"

Brianna grins broadly and nods.

With her hands on her hips, Kiowa declares, "That's just like having real parents."

"Children, we need to go back to school," Stephanie states.

"Hey, Miss Lily."

"Yes, Johnny."

"I'm going to have a new brother or sister."

"Congratulations."

"Okay, children. Let's go," Stephanie urges.

L ily walks into one of the three interconnected computer rooms in the east wing, places her hands on the back of Al's chair, leans over, and studies the display on his monitor.

He looks up. "Hi, Lily."

"Hi, Al. It's great to have a NASA engineer here who can access the satellites."

"They'd already tapped into several. I just added the nonpublic ones. There are still several that are top secret that I can't get into, but I can see that they're still orbiting. You know, I'm really surprised that so many are still on line."

"NASA had strong security, didn't it?" she guesses.

"Yeah."

"Maybe they're still operating."

"Could be. Would you like me to try to contact them? They might know a lot about what happened after communications went down. We could report it in our newscasts."

"Just don't open us up to getting attacked."

He laughs. "Lawrence can take care of that. I'm sure he can figure out something like putting it on a public website then we'd have our cover for the source of our news. He's got those GPS signals on the ID cards so encrypted that it'd take months for anyone to figure out we're in Nebraska."

"We're in Nebraska?" she rhetorically asks, her eyes wide in surprise. "I thought I migrated south; surely I wasn't that turned around. I know I was really stressed at that time, but not that much. Aren't we near the gulf? Mr. Patterson said we were. This doesn't look like the plains."

He tilts his head back and looks up at her with amusement. "That's what he wants them to think."

"Oh, I see." She heaves a sigh of relief. "You had me going for a minute there."

She asks, "Is there some way the satellites could help with the weather forecasting?"

"Already arranged."

"Good."

He again looks up at her. "Can we take a walk after supper?"

"Sure."

Lawrence walks in. "Lily, John Jenkins should be here in a few minutes."

"Okay, I'll be right there. I was just looking at Mr. Finke's workers. That's just normal activity, isn't it?"

"Yes," Al replies. "I have an alarm set to go off if any of them gets within a mile of the hospital, electrical stations, officers' quarters, or Armando's. It not only alerts us but sends a coded text message to the nearby Seals."

"You guys are great." She turns and walks into Lawrence's workroom.

He shuts the door. She looks at his face; his expression is unfathomable. It is a mixture of sorrow, concern, and unease. He obviously has more on his mind than their meeting with J.J.

"Lily, I need to talk to you a moment before he gets here."

She asks, "What's wrong?"

"We've found out who Thai is."

Since it appears to be a difficult topic for him, she patiently waits for him to continue. He takes his time.

After a moment, he clears his throat. "Serena managed to get her real name by explaining that we couldn't use nicknames on the ID cards and that we had to have her maiden name too. She was the very last one to come in for a card. She refused until Marie and Stephanie threatened her with loss of privileges and compromised and let her use Tyler for her last name."

"She was real reluctant, wasn't she? So what's she hiding?"

"I don't know why she was hiding her identity," Lawrence replies. "She didn't recognize me, so I have no clue what her motive was."

"You knew her?"

"Not really; she's my youngest sister."

Lily is flabbergasted. It clearly shows on her face. Speechlessness is unusual for the quick-thinking baroness.

He explains, "I didn't recognize her. She was about four when you caught me in your kitchen and I was so messed up that I hadn't been spending much time at home, much less paying any attention to another baby sister. And after I'd served my sentence, I spent as much time at your house as I could. I didn't want to end up in an adult prison. Juvenile hall was bad enough. I really didn't want to go home at all. I was afraid of what it'd do to me. It'd be sure to mess me up again just like it did before."

She closes her mouth then takes a deep breath. "What's her name?"

"Thelma Brighton."

"Does she know who you are?"

"I don't think so. I told Serena, Marie, and Stephanie not to tell her. I thought we should find out why she's so afraid first."

"She won't go see a counselor, so we may never find out."

He shrugs and blithely turns to another topic. "I have all your equipment ordered, so we should be set up in about two to three weeks for your confrontation with Mr. Finke."

198

"Good."

With a scowl, he states, "We still haven't been able to identify Rene's attacker."

"What's the latest tally?"

"She's eliminated every man who came from just before Mr. Patterson brought her to the clinic to the day she heard his voice in the hall."

"You're sure?"

"I'm sure of the list; it was complete. She marked off everyone she works with at the clinic and everyone else she's gotten to know. That left ninety-eight for her to listen to while Ralph talked to them."

Lily laments, "It's too bad that you couldn't narrow it down to those who came from Mr. Patterson."

"He doesn't sell anybody. Some of his have absconded while in other towns, so we had to look at everyone we redeemed during that time frame."

"That means something's wrong with our parameters," Lily suggests.

"We had her go over the list again. With a guard nearby she felt comfortable enough to wonder around the dining hall listening for his voice. She's double-checking the ones she marked off the list. Ralph was going to talk to you when she finished that, but I'm getting concerned."

"Ralph's been keeping the committee updated. I was wondering about the latest tally on the double checking?"

"About halfway," he answers. "She seems to be a pretty gregarious gal when she's not terrified of meeting up with her attacker."

Lily softly states, "That's what gets me about this: why didn't she meet up with him before a year had passed?"

"I supposed that he was recently redeemed. That's why we started with the newest and went backwards."

"My other question is: why hasn't she heard him again? It's been six weeks."

Lawrence shrugs. "That gets me too. That's why I brought it up. I think you're right about our parameters being wrong."

She raises her eyebrows. "Any suggestions?"

He shakes his head. "It's got me beat."

"Keep thinking about it and maybe something will spring to mind," Lily instructs.

John Jenkins, familiarly called J.J., opens the door and walks in preceded by the smell of sweat. "Am I interrupting?"

Lily sits down. "Nah, we were waiting on you. Pull up a chair."

He swings a folding chair around, sits backwards, and rests his forearms on the back. "Is there a problem?"

"We'd like to offer you a different job," she states.

J.J. grins. "I get to leave farming behind, huh?"

"Yes. We need to start an online bank because we're having a problem with the cards. As soon as I gave every adult a personal stipend, one person's balance completely disappeared courtesy of an unscrupulous vender."

"Did you confront him?" J.J. asks.

"Yes, but it's she said, he said. He says she bought more. I couldn't resolve it so told him that if we continue to get complaints, we'll put him on a no-trade list. Other than that, we need to have an account for everyone so they can only put on their card what they want to spend and their savings won't be available."

"How're they going to access their account?"

Lily replies, "We'll put in a couple of public-access computers in your office—"

"My office," he interrupts, with a wide grin.

She continues, "A few at the clinic, one at the ranch, and of course, the engineers already have plenty."

"That won't be enough anywhere except for the engineers."

"We'll continue to buy more until we have a sufficient number and if anyone wants to save up and buy their own, they can."

"That brings me to a question that I've had ever since you told us you were paying us," J.J. states. "How're those of us out here supposed to buy anything?"

"Lawrence is setting up a website with links to websites that we've determined to be legitimate."

"You're definitely going to need lots of computers."

Lily replies, "We know but we're too leery of the websites to place a large order, so we'll place another order as soon as each order comes in. It'll take a while to get this all set up so we have time especially since I think it'll take a while before people start spending their money. They don't have to buy necessities. We'll also set up sites for Jupiter and Mr. Patterson and maybe later for some of the other regional traders."

"That'll be a great convenience to buy from local vendors and cut down on the shipping problem. At least, I assume shipping is a problem; I've never seen evidence of mail service or shipping companies."

Lily informs him, "The regional traders have the only shipping capabilities."

"Will you eventually set up all the local vendors?"

"Jupiter's site will be for the entire market. They've always freely swapped merchandise there. It's almost as if the entire market is one store so no one's getting their feelings hurt over having just one website, especially since it saves everyone having to buy a computer. Jupiter is just the coordinator. Mr. Patterson will also have a site, but it will be mostly for food. Marie can then order online instead of over the telephone, and that'll decrease the errors inherent in verbal communications."

"How're you going to separate the personal stipend from the business allowance for people like Marie?" J.J. asks.

"She has two cards."

"What about children?"

"Their allowance is up to their parents."

Lawrence intones, "Oh."

Lily looks over at him.

"I think that might have been the straw that broke the camel's back with Thai. She said something about her allowance just as I walked out of the room."

J.J. asks, "Will the children need a bank account?"

Lily shrugs. "Let's leave that up to the parents. Maybe the older children will want to save, but I suspect the younger ones will want to spend theirs immediately."

"One last question: I'm a banker not a computer nerd. Do I have to learn how to set up the website?"

Lawrence answers, "We'll set up the basic site and let you tweak it and run the bank and be the human interface with everyone with an account."

"Okay, I accept the job," J.J. states as if there had been any doubt that he wanted to leave farming behind.

NINETEEN

Max leans back on the comfortable sofa and laments, "It's going to be hotter in August that it was in July."

Lily smiles as they sit side by side in the doctors' lounge, sipping colas. "Did the engineers get the ventilation fixed? It feels comfortable in here."

"They're still working on it. This floor is mostly done. It's the only one we're occupying right now, except for the minor emergency clinic in the former trauma center on the first floor. We can't open the nursing school until the classroom is ready, so we're hoping for the first week in September." He takes a gulp of cola.

She asks, "Is the helicopter flying yet?"

"They told me this morning that they only lack one part, something to do with stability, so it must be very important."

"They've started stockpiling fuel, so they must be confident they're going to find it," she states.

Lily takes a sip of cola. "What did you want to ask me? We keep getting interrupted before you get around to it."

He drains the last swallow, leans forward, and sets his empty bottle on the coffee table then rests his elbows on his knees and turns to look back at her. He smiles then his expression turns sober. "Well ... this is kind of hard to explain."

She swallows the last sip of her cola, leans forward, and sets her bottle on the table. With a smile, she turns her face toward his and props her elbows on her knees. "You can be blunt. It won't bother me."

"Okay. I'll be blunt." He grins with amusement then sobers. "It's been ten months since Paula died and you're a widow, so I was wondering if I could court you."

Her expression does not change as she stares into his eyes. Their faces are mere inches apart. He breaks their mutual stare and focuses on the floor. "Sorry. I didn't mean to insult you."

"I'm not the least bit insulted. I'm merely startled. This just takes me by complete surprise."

He looks up. "I've been trying to court you for a couple of months now, and it isn't working. I rarely see you, and we just talk about business."

"It probably isn't working because a romantic relationship with anyone has been the furthest thing from my mind for the last three years. Sorry I'm so dense," she apologizes.

He leans back, pulls his phone off his belt, glances at a text message, and looks up. "And we keep getting interrupted. I have to go, so think about it."

"Okay. I hope no one's dying, this time."

"I don't think so." He stands and walks out the door.

She answers her ringing phone.

Chivalrous Lieutenant Curtis Jones reaches up to help Lily down the ladder propped against the crumbling wall. The cavernous basement of the Grande Hotel is open to the elements and stripped of most partitioning walls and debris. A few officers dot the perimeter, keeping watch on the surrounding area. One glances down into the gaping pit as Lily steps onto the floor. With a bored expression, he turns back to his assignment as watchman.

As they walk across the floor, Lily whispers, "What's that smell?"

Lieutenant Jones leans toward her and whispers, "It was Ricky's job to haul the garbage to the dump outside of town, but apparently he found a shortcut. He boarded up an old laundry chute to make a ventilation shaft for the large room at the other end of the basement. It was—"

"Where was it vented?" Lily asks out of curiosity.

"Out of a third floor window; that room was also boarded to keep the smell out of the hotel. The room down here was stuffed full and the door boarded. He also filled a nearby abandoned building one block over. We hauled away everything down here ... except for the smell."

Commander Somerton stands near some partially demolished shelves in the remains of the wine cellar. He is clearly ill at ease. His thumbs are hooked in his belt and a dour expression hardens his face. He rocks between his toes and his heels. Lily stops in front of him and looks up. Because of his obvious discomfort, she makes no effort to break the tension with levity. Lieutenant Jones stops nearby, bows his head, and stares at the floor.

Commander Somerton clears his throat. "When they were demolishing this wine cellar, they discovered a hidden door. We'd like you to see what Mr. Barton was keeping in his secret room."

Trepidation sweeps a feeling of icy dread from the nape of her neck to her toes. She resolutely nods. Lieutenant Jones walks behind the last wine rack and opens the door. He stands aside and lets her enter. Commander Somerton walks in behind her. The young lieutenant closes the door, leaving the three of them alone inside the small, stifling hot room. A bright work light hangs from a nail on one wall.

She stares at the photos covering the wall above a crude wooden table.

Lieutenant Jones says, "The officers stopped the work immediately and took the prisoners back to the prison."

"I suggest you destroy it and not let anybody see it," Lily glumly states.

"I've already looked at everything."

She turns toward the lieutenant. "You didn't have to tell me that."

The commander's voice is gentle. "Jackie." She turns toward him. "Curtis and I are the only ones who've looked at the photo albums, and I've only looked at one. No one else has seen anything except the photos on the wall and they're pretty benign, mostly just photos of you from your childhood and around here."

Lily stares at the ten photo albums fastidiously arrayed on the long, wooden table. "My suggestion is still the same: burn it."

With acrimony in his voice, Lieutenant Jones almost growls, "I'd like an explanation. Here you are acting like a Christian and then I see this."

Commander Somerton sternly glares at the lieutenant. "Curtis, she gets a pass for being a 'wild child'. No one is responsible for their actions at a young age."

He scowls at his commanding officer. "I was talking about during her high school and college years when I called her a 'wild child'. It reminded me of the hippie era in the sixties."

"Curtis, may I remind you of those verses in First Corinthians[1], about midway through?"

Lieutenant Jones takes a deep, calming breath, and contritely nods.

"It lists all kinds of sins and then says, *and such were some of you.*"

Lieutenant Jones rhetorically states, "Paul was talking to Christians, wasn't he?"

"That's right. I don't think Jackie needs to give us an explanation. The past is the past, and it's between her and God."

Softly she says, "Perhaps it'd be better if I did give an explanation. As Christians, the three of us can be totally honest with each other. It could put Curtis at ease instead of leaving him at loose ends."

She smiles to soften the tension. "There's a reason why I left home at seventeen and never went back. I wanted to get away from my tormentors. My dad did solve the problem with Clarence by going to the sheriff when he turned eighteen. I didn't see him again until the migration three years ago. I didn't recognize him, but he obviously recognized me."

Tentatively, Lieutenant Jones asks, "So tell us: is Mr. Barton the young groom in that large photo where a cutout of your face has been glued over the bride's?"

"Yes."

"Who's the bride?"

Lily replies, "I have no idea. Like I said, I hadn't seen him since I was twelve."

"You were twelve when he was eighteen?"

"He was a little over five years older than me."

Lieutenant Jones releases his bottled up tension and his facial expression softens. "Oh. ... Would you mind explaining some of the photo albums?"

Reluctantly, she walks over and flips open an album. She stares at the first photo a moment then quickly flips a few pages and shuts it. She rests her palm on the cover as if trying to keep its contents from bursting forth. With her eyes riveted on the floor, she takes a deep breath. "This is family reunions. In that first photo, I'm the bawling toddler in my grandfather's lap and Clarence is about eight years old."

With wide eyes, Lieutenant Jones exclaims, "He's your family?"

She looks up. "We were distant cousins, fifth cousins I think. Our grandfathers were third cousins."

---

1 I Corinthians 6:9-11

"Maybe that note under the first photo explains your face on Mr. Barton's bride? Did your family intermarry?"

She shrugs. "I don't know. I was four the last time I went to the reunion. In fact, my dad and grandmother took me home early that time, after I bit Clarence."

The men's somber expressions rupture into laughter.

She sedately smiles, thankful that her honest but blunt statement broke the tension; therefore she adds, "He required stitches."

"Oh!" Lieutenant Jones wipes tears of laughter from his cheeks.

"I refused to go the next summer and soon after I learned to read, the wealthy relative who hosted the reunions made the front page of the paper. I managed to mouth out the first word of the headline: scandal. Mom grabbed the paper and burned it. There were no more family reunions."

"Is it possible that your grandfather promised Mr. Barton that he could marry you?"

She grimaces. "That note doesn't say marry. It merely says he promised me to him. It could be more like the relationship between my mom and his dad. Look at Clarence, his brothers and my brothers." She points toward the wedding photo. "Those groomsmen are his brothers and my brothers."

The men turn their eyes toward the central photo on the wall.

"Except for that skinny guy," Lily adds. "I don't know who he is, maybe the bride's brother. Anyway, all of the Barton and Gibbons boys looked alike. I'm the only one who looks like my dad at all."

"So ... you're saying ... that they're your half-brothers and ... half-brothers to Mr. Barton?"

"It appears that way, but I never asked."

Lieutenant Jones inquires, "What about the next album?"

She quickly flips through a few pages. "This is family photos. That skinny guy is my dad."

The young lieutenant tilts his head. "It looks like you're all fighting."

"That was a game," Lily replies. "You know, like that ancient movie with the police detective who practices martial arts with his Asian houseboy. Dad stopped it when they got too big. My brothers never studied martial arts. Soon after puberty hit, they started getting rough. Actually it petered out as soon as he made the oldest sit on the sidelines. It was too easy for him to take down just two, and they lost interest."

"Look at the last few pages," Lieutenant Jones requests.

Lily flips to the back and stares with astonishment at the photos. After a moment, she regains her composure. "I guess I blocked this from my memory. This was the day that Dad and I moved out. He could still easily subdue two, but I had trouble with two. … Wait a minute! Why'd I have two? I only have three brothers."

She leans closer, studies the photos then points at one combatant. "That's Clarence."

"Mr. Barton," the commander asks.

Lily nods. "Yeah. I was really angry. I slammed my foot into his knee and—"

"Is that the reason for Mr. Barton's limp?"

"Yeah, I ended his college football career and eliminated his chance to go pro. I injured my brother Tom too, pretty severely. I then turned toward Clarence, and he took off running. Well, as fast as he could hobble. I took off after him and met Granddad coming inside to see what was going on. I told him he broke his promise to me, and he said—"

"What was his promise to you?" Lieutenant Jones asks.

"When I was four, I demanded that Clarence be banned from coming over, and since I had requested it the way Granddad said I should, he granted it."

When Lily remains silent, the lieutenant prompts. "What did he say?"

"He said it had expired. I kicked him and knocked him against the kitchen cabinet. He had a concussion, a broken hip, and a fractured elbow." She turns toward the two men. "I guess you can see why Dad and I moved out that day."

Commander Somerton mutters, "I don't see why your dad didn't press charges against them. How old were they? They were adults, weren't they?"

"They were nineteen to twenty-five, but they were going to press charges against me in retaliation. Dad dropped the charges on them, if they would drop them on me."

"You did have a rough life, didn't you?"

Lily nods and opens another album. She silently stares at the first photo as if transfixed. Without looking at the rest of the photos, Lily closes the album and opens the next one. She slams it shut and stares at the blank wall.

"Who's the young man?"

"My first fiancée; he was murdered in what appeared to be a burglary. I always thought my brothers did it since they were still harassing me after I went to college, but Mr. Barton let it slip to Frank that he'd killed him. He didn't name names, but Frank figured it out and told me. Now, I see that it was all four of them."

She looks over at the men. "Do I have to look at all of these albums? I really don't want to relive these memories."

Commander Somerton points at one pushed against the wall at the back of the table. "That one is the one we'd most like explained."

She sighs then reaches to the back of the table and slides the album toward her. She pauses with her hand on the cover and takes a deep breath to steel herself for whatever awaits inside the dusty album—obviously the worst album of all. She slowly opens the cover and stares at the first photo. The men patiently wait. Tears well in her eyes, she looks up. "We thought this girl committed suicide."

"When was this?"

"I was eleven."

"So that's a long ago murder?"

Lily nods and flips the page. She slowly scans the photos of her bedridden mother who is surrounded by her three sons. In the next to last photo, Lily's oldest brother is holding a pillow. Fear wells inside her as she realizes her mother might have had an assisted suicide. She does not want to look at the last photo, but the desire to know overcomes her resistance. She quickly glances at the photo then stares at the wall behind the table. "I was twelve. She was very sick. We thought it was a natural death. … Maybe I should say, I was told it was a natural death."

She flips another page. "I was fifteen or sixteen," she says without emotion.

After flipping another page, revulsion sweeps over her at the sight of Clarence welding a hypodermic needle while her brothers hold her father down. She can barely articulate words. "I was seventeen. We … ah … I thought it was a heart attack. The doctor said it was probably a heart attack."

She looks up at the tall commander. Her cheeks glisten with tears. "You want to know if any of these happened here, if any of the murderers are here, don't you."

He nods. She quickly flips through the rest of the album, looks up, and wipes her eyes. "They're all people I knew in Washington when I was growing up. I didn't know some of them were dead, but I can safely say none of the murders are recent and Clarence is the only one of the murderers whom I've seen around here." She wipes her arm across her tear-streaked face.

"I assume the other young men are his brothers and your brothers?"

"Just my brothers, I didn't see any of his brothers but I did glance through them rather quickly."

"What about the two old men with them in a few of the photos, one of whom they murdered later?"

"My grandfather and Clarence's grandfather."

"Thank you, Jackie. I know this was painful, but we needed to know if any of these crimes were recent and who the young men were." The commander puts his arm around Lily's shoulders and escorts her from the room. "Take care of it, Curtis."

"One more question."

They turn back.

Lieutenant Jones is clearly ill at ease. He asks, "When did you become a Christian?"

She replies, "After being married for five years, I let my husband teach me."

"Thank you for explaining," the young lieutenant politely states. He picks up a paper shredder which an officer placed outside the door while they were inside. He sets it near the table and plugs it into an extension cord. As Lily and Commander Somerton walk across the expansive basement, they hear the rumble of the shredder as it devours the photos.

Lily knocks on Tommy Walker's door. She hears him shuffling about. She leans her head on the door frame while waiting. He cracks the door. With sadness in her eyes, she looks up.

"Hi, Lily. Do you need to talk?"

She nods.

"Just a minute."

She nods. He closes the door. She plops onto the step, wipes tears from her eyes then covers her face with her hands. She hears soft voices mixed with the muffled sounds of movement from within the cottage. He opens the door. She looks up as he steps past her onto the ground.

Susie Morrow steps out and strides down the path.

Tommy sits on the step and looks at Lily. His shirt hangs loosely on his thin frame. "Do you mind?"

She shakes her head. "I know Susie."

"And me?"

She nods. "We had some complaints so—"

"About me and Susie?" he asks with a frown creasing his brow.

She shakes her head. "It concerns public lewdness, so I was going to say I'm glad you keep it inside."

"Have you talked to those who are doing that?"

Lily shakes her head, "We'll do that after we have a decision from the council about what we should do about it."

Tommy turns their conversation to her obvious problem. "You look like your world's caved in."

"Yeah, sorry to disturb you." Lily wipes her face with her palms. "I'm glad you're here. You helped so much when Walt was having his problems. I wouldn't want to start over with another counselor." She is speaking of her oldest son, Walter Schwartz, IV.

"What caved today?"

"I had some things from my past rise up and hit me in the face."

Gently, he inquires, "Have you recalled some forgotten memories?"

She nods. "For the first four years of my life, I screamed to get my way. One thing I suddenly remembered today is that I bit someone. I bit him hard enough that he needed stitches."

"Who was that?"

"Clarence."

"You're talking about Mr. Barton, right?"

She nods. "He merely touched my arm with the tip of his finger to tease me. I leaned toward him and chomped down on his arm. My granddad decided to outlaw screaming. He demanded that I speak in a civil tone of voice and clearly state what I wanted and no more biting. He told me I had to do that or else."

"What was the punishment?"

She shakes her head. "I never found out what *or else* was. It was enough to know that it struck fear in my three older brothers. Whatever it was, it was strong enough that they left me alone when I calmly and clearly told them to leave me alone because Granddad told them they had to or else."

She tilts her head toward the clear blue sky. "I also tested Granddad. I clearly and calmly told him I didn't want Clarence coming over anymore. He looked at me in shock for a second then said he'd see to it and he did. … Well … I never saw him in my house again until …" She pauses for a moment.

He patiently waits.

"I saw some photos today that brought back another suppressed memory."

When her silence lengthens, he prompts, "Surely just remembering isn't what's brought you out here in tears?"

"No, but it's really hard to talk about it."

"Do you want to go over to one of the counseling offices for privacy?"

"Nah, this is private enough on your stoop. Your cottage is pretty isolated on this side of the main building."

Tommy chuckles. "Yeah, no one wanted the arsonist near them. They're afraid I might burn this place down, just like Mr. Barton's motel."

Lily smiles.

As a diversion, he grins and shakes his hands in the air. "I'm a pyromaniac because I smoked in bed and went to sleep."

She laughs.

"What do you recall?" he prods.

"It wasn't really things I recalled, though my memories were bad enough. It was photos of crimes committed by Clarence and … my brothers and … my grandfather and … Uncle Jonas." She takes a deep breath. "Well, Uncle Jonas wasn't actually an uncle. He was a third cousin to my grandfather, but everyone called him Uncle Jonas."

Tommy rhetorically inquires, "They kept evidence?"

Lily nods.

"They must have been proud of them?"

"Either that or arrogant."

"Having known Mr. Barton, I would say that arrogant is probably right."

He waits for her to speak, but she does not. He prods, "It must be hard to find out that your family is criminal?"

"I already knew it. I just didn't realize the extent of it. … I wasn't even close to knowing the extent of it. Probably my only close relative who was decent was my grandmother. Well, I'm just talking about my mom's side of the family, here. She—"

212

"Wait a minute. Are you including Mr. Barton as part of your family?"
She nods. "Uncle Jonas was his grandfather."

"Have you told me that before?"

"I don't know. Maybe."

"Oh … okay … ah … so your grandmother was nice?" Tommy asks to turn their conversation back to her problem.

"Yeah, she had a Bible that she kept hidden. Granddad would've hit the roof if he'd known. I caught her reading it once, and she swore me to secrecy. That's the only time I ever got an *or else* from my grandmother."

"What was her *or else?*"

"It wasn't her *or else*. It was Granddad's *or else*. It was what he'd do to her. *Or else* struck fear into my grandmother too."

"So you have a lot to talk about today?"

"I don't think I even want to talk about all of it, just enough to calm down," Lily admits.

"Then you can go work off your frustrations with the Seals?"

"It always helps to get on the mats and do something physical, but before I do that, let me ask how Rene is doing."

Tommy knows that Lily has said all she wants about her troubled past; he lets her turn their conversation to Rene's severe problem. He sheepishly grins, "She's decided that she dreamed the voice she heard in the hall."

"That would explain our inability to find him, but I take it from your expression that you don't think she dreamed it."

He slowly shakes his head. "It's not quite right. She'd just taken a shower and was standing up; how could she be dreaming? And I don't think it was a hallucination either."

"The other question is: why haven't we found him. It's been two months."

He shrugs. "She could be so terrified of him that she doesn't want to find him."

"So she's no longer able to recognize his voice?"

"That would be my guess, that she's subconsciously blocking it."

Lily covers her face with her hands. "How can we keep people safe here, if we can't find him?"

TWENTY

After Gary Brown eases his feet into the river, he looks over at Serena Hermann and asks, "Are they leaving you alone?"

She swishes her feet in the cool water and looks up. "It's getting better."

"Sorry, I can't be with you every minute."

"That's all right. George stepped in this morning and made Brett release my arm."

"He grabbed you!"

"I told him no and turned away. That's when he grabbed me, but George was nearby and settled it quickly."

"Did George threaten him?"

She smiles broadly. "Yeah: with the security committee."

"I guess I'd better not deck any of your unwanted suitors. I should just mention the security committee."

"I'm sure that if one of them takes a swing at you, no one would mind if you did. I'd defend you. That's for sure. After all, you are one of the guards around here. It'd be within your rights to use force on someone who's out of line, especially if it's Brett since he has a history of getting out of line."

He looks up at the bright moon. "Serena, would you mind if I ask you something about Mr. Barton's?"

"I guess not. I don't like to think about that, but you've already brought it to mind so go ahead."

"I hope this isn't too painful for you. Tell me if it is, and we won't talk about it again. Okay?"

"Okay."

"I was wondering why you were so compliant."

"James and I were both compliant."

Gary looks at Serena; her head is bowed. The reflection of the moon off the water is softly illuminating her gorgeous face.

She looks up. "We did it to protect our children. We did whatever he asked as long as he left our children alone."

"Did he keep that?"

"Yes. He never touched Jasmine. Sven was never in much danger of anything except being sold. I told him, I'd kill him if he ever did anything to either of our children."

Gary inquires, "Wouldn't Ricky have killed you if you did?"

"James had scavenged some drugs when Mr. Barton had them raiding the abandoned pharmacies. Ricky wouldn't have ever known what happened or who did it. And my threat was before Ricky came. It was even before Cisco came. It was back when we were just a bunch of coworkers and their families sticking together for strength in numbers. Mr. Barton hadn't taken full control, but he was beginning to show his true colors and there were no longer any police we could call."

"I hope this isn't too painful for you but since he was so far from being a decent human being, why didn't you go ahead and ah … dispose of him?"

She bows her head. "We didn't know of any better place to go and thought that it'd be better if we didn't fight among ourselves. At first, some still thought he'd hung the moon. It was really up in the air as to what would happen to all of us if something happened to the man who was claiming to be our protector. As things got worse, he was protecting us from the dangers outside our walls, especially Commander Tyler. He was worse than Mr. Barton."

He nods to indicate that he understands. "Things were pretty bad everywhere for a long time. There were no safe places."

"Someone's coming," Serena whispers.

They slip their arms around each other and engage in an apparently passionate kiss.

"Whooowee!"

"Al!" Lily whispers, "Let's go somewhere else. There're lots of little ponds on the river."

Serena breaks off the kiss. "Lily, it's all right. Come on over and sit by us."

Al grabs Lily's hand. "Nah, we'll go somewhere else."

She grips his hand and pulls him toward the couple.

216

"Oh, all right. We'll go sit by them."

She slips her hand out of his, sits beside Serena, quickly slips off her shoes, and dips her feet in the water. Al sits down and begins untying his shoelaces.

"Serena," Lily says. "You look happy now."

"I am. Gary's real nice and he keeps all those obnoxious guys away, most of the time anyway, so I have some peace."

"I'm glad to hear it. I talked to several of them and told them to look at your face and take a cue that they were ruining their chances with you. They needed to wait until you'd grieved for James before making any overtures, but they seemed to think that'd only give every other single guy a better chance of winning your affection."

Serena smiles and conspiratorially whispers, "But actually they're ruining their chances forever."

Al leans around Lily. "Didn't ruin Gary's chances; what'd he do differently?"

"He's nice and just offered friendship."

"That didn't look like friendship," Al exclaims.

Serena leans around Lily and stares into Al's eyes. "At this point that's mostly for show, but don't tell anyone."

Al slides his arm around Lily's waist. "I'd take that kind of friendship."

Lily grabs his arm and removes it.

Serena regrets calling Lily over; Al's unseemly behavior is making her uncomfortable. "I need to go check on my children. We'll see you later." Serena stands and slips on her shoes.

Gary dons his shoes and stands up. "See you later."

"Goodnight," Lily replies.

Lily pulls her phone and web-link device from her waistband and lays them and her keys beside her shoes. "Al, I'm going to cool off." She stands and wades into the pool fully clothed.

He pulls off his shirt and follows her into the pool. She dives into deep water. He dives and grabs her around the waist. She deftly removes his arms, flips above him and puts her feet against his back, pushing him deeper with a quick but gentle kick.

Within moments, she is back on shore, pulling on her shoes. She grabs her possessions and looks at Al standing in the shallow water. "What did you think you were doing?"

"Ah ... taking up where we left off when we were fourteen."

217

She grimaces. "Is that what you've been doing with all these requests to spend time with me?"

"Of course," he replies with a grin.

"Sorry, I misinterpreted your intentions."

A puzzled expression arches his eyebrows. "Oh? What'd you think I was doing?"

"Just being friendly, I guess. You have to realize that it's my job to talk to new people, to help them integrate into the community. I talk to everyone as often as they request. I'm really sorry if I led you on. I didn't mean to do that."

He steps onto the rocky shore and stoops to retrieve his shirt. "Can we walk back together?"

"Why?"

Al requests, "I'd like to start over."

"I'm not interested in starting over," Lily emphatically states. She turns and strides away.

"Are you mad at me?"

Lily replies, "I guess not."

"So what's going on?"

She stops and turns back. He is putting on his shoes and socks. She folds her arms across her chest. "Let me explain it this way. In high school, I chose you because you were small, timid, quiet, polite, and a whole lot of other things that my brothers weren't. You were more like my daddy. I no longer pick a guy using that immature method otherwise I wouldn't have ever married Walter."

He grins. "Walter definitely wasn't small."

She nods and walks away. He strides toward her and falls into step beside her, his untied shoelaces clicking against the rocks. "I'm still all of those things."

"But that's not what I'm looking for anymore."

"What are you looking for?"

"At the moment, I'm not looking for anything. I'm too involved in trying to make inroads against the barbaric system of slavery," Lily replies. "There's no time for a relationship."

"So there's no one else?" Al asks.

"I wouldn't say there's no one else."

Al mutters, "So there is someone else?"

"I'm not having a romantic relationship with anyone but I've had offers, several of them. Please don't take this as a problem with you. It's just not what I want to do right now."

"Maybe later?"

"Probably not," she replies.

"So my chances are slim to none?"

"Closer to none."

"That makes it sound like you don't like me," Al gripes.

"I've always liked you. You're a real nice guy. I've just matured and don't pick a guy for such shallow reasons as when I was fourteen. There're probably several hundred guys here with the same good qualities as you."

"Oh? So I don't stand out."

She protests, "I wouldn't put it that way. I think all the nice guys stand out, and the not-so-nice guys, like the dozen or so who've been after Serena, definitely stand out, just not in a good way."

He sighs. "I was really looking forward to maybe finishing what we started so many times way back there in high school but never finished."

She stops in her tracks. He stops and turns back; she is staring at him in shock.

Softly he says, "All the guys were telling me I was going to get lucky, and you'd take me away from the party up into the hayloft."

"Al! Something was going on."

"What?" he asks.

Lily shrugs, "I didn't know at the time. I kind of got a clue over the next couple of weeks from the way the kids treated me. I had suddenly and totally lost the popularity that I'd had since kindergarten, but I wasn't sure until this moment exactly what was going on. I could sense that something was going on; I just had no clue what it was. Daddy and Granddad were arguing and that's why I went and asked Daddy to take me to the house; I had to stop that."

Al shrugs his shoulders. "Why'd you have to referee the grown-ups? You ruined our good time."

Lily glares at him. "The other boys were probably going to beat you up that night."

"Oh?"

"Did they beat you up after I left?"

"Not that night," he admits.

"Posse told me you got beat up in December. He said that's why you moved."

"Yeah, Dad said the town was too rough so he found another preaching job."

"I tried to protect you," Lily states. "I called the sheriff a few times when I saw the guys waiting for you to leave Daddy's drugstore. You were in danger, dating the most popular girl in school."

"Oh?"

She looks at his still moist face. In the bright moonlight, she can clearly discern his baffled expression. She is also experiencing bafflement. "Let me ask a question."

"Sure, anything."

Lily gathers her courage. She is having doubts about Al's character. "You are a Christian, aren't you?"

He shrugs. "That's just our culture."

She takes a deep breath. "So ... you never took God seriously?"

"Nah."

She turns and strides away.

Al dashes after her and falls into step beside her. "I'd still like to—"

"Absolutely not!" she angrily exclaims.

He grabs her arm. Within seconds she pins him to the ground, twisting his arm behind his back and pressing her knee into the small of his back.

He mutters, "I'd forgotten you could do that."

"Let me get this straight: I'm definitely not interested, especially now that I know you better," she stridently whispers.

"Okay."

She releases her grip and stands.

With a smirk, he looks up at her.

"Don't follow me, this time." She turns and strides away.

Tommy Walker stands in the office door. Lily is sitting with her elbows on her desk and her hands over her face. "Lily."

She looks up. Her eyes are red; she has been crying. "Come on in."

He shuts the door, walks over, and plops into a chair. "Do you need to talk?"

"Yeah, and Max isn't here."

"You talk to Max about your problems?"

"We're friends. We just talk. Problems aren't off limits but mostly we just talk."

He raises his eyebrows. "Are you more than just friends?"

She bites her lip then smiles. "He's asked, but I haven't answered."

"Oh? ... What do you think your answer will be?"

"I don't know."

"Why not?"

"I'm busy."

"You shouldn't ever be too busy for a relationship. Do you like him?"

She smiles. "Of course, I like him. I just don't want anything to get in the way of keeping my promise."

"What promise?"

She inhales deeply, leans back in her chair, and looks at the ceiling. "When we first opened the nurses' clinic, I promised them I'd do something about the abuse of women in this awful culture and I'm still working on it."

"I don't see how Max would get in the way of that."

"I can barely find time to stop by and see him. He gets called away all the time. Sometimes I get called away. Something will have to give way for us to spend time together."

"Get Monkey to fix up a house for you in town. Then you and Max can spend the evenings together."

"I can't shirk my duties here."

"You don't have to; just spend a couple of nights a week in town, when Max isn't on evening duty."

She nods. "That's an idea. I probably wouldn't even need my own house. I think there's an empty bedroom in one of the nurses' houses."

"There you go. Now what else is troubling you?"

She bows her head. "I don't know that you're the right person to talk to about this?"

"You can talk to me about anything."

"Even Christianity?"

He shrugs. "I know quite a bit about it even though I don't practice it."

"What happened is: I just found out that someone who claimed to be a Christian doesn't believe at all."

"That sounds like an issue of trust."

Surprise engulfs Lily's face. She knows that Tommy is very perceptive, but his understanding of Christian values startles her. "I guess that's boiling it down to the gist of the problem. I thought pretty highly of him, and now I'd rather beat him to a pulp for his deceit."

Tommy laughs. "That's just about what my second wife and I did. Tonya and I were both hiding things from each other and it destroyed our marriage. The divorce was really acrimonious even though there weren't any children involved. I didn't make that mistake the next time. When I moved in with Cherry, she knew I had two exes and a daughter and I knew she had some exes. We both had baggage, but we were open about it."

She is thankful that he has diverted their conversation from her problems. He frequently speaks of his own troubles when counseling. His friendly conversational style has an uncanny way of relaxing his clients, allowing them to open up more freely. She was never able to open up to his successor when receiving counseling for her oldest son's problems. His strict avoidance of speaking of anything personal, though more ethical than Tommy's openness, made her uneasy. Since she is from a family with many secrets, she is guardedly leery of anyone who is obviously hiding something. It did not help that she knew the reason for his professional demeanor.

Knowing that within moments, she will be talking freely of her own problems, she inquires about his first wife, "What about Mary?"

"We just didn't get along. We're basically not compatible. She practices her Christianity, and my practices get on her nerves. Make no mistake; I never cheated on her, but we could both tell our fighting was getting to Jenny and she was only a toddler. Mary was showing signs of stress and I couldn't concentrate on what my clients were telling me, so we got a friendly divorce. Well, actually as soon as I moved out, we started getting along again and I asked if I could move back in but she said it'd never work between us." He smiles. "I love Mary but she's going to have to be just my ex but Jenny flourished and now we're enjoying our grandchild together."

Without pausing, he urges, "So tell me more about your hypocrite. Can you forgive him?"

"Yes. And I have many things that I need forgiven for in our relationship. I was far from perfect back then."

"You're on the right track."

She furrows her brow. "I'm surprised that you know so much about Christianity that you would urge me to forgive."

"Its good psychology: gets rid of stress and anxiety, etcetera, and if you can forgive yourself too, it keeps you from eating up your insides over your own mistakes."

Lily looks up at the ceiling for a moment then looks at Tommy. "I think I'm more disturbed that the hypocrite married my best friend. I mean that I got what I wanted out of the relationship at the time, and that single incident was just one of my many mistakes; my whole outlook on life at that time was one big mistake. But my best friend was a dedicated Christian, one of the strongest Christians I ever met. I learned a lot from her and her family about how to behave in a less selfish way, and now I know that she married a hypocrite. He was a hypocrite then and he still is now, so during her whole marriage, she was married to a hypocrite. That disturbs me a lot more than Al snookering me, especially since I was snookering him at the same time."

"Was he faithful to her?"

Lily shrugs. "I guess."

Tommy looks at her a moment then asks, "Can I get you to quit eating yourself up over your lying? I know that really gets you: the deceit in our way of life here."

"Lying is sinful. It's always going to bother me even though the reason is to rescue people from slavery."

"But you're not really lying," he contends.

"If it's deceitful, it's still lying."

"It's not a lie when you say you're the master, you really are."

"No, I'm not. We operate democratically here," Lily asserts.

"Yes you are; you just have everyone's permission to be the master."

She laughs. "I see your point, but it's still being deceitful to hide the democracy."

"It's nobody else's business. Now give yourself some slack and quit eating your insides up. That stomach pain is going to kill you. Has the doc figured it out yet?"

"Nah. It's mild, and he says we'll just wait for me to find a gastroenterologist."

TWENTY ONE

Al grabs his phone and punches in Brad's number. His tedious surveillance has paid off, turning a typical Friday into something other than mundane. It could still be a boring day, but maybe not. "A couple of Mr. Finke's men just turned onto our road."

"They're carrying their ID cards?"

"Yeah," Al confirms.

"Good. Keep tracking them, and I'll set up our intercept teams. Got names?"

"Glenn Corbett and Randall Laird."

Al states, "Todd, I couldn't get Brad on the phone."

"He's with the forward team," Todd replies.

"Randall was just dropped off in the hills, and Glenn is in the car and headed back toward town."

"Thanks, Al."

Brad holds perfectly still and keeps his breathing shallow as the intruder with a backpack slung over one shoulder walks within ten feet of his well-hidden position. When he disappears over the ridge, Brad quickly but quietly sprints up the hill. Ten feet from the ridge, he stops. In about a minute, Gary Brown stands up from his hidden position on the ridge. He looks back and signals. Staying about twenty feet apart, they dash into the small valley and sprint for the next ridge. Soon, ten guards are following the oblivious man who is now walking south along the river. Other trackers are hidden in the brush ahead.

Randall Laird stays on a sun-dappled animal path meandering through the brush near the river. He stops at the edge of the clearing surrounding the water tanks for the compound. He looks to his left and then to his right. There are obvious signs of recent work but no one is in sight. "Hello!"

Six armed guards stand.

"Whoa!" He slowly raises his hands and puts them on his head.

Brad curtly demands, "What's in the backpack?"

"Poison that I was supposed to put in the water."

"Supposed to?"

"Yeah. I had no intention of doing it. I've never hurt anyone in my life, and I'm not going to start now."

Brad walks forward and gently grips the strap of the backpack. Randall lowers his arm and allows Brad to take it. Brad steps back. Gary hands his rifle to John and walks over. He pats the man down. "No weapons. You can put your hands down."

"I'd like to request sanctuary," Randall requests. "I don't want to go back to Mr. Finke's."

Brad lowers his weapon. "Let's go see Mrs. Schwartz. What's your name?"

"Randall Laird."

Brad's face remains expressionless despite his relief that Randall is honest about his name.

As they start walking, Randall looks around. "Are all of you going in with me? It looks like you'd look for a second intruder, not that there is one, but it doesn't seem prudent to assume there's just one."

Brad calls out. "Stand."

Randall stops. Three men rise out of the brush at the edge of the clearing.

"Look back."

Randall turns around. He sees a dozen more men scattered in the brush behind them.

"Okay, back to work guys."

With wide eyes, Randall looks at Brad. "I never heard a thing."

Brad smiles. "Of course you didn't. Let's go."

Randall looks Lily squarely in the eyes. "Well, are you going to give me sanctuary?"

She stares across her desk at the nervous man. Four former Seals, Ralph, and Mr. Brashear quietly observe her interview of the intruder. "We give anybody sanctuary. I'll talk to you later about that, but for now I have one more question. What kind of work can you do?"

"I'm a mechanic."

She furrows her brow. "Why'd Mr. Finke give up his mechanic?"

"He didn't expect to loose me. I'm supposed to meet up with Glenn tomorrow morning."

"Are you his only mechanic?"

He shrugs. "I'm the only professional. I guess he'll miss me but some of the other guys were car hobbyists and could do my job, and anyway it wouldn't bother me at all if I left him high and dry. Say, this was more than just one more question."

"Your answer led to another question. I know mechanics are hard to come by so wondered about him sending you on a dangerous mission."

"It wasn't supposed to be dangerous. Just dump the poison near the intake pipe and get out of there, but nobody wanted to handle the poison. Of course I had no intention of handling it, so I volunteered. I couldn't resist the opportunity to get away. Fact is: I've been looking for a way to leave ever since I got there. He's the worst master ever."

"I need your ID badge," Lily requests. "You basically have no identity because we can't let anybody know you're out here."

He pulls his card out of his pocket and tosses it on the desk. "I don't care. Just treat me right and don't ask me to hurt anybody, and I'll be happy as a clam. It doesn't take much to satisfy me anymore."

"Gary and John will help you get settled. Guys make sure he fills out paperwork with Serena as soon as possible."

"You're going to give me a new name?" Randall guesses.

She grins and shakes her head. "Guys, fill him in."

A grin melts away Randall's apprehension. He stands up. "People with a sense of humor, I like that. Much better that being with a murdering thug."

The three men walk toward the door. John stops and turns back. "Are we going to do the coyote thing?"

Lily shrugs then nods. "I guess that'd be better than Randall not showing up at the rendezvous."

John grins. "Okay, we'll take care of it."

Randall raises one eyebrow. "What does it involve?"

"Just your clothes and a freshly killed goat; the coyotes will be delighted," John replies. "Let's get going."

"Hey!" The men turn back. Lily is holding out Randall's card. "We should leave this in his pocket."

John grins, steps back, and takes the card. The three men walk into the main room. John closes the door.

Brad, Todd, and Ralph move their chairs over to the desk while Mr. Brashear takes the one Randall vacated. "Suggestions," Mr. Brashear solicits.

Lily grins. "The usual."

Ralph solemnly nods. "The usual."

Brad and Todd laugh as Mr. Brashear looks around in perplexity. "Okay, guys. What is the usual?"

She bites her lower lip then answers Mr. Brashear's question. "We hide it."

With a thin-lipped grimace, Mr. Brashear stares at her. Brad licks his lips while Todd pulls on his earlobe. Lily bites her tongue. Only Ralph remains stoic, easily hiding his urge to laugh.

She looks down at the backpack on the floor beside her chair; the teasing is suddenly forgotten. "We need to find out what the poison is and handle it carefully in the mean time."

Mr. Brashear sighs. "Too bad that guy was not the least bit curious about what he was handling."

She leans forward and nods. "We know there aren't any observers in the hills, so have the guys dig some shallow graves. Then it'll look like we've had some deaths if someone comes snooping around. Later today, we'll take some volunteers to the hospital, carry them in on stretchers, and carry them back out with sheets over their faces. If possible, we'll do that when Mr. Finke sends someone to observe so we can be sure he knows about it. It might take several days to achieve that result. Maybe, just maybe, we can draw Mr. Finke out into the open and get something we can use against him; maybe."

"When do we take the poison to the hospital for testing?" Mr. Brashear asks.

She glances at Brad, Todd, and Ralph. They shake their heads slightly, undetected by Mr. Brashear. She drums her fingers on the desk. "I'm not sure we want to do that. We can't be seen with the backpack and I don't think anybody wants to take it out and handle it, not even with gloves. At least, not until we can find out what it is. We need to get expert advice from the doctors before we do anything with it, especially since we may not have any way to test it. Until then we'll keep it locked up."

Todd inquires, "Didn't you tell me you're bidding on Edward Ulmer?"

"Does he have expertise in this?"

"He earned a degree in chemical engineering then decided to enter the military, so I suppose he'd know something about most any poison."

"Let me check on him." She picks up her web-link device, turns on the power, and taps the screen. "Here he is. Someone just topped our bid. I'll call Lawrence and tell him to make sure we get Edward. How much time is left?" The men lean forward as she taps. "It's four o'clock. We have one hour before bidding closes for the week."

Mr. Brashear inquires, "That means he should be here Monday?"

She looks at him and shrugs. "It depends upon where he's coming from. It will be some Monday within a month … probably within a month."

"Can you tell where he is coming from?"

She shakes her head. "I won't know anything until I get to the prison Monday morning and then I'll just find out whether he's there or not."

"So he might get here in three days or twenty-four days," Mr. Brashear states.

"Maybe. There's really no communication in this area. Prison transport is kept completely secret. Let's get this bag locked up and then I'm going to go watch over Lawrence's shoulder until bidding closes. One other thing: we need to watch for Glenn when he's supposed to meet Randall. I'll inform Al when I go see Lawrence."

Mr. Brashear guesses, "To make sure he sees the staged death?"

"It's more to see if he comes to pick up Randall. That'll tell us about his original intentions and maybe the danger of handling the poison."

With her hands on the back of Lawrence's chair, Lily bends over his head, staring at his monitor.

Al stops in the doorway. "Lily."

"Not now. I'll talk to you after five."

"I want to apologize."

"Later, this is important," Lily stresses.

"Is it about that intruder?"

"Yeah, now leave us alone. Oh sorry to be so rude. I'll see you after five. I have an assignment I need to tell you about."

Lawrence positions the pointer over the send icon. "Okay, I have the bid ready to go. Thirty seconds."

"Don't wait too late."

"I can't give them enough time for a counter bid."

Al walks over and leans toward the screen.

"Fifteen seconds. Okay, our bid is ... entered and ... we have it!"

She pats Lawrence's shoulder. "Thanks."

"Is that somebody important?" Al asks.

"Yes," Lily replies.

"Something to do with today's intruder?"

"Yes, Al. Your apology is accepted."

"Thanks. Tell me about this guy that's so important? Would he have expertise in poisons or something?"

"Yes."

Al offers, "Maybe I can help there?"

Surprised, she blurts, "What do you know about poisons?"

"I've been researching them ever since you found out that the water guy was the one threatening the commander," Al admits.

"Oh."

"Yeah, come in here and let me show you what I've learned."

As they walk through the connecting door, she asks, "What have you learned?"

"A lot. I have it bookmarked and sorted by types. So what do you know about the poison? At least, I assume that the intruder brought some since you're looking for information," Al replies.

"He didn't know what it was. He's an auto mechanic, not one of Mr. Finke's engineers. He said it was a clear liquid that Mr. Finke handled with rubber gloves and put into a glass jar then into a plastic bag and wrapped with towels before putting it in the backpack."

Al suggests, "We should look at it."

"We don't want to touch it. We've locked it up without opening it since that seemed like extreme caution. It would have to be pretty concentrated for a small jar to be effective in our large water system."

"So you don't even know if it is a clear liquid? Maybe it's a bomb instead."

Lily shrugs. "We considered that but the guy appears trustworthy. He was using this as an excuse to escape. He had no interest in the poison. He wasn't going to touch it at all, and he had no qualms about staying in the same room with it. He was nervous about us but completely at ease about the backpack. If his intention was a suicide bomb, he wouldn't have had any reason to be nervous about us. Or at least, he doesn't think it's a bomb and the rubber gloves were in one of the outside pockets so he could use them to get it out and he was told to put it in our water system, not walk into a populated area with it. At least, he said he was told that. Mr. Finke is pretty wily, but I don't think he's capable of thinking that many chess moves ahead. We have guys with expertise in defusing bombs, but they don't want to mess with a poison until we know more."

"But we need to find out all we can about it?"

"Al, what we want to know is: what symptoms it should cause so we can fake some believable illnesses."

"Oh, deceit!" Al laughs. "Okay, let me sort my research by appearance and the ability to be absorbed through the skin, and we should assume odorless and tasteless."

"Or ingested," Lily adds.

Al pushes print. "Okay, there's your list of most likely symptoms."

"Thanks. This will really help," Lily says.

"Thanks for forgiving me. I was just ticked off the other day. I didn't know that you'd changed."

Lily admits, "I think I was more disturbed that you'd married Cathy. I know she's a true believer and was saving herself for marriage and it was a shock to suddenly discover that … ah … you weren't what she and I both thought you were."

He laughs.

Anger flashes in her eyes. "What's so funny?"

"We were thirteen when we met at camp Lucky Lake and I had a bunch of lies that I used with girls and it usually got me what I wanted and," he shrugs, "I fooled her too."

Lily glares at him in shock and dismay. She is particularly shocked that he dated her after Cathy, who had always thought she and Al were 'going steady' from the beginning. Lily had always assumed that they meet at camp after she and Al dated. She stands, grabs the paper from the printer and stalks out.

She immediately turns around and walks back in. "I forgot to tell you about your assignment. We're going to have to put away our differences so we can work together."

"So no more discussion of the past huh?" He grins.

"That'll work. Now on to tomorrow morning's problem; we need to know if Glenn comes to pick up Randall and if anyone comes to observe our graveyard or watches us take our fake poisoning victims to the hospital."

TWENTY TWO

Max opens a bottle of cola and hands it to Lily. "This guy's serious."

"Yeah, does everybody know to use only the water we bring in for all drinking, cooking, and teeth brushing, etcetera?"

He opens another cola. "Yeah and also to keep quiet and pretend we don't suspect a thing. We'll reiterate it to make sure. I think we need to keep our water lines flushed, so we'll need to run the taps more than we did before this happened. Do we have the funds to do that? Water's pretty high, I hear."

"We have plenty of funds. And that's a good suggestion for another reason: this way our bill won't go down and alert Mr. Finke that we aren't using his water, but it also shouldn't be obvious that we're flushing our lines."

He sits beside her, leans back, and sighs. "When's this going to be over?"

She shrugs. "I haven't managed to talk him into meeting with me yet. We may have to go to Plan B. Yesterday's attack kind of spurs us in that direction anyway." She leans back on the soft sofa in the doctor's lounge.

"What's Plan B?"

"We haven't decided, but it wouldn't require Mr. Finke's voluntary involvement." She takes a sip of cola. "Maybe, if we can double the size of our military, we could raid the water facility without putting the whole town in danger. Right now we're concerned that he could slip poison into the water main before we could stop him."

Max says, "The guards are giving us frequent reports to allay everyone's anxiety. It helps to know everyone's doing everything possible to keep us safe. They're particularly happy with the alarms Al has set on his computer, and it helps to know how easily they tracked and caught Mr. Finke's man when he alerted them."

"Yeah, Al's keeping his cot in his computer room."

Max lifts an eyebrow. "That's dedication."

"We're all kind of dedicated to surviving."

Lily watches him gulp his cola. "I'd like to apologize."

"For what?"

"For not noticing that you were interested in me."

"I probably wasn't clear about my intentions."

"I was probably too focused on my task. It's kind of all consuming."

He takes a gulp of cola. "I understand that. Being medical director is kind of all consuming too. I never did covet being the boss. I'd rather just practice medicine. At least this is Saturday, and there's no clinic and no work on the upcoming nursing school. Now, that's going to be a job!"

He suddenly chuckles and looks over at Lily. "What do you suppose our pretend patients are doing down there with an ER full of idle medical personnel?"

"I hope they're having a party just like we're doing."

"I hope no real emergencies come in and see the merriment."

"Ralph and John are guarding the door," Lily states.

"Have you made any progress on the other barons?"

"Mr. Kasper appears to be softening. I hope he doesn't renege and back out of our deal."

"What deal?"

"Just a business deal. I haven't pushed him to commit to the co-op. I'm trying to build relationships with all the barons, but he's the only one with whom I've made any progress other than Mr. Patterson who's always been with us. Some of the others seemed like they wouldn't object then the next time I saw them they were vehemently opposed to a co-op. Just a bunch of wafflers. That's what they are; just blowing around with the wind." She gestures violently with her free hand then sits erect and sets her bottle on the coffee table.

"Something must have just occurred to you," Max guesses.

"Yeah, he killed an officer and tried to kill some of us."

He counters, "You don't know that for sure. As dilute as it would've been, it might've only caused some mild sickness."

"He might not know how large our water system is. He might have intended to wreak havoc. It makes me think, though, that he might have intimidated some of the other barons too. I knew he could intimidate them. Why didn't it occur to me that he might have already intimidated them?" She stands up.

"Where're you going?"

"A group of the Seals are out at the shooting range. I'm going to task them with looking for recent graves and when I get home, I'll see what Lawrence and Al can discover about recent deaths by comparing the ID cards with the register of each baron a few months ago. I'll come back and get my 'dead poisoning victims' after I talk to the Seals."

"We didn't get to talk about us?"

"Oh," she mutters. "Well, I'm making arrangements to stay overnight with some of the nurses about once or twice a week so we can spend time together in the evenings."

He smiles. "So it's a yes?"

"It's not a no."

His face falls. "But you haven't given it much thought."

She leans toward him. "I've given it some thought but haven't decided yet. As long as things are so unsettled, it's really hard to make a decision about something personal, something so momentous."

Disappointed, he watches her stride out, occupied with her suddenly conceived task.

Brad cocks an eyebrow. "I hear you're the best shot."

Lily smiles at her challenger. Ralph Merrell folds his arms and leans against the SUV. One corner of his mouth tilts up. John Thorne slams the driver's door and leans against the fender. He covers his grin with his hand. Even the two Seals stationed as guards on the hills at the entrance to the box canyon focus their attention on Brad's obvious dare.

She tilts her head. "Okay. What I came for can wait a few minutes, but I need to go soon."

Brad turns to one of the men. "Put up a new target."

"On which one?"

"Number five," Ralph suggests.

John grins. "Oh ... challenging!"

Ryan Sealy calls a halt to practice, not that anyone has fired a shot since Brad's challenge. They have been pretending to check their weapons, reload, or study their aim. As one, they lower their weapons and turn around with grins of anticipation. Lieutenant Williams allows his eyes to slyly take in the curves of the baroness; he fervently wishes that the powerful baroness was not out of his league. Two men race to the most distant hay bale and put up a new target while she chooses a rifle and reloads.

Lily looks up when they return, steps up to the firing line, assumes a braced stance, places the rifle against her shoulder, and checks the sights. She lowers the rifle. "How're the sights on this one?"

"True," someone replies.

"The first shot doesn't count." She steadies her stance and takes aim. She raises the rifle slightly then lowers it then raises it again.

"Five degrees," John states.

She adjusts her aim and fires. All eyes focus on the target.

Todd raises a pair of binoculars. "Bull's-eye."

"Okay, that one doesn't count," Trevor Nichols jokes.

She fires five more times. As soon as she lowers the rifle, two men race to the hay bale and replace the target. With excitement clearly evident, they sprint back and hold up her target. The men gather around. Ralph walks up behind the group.

Trevor clears his throat. "You can't repeat that."

With a wide grin, Ralph says, "She can waste all the ammo on bull's-eyes. She has an unusually steady aim."

"Okay, guys," Ryan announces. "This is your goal. First man to match this gets a week's extra vacation."

Trevor inquires, "That was a stationary target. How's she at moving ones?"

"I'll get some." John dashes to Lieutenant Williams' car and kneels beside the front wheel.

Brad watches with astonishment. "You're stealing an officer's hubcaps!"

John looks up. "Doesn't look like he minds."

The amused lieutenant grins. "Just small dents; no one will notice."

Within moments, Lily stands at the firing line with four men spaced in a semicircle behind her, each holding a hubcap. Ralph's carefully spaced verbal signals mimic the automatic launches of skeet. She expertly hits the first three. Each metallic ping echoes off the rocky hills surrounding the rifle range. The hubcap hurled by Lieutenant Jones sails backward, skips across the roof of Lieutenant Williams' car, and rolls into the brush.

Lieutenant Williams walks over, glares at the scratches on his car, and turns to face Lieutenant Jones with mock disapproval.

"Sorry," Lieutenant Jones apologizes.

"Okay, guys," Lily says, "enough playing around. I have a job for you. Let's get to it."

Lieutenant Williams looks at the capable baroness with new respect. Ralph had said she was a crack shot, but he now knows that it is no exaggeration.

Doug Kasper jots down a note, slips his memo pad into his shirt pocket, and searches the market for the other customer with whom he needs to speak.

"Do you have a death wish?"

He pales as he recognizes Matt Finke's voice and turns to face the conniving and ruthless power baron, the heartless brute who gouges everyone with high rates for water, a vital necessity. With trepidation, he looks into the cold, steely eyes on the narrow face and swallows. "Of course not."

Matt waits for a man laden with a load of pipe to pass. On the unusually hot August morning, the noisy market bustles with activity. Their conversation will not be overheard even though they are surrounded by hordes of shoppers, vendors, and delivery men. "If you keep talking to Mrs. Schwartz, you'll meet an early demise."

"It's just business."

"Business?"

"Yes. She has quite a head for business, and I'm finding her suggestions to be quite helpful," Doug admits, hoping to appease the irate brute.

"How entangled is she in your operations?"

"She merely makes suggestions. She doesn't intrude."

"Really?"

Doug nervously nods. Sweat rolls underneath his collar. He shifts his weight but doesn't dare lift his hand to wipe the copious beads of sweat from his brow.

Matt's tone of voice remains demanding. "Is she pushing for the electric co-op?"

"No. We stick to business and ... ah ... general conversations."

"If you get too involved with her, she will as soon as she has you firmly in her snare."

Doug swallows. His voice cracks, "I don't think so."

"Do you have a reason for that or are you naively thinking the best of your business partner?"

"She's not my business partner, and I do have a reason for thinking that."

Matt glares at the trembling man for a moment. "Well, out with it! What's your feeble reasoning?"

Doug takes a deep, calming breath and steels his nerves. "We've talked about it, and she thinks the assault against our way of life is going to come from outside."

"What does she mean come from outside?"

"Rebel bands; there are rebel bands with political motives. They're antislavery and violent. We have to band together to meet the challenge which is sure to come."

"Oh, is that what she says?" Sarcasm infuses Matt's rhetorical statement.

"That's the gist of it. Perhaps you should meet with her. I think you'll find it quite interesting."

"Oh, really?"

Doug wipes the sweat from his brow. His tension eases—slightly. He shifts his weight. "Yes. I resisted meeting with her since I'm opposed to the co-op, but when I finally confronted her, I was pleasantly surprised. Find out for yourself what she's all about instead of just assuming or ... ah ... listening to gossip."

Intending to intimidate, Matt Finke leans toward the plain-looking man who dares to voice a dissenting view. The meeker man cringes. With their noses inches apart, Matt Finke commands, "Until then, until I say so, just cut if off with her!"

"Ah ... I kind of can't." Doug's stomach churns; his legs feel like jelly.

"That's what I thought! She's got you in her clutches, doesn't she?"

"I ... ah ... owe her money," Dough admits merely because he has been backed into a corner. His assessment is that it is an extremely dangerous corner and his demise is imminent unless he can pull some rabbit trick out of his hat.

"You're borrowing from her?"

"I'm after profit, that's all."

"You're a goner!" Matt snarls. "She'll be making her demands, and you'll kowtow to her wishes because she's got her claws into you and that will be the end of you. Mark my word!"

"No, really; she's not like that."

Matt lowers his voice. "Someone's going to find your body soon."

Doug capitulates. "What do you want me to do?"

"Get out of her clutches and quit meeting with her."

"I can't do that. Well, I can probably quit meeting with her."

"Give her the money back."

"I can't; I spent it. ... All of it. I'll quit meeting with her and pay her back as soon as possible." Doug's eyes light up. "Wait a minute. Would you be happy if I soaked her?"

"What do you mean?"

"I could borrow more and ... not pay her back. How's that?" the meek baron offers.

"That's an idea. You will have to meet with her though."

Doug nods. "Of course, but I'll be as conniving as I can be and dupe her out of as much as I can."

"Fine, you may have a long career here. But I'd better not ever hear that you're for this co-op."

"Yes, sir. I'm definitely not for the co-op; never have been, never will be."

TWENTY THREE

Lily stops and looks up at the tall Southern gentleman. There is no smile on his face. She did not expect one, not when asked to meet at the hospital. "Commander, what did you want to see me about?"

His soothing drawl does not soften the sadness of his message. "Mr. Patterson was the first to use the new helicopter service."

"Sorry, how is he?"

"He died a few minutes ago."

"Sorry. Is his son here yet?" Lily asks.

"No, but we've called him. He was already on his way back and should be here within the hour."

He looks at the young man with her. "Where's Judge Hahn?"

"He's too ill to come. He'll probably die within days. We—"

The commander interrupts. "There's nothing the doctors can do for him?"

She shakes her head. "He's resigned and ready to meet his maker. We do have another lawyer. This is Raymond Harris. He's been here about three weeks. Ray this is Commander Somerton."

Ray holds out his hand. "Glad to meet you."

The commander firmly grips the attorney's hand. "Glad to meet you."

Lily inquires, "What's going on? Does this have something to do with Mr. Patterson asking to see Judge Hahn a while back?"

"Yes, he wrote his will. We'll need Mr. Harris to read it in front of Reginald."

Reginald Patterson and Dr. Maxton walk out of the morgue and into the hall. Max nods at Commander Somerton and walks away.

Reginald looks up at the tall commander. "I'll try to get the funeral arranged for tomorrow afternoon. Now why'd you want to see me?"

"Let's step into this room."

Commander Somerton opens the door and politely motions for Reginald to enter. The room has been recently cleaned and furnished with chairs. Lily Schwartz, Ray Harris, Eva Johnson, Linda Owens Jones, and Lou Piedmont are seated in a circle of seven chairs, waiting for the two men. In anxiety, Eva and Linda clasp their hands tightly. Lily, Ray, and Lou appear relaxed. Seated on one side of the door are Ralph Merrell and John Thorne. On the other side are Lieutenants Williams and Jones. Three are alert and watchful, as guards should be; however Lieutenant Williams allows Lily to dominate his attention.

Reginald stops and stares at the solemn group. "What's this about?"

Commander Somerton closes the door. "Please have a seat."

With anger, Reginald raises his voice. "I demand to know what's going on here!"

The commander sits down and calmly pleads, "Please have a seat, and we'll get to that immediately."

Reginald snorts in disgust but obediently plops into the remaining chair. He crosses his arms, a posture of defiance.

"Your dad wrote his will a few months ago. We need to read it."

"What's it say?"

"I don't know," Commander Somerton replies. "Mr. Harris will read it. He's an attorney."

Reginald Patterson looks at the floor for a long moment. He then looks up at the commander, whose worried expression does not adequately display the turmoil roiling within. Reginald's face, however, fully reflects his anger. "So I don't get anything?"

Lily states, "You know the business, the routes, the traders, and the workers. I suggest that you continue to do for the estate what you did for your dad. You'll be a great asset. As co-executor, what do you think, Commander?"

Disgruntled that she tossed the ball to him, he resolves to support whatever she suggests. "Sounds fine to me. What do you think, Mr. Patterson? Would you be willing to continue in your current capacity?"

"But I wouldn't own anything."

Lily ties to diffuse his tenuously controlled anger with a smile and soothing words. "I think you'll find that it doesn't really matter. Ownership is just a matter of the name on the system. There is no legal ownership yet, since no system of law has been reinstated. What does matter is that this is a well-respected and lucrative trading business, and we've been tasked with the responsibility to see that it continues to prosper during the transition phase."

"Why'd my dad do this?"

Lily looks at the commander.

Wishing that he could be a silent partner, he shrugs, more from resignation that he must answer than as an answer to the disinherited son's question. "He didn't say. He gave me the sealed will and a letter of instructions telling me who to gather for the reading. I didn't know I was being named executor until Mr. Harris read it. Neither did Mrs. Schwartz. I told her this morning that there was a will and her presence was requested." He looks toward Eva, Linda, and Lou. "I guess the three witnesses knew they'd signed a will but didn't know what it contained?"

Lou answers for all three. "That's right."

Reginald heaves a heavy sigh of apparent resignation. "Okay, I guess I'll have to acquiesce to this. So what do we have to do?"

Commander Somerton shrugs and looks at Lily.

She takes charge since it has become increasingly obvious that the commander is refusing to take the leadership role. "We'll need his web-link device. My computer guy will set it up for you. He can program it so you can use it for all transactions and send them to us. Since we're not experienced regional traders, we'll intrude as little as possible. We'll merely look the transactions over and authorize them. The system that's been set up for my other enterprises works very well. We've pretty much worked the bugs out of it by now, and I suppose it'll work for a trading company pretty much like it works for the electric utility. It should be easy to set it up for two executors instead of one. Let me know if you think something isn't working as well as it should, and I'll have him fix it. I think we'll get along just fine. The only thing that'll be much different is I think you'll have to spend more time in town instead of going on the routes. We need you to handle many of the tasks your dad did. The three of us can meet as necessary and iron out the details."

"What about the funeral expenses? I need to take care of that immediately," Reginald politely requests, although he is hoping to find some bone of contention and keep his relationship with the executors volatile.

The commander offers, "I'll call Marvin and have him put the funds on your card. He should be able to do that within a few minutes, and you'll be all set to go. Do you have an estimate of how much you'll need?"

Reginald shrugs.

"Call me when you figure it out. I don't think it'll take more than a couple of minutes. Also, after we get the system set up for the estate, I'm going to let Mrs. Schwartz take care of the day-to-day details and the financial side. She's much better at business than I am. I'll consult with her as needed."

"How long is it going to be an estate?" Reginald demands.

Commander Somerton looks at Lily with pleading eyes.

She turns back to Reginald. "That depends upon when we can convince the other barons to agree to other types of entities. That's going rather slow. We'll have to keep it as an estate until we can follow your dad's wishes and reorganize it as an autonomous entity. Then you will have ownership."

He snorts in disgust, "But not a majority interest! Well, I'll go make the funeral arrangements and call you." He rises and stomps out, making no effort to hide his anger.

Lou rises. "I don't suppose you need us anymore?"

The commander shakes his head. "Thanks for everything."

"No problem. We were glad to do it for Mr. Patterson." Lou, Eva, and Linda quickly exit the room as if escaping from the principal's office after being caught breaking a school rule and receiving a mere scolding.

Commander Somerton turns to Lily. "How're you doing?"

"Mr. Finke actually spoke to me on Monday. He was almost friendly," Lily admits.

"Almost?"

"Yes. He briefly mentioned being open to meeting with me sometime. But his tone was anything but friendly, actually more arrogant than usual."

With a glimmer of hope in his voice, the commander seeks affirmation of progress. "So he's willing to talk about a co-op?"

"He's thinking about talking with me, no mention of the co-op. That's all, but that's more than before." She draws a deep breath.

"I'm worried about you meeting with him. Murder apparently doesn't even cause him to blink."

She nods toward Ralph and John. "I have two bodyguards now, a policeman and a Seal. What could be better than that?"

"Has the equipment come in yet?"

She shakes her head. "I'll let you know."

"What if he doesn't meet with you?"

"We've discussed Plan B and came up with one suggestion, but it's dangerous."

"How dangerous?" the commander inquires as fear quivers inside his belly.

"It puts an infiltrator inside Mr. Finke's."

"How would you do that?"

"We set up a fake auction for Mr. Finke and force him to buy one of the Seals," Lily explains. "Lawrence says he can do it."

"How do you make him take your man?"

"He loses all other bids."

He nods. Her plan might work. "What does the infiltrator do?"

"Observe and see what the possibilities are, how loyal Mr. Finke's people are, etcetera."

"That's dangerous, but it may be an option that we'll have to take."

She nods.

He sighs. "How do you think Reginald's going to take this?"

"Not well." She looks over at John. "What's your take?"

"You're right," John replies. "He already has a plan."

Commander Somerton sits erect. "What's his plan?"

The perceptive guard shrugs. "When he ended the conversation and left, that means he's decided to do something other than argue but his attitude says it's not going to be acquiescence."

The commander rises. "I guess I don't have to warn you to keep a watch on him."

John grins. "We've been keeping a watch on him for a long time."

"Watch yourselves. I'll be seeing you." The commander and his lieutenants exit. Lieutenant Williams takes one last glance at Lily before he steps through the door.

John and Ralph stand as Lily rises. She looks up at the two tall men. "Let's go see what Mr. Kasper wants."

Lily takes note of Doug Kasper's worried expression and smiles. "Sorry I couldn't get here earlier this week."

"That's okay. I'm in no particular hurry."

To break his uneasy silence, she states, "I'm glad it's nothing urgent."

He looks at the ceiling.

"It appears to be something important. I can tell by your reluctance to address the issue."

He looks at her. "Sorry, but it's very difficult for me to make this request." He looks down at his clasped hands. His knuckles are turning white. He unclasps his hands then again clasps them.

She watches him closely, waiting for his request. It quickly becomes obvious that the burden of conversing falls on her. She breaks his uneasy silence. "You don't ever need to be reluctant to talk to me."

He looks up. "I understand that. This would be hard for me to bring up with anyone." He breaks off his stare and looks at the ceiling.

She glances at the ceiling. Amused, she assesses his literal ceiling as not being in danger of falling but something in his world does appear to be caving in. She decides to draw it out of him with a game of twenty questions. "Have you found a new supervisor?"

"Yes."

"How's he doing?"

Doug replies, "He wasn't familiar with this type of work, but Ramiro is helping him and together they're doing a great job."

"How's Ramiro's English?"

"Improving."

"It's too bad Roberto suppressed such a talented man," Lily states.

He shrugs.

"How much does he have to relearn?"

"A lot. Roberto had his English completely jumbled up and had him convinced that he was getting senile. I really appreciate your guy picking up on that."

She nods her thanks. "Have you received your shipments of breeders and layers?"

"Oh yes, last month."

"The engineers have told me the equipment is running smoothly and my supervisor of supplies is delighted with the processed chickens. Exactly what is bothering you? I've run out of guesses."

He wipes his sweaty brow, sighs then lays his hands on his desk and looks down. His silence is again extended.

"Come on, out with it or … shall I leave?"

He looks up with horror on his face. "Don't leave; I'd be in big trouble then."

She leans back in her chair, thinking of Mr. Finke and wondering what threat he has made against mild-mannered Doug. His lips are pressed into a thin line and his eyes plead for help. She leans forward and motions for him to lean forward. He brings his face within inches of hers. She cannot let on that she knows about Mr. Finke's brutal ways so whispers, "You're going to have to tell me, or I'll have no choice but to leave."

He breaks off their unblinking stare and looks down at his clasped hands. His knuckles are again turning white. His whisper is raspy and breaks with emotion. "I need to borrow more money."

She smiles. "What do you need to buy? More personnel, more breeders and layers, or do you need to improve your buildings?"

He relaxes—slightly—and looks her in the eyes. "I don't plan to spend it. I'll give it back to you later."

She raises her eyebrows. "Let me guess. You've been threatened?"

He leans back in his chair then quickly leans forward again and shakes his forefinger in the air. "I didn't tell you that!"

She smiles. "Of course you didn't."

He drums his fingers on his desk.

"How much do you need to borrow?"

"A lot."

"Twice as much as you already borrowed?"

He raises his eyebrows in surprise then takes in a big gulp of air. "I think that'd do it, and I can't pay you any back until … until …."

"Until the threat ceases?"

"Yeah! Until the threat ceases. That's a good way to put it." He wipes his face with his sweaty palms. They are sweaty because of fear; his air-conditioned office is pleasantly cool.

"And you are talking about not paying back any on the first loan either, aren't you?"

He nods.

She pulls out her web-link device and taps in the loan. After putting it back on her waistband, she looks at him and allows the silence to lengthen. She patiently waits for him to make inquiries into her plans for diffusing the threat. She is surprised that he doesn't pull out his web-link device and check the loan. She gives him several more seconds to make subtle inquiries, while wondering if he is capable of being subtle. Her assessment is that he is transparent and incapable of deceit. After giving him sufficient time to phrase a question, she stands. "I'll be going."

"Okay. I'll be seeing you around, but we can't meet anymore."

She sits back down. He is either very cunning or completely cowed by Mr. Finke. Her guess is the latter.

He looks at her in surprise. "I thought you were going?"

She clears her throat, leans forward, and whispers, "I was testing you to see if you were getting yourself out of danger by becoming a snitch who was supposed to find out if I knew anything or if I had any plans, etcetera."

He waves his hands back and forth in front of his face, palms out. "I don't want to know anything. I told him I was going to be very cunning and conniving, but I couldn't do it. I want to live my life in peace and stay out of it. This is all about the co-op, and I don't want any part of it. I just want to run my farm. I promise I'll pay you back. I don't know when, but I promise I'll repay you."

She smiles. "Okay, but I think you should spend at least some of this new loan for the sake of appearance. Expand your operations, improve your buildings, and buy more breeders and layers."

"I think I have enough for the market here. I don't need any more."

"Expand your market."

He looks at her in surprise.

"Mr. Patterson bought a truck to transport frozen fish. Go see Reginald Patterson and see if he can find a market in the surrounding towns for frozen chicken."

"I'd rather deal with Patterson, Sr."

"He died this morning. Reginald is running the business. The funeral will be tomorrow so Friday or Monday would be a better day to speak with him."

He smiles. "Okay. I should have known that you'd have some way to make the best of this situation."

"You're not going to tell me who threatened you, are you?"

He shakes his head. "He'd kill me."

"I understand; I won't press." She rises. "And I should catch you in public and get on to you for not meeting with me and for not paying me back. Understand?"

He smiles and nods. Suddenly he is completely at ease. "You're good. You're really good at this."

TWENTY FOUR

After shaking hands with Reginald Patterson, Lily walks away from the open grave. Ralph and John follow on her heels. Jack follows at a distance. She stops beside Curtis and Linda and turns back toward the procession paying their respects to the elderly trader by giving their condolences to his well-dressed son, despite the fact that they have no respect for the dishonest young man. She glances over the crowd gathered in the neglected cemetery. It is a large turnout, perhaps as many as five hundred. The talented and genial businessman was well respected, a very honest trader.

Never has she seen the local population dressed in their finery. Since Mr. Barton's demise, even the most powerful barons have fallen into the habit of dressing casually. But to honor Mr. Patterson, the silk suits and ties have been retrieved from mothballed storage and the white shirts stiffly starched. The authorities appear to have only one uniform but every officer's uniform is spotless and sharply creased, reminiscent of Commander Tyler's meticulously dainty appearance. Lily has donned a dark skirt, dressy white blouse, and black flats instead of her usual uniform of jeans, loose blouse, and canvas shoes. Marie even managed to procure a pair of hose for her to wear for the occasion; however she regrets having worn the clinging nylons on the hot and humid August afternoon.

She glances around at her guards, scattered among the crowd. Other than Ralph and his elite squad, she brought only former military men. Commander Somerton's men are out in force but gravitate toward the well-trained military men as if they feel a need for protection. Only Lieutenant Williams and the commander freely mingle with the crowd. Ann Somerton hangs onto her husband's elbow and smiles as he introduces her to one person after another. For safety, all the officer's wives stay within the heavily guarded confines of headquarters. This is a rare social occasion for Ann, which she is obviously enjoying. Four officers and Todd tail the couple for her protection.

Lily looks around at Linda, Eva, Lynnette, and the other women who came because they knew and loved the affable gentleman who frequented the clinic. Despite the heavy complement of guards, something about their presence makes her uneasy. Her thoughts turn to the raid four months ago. She tries to recall who commented that more guards would have been more unarmed targets for the raiders.

The procession ends. Reginald turns and speaks to a man waiting behind him. He signals several men on the outskirts of the proceedings. They pick up shovels and walk toward the grave. Reginald walks toward the line of cars on the dirt road running through the large cemetery on the edge of town. Lily turns and starts walking toward their vehicles. In addition to both vans and the SUV, she brought two cars assigned to the hospital and three of the pickups belonging to Mr. Barton's estate so she could transport as many guards as possible without being obvious by bringing the bus. Add all of the officers present and at least twenty percent of the attendees are security personnel.

A shot is fired. Commander Somerton collapses as pain sears his lower back. Ralph grabs Lily and turns her away from the assailant. The second shot pierces his hip. He pushes her behind a large headstone and collapses beside her. Jack quickly applies pressure to Ralph's profusely bleeding injury. Lily ignores the painful scrape on her knee and cradles Ralph's head in her lap as he lapses into unconsciousness. Tears stream down her cheeks.

Curtis pushes his young wife behind a headstone and pulls out his pistol. He searches in vain for the gunman among the terrified crowd. John crouches beside him and keeps his eyes focused on the calm assassin. He lightly touches the lieutenant's arm. Curtis surrenders his pistol to the marksman. John aims at Reginald as he purposefully moves among the scrambling crowd. Soon he will be within range for an accurate pistol shot. John is thankful that he has fired the young lieutenant's gun. Two days ago he assisted Curtis with the scavenged weapon, so he is not shooting blind with an unfamiliar weapon. The crowd is scattering in a general outward direction reducing the chances of John's shot causing collateral damage. A fleeting moment in the clear is all John needs to drop the irate son of the deceased baron.

Those nearest Reginald lunge forward at the sound of the third shot. A few dive for the dirt. Then all stop and look back. Reginald is sprawled face down on the parched grass in the neglected cemetery. His arms are at his sides. His small, easily hid pistol rests between his thigh and right hand. A pool of blood gathers underneath his head and slowly soaks into the dry earth. With his gun drawn, Lieutenant Williams breaches the circle of onlookers and approaches the fallen brigand. Cautiously, he kneels and touches two fingers to Reginald's neck despite the obviously fatal head wound. He holsters his pistol, picks up Reginald's, and stands.

John hands the pistol back to Lieutenant Jones. "You take the credit. I wasn't supposed to be armed."

Lily smiles as she looks up at newly appointed Commander Bruce Williams.

He returns her smile and lets his thoughts run wild. For the first time, he feels that his status is equal to hers. They are standing in the vacant hospital corridor around the corner from the bustle of activity in the intensive care unit. He takes notice of the mixture of aromas emanating from the disheveled baroness. A refreshing scent of soap is evident in spite of her sweat from being out in the sun for hours. There is also the smell of the grass from the stains on her clothing and the antiseptic on the bandage on her scraped knee.

"You seemed surprised that Robert so quickly authorized a successor before he went into surgery."

She nods.

She then steps closer for confidentiality. "I know he takes his responsibilities seriously. I was just surprised that he was clearheaded while in so much pain."

He stifles his thoughts and tries to concentrate on their conversation, but her step toward him has overloaded his senses. He has taken her approach as a sign of interest in him, sending his expectations spiraling into the stratosphere. "He'd already talked to all the lieutenants about a succession plan. That's one thing your men have taught. Succession of authority must be clearly delineated and changes ready to implement at a moment's notice despite the turmoil of the situation."

"I guess we call you Commander Williams now?"

He grins, pleased with the fact that she called him commander. As a ploy to get into her good graces, he feigns humbleness. "I'm merely the interim commander. Robert is still commander, just in case he recovers. He seems to think he won't."

Sadness swallows her face. "They said he probably won't recover function in his legs. They've already stashed a wheelchair in his room to make sure one's available for him. Even if he recovers it'll take some time, so I'm guessing that you're more than just the interim commander."

"It wouldn't bother me either way. Oh, Robert's condition bothers me. I'm just saying it doesn't matter to me which one of us is commander. We have the same agenda." He silently chastises himself for blundering because of her overwhelming presence. He does not want to come across as a tongue-tied, socially inept jerk. This is his chance, one that he has been craving for a long time, and he does not want to squander it.

"How's Ralph?"

Tears moisten her eyes. "They don't expect him to be paralyzed, but he lost a lot of blood. The bullet pierced a major artery. He's in serious condition. It's really touch and go right now. Our new blood bank is doing a booming business."

He leans his head close to hers. "The helicopter saved his life."

She nods. Their faces are mere inches apart. He is delighted that she does not recoil. He again takes this as a sign that she is interested in him—a personal interest, not merely a professional relationship. He quickly slips his arm around her waist. She pushes against his chest. He does not release her but tightly holds her as she struggles. He easily counters every move she makes as he visualizes her stunning face framed by a pillow.

Lily ceases her struggle and looks into his eyes. She senses no malice. Instead his eyes reveal sheer joy. She keeps her face away from his. She has no intention of consenting to his advances; she is merely gaining time to think. She is trying to recall a method of close-quarters fighting she studied several years before. She quickly abandoned it after finding it to be excessively brutal but now brings to mind every move she still remembers. As she calmly continues conversing, she will slowly reposition herself into a position such that she will be able to execute the move she selects as the most likely to catch the very capable interim commander off guard. "What do you think you're doing?"

His utter delight lights up his face with a broad smile. "Ah ... making it with the pretty lady." He rues not having a more suave answer; he is in grave danger of losing the opportunity to impress her.

Lily moves one foot slightly. "With what I know about you, why would you even try that?"

For lack of a better idea, he decides to impress her with feigned altruism. "I was hoping to make a stronger alliance with the most respected baroness. I want to retain the progress Commander Somerton has made by strengthening his network of relationships, and I know you're a bit peeved with me. I want to make sure there're no steps backwards during this interim phase."

She keeps her expression neutral to avoid revealing her utter disbelief of his statement and moves her hands slightly. "Let's keep our relationship strictly professional. No honest person has to use backhanded methods with me. In fact, such tactics backfire. I'm now more peeved with you. You've definitely made a backwards step. So let me go," she demands. She is hoping he acquiesces; it is a better alternative than the move she is considering.

He grins mischievously, convinced that she is merely playing hard to get; it is a game he has seen many women play. He reasons that he is powerful, physically attractive, and congenial; he has always been able to select the most attractive, unattached female present and preempt the attention the other men were lavishing on her then deftly play her hard-to-get game. Though he is now after a lasting relationship, he naïvely expects success from the same tactics. "What if I don't want to?"

She repositions one arm. "You know you're pretty good to counter all my moves."

He shrugs. With no intention of letting her go, he tries to distract her. "You know you had an observer when you took down Commander Tyler."

"Oh really? Who?" She shifts her stance.

"Buster."

She makes a small adjustment in her stance. "So you knew all along?"

He chuckles. "I knew from the moment that Ralph warned me that you were a marksman. I was pulling my gun instead of unshackling his ankles, and he told me I was a dead man if I tried it. I knew he meant it."

She stifles her surprise, calmly states, "You knew Ralph?" and makes another small move.

"I meet him a few times, but I don't think he remembers me. If he was all right with you going into that alley for a showdown with Commander Tyrant then I knew you had to be good, very good."

She keeps her muscles relaxed as she steadies her stance. "Where'd you meet him? Did he arrest you or something?"

Commander Williams laughs. "Of course not; I'm a … I was a Texas Ranger."

"Why've you been hiding your skills? You could've been helping Commander Somerton train the officers." Almost prepared to take action, she visualizes each tiny step of her selected tactic.

"I hid it for the same reason you hide your skills."

She raises her eyebrows and postpones her move. Their conversation has captured her attention.

He continues, "I'd have been signing my death warrant, if anybody had known. They'd have plotted and killed me out of fear that I'd kill them. I saw it happen several times."

"Who would've killed you?"

"The other officers or the commanders: the prior commanders, not Robert of course."

A thoughtful frown furrows her brow. "Is that why you didn't become a co-commander after the coup?"

"Yeah. Spencer asked, but I suggested Robert instead. I didn't think things were stable enough for me to enter the limelight, and I was concerned that Spencer might be overthrown very soon and the usurpers would take his co-commander down too."

"Are you the reason for Robert's success?"

He laughs. "I've supported him from behind the scenes. He's a good man, a very good man, but with absolutely no training in law enforcement."

She gives him one last chance to release her. "I think it's time you let me go."

He grins and shakes his head. She grabs a pressure point and squeezes.

"Ahhhh!" He releases her.

She steps back and releases her grip, delighted that he immediately acquiesced and that she does not have to follow through with the brutal takedown.

"You must've studied with bouncers. You know that's an illegal move?"

"Not for a petite woman defending herself from an aggressor."

He realizes that he misjudged; she has no interest in him. Disappointment floods his senses, but he realizes that he should have guessed that she would not be open to a liaison. That she requested Bibles from Buster before requesting ammo should have been a dead giveaway. He did know as soon as Buster delivered his report that he had no need to fear the baroness. Someone who requested Bibles would not slaughter her enemies or seek political dominance for selfish reasons, but he never even considered the moral implications in regard to her 'private' behavior. That was probably blindness on his part due to his unwillingness to give up his dream, his fantasy of her.

He seeks to recover some semblance of dignity and refocus on his job of bringing stability to the community. That she is a major player in the community requires that he regain her respect; he needs her support. His blunder must be pushed into the background. "Okay. I misjudged. I won't hit on you anymore."

"I don't see what you were waiting for? With Robert as commander, why weren't you working with him toward making a difference? Surely you were no longer in danger."

He is amazed and delighted that, without the least hint of anger, she has so quickly returned to their conversation as if nothing happened between them. He forces his thoughts to her question. "It was obvious that all of the other officers were untrained. Even with Robert as commander, I assumed if I appeared trained, I'd be a target. It'd only take one jealous, ambitious officer to take out a competitor, so I bided my time until I could move up in the hierarchy without drawing suspicion. Now with all of the officers receiving training, it no longer matters. I was waiting for a time when I could be effective and I think that time has finally come, especially since they elected me as Robert's successor. All of the lieutenants have become excellent officers. I no longer feel threatened."

"Just be an honest commander," she softly but sternly demands.

"I will," he promises. "That's of paramount importance."

"You'll also need to champion the rights of women."

"I will!"

She shakes her finger at him. "You said that too quickly and too emphatically."

He shrugs. "Why do you say that?"

"Because of the way you just treated me."

"Oh? Okay." He sighs as he realizes that she will never let him forget his trespass, but instead of a fit of ineffective anger, she will skillfully and effectively force a permanent change in his behavior.

Lily crosses her arms. "I'm going to watch you on that."

"You know I'm trustworthy. I treated Josie all right, didn't I? I could have gotten away with anything, and she wouldn't have ever said anything. But that's why we deposed Commander Blakely: to put a stop to that in the prison."

"But you didn't treat me right."

"Okay, I'm sorry. It won't happen again. I just misinterpreted signals," he apologizes, hoping he can regain some of the ground he has lost with the powerful and determined baroness.

"Not with any woman."

"Okay, not with any woman. You're really adamant on this aren't you?"

She nods. "Have you ever been married?"

"No."

"That's not what you told Josie."

"I was trying to make a good impression so I told her that my wife had died but it was my live in who died."

"You need to be honest with her," Lily insists.

"You think so?"

"If you want to continue your relationship as an adopted uncle, you'd better come clean. Otherwise you'll end up with one irate ex-niece. So do you have children?"

He grimaces. "Just one."

She looks askance at him. "So you were lying about that too?"

He nods.

"You don't look the least bit happy about having a child."

He shakes his head. "It was the first one, the first time, and she came after me for child support. It's dogged me ever since. I never even saw her again, just sent her money. Well ... until the terrorists' attacks."

"No visiting rights?"

"I never even requested it. I don't even know her name. I just made sure it never happened again."

She grimaces as she looks up at the tall man—the not-so-honest commander. "Next time you come out or Josie comes in, why don't you be honest with her?"

"Do I have to?" he pleads, hoping to avoid the ego-busting admission of dishonesty. He would rather just disappear from Josie's life than apologize.

She sighs. "Of course you don't have to but if you want her respect, you'd better."

He knows that to have the respect of powerful Baroness Jackie Schwartz, he has to follow her advice, even if he thinks it is ill advised.

Commander Williams casually strolls through the busy market. Over the last hour, he has noted the presence of every officer assigned to patrol. Each has been diligently patrolling his assigned area, and that is an improvement. The training is making a difference.

A familiar voice behind him suddenly snarls. "I hear you're the new commander."

Commander Williams turns to face Mr. Finke. "That's correct."

Mr. Finke sneers. "Do you know about Officer Hayes?"

The interim commander readies himself for a quick draw of his weapon, if it should become necessary. He silently rues the fact that the nearest officers have not been sufficiently trained for a potentially deadly situation. He takes note of Mr. Finke's men nearby and carefully moderates his voice to keep his fear undetectable. "Yes."

"How many officers are you willing to lose?"

"None."

"So Officer Hayes is sufficient?" Mr. Finke guesses.

Commander Williams counters, "His death was unnecessary."

"Unnecessary? Commander Somerton was pushing for this co-op. Just be sure you don't ever push for any changes in our way of life."

"I have no interest in the co-op. Never did, never will."

"That's good to hear. So what are you going to do about Mrs. Schwartz and the changes she's pushing for?"

The commander replies with a confident voice, "Nothing."

"Nothing!"

"That's right: nothing. She's alone in her struggle against our system. Slavery is working just fine, and there's no need to change anything.

Everybody knows that. Leave her alone, and her movement will die for lack of support."

Mr. Finke places his hands on his hips. "What about the politically motivated bands of bandits who're using violence to overthrow slavery?"

"I haven't heard about them, but don't worry. Our forces are strong. We'll be able to take out any little band of bandits, whether they're politically motivated or just mere criminals. We certainly cleaned up that bunch who hijacked Mr. Patterson's truck, before they had a chance to do any significant damage."

"I think I'm going to like working with you," Mr. Finke declares.

"The feeling's mutual."

"So you think we have nothing to fear from outside. Slavery isn't being overturned in other areas?"

"Not that I know about. None of the transport officers have reported any problems in the areas around here," the commander asserts.

"That's good to hear. I'll be seeing you."

"Good day, Mr. Finke, and don't worry about a thing. I'll see to the safety of the town. And remember: no one is taking Mrs. Schwartz seriously."

Mr. Finke nods and walks away.

Commander Williams puts his hand over his mouth to hide his grin. His thoughts are focused on his crafty deceit; he easily manipulated the power-hungry baron. Merely tell a person what he wants to hear, and you have him eating out of the palm of your hand. He would like to employ the same technique on the powerful baroness, but she seems to see right through a person and read their inner motivation.

He rues the distraction of his thoughts wondering back to the attractive baroness, who is still out of his league, and forces his thoughts back to Mr. Finke. He would like to be the one who takes out the little weasel, as he thinks of him, but realizes that it will be Jackie or one of her bodyguards who will have that privilege. As he watches the sinister baron disappear into the market, he thinks: *Goodbye, Mr. Finke! We'll be replacing you with somebody trustworthy. Soon! Mr. Finke, enjoy your last two weeks on this earth!*

TWENTY FIVE

Lily rouses from the heat-induced sleepiness of the sweltering afternoon and picks up her ringing phone. "Lawrence, what've you got?"

Amusement is clearly evident in his voice. "You have a real nasty reply on instant messaging."

"From who?"

"Howard Wood."

"Oh, our former senator. How nice. I'll be right there."

She dashes from her office, into the east wing, and into Lawrence's cluttered lair. She plops into the chair beside him and quickly scans the vehement tirade against her and the brutal system of slavery. With a relaxed, pleased smile, she jubilantly declares that the man who dares to voice his dissent against the brutal but well-entrenched system of slavery is, "A man after my own heart."

Lawrence laughs. "I guess he didn't like you trying to redeem Mindy."

"He sure doesn't. But I had to go really high to force a reply."

"I'll say. You haven't ever paid a hundred thousand for anyone, have you?"

"Nah, fifty thousand for Lucas was the highest. Well, let's reply."

He selects reply and places his hands over the keyboard.

She dictates, "Senator, I agree wholeheartedly. Just as you are, I am a protector. Ralph has been my bodyguard for over two years. I would like to reunite the family. It doesn't matter to me whether they live with me or with you. And if you know where their children are, we should strive to reunite them with their parents. Lawrence, move that last sentence. Put it before: It doesn't matter to me. ... Okay. At the present time, Ralph has been injured—change that to: severely injured. ... And his condition is serious. His life still hangs in the balance. Take out: still. ... If possible, I would be willing to pick up Mindy instead of having her travel through the prison system. After he has recovered, I suggest that we let them choose where they live. Okay Lawrence, give him my phone number too, and we'll see where this takes us. No, wait a minute. Go back and add or somewhere else after with me or with you."

"Are you hoping he's actually protecting her? After all, Mr. Barton claimed to be a protector."

Lily replies, "From what I know about the senator, I'd expect him to be a noble man. Walter followed politics closer than I did, and he admired Senator Wood."

"So did my mom. The only time she ever voted was when he was up for reelection."

He holds the pointer over the send icon. "Now, knowing that we have no assurance that instant messaging is secure, do you want me to send this revealing message?"

"For Mindy, I most certainly do."

"Okay, that's done."

Two days later, on a sweltering Friday afternoon in late August, Lily instructs, "This is where we stop."

Pat Cooper applies the brakes and slows the tractor-trailer rig to a crawl. He pulls into the parking lot of an abandoned truck stop. A couple of armed men stand just inside the vandalized building. Lily checks the nine millimeter pistol in her waistband behind her back. Brad Kraft opens the passenger door and descends to the ground. He steps to the side and points his rifle toward the ground. John Thorne follows. He steps to the other side and points his rifle downward. Lily climbs down and walks toward the building. She pauses beside gas pump number five as instructed by former senator Howard Wood.

A man with a mane of untamed white hair steps into view inside the building. He scans the area then walks out the door and toward her. He stops five feet away.

She is surprised at the unkempt appearance of the usually well-groomed, middle-aged politician. His trials over the last three years appear to have aged him considerably. She wonders about their living conditions. They might be barely eking out a primitive existence without a barber or even an iron. Perhaps they do not have electricity. She immediately recalls his instant messages and realizes they must have electricity. "Hello, Senator."

"Hello, Mrs. Schwartz."

"Did Mindy assure you that I'm legit?"

"She did. She didn't recognize Jackie Schwartz but when I told her Lily Schwartz, she recognized you immediately. She and their three children are ready to go. Did you have any trouble getting here?"

"My military men took out one small group of bandits who attacked."

"Did you sustain any injuries?"

"No," Lily replies.

"Your guys are good, huh?"

She nods. "Do you know Commander Perkins?"

"He runs that town you passed through. We stay away as much as possible."

"Did you know he's protecting people too?"

"No," he replies.

"Perhaps you could work with him to improve conditions in this area."

"We don't want to jeopardize our safety. We're irritated that he came out and forced us to register on that diabolical slave registry."

"If you weren't on it, I wouldn't have found Mindy and we wouldn't be reuniting the Merrell family."

He sighs and reluctantly admits, "That's true."

"Isolationism isn't going to be safe in the long run."

"The world is too uncivilized."

"It's changing," Lily counters.

"It is? People are abandoning slavery?"

"Many are willing. They just need a leader to step forward."

He stares at her with skepticism.

"I'm on the cusp of changing the system in Somertonville."

"Really? How'd you do that?"

Lily replies, "Years of networking and strengthening our position in the area."

"How'd you strengthen your position?"

"We developed a strong economic presence in the community, trained our men as guards, and established a military."

He admits, "I don't have the resources to do that."

"You could develop them."

"How'd you develop them?"

"We found a service we can sell to others and use the proceeds to redeem our loved ones from the barbaric system of slavery. We started with just twenty-five women and children. Now we have well over a thousand. In fact, we passed one thousand a long time ago. It might even be up to two thousand now. Our economic presence and influence in the community is significant. We have the kind of sway you used to have in the Senate and in your party."

He grins. "You said *your party.*"

"I'm too independent to desire party affiliation."

With a mixture of amusement and surprise at the humility of the powerful baroness and her unabashed truthfulness, he rhetorically asks, "You're not trying to impress me, are you?"

She shifts her weight and soberly retains her all-business demeanor. "I'm not trying to impress you with me. I am trying to impress you with the opportunities open to you to make a difference. We don't have to see eye to eye to be allies."

"Okay. Now back to your methods. You're saying that you participate in the slave culture?"

"We redeem our loves ones and the occasional stranger in need. I never sell any of our residents, not even a stranger who has turned out to be problematic."

"How'd you get started with the military?"

She looks down at the ground and then back up. "One of the women we rescued is the wife of a Navy Seal. I searched for him and eventually found him. He has replaced Ralph as my bodyguard and is standing over there by the cab."

He looks over at the two armed military men standing alertly by the cab.

"There's someone I want you to meet," she states.

He glares at her. She signals. Brad walks to the trailer, raps five times then returns to his position near the door. The rear door of the trailer opens. The men inside the building suspiciously aim their weapons toward the activity. An unarmed young man jumps to the ground. He strides toward Lily and the senator.

She smiles. "Do you recognize him?"

"Perry Graves, my nephew."

"Yes. He and four of his buddies are willing to stay with you and be the start of your military force. We can't spare any weapons, but we have an officer with us. He came along to make a purchase of weapons and ammo for the authorities. He could advise you on procuring weapons."

"I don't know that I want a military."

"It's for safety, not for using force against others. You must use political means to form alliances to bring about change in the abusive culture. Fear will never be a good ally. You can't use force to effect lasting change, but you mustn't live in fear of others either. Perry and his men can tell you how we've brought about change and help you get started here. You don't have to copy our methods, just use them to stimulate discussion and consider your options here. One of the most important elements is a good relationship with the local commander, and I have information from a reliable source that Commander Perkins is a good man."

With skepticism, he glares at her.

"I'm known as an honest and fair baroness. I'm well respected and trusted. You'll have a leg up on that. You're already known as honest and fair, and you're definitely well respected and trusted. I had to prove myself in that respect. Others will listen to you. Like I said, people are waiting for a leader to step forward. You could be that leader."

"Very well; I'll consider your suggestions, but I make no promises."

"We never ask for promises."

He looks at the ground. "I'm not sure how we'll manage to ... ah ... increase our influence."

"I have an unofficial bank and am willing to loan you a grub stake to get you started in some enterprise."

Without blinking, he stares into her eyes. "Unofficial since there's no government to issue a banking charter."

She nods.

"How much interest do you charge?"

"I've never charged interest. Banking isn't one of our for-profit enterprises. I've been helping beleaguered but honest barons get a leg up over the despicable, threatening charlatans who are ... who are ... trying to get them to ... ah ...."

He suggests, "Toe the line, their barbaric line?"

"Yeah, their extremely barbaric line."

"I'll consider your suggestions."

She replies, "Thank you. I look forward to working with you."

"I'd like to speak with you alone for a few minutes," he requests.

Perry states, "Uncle Howard, I'll wait by the truck."

He thrusts his hand toward Perry who smiles and steps forward. They shake then Perry strides to the trailer.

The white-haired gentleman steps toward Lily and lowers his voice. "Mindy told me that Walter Schwartz is your husband."

Surprised, she replies, "Yes, did you know him?"

"I met him once. Do you know Lawrence Brighton?"

She arches her eyebrows even higher. "Yes, do you know him?"

"I never met him. How are they doing?"

Solemnly, she states, "My husband was killed soon after the terrorists' attacks, but Lawrence has been with me for about two and a half years. He was one of the first two that I redeemed. That's really how I got involved in the slave system. I saw him on the auction block, had the means to redeem him, and could not leave him in slavery. He'd married shortly before the terrorists' attacks and hadn't even seen his son. They now have two children and a third on the way."

With obvious pleasure, he states, "So you have the whole family?"

"There's always more extended family we can search for, but I have all of those closest to him. What's your interest in him?"

Obviously embarrassed, he clears his throat. "He's my son."

"Now I can see why you didn't want to meet him."

"I'm sorry that I felt that I couldn't. I'd have liked to get to know him."

"I know this was confidential. May I tell him who you are, now?" she requests. "He wants to know."

"I'd like that. All reason for keeping it confidential is gone. I wish I'd … ah … gotten to know him. Now that our way of life has been destroyed, it's given me a whole new perspective on what's important. I've missed … ah … a lot by not getting to know him. I now wish that I'd given up my political career when Walter informed me that I had a son."

"Perhaps after travel is safer, you can meet."

He nods. "I'd like that. In the mean time, I'd like you to tell him my story, how such an upright man as I, got his mother pregnant."

"I don't think youthful indiscretions need to be explained."

"I wish it were that simple." His expression clearly, but subtly, conveys his insistent determination.

She stifles her sigh of resignation. "Very well."

"I'll be brief. It was the night before my wedding. I had a very sedate bachelor's party. Near the end, one of my acquaintances—he can hardly be called a friend—crashed the party. He must have put something in my drink because I left with him. I wouldn't have ever done that; I didn't trust him at all. He took me to his apartment where several of his buddies and some girls were partying. I eventually realized they were high school girls who were ecstatic to be partying with college guys. To make a long story short, they plied me with booze—which I never drink—and I woke up in the bedroom.

"I began to sober up—since they hadn't been plying me with booze for a while—and begin plotting my escape. I knew where Eugene kept his emergency key, so I went out the window and took his car.

"Later, I sobered up enough to realize the gravity of my situation. I was obviously still under the influence. I was speeding and driving erratically. I was also in a stolen car and didn't have my license or insurance and I'd just ... ah ... maybe ... ah ... been with a minor. I didn't know at that time what had happened, if anything. And," he emphasizes, "I was the youngest son of Senator Woods. My oldest brother was making his first bid for office. I immediately slowed down then turned around and went to the restaurant and got my car. Then I went to Eugene's apartment. The door was open and everyone was totally plastered. I grabbed all my clothes, made sure I had my wallet, and split.

"Please tell Lawrence that his dad ... that I'm ... that I'd never ... oh, I don't know how to put this."

"I understand," Lily soothingly replies.

"I'm a politician and here I am at a loss for words."

"It's difficult. I suppose there's a reason why you didn't bring charges against your buddy."

"Don't call him my buddy. Eugene was more of an adversary. He tormented me all through college. He was always baiting anyone who professed to be a Christian. If he found any little chink, any little indiscretion, he'd spread an exaggerated version all over campus. He looked like an angel with those dimples on his boyishly good-looking face, but he was a devil."

She unwittingly smiles as an image of Mr. Lorne pops into her head.

He angrily glares at her. "What's so funny?"

She suppresses her amusement. "I'm sorry if my reaction offended you, but that description of Eugene reminds me of one of the most despicable barons in our town."

"I wouldn't be the least bit surprised if Eugene Lorne was a brutal slave master now."

Surprise registers on her face.

He looks at her with shock, not mere surprise. "Don't tell me it's him?"

"I don't know his first name, but his last name was Lorne."

He squints. "You said was?"

"He's dead, and you may be amused to learn what happened."

"Oh, really." He pushes his hands into his pockets and glares at the assertive woman.

"Yes."

"Now you've made me curious," he states.

"It was accidental."

"Why would I be amused at accidental?"

Lily reports, "One of his slaves pushed him down the stairs."

"Accidentally?"

"He … ah … got out of line with her daughters and she confronted him. He pushed her. She pushed back."

He looks at her with a blank expression for a moment, then relaxes, suddenly comfortable in the formable presence of the petite baroness. "Was she punished?"

"Her husband confessed and got the firing squad."

"I'm so sorry."

She smiles to reassure him. "She recently remarried. He's a very nice young man who'll be a great father to her three young daughters, and I think they have a son on the way."

"That's good to know. Say, did he have two moles—"

"Yeah," she interrupts, "on the left side of his neck?"

"Yes. So, it was him! Well, back to your question before I got sidetracked with vehemence for Eugene. Sorry about that. I shouldn't be so vindictive in my thoughts about him. Okay, I'm off track again. Back to your question: why I didn't press charges.

"I was thinking about my wedding and my lovely young bride and my acceptance to a prestigious law school and following my dad into politics and Bill's first campaign and that it'd be a he said, ah … I said situation if I said anything about Eugene's dastardly deed, especially without the least bit of proof. So no, I didn't bring charges against Eugene. I didn't want to face any scandal. It probably would have sidetracked my dad's well-established political career, and I'm sure it would have cost my brother the election." He takes a deep breath.

She takes the opportunity to query, "I didn't know you were married?"

"She had it annulled. I ... ah had trouble getting over Eugene's dirty trick."

"I'm surprised you didn't remarry."

He shakes his head. "I was thrown for such a loop, that it was years before I even considered it but by then almost all the single women my age were divorced. The few dates I had were agonizing. I gave up and threw myself into my career. I thought maybe a little later I'd find a chaste widow."

She smiles to hide her discomfort with hearing his confession. "Thanks for letting me come get Mindy and their children. Are you ready to make the trade?"

"Yes, just tell Lawrence that his dad ... that I was just young and perhaps a bit naïve and got Shanghaied by an unscrupulous adversary. And I know that money doesn't make up for ... me ... ah ...."

"I understand. I'll tell him."

"And I hope he had a very nice wedding, and I'm sorry his computer business didn't pan out."

"You know a lot about him."

"Walter kept me informed, and I footed the bill for everything."

She hides her surprise. She had wondered why her husband wasn't disturbed about losing fifty thousand on Lawrence's ill-fated computer venture, but it never occurred to her that someone else was financing it.

TWENTY SIX

Pat Cooper slows the tractor-trailer rig on the downhill slope. Brad Kraft pulls his vibrating phone from his pocket. Lily Schwartz leans into the cab from the sleeper section. She is thankful that Mr. Hobbs has managed to increase phone coverage between towns. Coverage is not complete. There are dead zones on the more remote stretches of road, but his ingenious blend of amplifying antennas near each town and camouflaged, off-road relays strategically placed on high ground has enabled them to remain in contact most of the trip. In addition, Al said something about the satellites coming back online had enhanced phone service in the remote areas.

Brad slips his phone into his pocket. "Al says bandits are beating someone up." He puts his binoculars to his eyes. "Rescue her?"

"Definitely," Lily replies.

"Mindy, stay put—again. We'll leave a Seal to guard you and the children." Lily's repeated assurance is not to inform Ralph's wife, who has been through the same scenario a couple of hours ago, but for her peace of mind and reassurance that she and her children will be safe again, just like last time. Lily grabs her rifle.

As they slow to a crawl, Lily observes the melee. A slender black woman is being beaten by a bearded white man in a blue baseball cap. Six armed men, also with beards, are egging him on. A sedan and a pickup are parked at angles on the side of the road. Behind the vehicles is a small clearing and behind that thick brush extending over rolling hills to the horizon.

Brad pulls out his phone and informs Todd Jenson of the situation. Todd is in the trailer with three squads of armed guards, both military and Ralph's elite force. Brad slips his phone—on speaker mode—into his shirt pocket.

The bearded men take notice of the slowing semi and swing their weapons toward it. Brad is aiming his rifle out the window. John Thorne is behind him, his rifle beside Brad's head. He would lose an eardrum if John fired, but that is better than losing his life. Lily is stacked behind John.

The color drains from Pat's face and beads of sweat glisten on his forehead. He keeps his foot on the brake and resists the urge to floor the accelerator—the usual practice, despite the condition of the roads. Even with a bribe for the bandits, drivers never slow down. There is no confronting the armed and trigger-happy thieves. Bribes—mostly food— are left in desolate areas which provide no cover for the ambushers. Quick signals are exchanged, giving the location of the drop. No signal means bullets as they pass. No bribe at the site means an ambush for two or three trucks from the same trucking line. The singular law of the lawless road bandits, pay the bribe or die, is strictly enforced without mercy. It is, however, a one-sided arrangement; they ambush truckers despite complete compliance if they wish to steal the entire load.

Brad barks the signal. "Now!"

Todd relays the order to his men. The rear doors swing open. Armed men leap onto the pavement. By the time the semi comes to a complete halt, the standoff is in place.

"Back off!" Brad orders.

The unarmed man in the blue cap calmly looks at the large, well-armed group descending from the rear of the trailer and spreading out in a large semicircle. He hears their boots on the pavement as a group dashes to the front of the semi to enlarge the semicircle as far as possible. It would be a decidedly unequal confrontation even if they weren't obviously a military unit. He releases the woman and backs toward the sedan, motioning for the others to back away. Most of them slowly back past the vehicles and attempt to take cover.

Todd at the rear of the trailer and Ryan Sealy in front of the cab, reposition the teams under their command into a wider arc. It is impossible for the bearded bandits to get out of the line of potential fire without making a risky dash for the brush, some distance away. In addition, two snipers appear on top of the trailer; their job is to prevent any bandits from escaping across the clearing behind them and to search for any bandits who were already in the brush. The man in the cap looks up at the two snipers. He then leans against the sedan and casually crosses his arms and ankles.

Brad opens the door and climbs down. John follows then Lily. The man in the blue cap focuses his attention on the petite woman aiming her rifle at his head.

"Miss!" Lily glances at the woman. "Come with us."

"My daughter!" she yells in anguish. "They have my daughter."

Lily turns her attention to the arrogant man leaning against the car, assuming that he is the leader. "We'll take the daughter too."

A young man walks out of the brush and across the open space. He is unarmed and also sports a full beard and a blue cap. He walks around the pickup, leans against it, and crosses his arms. He looks over at the man and crosses his ankles in obvious emulation of a man he idolizes. He turns his arrogant gaze to Lily. "She's dead."

Recognizing her son's voice, Lily holds her breath. The woman wails. Lily recovers her composure and demands, "Get in."

"My daughter!"

"Just get in," Lily sternly demands.

"Mom," the young man calls. "Aren't you even going to speak to me?"

Lily looks at Walter "Walt" Schwartz, IV. "I wasn't planning on it. We'll just take the woman and leave."

"Mom, why'd you shoot Gyp?"

"I didn't shoot him. I beat him up when he pulled that knife."

"I don't mean when we broke in to get my clothes. I mean when we … ah … they shot Dad and my two bratty brothers."

"Well then, Walt, you know why I shot him. Say, Gyp's name wouldn't be Barton would it?"

"Yeah and quit calling me Walt. You know I'm Cuatro."

"No thank you, Walt. I'll call you by the name your father gave you."

"Mom, you're so cruel! Why won't you call me Cuatro? It's just a little thing. You don't ever give an inch do you?"

"You didn't obey us, so no privileges."

"Why didn't you just let me have my clothes that day? That's all we came for, just my clothes. We told you that."

Lily replies, "For one thing, you broke in. It was over a thousand dollars in damage and more important: Gyp pulled a knife."

"But why didn't you let us have my clothes? Why'd you have to beat both of us up?"

"Will was there. Why do you think I was home that day instead of at work? He was sick, and I had to take a sick day. No one who broke in and pulled a knife was going to get near him. You'd already proven that you had no qualms about injuring him and Wes. I found myself actually relieved that you'd run away, especially after that!"

The man leaning against the sedan lifts his chin in arrogance. "That's a Patterson truck. We'll be taking out all of them now."

She looks over at the bearded man in the cap. "Bob Gibbons! I didn't recognize my own brother either."

"Mom," Walt calls. "Uncle Bob told me about the martial arts lessons you took when you were small. He said you quit when you were twelve, so how did you remember enough to take down both Gyp and me when we came for my clothes?"

"I took up martial arts again when I left for college and continued them until the terrorists' attacks."

Walt exclaims, "All those exercise classes were really martial arts?"

"And gun safety and target practice, so don't think that I don't know how to use this rifle."

Lily turns back to Bob. "What're you doing all the way down here?"

Bob grins. "By the way, it's Bob Royal. Our name never was Gibbons. We just went by Gibbons because Mom was married to your dad."

"I'm not surprised."

Bob gloats. "We turned your son against you!"

"I've already figured that out. And by the way, Mr. Patterson is dead. We borrowed his truck for this one trip."

"Which Patterson?"

"Both," Lily replies.

"Really? What happened?"

"Senior died a natural death, and Junior decided to take out the executors of his dad's will. He was shot by an officer."

"Wills, huh? You're getting very snazzy there, and you can be sure Senior didn't die a natural death."

Although she would like to know more about Mr. Patterson's demise, she ignores his remark and changes the subject. "Let me ask you a question?"

He nods.

274

"Why'd you kill Mom?"

"She asked us to. She was dying and in pain. She wanted to end it."

Tears stream down Lily's cheeks. Even though she already knew, it pains her to have her mom's assisted suicide confirmed.

"How'd you know about that?"

Lily replies, "Clarence kept photos of all the murders you guys did. I'm surprised that you got away with so many."

He grins.

"Why'd you kill my dad?"

Bob laughs. "Because he took you away; he moved you into that apartment above his drugstore."

"Is that why you killed my fiancé and my aunt and uncle and the sheriff? Is that why you killed everybody, just because they helped me?"

"Yeah."

She clamps her lips into a thin-lipped grimace, her emotions on a roller coaster. She begins mental coaching: *Stay calm. Stay focused. Take a deep breath.*

Bob tilts his head back and stares at her. His grin broadens into an arrogant sneer which can be detected in spite of his full beard.

She speaks softly, "Why didn't you kill Posse? He helped me?"

"That's that old preacher, isn't it?"

She nods.

"They weren't home, so we trashed the house. Before we got around to going again, the sheriff came over asking a bunch of questions. Granddad embellished his answers and told us it'd be worse than death for a preacher to a registered sex offender."

"Now let me ask you a question," Bob demands. "Why'd you kill Tom?"

Lily cautions herself: *Stay focused! Don't roll you eyes! Take a deep breath.*

"No answer, huh?"

"I have no idea what you're talking about," Lily replies.

Bob grins. It is a sly malevolent grin. "He was with Gyp."

She raises her eyebrows in complete and utter surprise that her brother was with the group who killed her husband and two younger sons. "He was?"

Bob nods.

"What was he doing down here?"

"First, you tell me why you shot him."

"If he was with Gyp, you already know why. They shot my husband, two of our sons, our neighbor, and his four sons. All of them in the back. And they were coming after us. It was self-defense."

"You didn't recognize Tom?"

"I didn't even go look at them," Lily admits, thinking about the fact that she and Marie sent Angel over to pick up all of their attackers' guns and ammo while she and Marie dug the graves. "We just took care of our own dead, all eight of them. Now—"

"Mom!" Walt angrily interrupts. "You didn't even recognize me!"

She again raises her eyebrows.

He whips off his cap and pushes his hair back, revealing a scar. "You shot me!"

"Oh," she calmly intones. "You're the one who got away."

"You didn't recognize me," Walt repeats.

She shakes her head then turns back to Bob. "You still haven't answered my question, so tell me why Tom was here."

"Clarence called. He'd found you. Tom came to get you."

"Oh? … He and Clarence were always tight, weren't they? Let me ask another question. Why'd you kill Granddad? He definitely never helped me. We were always butting heads."

"He didn't keep his promise."

"I know he didn't keep his promise to me, but that wouldn't upset you. So what promise are you talking about?"

"You."

In shock, Lily exclaims, "Me!"

"Yeah, you!"

She is totally appalled that her granddad's promise was not just to Clarence but to her own brothers too. "That's sick!"

Bob laughs. "Not as sick as you think."

Focus Lily, focus! Don't get caught up in this! Get out of here! Take the woman and go! She turns to the woman. "Let's go. Can you get up?"

"You won the beautiful baby contest."

Bewildered, she turns back to Bob.

"Clarence and Tom asked for you so Granddad and Uncle Jonas set about getting you."

Focus Lily, focus!

"They took care of your mother."

Lily scowls. "What do you mean they took care of Mom?"

Bob laughs. "Not Mom, your mother."

"What?"

"They killed your mother. Then Mom began frequenting your dad's drugstore and a year later, they married."

She stares at Bob with her mouth hanging open, thinking: *he's my stepbrother!*

"But we never got you. You did everything but spend time with us: screaming fits and spending every moment at your dad's drugstore when you were small. Then there was gymnastics, ballet, karate, piano, summer camps, cheerleading, and everything else you could think of. When you were home you locked yourself in your room to 'study'. We never believed you were really studying that much."

"Home wasn't fun with you guys pestering me continually," she retorts. "Of course I wasn't going to spend any time with my tormentors."

Lily looks over at the woman. "Let's go. Now! Get in the cab."

The battered woman wipes her face with the back of her hand. "I want my daughter's body."

Lily sternly exclaims, "No! We're not taking any dead bodies! Get in!"

"Not without my daughter!"

Lily reaches over and takes John's rifle. Brad signals and the men methodically cock their weapons, taking the attention of the bandits away from John as he grabs the woman and carries her, kicking and screaming, into the cab.

Bob derisively yells, "Hey, Lily! Do you want to know what we did with your trust fund after you disappeared off the face of the earth?"

She climbs into the cab without turning back.

"We all got new cars, put a real nice sound system in the barn for the parties, and bought two more dairy farms: one for each of us, and gave the rest to Clarence as restitution for you ruining his football career. He was—"

The slam of the door cuts off Bob's taunt.

Tears roll down Lily's cheeks as she enters the sleeper section. She is not crying over her stepbrothers' embezzlement of her trust fund. She is grieving over the relationships stolen from her by the interlopers she used to call family. She thought she was staying one step ahead of mere tormentors, but in reality, she was merely thwarting their moves in a perverse 'game' in which she was the blind prey. She fears that their betrayal will scar her soul even more than their continual tormenting has already done.

Lily takes one last look at the terrified woman. John securely holds her. Blood is streaked around the sleeper section from scratches she inflicted on his arms before he physically subdued her. It is unlikely that mere words will calm the distraught mother. Lily glances at Mindy and her children huddled in a corner, behind the Seal guarding them. They are terrified.

Lily leans into the cab. "What's the plan for rescuing the girl?"

The woman ceases her struggle.

Brad points at the curve in the road. "When we're behind this hill, we'll be out of sight. Pat will slow and team two will jump out. Pat will speed up. They'll see the truck pass through that valley. It'll appear that we haven't stopped. Pat will stop around the next curve. Team three will guard you until they return. Team one is already hidden in the hills on the other side of the road. They'll keep track of them so they can't vanish before team two arrives. We'll have a two-pronged attack."

"I'm glad you anticipated this since I had no chance to signal," Lily states.

Brad looks at John.

John confesses, "That you didn't want the dead bodies was a clear signal to me. I relayed it to Brad."

"Thanks," Lily states and turns back to Brad. "Bring back the girl, dead or alive and—"

"Alive?" the mother screams with a mixture of anger and surprise. "That punk said she was dead!"

Lily turns toward her. "Walt's a liar. That's why I didn't want her dead body. There's only one way they could give it to us."

Lily turns back to Brad. "Bring back the bodies of Walt and Bob."

"Bodies?"

"I don't think you'll be able to take them alive, but if you do, I guess we can put them in prison. Don't bring back any other bodies; let's just bury family, no strangers. If you don't stop Walt and Bob, they'll continue to give us problems just like Mr. Barton did, so if at all possible, don't let them escape."

"You can let go now," the woman requests with calmness. John releases her.

She moves away and looks at Lily. "Thanks for burying my daughter too?"

"I hope she's alive," Lily replies.

"There's another girl."

"Okay, we'll bring her back too."

The woman lifts an eyebrow. "Where're we going?"

Lily smiles and takes a calculated risk. "To Jupiter."

"Jupiter! You know Jupiter?"

"You're Marissa Rae Worthington, aren't you?"

She nods vigorously. "How'd you know?"

"He described you."

"Just from a verbal description, you recognized me? You're good! I don't know anybody who can do that. So where's my husband."

Lily replies, "He has a stall in the market. We've been trading with him for years."

"How is he? Oh, he's probably just fine, isn't he?"

A satisfied smile lights Lily's face. "Yes, he's fine."

The truck slows. They listen to the doors opening and the men's footsteps as team two exits. The doors slam and the truck gains speed.

"Where does he live?"

Lily shrugs. "I don't know."

Marissa bites her lips.

"Are you wondering if he has a place for you?"

"I guess I am."

"If he has to arrange new quarters, we have room for you in the interim," Lily offers.

"How long can I impose on you?"

Lily laughs. "There's no such thing as imposing on us. Friends take care of each other, and that's what we consider Jupiter. There won't be any time limit from us on how long you can stay, but you and Jupiter may be anxious to get settled. We'll take you to the hospital first and get your injuries taken care of. We'll call Jupiter to meet us there."

"Pardon me," Mindy Merrell says. "How long is this raid going to delay us?"

LYNN VADNEY

Lily looks at John.

He shrugs. "I'd guess a minimum of two hours. They have quite a trek, there and back."

With his phone to his ear, Brad looks back. "I gave the go-ahead for team one to begin the assault. They have determined that the bandits have no backups waiting in the brush, so it poses no danger for just one team. That should speed it up even if they only manage to keep them penned down, and if the area remains clear, we can drive back to pick everyone up. That'll be better for the girls' safety."

Lily nods then reaches over and pats Mindy's knee. "I know you're anxious, but I'm sure Ralph is going to be all right." She almost adds *we've all been praying for him,* but decides that might reveal more about Ralph's condition than she wants to reveal. There are two problems about which she has not told Mindy. Ralph hit his head on the nearby tombstone when he fell; it resulted in a concussion. He was also near exsanguination by the time they were able to start his first blood transfusion. Only rapid infusion of fluids, continuous CPR, and valiant efforts by their lab tech to find matches from among the hordes who lined up to give blood saved his life. Whether he has irreversible brain or organ damage is still unknown.

"You said he's in serious condition, didn't you? Doesn't that mean he could die at any moment?"

"I think the crisis passed in the first twenty-four hours."

"Didn't you say he was still in ICU and unconscious when you left this morning?"

Lily replies in the most upbeat fashion possible, "They also said his blood pressure was good and his heart beat was regular, and they're expecting him to wake up at any time."

Mindy's youngest, her only daughter, bursts into tears.

Lily tries to reassure the young girl. "I'm sure your dad's going to be all right."

Mindy softly states, "That's not why she's crying."

The young girl wails, "I can't have a tea party with Daddy!"

Lily leans closer. "As soon as he wakes up and the doctor says it is okay, you can have a tea party at his bedside. I'll find you a tea set."

The mollified girl pats her backpack. "I have my tea set. I couldn't take my table and chairs, but Daddy never sat in the chair anyway. He said he didn't want to break it. I told him I wanted him to be comfortable. I didn't want him sitting on the floor, but my daddy says that sometimes we

280

endure pain for those we love. My daddy says we should never be afraid to stand up for what's right, and we should never be ashamed of what we do. If we're ashamed then it's something we shouldn't do. Daddies can have pretend tea parties with their girls; they don't have to be afraid of what people say about it. He said girls should be able to play football if they want to but that he doesn't think anyone should play football; it's too rough. Also wrestling and boxing are too rough. They're not good things to do since you can get hurt. Daddy did track and baseball and cheerleading, and he was team captain. Daddy says boys can be cheerleaders and girls can learn to shoot. Daddy says I have to be good no matter what people say."

Lily steals a glance at John. He is taking it all in—the wisdom the child gleaned from her dad. Lily wonders if he is going to take a page from Ralph and have tea parties with his girls. She resolves to find a tea set for the two Thorne girls. *No,* she corrects herself, *tea sets for every girl on the compound.*

Lily looks at John's arms, turns to the first aid kit, and opens it. It is empty.

TWENTY SEVEN

Gary Brown plops on the porch of the doctors' residence in the securely fenced compound behind the hospital, leans against the wall, and closes his eyes. John chuckles.

Lily looks up at John. "What's so funny?"

"It just occurred to me that I finally went on one of those reconnaissance missions that you promised me when I first came."

She smiles and softly raps on the door. "Yeah, it certainly took a long time to get around to it."

Max opens the door.

Lily states, "You wanted to see me as soon as I got back?"

"I couldn't sleep while you were gone. Come on in."

She steps inside. "My shadow's with me."

John steps inside. "We promised Ralph that we wouldn't leave her side."

A crooked smile tilts up one corner of Max's mouth. "He's unconscious."

"We promised him anyway. I hope he heard us. We want him to be at peace and focus on getting well."

"Well, go in the kitchen and get whatever you want. You've had a long trip, twenty hours."

"I'm not hungry, but I am very sleepy. We've been awake and on high alert the whole time. I'll just plop down on this new rug and take a nap." John stretches out on the floor and puts his arm over his eyes.

Lily walks over to the sofa. "He's already heard everything that I'd like to talk about."

Max sits down beside her. "So we're not going to talk about—"

"No. I have too much on my mind so—"

"Let me ask about Mindy first."

"We got her and their children. They're fine and have been protected by Senator Wood the entire time."

He puts his arm around her shoulders. "Does she know how serious his condition is?"

"I left it to the doctors to tell her. I didn't want to do it, at least, not while we were on the road."

"That's probably wise, but she may get mad at you for hiding it," he warns.

Lily shrugs. "She was, but I explained that I didn't want to tell her in front of her children. I wanted her to do the talking to them."

"I can see the wisdom in that."

"We also got Jupiter's wife and oldest daughter and another teenage girl."

Max furrows his brow. "I know you've talked about Jupiter, but I've forgotten who he is."

"Julius Worthington," Lily replies.

"Oh yeah; Teddy regaled me with the football exploits of Julius Junior and Senior just the other day. That's great. How'd you get them?"

"Bandits were beating them up."

Max exclaims, "Whoa! It must've been a rough trip."

"We took out three gangs of bandits, one on the way there and two on the way back. That's why it took us so long."

"Any injuries?"

"None other than Marissa and the girls."

Max looks over at John's bandaged arms.

"Marissa scratched him before she figured out we were helping her. They're not very deep."

"What about the bandits?"

"All dead," she reports.

"Sorry, is it disturbing you? How many did you shoot?"

She lays her head on his shoulder. "None. It's just that my oldest brother and Walt were two of the bandits."

"I'm so sorry." He puts his other arm around her and pulls her close.

She snuggles against his neck. "Both girls are in comas. Bob and Walt are the ones who put them there. We have no idea if they'll survive."

"Is that where the helicopter went?"

"I gather you weren't on emergency call."

"No, I had difficulty keeping my mind on work with you in danger. I had to swap some call around and lighten my load today. I couldn't focus. You didn't consider bringing the bandits back and putting them in prison?"

"None of them had any intention of surrendering. Two groups shot first. The third had the two girls and Marissa was in tears. We stopped down the road and the Seals went back to rescue the girls. It's really dangerous to travel. I'm surprised so many patients come from other towns and that the traders don't lose more men."

With concern, Max asks, "Does it bother you that you lost your brother and son?"

"Yeah, but I'm fairly certain that they sent those raiders three months ago. That's what I want to talk about. And I found out that I killed Tom, my middle brother, three years ago. He was with Clarence's sons when they shot Walter and the others in the back. They're not even my brothers. They're my stepbrothers. And they came down, just to capture me. Maybe I don't want to talk about it. Maybe I just want to cry on your shoulder, especially since Walt was there too, and he has no remorse over killing his dad and brothers. And I shot him in the head, left a scar on his scalp."

"Jackie." They look at John. He has lifted his arm and turned to look at them. "I think God was preparing you for the last three years. Only the strong have survived, and He made you strong."

He turns his head away and puts his arm across his eyes.

Lily snuggles against Max. He tightens his hug.

She whispers, "What really gets me is why my dad stayed. Surely he recognized the turmoil. Why didn't he take me and leave? He did leave, but not until three years after my stepmom died and then I was forced to go back when he ... died." She cannot bring herself to say murdered.

Max gently strokes her hair. "Why don't battered women leave their husbands? Stress has a way of taking a toll and keeping you chained up and afraid to make a change."

"Like all the people now who stay with an abusive master."

"That reminds me," Max interjects. "Commander Williams came by when he couldn't get you on the phone. A woman killed her master, and he wants you to go out to the prison and talk with her. See if you can make sense of her story."

Lily heaves a sigh. "I guess she was bold enough to make a change; wrong change but nevertheless, a change."

She is quiet for a moment then knits her forehead. "Another thing I don't get is why Daddy made Bob the executor of his will."

John speaks without raising his arm. "From meeting Bob, my guess is that it was a forgery."

"I hadn't thought of that. I guess you're right, but we'll never know. Everybody is dead now ... except Dale."

Max asks, "Who's Dale?"

"My youngest brother ... well ... my stepbrother. It's going to take a while to get used to that." Actually she is having difficulty assimilating all of the recently unveiled secrets of her childhood. She had suppressed the most distressing memories, and now the deluge of suppressed memories and new revelations is overwhelming her emotions.

Dr. Chris Morris looks at Gary Brown, asleep beside the front door. He softly chuckles as he quietly turns his key in the lock and steps inside. He looks at John Thorne asleep on the floor then looks over at the sofa. Max is asleep with his head tilted sharply back against the wall. Lily is asleep, snuggled in Max's arms. Quietly, he closes the door and slips off his shoes.

Dr. Ed Randolph walks in from the hall. "Anyone want breakfast?"

Dr. Morris strides toward the hall and speaks softly. "I'm beat. I'm going to catch a few zees and then go back and check on the patients I spent the night with."

John takes his arm off his eyes. "What're you making?"

"Sausage and eggs."

Dr. Morris turns back. "Okay. This is Saturday. I'll eat and go in a little later."

John hops up. Max rubs his aching neck.

Lily stands and stretches her arms above her head. "How long did we sleep?"

John grins mischievously. "About three hours. I'm refreshed and ready to go. Come on sleepy heads; let's eat."

Lily and Max follow him into the kitchen. Dr. Randolph opens the refrigerator and tosses a loaf of bread to Dr. Morris. He steps over to a cutting board. John picks up dirty dishes from the table. Max flips open the coffee maker and pulls out the used grounds.

Lily puts her hands on the back of a chair. "Do you know what this reminds me of?" They glance at her as they work. "It makes me think of a family eating together or a group of friends getting together. Normal life, that's what."

With a skillet in one hand and a package of sausage in the other, Dr. Randolph turns toward her and grins. "It's not the least bit normal for three doctors to be living together in a three bedroom house and making their own breakfast."

Everyone laughs.

Lily holds up her hands. "Hey, I'm trying to find your wives and children. Then it'll be more normal around here. And you do have maid service. Do you guys have a dish cloth I could use to wipe the table? You make quite a mess in between cleaning days."

John sets a pile of dirty dishes in the sink, turns on the tap, picks up the dishcloth, and puts it under the stream of water. "Jackie, I'd like to tell you that I'm glad to be a part of what you're doing around here, and I want to thank you for putting up with me during those first two weeks when I gave you so much trouble."

"We had inside information on dealing with you."

He wrings the dishcloth and tosses it to her. "You knew what made me tick."

"That's right." She begins wiping the table. "Stephanie was uneasy about reconnaissance missions but knew you'd latch onto the idea."

"She was right to be concerned," John remarks. "This trip was a real eye opener. I thought I knew what was going on from being on my own for two and a half years, but I didn't."

Lily asks, "You were in the east, weren't you?"

"Yeah, the Midwest and the east."

"I gather it wasn't so dangerous there?"

"No, it was just as dangerous, just a different kind of dangerous. It was less organized than here, every man for himself. Of course, I've been here almost a year. It could be more organized there now."

Gary Brown opens the door and walks in. "Are we having breakfast? Do I smell sausage?"

Someone raps on the front door. Gary jumps up and returns in a moment with Lieutenant Curtis Jones.

Dr. Randolph motions at the food on the table. "Have some breakfast."

"No thanks. I've already eaten. My bride is a wizard in the kitchen."

Curtis sits down. "Man, John! What happened to your arms?"

"Distraught mother, but she's okay now that we rescued her daughter."

Curtis lays a large manila envelope on the table and pushes it towards Lily. "I found these taped underneath that table in Mr. Barton's secret room. I thought you'd like to have them."

With trepidation, she pushes her empty plate away, picks up the envelope, and opens it. She slowly pulls out a handful of yellowed and brittle newspaper clippings. She carefully unfolds the top one and smooths it out. "Oh, thank you. This is about me winning the beautiful baby contest." She quickly scans the article. "My mother's name was Lillian ... and she was a gymnast. She trained for the Olympics but was sidelined by an injury. Wow!"

John grins. "You take after her."

Curtis clears his throat; she looks up at him. "I read them."

Her lips tighten into a thin-lipped, impish smile. "I was going to leave out that her diva personality contributed to the decision."

John's grin broadens. "You definitely take after her."

She shakes her head in amusement and turns her attention back to the riveting clipping. "Both my parents had PhD's. I didn't know that. They moved to a smaller town and opened the drug store to get away from the city and have a slower paced life. Why'd I have so much trouble in school, if both of my parents were so smart?"

"Stress," Max and John reply.

She shrugs. "I guess that explains the chess."

Max grins. "Do you play chess?"

"I did when I was a child. Daddy was teaching my brothers, and I was sitting in his lap the whole time. When I was five, Bob was teasing me and I got tired of it. I told him I'd go swimming if he beat me at chess."

John knits his brow. "Swimming sounds like fun."

"It was winter ... in Washington."

"That wouldn't be fun unless you were a polar bear."

"I'm definitely not a polar bear," Lily needlessly exclaims.

John guesses, "I suppose you beat him?"

"Nailed him in about ten minutes."

"Did you play a lot of chess?"

"For about two weeks then they got tired of losing."

Out of curiosity, John inquires, "I thought you had a Master's degree? You couldn't have gotten that without doing well in school."

"I did better in college after I came to Texas and got away from my brothers' harassment. I also did better in high school after I began using studying as an excuse to lock myself in my room to get away from my brothers." She knits her brows. "I guess I started that in junior high, but it was a struggle until I got completely away from them."

Dr. Randolph grins. "You could've been an intellectual snob just like us three docs." Dr. Morris snorts in mock disgust. Dr. Randolph continues, "But you aren't the least bit arrogant."

She bites her tongue to stifle her laughter as she unfolds the next article. She sobers as she stares at the poor quality newspaper photo of the mother she resembles but does not remember. Tears roll down her cheeks as she reads about her mother's unsolved murder. She wipes her face and goes to the next clipping.

John leans toward her as she smooths the brittle paper. "That trophy is bigger than you!"

"Yeah."

"Is that your teacher?"

Pride is clearly evident in her voice. "That's my daddy."

John guesses, "He had a black belt?"

She nods.

"How many degrees?" John inquires.

"I don't know."

John raises his eyebrows. "You don't know?"

Lily shakes her head. "I said a million from the time I was small and never asked. He was kind of a volunteer part-time instructor at the dojo, helping the masters hone their skills."

"Who'd he learn from?"

"His grandfather, his mom's dad," she replies with a big smile. "His father, my great-great-grandfather, was from the old country and became all-American except for his dedication to martial arts."

"Which country?" John asks.

Lily shrugs. "I don't know. I never asked."

"Why not?"

Sadness swallows her face. "I lost both parents when I was young and didn't get a chance to ask those questions. I have a lot of questions that I'll never be able to ask."

Lily looks up at the quizzical Seal. There is a reason he can so easily gather intelligence. His inquiries are infused with interest and curiosity without even a hint of anything negative such as disapproval, incrimination, or especially a tone of interrogation.

She continues, "But I do have a photo of an ancestor from another branch of the family. It was taken in 1865 when the Chinese were building the railroads."

John rhetorically queries, "So you're of Asian descent?"

She laughs. "I'm somewhere around twelve and a half percent. My great-grandfather married a descendant of the one I have a photo of, but she was mostly just American. My grandmother married a man named Gibbons, which obviously isn't an Asian name."

"I thought mixed marriages would have been frowned upon in that day and time?" Dr. Randolph remarks with an edgy tone in his voice, indicating his elitist disapproval of interracial marriages.

"Yeah," Lily concurs. "But people are people, and they do what they want despite the disapproval of their family and just suffer the consequences."

"So they were disinherited?" Dr. Randolph guesses.

"Some of them," Lily replies, "and the outcasts lose track of extended family, but somebody ends up descended from the scandalous, isolated side of the family. That's one reason that I'm not from a large family."

She puts aside the photo of her father.

"You look happy," Max states.

Lily looks up at the ceiling and furrows her brow in thought. After a moment, she turns to Max. Her expression softens. "I guess I am. It's a great relief to know I'm not related to those self-centered, murderous tormentors that I used to call my brothers. I'd much rather be related to those who defied tradition and scandalously entered into an interracial marriage. I feel very content; very happy; very upbeat. I even feel confident that we can conquer our difficulties here and turn this brutal society around into one that respects everyone."

Lily reaches in the envelope and pulls out more papers. She picks up a photo. "Mother looks a lot like me."

"Don't you mean you look a lot like her," John teasingly corrects.

She nods then unfolds the next piece of paper. Her eyebrows arch. "This is my birth certificate. My name is also Lillian, and my mother's name was Lillian Jacqueline. … And I was born in California!"

"Why is that so surprising to you?" John inquires.

"I just thought I was born in Washington, where we lived from my first memories." She sighs. "This is why I couldn't get my birth certificate."

John guesses, "You only looked in Washington?"

Lily nods. "Walter wanted to take me on a cruise to the Caribbean for our honeymoon, but I couldn't get a passport without my birth certificate."

"Where'd you go instead?" John asks.

"No where."

"No where!"

"Yeah. We got married on a weekend in December and had to go back to school on Monday, so the honeymoon was planned for after the spring semester but by then I was six months pregnant."

John laughs. "Never got your honeymoon."

"That's right. All vacations after that included children."

"All in the U.S."

Lily nods.

John clears his throat. "I hope I'm not being too personal, but may I ask a question about your trust fund?"

"Sure."

"I thought you said your dad ran a drugstore. I can't see that being a wildly profitable venture, so I assume that your trust fund came from his prior career."

Lily shrugs. "That's another of the questions I never got to ask. I knew Daddy had money, and he always called the drugstore his hobby. It was a place for him to play chess with all the old men who loved the game. That first article I read didn't elaborate about his prior career. Here, you can read it."

She shuffles through the clippings and hands it too him.

"Jackie."

She looks over at Lieutenant Jones.

"Commander Williams would like you to come over to the hospital and talk to a woman who killed her master."

"I thought she was in prison."

Dr. Morris stands. "She was injured. I vote for self defense—if we had anything that even resembles justice and law around here! Well, I'm going to get a little shut-eye and then go back and check on my patients."

TWENTY EIGHT

A grimace tarnishes Lily's face as she exits the patient's room. She closes the door and lets relief wash away her pained expression. She nods at the officer seated beside the door. A door opens down the hall. She looks up. Commander Williams exits the stairwell and turns toward her. She walks briskly toward him, mainly to put distance between her and Dorothy Worsted.

He grins in amusement at her obvious discomfort. "Profanity laced tirade?"

She waves her hands back and forth. "Yeah, I'm the cause of all her problems because I didn't buy her two years ago … or whenever it was when she was on the auction platform."

He laughs. "Is this that woman, the one that you wouldn't buy?"

She nods. "I don't know what to do with her. I'm not willing to take her. I offered if she'd conform to some behavior and language requirements but …." Lily shrugs. "She'd be more trouble than she's worth. She'd cause problems anywhere. Well, I really shouldn't say that."

"It's true, she'd cause problems anywhere."

"I was talking about implying that she's worth less than another person."

"So what do you think we should do with her: put her in prison?" the commander suggests for lack of a better option.

"I don't think that's appropriate. She's obviously been abused, so I think she has a valid self-defense plea. What're you doing about the baron's enterprise?"

He frowns. "It was two brothers. Well, there used to be three a long time ago. The remaining brother is now the sole baron, so we can't finagle you into running this one. I'll see what I can come up with for her since giving her back isn't an option. He'd kill her for killing his brother."

A smile replaces his frown. "Officer Garcia has been telling me about your trip. He said you had warnings each time you ran into bandits, that your computer guy was tracking you on satellite."

The furrows on her brow soften. "It was a life saver—literally."

"I talked with Marvin, and he's going to expand our command center so we can take more advantage of the satellites. It'll mean using more officers as dispatchers, but I think that'll be more effective in the long run. We have an officer, Donald North, who washed out of training. He's been our clerk for the ID cards, but now that we're over the initial hump of the system, Marvin has been training him as a dispatcher. Donald's delighted; the idea of being in law enforcement enthralls him. He just can't stand being around guns, afraid he's going to shoot himself in the foot. He had trouble with the typing involved in the ID cards. I'm sure he only mastered that because it was so repetitious but anything that goes in his ears, sticks forever. He'll make a great dispatcher; no detail of a call ever gets lost."

"That sounds good. The men have been telling me how well things are going and that the crime rate has decreased."

"Yes, it has; an actual documented lower rate," Commander Williams states with pride. "I'm going to look at working on the roads to the nearby towns. I'll start with the road to the northwest. I'll contact the commander in the next town and see if he'll agree to a cooperative effort to clear the road of bandits. It'll make travel much safer and decrease the cost, both cargo and human, for the regional traders. We can start repairing the roads between towns, if we can make it safe enough for a road crew. Mr. Hobbs can then get rid of the last of those dead zones. We desperately need good roads and phone service between towns. It'll probably increase usage of your hospital too."

She laughs. "Our docs are already overworked."

"So get more."

"I am."

She scowls. "There's something one of the bandits said that I'd like to run by you. He said Mr. Patterson's death probably wasn't a natural death."

He laughs, not in merriment but at the irony of the situation. "I'm not surprised. Reginald had deals with the bandits. Most of the truck drivers do. It's the only way to secure safe passage. You either shoot it out or cut deals. Mr. Patterson was vehement about trying to get away from funding their lawless lifestyle. What'd your docs say about it?"

"They weren't looking for foul play. They didn't have any reason to, so we'd have to dig him up and do an autopsy to find out. There's also the possibility that we wouldn't find anything since we don't have the capability to test for most poisons. However he did it, it wasn't obvious."

"I don't suppose it matters with our only suspect dead," Commander Williams states.

Without pausing, he asks, "How're you doing with Mr. Patterson's men?"

She replies, "I had them elect four supervisors, one for each major route. They seem to be doing well, but they never said anything about the bandits. Now that I've made a trip, I'm going to talk to them about using the satellites for early warning. Maybe we can short circuit the pirating."

"A couple of your Seals on each truck would probably do the trick."

"I think it'd take more than two. But at least three of the gangs between here and Perkins have been eliminated."

"That's a great start. Is it accurate that it's forty miles to Perkins?" he asks.

"Not as the crow flies. You go northwest to one town then east northeast to another then almost due west to Perkins."

"I bet it's not fifty miles to Crutchfield either."

"Probably not. Maybe when you and the other commanders have made the roads safer, we can survey the area and make an accurate map. Mr. Hobbs's phone brochure isn't very accurate."

He puts his palm against the wall and leans on it. "Is Mrs. Somerton okay with moving into your complex by the hospital?"

"Yes. She wants to be close to Robert. We have her in with Lieutenant Jones and his wife for now, but we'll fix up a wheelchair accessible house for them."

"Good. I was hoping she wasn't mad at me for kicking her out of their house, but Marvin has his command center all set up in there and that wouldn't be easy to move. Neither did we want it out of service for a while. It's essential; we couldn't function effectively without it. We're going to set up a backup command center, but that's going to take a while."

Lily reports, "She had no complains about the way you handled it."

"I'm glad. What're Jupiter's plans for his wife and daughter?"

"For now, Marissa is staying with some of the nurses so she can be close to their daughter. Or maybe I should say she will stay with the nurses; she hasn't left the hospital yet. Jupiter also plans to spend as much time at the hospital as he can. He'll work on housing arrangements later. We told them there's no hurry."

"Will they live in one of the houses here?"

"I'd like to offer that, but for now they're still in crisis mode. I don't know anything about Jupiter's current accommodations. Do you?"

"All the vendors stick together. It's a like a trade association. Alone each one is vulnerable but united they protect each other."

"So that's what he meant when he said he had friends that first time I traded with him?"

He grins. "Yeah."

"So ... we already have an organization very similar to a co-op, a long-standing organization?"

"Hum ... I guess we do," the commander admits. "But I don't think it'll be a very persuasive argument with Mr. Finke."

She shakes her head. "We're still on track with our current plan. What I was really meaning is that after Mr. Finke is ... ah ... persuaded to see things differently perhaps the other barons will be easier to convince."

"I'm sure of that."

"That's good," she absentmindedly comments as she evaluates the sound of confidence in his statement. It is probably unsubstantiated overconfidence.

He tilts his head to the side. "When is Josie coming back to town?"

"I don't know of any plans for that."

"Would it be okay if I went out to see her and her mother tomorrow morning? I'd like to meet her young man too. He wasn't around when I settled Buster into his house."

"How about tomorrow afternoon? If you'd like, why don't you come for lunch."

"What time?"

"They serve from eleven to one."

"Okay. I'll see you then."

She smiles and walks away. Commander Williams takes a deep breath, walks over, and knocks on Dorothy's door. He is met by a stream of profanity. The officer on guard duty closes his eyes and leans his head against the wall.

Commander Williams looks down at the seated officer. "Getting hard to listen to huh?"

The officer nods.

After another deep breath, the commander pushes the door open slightly. With a commanding tone of voice, he declares, "This is Commander Williams. Answer without profanity. May I come in?"

"I don't give a ... ah ...."

He opens the door, walks over beside her bed, and looks down. She glares at him. Her wrists are securely held in padded restraints. He states, "We're having trouble finding a place for you. Almost everyone I've talked to expressed their opinion that you have a valid self defense plea."

He purposefully omits that he has only talked to a few officers, the doctors, and Mrs. Schwartz, since he won't be able to get a valid comment from the other barons until brutally persuasive and overbearing Mr. Finke is out of the way.

Her expression softens. "Thanks."

"The doctors want to keep you here a little longer, so we'll need to make a decision soon as to where you'll go."

She looks up with a dejected expression. "I think I'd rather go to hell than where I've been."

"Perhaps we can find some place a little better than that."

She shrugs and looks away.

"Since you've shown that you can speak without using profanity perhaps we could come to some kind of agreement."

She looks up. Skepticism is etched on her face.

"If you can eschew the profanity and moderate your argumentativeness, I'd consider taking you."

"Do I have to share your bed?"

"I need a cook and a housekeeper. If we both fall in love we can share the bed, but I can guarantee you that I'll only fall in love if I enjoy your company."

"And if you don't enjoy my company?"

He shrugs.

"Beat me?" she glumly inquires.

"Nah. If you're not a good cook and housekeeper, I'd just sell you."

"That'd just send me to another da ... wretched baron."

He nods.

"I'm not the best cook," Dorothy admits.

297

He shrugs. "You're probably better than me. And Marvin and Donald can't cook worth a flip either."

"So I'd be cooking and cleaning for three guys?"

"We could probably find some help for you."

She cocks one eyebrow. "Do you need an answer now?"

"No, but I do need it before the doctors release you otherwise I'll have no choice but to house you in the prison. I'll check on you tomorrow," Commander Williams states.

"Is there any chance of getting out of these restrains?"

"I'll check with the medical staff. Be nice to them and maybe they'll consider it. I will keep an officer outside your door—two if necessary."

"Thanks," she uncharacteristically states. "Nobody's ever been this nice to me. I'll give it a good try."

Commander Williams exits the room, strides down the hall and into the stairwell. Hidden from the officer's view he stops and leans against the wall. Being commander is harder than he thought it would be. He has to find a solution even when no one else is able to even make a suggestion.

Max opens his eyes and looks over at Lily. She is sitting on the coffee table with her elbows on her knees and her chin in her hands.

She smiles. "Ed let me in. I didn't want to wake you."

He rubs his hands over his face to wake up and ascertain his need for a shave. "I can sleep now that you're back. Last night, I was probably just as alert as all the military guys with you. Twenty-two hours without sleep shouldn't bother me, not after all the call I've endured, but I still feel beat even after sleeping the entire time you were at the hospital. How long were you gone?"

She shrugs. "I'd guess it took me about five hours. Did you eat lunch?"

"No. What time is it?"

"About two."

"I don't feel hungry. I guess that's to be expected since I haven't done anything except sleep. Ed's a great cook so that breakfast is probably sufficient for the entire day anyway."

Lily laughs. "I guess you're going to miss him."

He looks at her in surprise.

She grins. "I called Lawrence to see what happened with the bids yesterday. His wife appeared about mid-afternoon, and we got her. Monkey's already been informed and will start working on a house for the Randolph's on Monday."

"Is she going to move in here until it's finished?"

She cocks an eyebrow. "You remember that there's no guarantee that she'll be here this Monday?"

He nods. "That anesthesiologist isn't going to move in here after Ed leaves, is he?"

"No, it appears that he needs his own place."

He smiles. "Have you considered my offer?"

She raises her eyebrows. "You make it sound like a business deal."

"You know I'm not good at this dating thing. It took me seven years to get a date with my wife."

"I'm not good at dating either. My practice was to turn down all dates, some politely, some cruelly depending upon what I thought of the guy."

He inquires, "How did you get together with your boyfriends?"

"I initiated everything, usually to get back at some arrogant guy who was flirting ... except with Walter."

"What was so different with Walter?"

She looks down at the floor then back up. "I learned that I could trust him. You know what the Bible says." She paraphrases, "Those who can be trusted with the little things can also be trusted with the big things.[1] Walter could be trusted in everything, absolutely everything."

"Do you trust me?"

"You know I do?"

"So."

She shrugs. "I guess you could take me to Armando's or Guzman's."

He sits up. "How about tonight? How about an early supper?"

"I'll have to take an entourage of guards."

He laughs. "I guess this is what it'd be like to date the president's daughter."

"Okay. How about four o'clock?"

"Sounds great!" Max exclaims. "So this is a yes?"

"I don't know."

---

1 Luke 16:10

"What do you mean you don't know? You've agreed to a date. What's the problem?"

She shrugs. "It's hard to make a decision about something so momentous."

"What do you mean momentous? You've said that before, but I don't understand."

"It's hard to shift gears. I have things to do." She shakes her head and gestures with her hands. "Committing to something else is just ... so ... so beyond what ... ah ... what I've had on my mind for the last three years."

He leans toward her. "Look. This is just a date. Commitment isn't what I'm thinking about, at least not at this time. I'd like to spend time with you with the possibility of commitment off somewhere in the future."

She sits up straight. "Oh?"

He raises one eyebrow. "Have we failed to communicate?"

"I guess. I was probably skipping the beginning. My relationships always progressed rapidly, except with Walter. It took me a while to look at him as a potential boyfriend or even a friend. I turned him down when he asked for a date and went over and sat by Steve."

He reaches for her hand. "Let's progress rapidly enough to get you over on this couch beside me."

She smiles and allows him to guide her over beside him. He warps his arms around her shoulders. She looks into his eyes and smiles. "Tommy thought it was obvious that I like you."

"Is it obvious to you?"

She shakes her head, looks down then back up at his face. "Well, there're several different variations of like. I would say that I feel a kinship with you because we have so much in common. We've shared our backgrounds. We enjoy talking. I look forward to seeing you. There's a definite attraction. I feel safe with you. But as to a closer relationship ... well ... that's an unknown."

He gently strokes her cheek with the back of his left hand. "That's why I wasn't asking for a commitment to anything other than continuing to see each other. I just want to see you. I think I'd like something to develop, but I'm in no hurry."

Complete relaxation washes over her muscles, dissolving all tension as she gazes into his eyes. He stops rubbing her cheek. His index finger is poised at the corner of her eye. He smiles then slowly brings his finger down across her cheek. She smiles and leans her head against the back of the sofa. He leans over and nuzzles her neck. She slips her arm around his neck. He relishes the feel of her cheek as he brushes his lips across it.

He lightly brushes her lips with his. She pulls his head closer, pressing their lips together.

She abruptly breaks off their kiss and slides her check against his, gripping him tightly around the neck.

He holds her in a quiet but tight embrace then pulls back and rests his forehead on hers. He gazes into her dark brown eyes.

She looks into his eyes, smiles then lays her head on his shoulder. "This is more restful than eight hours sleep."

He laughs.

"Do you know what I mean?" she asks.

He shakes his head.

"I go to sleep thinking about our problems and wake up thinking about our problems. This is the only thing I've done in the last three and a half years that's taken my mind off our problems."

He grins. "You're saying that you haven't had a restful night's sleep since the first terrorist attack?"

She pulls back and looks into his face. "Yeah. I've been thinking I couldn't possibly work a relationship into my busy schedule but in actuality, I need to. … For the sake of sanity, I need to. Even that pain in my belly is gone … for now."

"That's really good news. Perhaps it was a sign of stress. So let's have a little more sanity and see if we can keep it away," he suggests.

She understands his oblique figure of speech: have a little more sanity. She pulls him toward her.

Dr. Morris opens the front door. It is well oiled and does not make a sound. He steps inside. His soft-soled shoes make no noise. He turns back to close the door and stops, facing the sofa on the far side of the room. "Whoops!"

They break off their kiss and turn to look.

He grins. "Caught ya'!"

TWENTY NINE

After visiting with Uncle Buster, Commander Williams pushes open the door from the east wing, steps into the main room, and walks among the furniture and dividers. He finds Josie, her fiancé, and her mother seated on a sofa in the corner. Max and Lily sit several feet away. Jeff Clark and Jenny Walker are also nearby. A few other couples are scattered about enjoying a lazy Sunday afternoon.

Excitement lights Josie's eyes. "Uncle Bruce!"

He smiles and sits in an armchair opposite their sofa. "Sorry I'm so late, but Buster wanted to walk out and visit Rose. He's a little slow and getting slower."

Josie replies, "I know. I walk him out there every day, all fifty feet or so, and it takes an hour."

"I also had to profusely apologize for not coming out to see him sooner."

She nods. "He's been asking about you, wanting to know when you'd come."

"Is this your young man? What's his name?" Bruce Williams asks.

"Brian Ladd."

"I'm glad to meet you, Brian." He holds out his hand.

The nervous young man leans forward and shakes hands. "Glad to meet you, sir."

"You can call me Uncle Bruce."

"Thank you, sir ... I mean Bruce ... ah ... Uncle Bruce."

The commander casually laughs. "There's no need to be nervous. I'm not her father. I'm merely an unofficially adopted uncle who's going to give the bride away. I'm not even the commander to you. So kids, when's the wedding?"

A smile lights up Josie's face. "We've decided on October tenth. We're trying to make the date easy for Brian to remember. Dad always had trouble remembering their anniversary. Mom says most men do. Our birthdays are both on the tenth so that should make it easy. So we're getting married on the tenth day of the tenth month."

"That sounds like a good idea."

He looks down at the floor then back at Josie. "I have another purpose for coming out today. This isn't totally a social call or just to meet the groom. I wasn't totally honest with you the first time we talked. Jackie tells me I need to be honest with you otherwise you'll be as peeved with me as she is."

"Who's Jackie?"

"Mrs. Schwartz."

"Oh, yeah. I hear her called Jackie all the time." Josie grins with amusement and a twinkle flashes in her eyes. "Well, Uncle Bruce, what lie did you tell?"

He looks at the floor and then back into her eyes. "I haven't ever been married. It was my girlfriend who died during the lawlessness."

Josie says, "I'm still sorry she died."

"Thank you. I also have a daughter. She'll be eighteen on September the tenth."

Josie and her mother Josephine both turn pale. Josie's eyes widen. She looks over at her mom then back to him. "I'll be eighteen on the tenth."

A puzzled frown creases the commander's brow. "I thought you were going to be twenty."

"Well … I lied too, but I have a reasonable explanation." Josie takes a deep breath and nervously chatters, "I skipped a grade in elementary school and was teased all year. Next year with a new class, I just added a year and they didn't tease me about being the baby of the class. In junior high and high school, I got to take some advanced classes and test out of some classes so I added another year since I was going to graduate when I was only sixteen. When I got kidnapped, I added another year but dropped that when I talked to you."

"It sounds like you're one very smart girl," Bruce compliments then looks over at Josephine Vaughn.

She has a thin-lipped grimace on her face.

He takes a deep breath with the intent to calm his emotions. It does not work. "Are you Jody Simmons?"

"Yeah. Are you Jeff Williams?"

He nods.

Lily takes note of the rising hostilities and whispers for Max to ask people to move away. She signals Jeff Clark to do the same. She walks over and sits near the smoldering volcano. Josie's lips are pursed and her brow is knit into tight furrows of worry. Brian appears ready to disappear into the crevasses of the sofa. Jody's pale face reddens as her anger rises. The capable commander, in uncharacteristic fashion, looks like a wild animal caught in a car's headlights.

Josie snaps, "Have you been lying about your name too?"

The commander takes a deep breath, ruing the fact that what was supposed to be an air-clearing confession has landed him in hot water over long ago indiscretions that he would like to forget. He regrets following Jackie's suggestion. He should have left well enough alone, but felt he needed to get into Jackie's good graces after his embarrassing gaffe with her. He explains, "People started killing all law enforcement officers. That put me in danger since I was a Texas Ranger. I started using my middle name for survival. So it's not a lie. And I didn't know your mom's name after she got married, so I didn't recognize Vaughn."

He looks over at Jody. She glares at him. He turns his eyes to the floor.

"Look at me!" Jody demands.

The commander meekly complies.

"I believed your lie," she states with barely contained rage.

"I believed it too. The kids at camp were all saying that. I didn't know it was just a pickup line. I thought it was true."

Josie timidly asks, "What lie?"

Jody turns to her daughter. "I'll tell you about Camp Lucky Lake later."

Lily gasps. They turn to her, suddenly aware of her presence. She takes a deep breath and explains, "I know about Camp Lucky Lake."

Bruce rhetorically inquires, "You went to camp there too?"

Lily replies, "No, but I know someone a little older than you who went there."

"Jeff!" Jeffery Bruce Williams turns back to Josephine "Jody" Simmons Vaughn. "I'm not through talking to you! You deserted me."

305

"Let's talk privately," he calmly suggests despite the turmoil raging within his gut.

Recognizing the wisdom of his request, Jody signifies her acquiescence with a nod.

They look at their daughter. Tears are rolling down her cheeks. Her fiancé is too intimidated to offer any comfort or support.

"I'm sorry, sweetheart," Jody soothes. "I should have told you about this."

"Mom, I understand. I figured it out a long time ago. I understand all of that. It's just … it's just that … I'm scared!"

Jody grabs her daughter and hugs her tightly. "What's scaring you?"

"Ah … I didn't tell you what happened at the prison."

Jody's eyes flash at Bruce. He puts his hands up in a defensive posture. "Hear her out."

Her anger does not abate.

Lily interjects, "Josephine, its okay. Nothing happened. Let her talk."

Jody takes a deep breath. "Okay, darling. What's so scary?"

"Mom, you remember what I told you about the other place?"

"Uh-huh."

"I thought I could have a very nice officer protect me here."

"Oh?"

Bruce inhales and forces a soothing smile onto his face. "You do have a very nice officer here who will protect you."

"Yeah … but I made a play for … my dad!"

Jody hugs Josie tighter. In anguish, they rock on the sofa.

"Hey," Bruce softly calls.

They look at him.

He smiles. "If your stepdad shows up, he's still your dad. I was too young to be a dad, so I wasn't. Your dad can give you away. I'm still your Uncle Bruce. Okay?"

Josie nods.

"Now let's quit scaring your young man. That may be one reason why I never married. I never wanted to go through 'meeting the dad' again. Don't worry about what happened at the prison. Nothing happened except your natural instinct for self-preservation."

Lily strides down the east hall with a scowl darkening her face. She opens the door to Al's office and quickly closes it. She leans against the wall and waits. Within moments a woman dashes out and strides down the hall with her head down.

Lily waits a couple of minutes then knocks on the door.

"Come in," Al calls.

She opens the door and looks in. With a scowl, she sternly demands, "You have a lock. Use it! This is ... was ... an office. It's a long-standing habit to walk in."

She walks in, shuts the door, and turns down one corner of her mouth in a frustrated scowl.

He smirks. "You're obviously mad at me."

When she does not elaborate, he sternly demands, "Well, what is it?"

She pulls a chair away from the table, sits down, and glares at him for a long moment. Then she furrows her brow and answers, "Those lines you used at Camp Lucky Lake."

He shrugs. "Why are you mad about that? You weren't there."

She stares at the ceiling in disgust. To calm herself, she holds her breath for a moment then slowly exhales and looks at him. "Did you hear them from someone else, or did you make them up?"

"I made them up. Why?"

She presses her lips together, bites them then leans toward him. "Years after you went to camp, somebody was still spreading those lies around."

He laughs.

She glares at him. "Some of them believed them."

"Why are you bringing this up?"

"Because actions have consequences; what you do affects others. Lies hurt others. No one lives in a vacuum." She stops and takes a deep breath. "You do a really good job around here. We appreciate that so don't get me wrong, but I hope you'll be more responsible in the rest of your life."

He shrugs. "I don't see why you're so upset. This didn't hurt you. What's the big deal? Dolts are responsible for their own actions. If they believe a lie, that's their problem."

She glares at him. "I care about others. So yeah, if your actions hurt them then you've hurt me."

"I still don't see why you're so mad."

"You have no remorse." She throws her hands in the air in frustration. "Give up your archaic view of religion and lighten up!"

Not rising to his challenge, Lily calmly replies, "I know how much it hurts for someone to be cruel. That's why it hurts me so much for someone I know to be hurt."

"You're naïve. It's every man for himself. No one is going to look out for others and have their best interests at heart."

"You're impossible." She stands and walks out, leaving the door open.

His laughter echoes down the hall.

She turns around, walks back, and leans against the frame of the open door. "I'm sorry. Perhaps I shouldn't have challenged you on this. I know neither of us can do anything about the past, but it bothers me that you have no remorse. I used to think that you were a nice guy—a nice guy that I led astray back when I didn't know any better."

She lowers her head and looks down at the floor. "Look Al, I thought we could just ignore the past." She turns her eyes up and looks at him askance. "But we can't. We are never going to be able to go back to the relationship we had. And I'm not talking about high school. I'm talking about after we were both married and were just friends. It's not going to happen. So I'm going to try to forge a new relationship with you which will be hard since I don't exactly trust you anymore."

He laughs.

She scowls.

He raises his eyebrows. "Just friends? I was willing to be more than just friends."

Her jaw drops. He smirks.

After a moment, she regains her composure. "Did you put a cryptic note in my Bible?"

"Yeah, I knew Walter had a meeting Sunday afternoon and your kids had that party. Cathy and her parents were taking ours to the zoo. I figured we were both free, so I rented a room and managed to slip the note in when you left your Bible on the pew."

She glares at him.

"It wasn't the first time I tried it. I did it a few months before when we were visiting Cathy's parents but didn't manage to slip the note to you."

She rolls her eyes.

"Look, I'm a hypocrite," Al admits, "so I thought you were too."

She sighs. "I didn't find the note."

He raises his eyebrows. "You didn't?"

She shakes her head.

He guesses, "Walter found it?"

She nods. "It fell out about a month later along with all the Bible class papers that my boys always gave me. Walter picked it up. Neither of us could figure it out. We assumed that he picked up a piece of paper that was already on the floor."

"I guess it didn't cause any problems between you two?"

She shakes her head. "But it could have. It's like I was saying: actions have consequences."

Al grins. "But it would have been so much fun."

Lily stares at him in shock. She is ruing the fact that the compound is a haven for anyone. The security committee is continually deluged with complaints, both valid problems and petty gripes. She now wishes that she had been more discriminating when selecting people to rescue. Exactly how she could have predetermined in advance who would work out or not, she does not know. Al would have slipped through, as an old friend, since she had been completely deceived by him.

She recovers her composure and states, "The security committee is drafting a policy on public lewdness. There are a number of people around here whose behavior has been inappropriate. It's becoming a problem and is something we're going to have to deal with, so keep your door locked. It won't be fun to go before the security committee."

She turns and walks away. This time there is no laughter from Al.

Tommy plops down on his doorstep and looks over at Lily. She is covering her face with her hands. "Al has revealed more of his true nature, hasn't he?"

Lily lifts her head and nods.

"Let me guess," he states. "He has admitted that he was unfaithful to his wife."

She looks up at his face. "Not in so many words, but he has implied it."

She focuses her gaze on the hard-packed dirt below her feet. "He admitted that he attempted it. He tried to set up an assignation with me, so I can only assume that I wasn't the only one and that he was successful with someone else."

Tommy furrows his brow in puzzlement. "Did you suppress the memory? Is that why it is now a 'new' revelation?"

Lily shakes her head. "He left an unsigned note in my Bible. We didn't find it for a month. By then we didn't have any reason to connect it with him. It never even entered my mind that the note was for me."

"But it was in your Bible," he states with emphasis on the word your.

"My boys always gave me their take homes, and—"

"What're take homes?"

She replies, "Those handouts in Bible class: drawings, coloring, puzzles, and things. My Bible was always stuffed with them. One of the boys picked up my Bible, and all the papers went on the floor. Walter picked them up and we just assumed that the note had been on the floor, not in my Bible."

"Was that the only time Al tried that?"

Lily shakes her head. "He admitted that he tried it once before but didn't manage to get the note into my Bible."

"So now you have reason to believe he was unfaithful."

She nods.

"But still an assumption," he adds.

She nods. "I know that Cathy wanted a Christian husband more than anything in the world. She always said *Christian husband or old maid, no other choice.*"

"And now you know she got sold a bill of goods."

"I knew that a couple of weeks ago, but I didn't have time to deal with it because we were too wrapped up in Mr. Finke's attack. I was just hoping that Al had changed and made a good husband, but after today, I know he's always been the same. Deceit is his middle name. He has the morals of Brett with some of the charm of Frank."

"Do you regret redeeming them?"

"I regret redeeming Brett. I shouldn't have taken a chance on a stranger without any information."

"But other strangers have turned out all right," Tommy contends.

She looks over with her eyebrows raised. "I had a little information on all the others, at least the look on their face in person or in a photo. Brett was the first stranger after we went to the online bidding, and I didn't even have a photo to look at. Since he attacked me during his interview, I never did that again. I never bid on another stranger until Lawrence added the ability to post photos on the auction site."

THE STONE IS TURNED

Tommy tries to change her focus. "You really care about others."

"That's why we have to be successful around here," Lily states. "We have to keep people out here safe and also do something about the problems in town."

"You've bit off a big chaw."

She nods. "We'll do our best. It isn't enough, but we'll try."

"It is enough," he contends.

"It isn't enough."

"Our best is enough. It's all we're expected to do. We can do no more."

She looks over at him. "Who expects us? Are you referring to God?"

"I guess. ... I guess the Christianity around here is beginning to rub off on me."

Lily smiles and thinks *now converting you to Christianity, that would be a 'big chaw'.*

THIRTY

Upon leaving the compound, Commander Williams stops before Lily and Max, who are sitting on a sofa near the front door. He contemplates his options for a moment then seeks her good graces—again. "Thanks, Jackie. This afternoon was difficult, but I'm glad you urged me to come clean."

"I'm glad it turned out all right," Lily replies.

"Yeah. All these years, I wasn't even seeing my daughter as a real person. She was just a great inconvenience, just a reminder that I'd been hornswoggled. Now she's a pure delight, and Jody and I have a chance to make amends. I think my subconscious mind must have recognized Josie and that's what drew me to her that first day. I became unreasonably protective when that officer merely looked at her. I'm glad she already has a beau; otherwise I'd be filled with great anxiety right now. I'd be afraid some selfish little cretin was going to ...." He looks down at the floor then back up. "Brian seems like a very respectable young man. I'll be seeing you."

"Bye."

Lily watches him walk out the front door. Jack, John, and Brett walk into the main room from the west wing. She turns toward them; her face drops. "It looks like I'm going to get called away again."

Max laughs. "Or maybe, I'm the one they're coming for."

"That looks like a black eye. I think the nurses have already taken care of Brett. I see an ice pack in his hand."

The three men stop before them. Brett puts the ice pack on his left eye. She stifles her amusement to at least appear objective. "Brett, what did you do?"

"Nothing! Gary just hauled off and slugged me." He is speaking of U.S. Navy Seal Gary Brown.

Lily replies, "Since I'm very familiar with your definition of nothing, we'll convene a special session of the security committee Monday afternoon to deal with this continuing problem."

"Hey, Gary's the one at fault!"

She rises. "Let's go in my office for privacy while I get your side of the story."

He reluctantly trudges after her, followed by Jack and John. They take their place as guards and sit down in chairs outside the office door. She closes the door then follows Brett over to her desk. She sits down, puts her elbows on the desk, intertwines her fingers, and rests her chin on them.

He drops the ice pack on the desk, plops down in the chair, and looks up. His expression is as close to innocent as he can consciously make it. "I didn't do nothing to him, absolutely nothing!"

"Let me write down the basic facts." She opens a drawer and takes out a pen and a sheet of paper. "First I'll put down incident report and the date and time. Now, besides you and Gary, who else was there?"

"Serena."

"Where were you?"

He sighs.

"I don't want to have to repeat questions. Where were you?"

"In her cottage," Brett reluctantly concedes.

"What were you doing?"

"Nothing."

Lily contends, "Nothing cannot be an answer; even sleeping is not nothing."

"We were talking."

"All three of you?"

"Just Serena and I. Gary didn't say anything when he came in. He just hauled off and slugged me."

"What were you talking about?"

"Nothing. Oh, I guess you won't accept that answer. I said *hi* and *how are you* and stuff like that."

Angry that she has to repeat her question, she demands, "What'd she say?"

"Oh ... not much. Gary came right away, so we didn't have time to talk."

"What did she say?" Lily repeats, careful to keep her tone very calm.

314

"I don't remember. Gary's fist must have knocked the memory right out of me."

"How'd you get into her cottage?"

"She let me in."

Lily wonders about the truthfulness of his answer but merely continues her interrogation; she will address that issue later. "Did you knock or something?"

"Yeah, I knocked. She opened the door."

"Is there anything you'd like to add to this?"

He shakes his head.

"You wait here while we go talk to Gary and Serena, and you need to put that ice pack on your eye; it's not doing the desk any good."

Gary Brown opens the door of Serena Hermann's cottage.

From the bottom porch step, Lily looks up at the tall Seal. "I need to talk to Serena while John talks to you, so we can get all three sides of the story for the security committee."

"Okay." He steps out.

Lily enters the cottage then turns back. "Gary, we've been having some troubles with public lewdness around here, so the security committee is drafting a policy. I don't know what it'll be yet, but you and Serena probably shouldn't be so passionate with your goodnight kisses at her door. Parents are disturbed that their children are seeing it."

He nods.

She closes the door, walks over to the bed, and sits beside Serena, whose eyes are red and her face streaked with tears. She puts her arm around Serena's shoulders. "Tell me what happened."

"Gary and I came back from a walk and stood at the door for a while, kissing and talking. Soon after he left, Brett knocked. I asked who it was and he said he was Gary and forgot something. I thought his voice sounded a little different but it was through the door, so I opened it. Brett pushed his way in and grabbed me. I screamed. Gary ran back and pulled him off. Brett took a swing at him and Gary decked him." She holds her arms up. "I'm getting bruises where he grabbed me.

"Lily, there's something else you should know before taking this to the security committee. Brett used to come see me at Mr. Barton's at least once or twice a week."

"So he thinks you should be providing the same 'service' now as you did then? I see. Do you have anything else to add?"

Serena shakes her head.

"I'll be going now."

Lily stands then looks down and asks, "Are you going to be all right?" She asks this because of Serena's unusually sad demeanor despite the almost benign accounts that both Brett and Serena gave of the incident. Either both are lying or there have been unreported incidents of a more serious nature in the past. Or it could be that something else is bothering the young widow.

"I'll be all right. I know that Gary will protect me," Serena replies then suddenly blurts, "No, I'm not going to be all right!"

Lily sits beside her and wraps her arm around Serena's waist. She buries her head on Lily's shoulder.

Lily gently inquires, "What'd he do? What's wrong?"

"It's not Brett. It's Gary."

"Gary? What'd he do?"

"Nothing; it's not him. Lily, I think I've fallen in love with him."

"Oh," Lily intones. "So that's the problem."

"He's just spending time with me to protect me. This is all pretend. How do I make it real?" Serena pleads.

"Why don't you try talking with him, maybe when all this with Brett is over?"

"What if he isn't interested? Then I would have blown it. I'd have ruined my chances with him ... and lost a friend and my protector too."

"Serena, I think Gary's been interested in you all along. If he wasn't, I doubt if he'd spend all his free time with you, especially with the way you're always dropping hints that you'd like something to develop. Instead, he'd have just brought it up when we discussed security and we'd have assigned guards to you all the time, just like we do when Gary's not around."

She looks up. "I have guards when Gary's not here?"

Lily nods. "Brett doesn't bother you when Gary is off on some assignment, does he?"

"I just assumed that Brett was at work."

316

Lily smiles. "Your expression tells me you're feeling better."

"Yeah. I'll think about talking to Gary, maybe feel my way around and try and assess his feelings before I come right out and tell him how I feel. But thanks. You've pointed out the obvious. I should have guessed it, but I'm just so used to men paying attention to me. That's the bane of being considered beautiful. I can't ever guess which kind of attention they want to give me. I almost didn't accept a first date from James and so almost unknowingly lost the love of my life. I know Gary gets a kick out of our little sham but it's all in public, never in private. Tonight is the first time he's ever come inside my cottage, and it was only because Brett had pushed his way inside."

Serena looks across the darkened room. She can barely see Gary's prone form on the mat beside the door. He is her assigned protector for the night. It is also helpful to know that two guards are stationed outside to watch for Brett.

"Gary."

"Yes."

"You don't have to lie on the floor. You can join me in bed."

"Tomorrow, the committee's going to question us about everything that happened today and before today and tonight and tomorrow. I'll stay down here. I'm just a guard to keep you safe."

She stifles her sigh. "Gary."

"Yes."

"I'd like to stop the sham."

"Okay," he agrees. "I'll arrange for other guards tomorrow."

"Gary."

"Yes."

"I think I know who I like."

"Okay. If he's agreeable, I'll turn guard duty over to him tomorrow. Since it's so late, I'll take care of guarding you tonight."

"Gary."

"Yes."

"You're the one. I'd like to make it real."

He is quiet for a moment. "You're not just saying that because of Brett, are you?"

"No, I've been thinking about it for some time now."

"Okay. After this is all over, we'll start a courtship. Until then I'm just a guard, and there'll be no more sham. Goodnight, Serena."

"Gary."

"Hum?"

"Could you hold me for a moment or something?"

"They're going to question us about everything we do. Are you upset about Brett?"

"No. ... Well ... I am upset about Brett, but I want you to hold me because I fell in love with you about a month ago."

He is silent for a moment. "Serena, trust me on this: no courtship until after the committee proceedings."

Disappointment is clearly evident in her whispered concession. "Okay. But after this is all over, you'll stay here?"

"Shouldn't we wait a while on that, or are you afraid of Brett?"

"It has nothing to do with Brett."

"That's good, but I'd like to ... ah ... try out our new relationship for a while before we make any commitments. Is that all right?"

"Okay. That sounds reasonable." She sighs. "I guess I pulled a surprise on you tonight. If you haven't been thinking about us that way, you should have some time to get used to the idea."

He admits, "I've been hoping from the beginning that I'd be the one you'd like."

"So what's the hold up?"

He shrugs despite the fact that she cannot see him in the dark. "How about—once we decide—we have the wedding as soon as possible?"

"Okay," Serena agrees. "It should only take about a week to plan everything. It's becoming routine to have a wedding around here."

"I hear the most time consuming requirement is the premarital counseling."

"Yeah, that and they've started ordering rings which take a couple of weeks."

A hint of disappointment infuses Gary's tone. "I thought you said it'd only take a week?"

"Let's go ahead and order your ring. And if you don't mind, if you're not the sentimental type, I'll use mine. We're kind of stingy around here.

We've been using the same wedding dresses over and over. We have several sizes and styles now, so I'm sure one of them will be perfect for me."

"Wait until Tuesday or whenever the security committee has settled this matter with Brett, before you order my ring," he urges.

"Lawrence will need your size. So why don't you go in and order it."

"Okay."

She whispers, "Gary."

"Yes."

"I love you."

"I love you too."

THIRTY ONE

Brett and Lily remain seated while Serena, Gary Brown, the security committee, and other concerned parties leave the office. Brett stares at the floor until the door is closed.

He looks up. "That's not right!"

She keeps her voice soft. "What's not right?"

"He doesn't get punished for hitting me!"

"That's the decision of the security committee based on all testimony."

"They planned those lies against me!"

"They say they didn't."

"They had time to plot their lies!" He stabs his thumb at his chest. "I was telling the truth!"

She holds her hands out, palms up. "The security committee believed them, not you, so that's the way it is."

"Everyone here has had it in for me since day one!"

She stifles her sigh of exasperation. "What do you mean everyone has it in for you?"

"Well, to start with: you broke my ribs right off!"

She leans toward him and softly whispers, "You attacked. I didn't mean to break your ribs. You fell against the table. It just happened."

He leans back in his chair and crosses his arms.

Lily continues, "I gave you some advice, didn't I: about how to court a woman?"

He nods. "Yeah, but it didn't work. It was going fine but real slow then they found out about each other and poof! They were both gone, and they warned all the other women."

"Women don't find competition … ah … acceptable."

With compassion, she gazes at the forlorn man. "I checked our list. Your wife and children are on it. I'll try to find them as soon as possible."

"She's my ex. We don't get along. She's only on the list because you said you didn't want to separate children from their mothers."

Lily changes the topic in an effort to mollify the frustrated and irate man. "You have to admit that the committee let you off easy."

"Same ol' same ol'," he mutters.

"We don't have many options here. Prison or another chance, that's our only choices. Just don't let it happen again. You've been warned that prison awaits you, next time."

"You could sell me," Brett suggests.

"I have no intention of selling you. I could be sending you to some place worse than prison. Just be nice to all the women and maybe they'll quit warning everyone. We're getting to be a very large operation. Maybe you'll find someone someday."

"Humph!"

"Look, there're lots of other guys out here in the same boat. You're not the only one. So what're you so hot about?"

"I don't see why Serena won't." He looks at his feet then back up at her. "Do you know what they did just because I asked?"

"I don't particularly want to know," Lily admits.

He snarls, "I think you need to know what goes on around here!"

Lily rolls her eyes. She considers this tactic merely another angle of his verbal assault. She genuinely doubts his truthfulness. She reconsiders. She is certain he has been attacked although he has vehemently denied it. Now, it appears that he might be ready to admit it.

He leans forward. "I politely approached Serena a few days after she got here. James was with her, but I didn't think anything about it. That wasn't unusual at Mr. Barton's. James told me she didn't do that anymore and not to bother his wife. I tried again later when he wasn't around, and Serena told me the same thing. Then I got a note to meet her at the river later that night. Do you know what happened out there?"

She stares at him with a grim expression clouding her face. A name pops into her thoughts: Frank—always her first suspect when questionable activity is involved.

"James, Frank, and some other guys were there. Serena wasn't! They beat me then held my head under water until I thought I was going to drown! They did it again and again! I had to swear that I'd leave Serena and all other women alone!"

322

Lily sits up straight. "Was that also what happened that time you were running through the brush?"

"There was some guy chasing me!"

"I saw him too, but wasn't that the reason Frank asked for you? So he could ... ah ... do that to you?"

He nods.

"Why didn't you report it? He's not supposed to be abusing anyone, no matter what they did?"

"He said he'd drown me the next time ... but he didn't. ... He said that every time: that he'd drown me next time, but he never did."

She is saddened to learn that he has been repeatedly abused, despite the fact that she already suspected it. She realizes that it is partially due to their lack of an effective judicial system. Surmising that Brett's abuse started before Serena arrived, Lily asks, "Who was it?"

"It was Frank and ...."

She clarifies, "I mean, who was the woman before Serena came?"

"Oh ... ah," he stammers. "I didn't know Angel was only fourteen."

Anxiety grips Lily at his mention of the puckish, yet, vulnerable teen.

"I quickly let her go, but Frank got mad anyway. Before that it was Susie, but she chased me with a knife so Frank didn't really need to beat me; I wasn't going to bother her ever again."

Lily loosens the talons of her anxiety by turning the conversation back to the slightly more benign topic of his pursuit of Serena. "So you thought that with Frank and James both gone, you had a chance with Serena?"

He nods and looks up. She is leaning back in her chair with her arms crossed. He leaps up.

Lily opens her office door. John looks up. At her disheveled appearance, he leaps from his chair.

"I've already called for the helicopter," she states.

John looks at Brett, writhing in pain.

"I need you to go get a nurse."

In shock, he stares at her, mouth agape, as he backs toward the clinic. "Is this what you do when the security committee doesn't sufficiently punish someone?"

She shakes her head. "No, he attacked. He's headed for prison when he recovers."

John turns and dashes toward the nurses' clinic.

Lily looks over at Tommy Walker, waiting patiently on an overstuffed chair. He stands up, saunters over with his hands in his pockets, and looks into her office. He turns to her. "I've come to tell you Rene identified her attacker, but it looks like it doesn't matter anymore."

Her eyebrows shoot up. "It was Brett?"

He nods.

"How could that be? We got him three or four months before Mr. Patterson brought her to me. … Oh!" She slaps her hand over her mouth.

He arches his eyebrows, silently urging her to share her sudden thought.

"I guess that explains the disappearing acts he used to do and why we couldn't find him anywhere."

Tommy guesses, "He hasn't done that since Reggie died?"

She shakes her head. "It never seemed plausible that he was going into town and coming back, but I guess he was hitching a ride with Mr. Patterson's delivery men after all. At least he was hitching a ride one way and walking or something, since we only get deliveries twice a week; he was never away for three days."

"Maybe Reggie was giving him a ride back and dropping him off in the hills," Tommy suggests.

A puzzled look falls across Lily's face. "There's one other thing that I don't understand. How did she manage to recognize his voice? We've had Brett under constant surveillance for over a week. Rene hasn't been near him."

Tommy pulls his phone out of his pocket. "I recorded his voice. I became suspicious of him after what he did to Serena, so I checked it out.

"I'll go tell Rene that she's safe." He shoves his phone in his pocket and saunters off.

THIRTY TWO

Lily and Gary Brown walk down the long corridor from the hospital and into the clinic hall. Her oversized white coat swirls just above her ankles; the long sleeves are rolled to her elbows. His coat is only slightly tight across his shoulders but he has left it unbuttoned because it does not come close to buttoning across his broad chest. The sleeves are about an inch too short. He has rolled them a couple of times to hide the misfit. But there is nothing he can do about the length other than wait for the seamstresses who are waiting on a shipment of fabric; the last shipment fell victim to road bandits. To complete his official look, he carries a clipboard and two pens jostle in his breast pocket.

At Jupiter's suggestion, Lily has agreed to search for the families of all the vendors. When she offered to search for his family, he stated that he could not allow her to search for his family without extending that privilege to the others who have no way to search for their own. However, like many other things about the compound, it must remain a well-kept secret.

Eva steps out of an exam room and signals. They walk into the room. Eva follows and closes the door.

Lily looks at the man, one of the vendors from the market. "You'll be here until noon. Is that too long?"

"Guess not."

She turns to Eva. "Okay, this is the last one this morning." She pats Gary's arm. "Our new 'orderly' Mr. Brown will schedule appointments for everyone else who comes in for one of these special 'MRIs'. The break room will be his office today. About how many people are crowding the waiting room?"

Eva looks at the man sitting on the exam table, silently passing the question to him.

He shrugs. "I'd guess about twenty. At least, that's how many were there when I was called in a couple of minutes ago."

"Okay." Lily turns to Gary. "Two every thirty minutes is four per hour. That'll be sixteen this afternoon and the rest on Wednesday."

"They're not going to like that," the man states.

Lily explains, "Everyone who gets in by Thursday will be in the same boat. I'll have their relatives on my list and will get to search for them on Friday. So that's another sixty-four for this week. Will that get everybody?"

He shakes his head. "Another thing I don't understand is how you'll be able to search for so many people in just one day. Surely you'll miss somebody just by accident."

"I have staff to help search for names," she obliquely replies, not willing to reveal that her bidding on the slave auction is totally electronic, "and there's really no rush. Another few weeks won't make much difference."

He argues, "That's a hard concept to grasp too."

"Let me explain it like this: out of ten thousand or so on our list," she says speaking of their complied list of family and friends of everyone under her capable care, "I average thirty-five per week. What's that percent?"

A frown clouds the man's face, "Less than one."

"Don't get discouraged. It just means it might be three months before I find the first person. We need to get started but one week isn't going to make that much difference, nothing to get hot over."

He takes a deep breath. "Okay. Now how much does this cost?"

"I won't bill until we get someone," Lily replies.

"How much does it usually cost?"

"The average is six thousand."

He cringes. "Ouch!"

"How many are on your list?"

"I'm going," Eva says.

Lily nods. Eva hands her the 'patient' chart, slips out, and closes the door.

"I guess I could pare it down to closest family," the man suggests.

"No need for that. You don't know who's survived. Put them all on," Lily urges. "We'll probably only find a few. So how many are on your list?"

"I have a big family: forty."

She slowly nods. "I can see why you'd be worried about the cost, but once you have family here, they can share the cost. Why don't we go over to the hospital, so they can use this room?"

She turns to Gary. "Have you got it?"

"Yeah, two every half hour from one to five this afternoon and if—"

"Four-thirty," she corrects.

"Okay, we need to be finished by five not starting on the last two."

"We'll probably be here 'til six but taking two more at five would keep us here until almost seven."

"Okay. If I can't answer their questions, I'll call." Gary checks the phone in his pocket.

She nods and looks down at the chart. "Mr. Johnson, let's go and no questions until we get to the waiting room over there."

Mr. Johnson nods in agreement. "Jupiter warned us that this has to be kept completely quiet."

Lily and Mr. Johnson meet John—also wearing a white coat, slightly too small—and a 'patient' at the door to the waiting room. A guard sits in a chair beside the door. Lily looks at John; anxiety is etched on his face. "Mr. Thorne, you call the next patient and let me talk to this one for a moment."

He hands her the chart he carries, picks up the top chart from a stack on a small table, and enters the waiting room. She slips Mr. Johnson's chart under the pile and turns toward the door. John and a patient exit and walk over to the MRI room, where the idle machine looms over the activity completely unrelated to health care. John glances back. His brow is sharply creased and his jaw slowly grinds. She smiles to reassure her anxious bodyguard.

Lily enters the waiting room, followed by the two patients. "Mr. Johnson, please have a seat."

She closes the door and glances at the chart in her hand. With a smile, she looks up at the burly man beside her. "Mr. Valdez, I need to get a message to the vendors that we're being too obvious. Too many 'patients' are coming. Jupiter was supposed to instruct that only fifteen come each day. We need to slow it down before someone gets suspicious."

"We're all anxious to turn names in," Mr. Valdez contends, accurately conveying the attitudes of all the vendors who have suddenly been offered the opportunity to search for loved ones.

"It's not possible to go any faster."

"You have more people. Get a few more set up in there," Mr. Valdez suggests with a hint of sternness in his tone.

"We only have two laptops. We've ordered two more, but it'll take two to three weeks for them to get here."

"Scavenge some."

"We depleted that a couple of years ago. Can you subtly spread the word that they need to have patience? Mr. Brown is speaking to those already in the waiting room and making appointments for them to come back later. See if you can head off the flow coming in. Here hold your chart a moment."

He holds the open chart. She scribbles a phone number on the corner of the mostly blank page and tears it off. She takes the chart and hands him the phone number. "This is Mr. Brown's phone. Have people call and schedule an appointment instead of coming in. That'll be much less obvious than everyone coming in twice. But tell them not to swamp him; he has to schedule those in the waiting room first."

He slips the paper into his shirt pocket. "Will they all be able to come in by Thursday?"

"No, some will have to come next week or maybe even the next."

"We thought this was the only week."

Sudden insight lights Lily's face. "So the problem is miscommunication. We'll continue this from now on. We'll just cut it down to once a week once we get past the initial rush. The major problem now is that we can't let any of the barons know what's going on and the packed waiting room down there is making it too obvious."

"Okay," Mr. Valdez agrees. "I'll head off the stampede. None of us wants to ruin this opportunity, but we are all very anxious to get started."

"Thanks." She opens the door for him and nods at the guard. Mr. Valdez steps out; the guard rises to escort him to the exit. She closes the door and leans against the wall for lack of available seating.

She pulls her phone off her waistband and taps in Gary's number. "Mr. Brown, I've given out your phone number, so they can call for appointments. … Okay. Bye."

She puts up her phone and pulls out her web-link device. She lays the open chart on a table by the door, enters Mr. Valdez's information into hospital billing, closes the chart, and returns the device to her waistband.

She looks up. "Mr. Johnson, I know you have more questions."

"Why can't we write our lists down? We could all write at the same time."

For the tenth time this morning, she answers, "No paper trail. It's too dangerous. We have barons here who would resort to murder if they found out that I'm redeeming your families for you."

"That's why the subterfuge, huh?"

She nods.

"When you find someone they're going to be on your slave registry, aren't they?"

She nods. "Yeah, even though you've paid for them, but just consider that a formality and temporary."

"Since most of us aren't listed as slave owners and can't 'purchase' our families from you, how're we going to work this?"

This question is new, apparently most of the vendors have not thought that far ahead, so she shrugs. "Suggestions?"

The men look at each other and shrug. Mr. Johnson looks at the floor and then back up. "We don't know."

"Okay. We're hoping for more freedom someday, but in the meantime, … we have to find a workable solution."

Mr. Johnson sighs. "What's Jupiter doing?"

Lily replies, "His wife and daughter aren't on the slave registry, so it's a different problem."

"But he still has a problem. Let's start with his solution and see if it'll fit ours."

"We haven't discussed it yet," Lily admits. "His daughter will be in the hospital for a long time. She's still in a coma so Marissa will be staying in one of our houses to be close to her. So you see it's a very different problem. We're hoping none of your family is in the same circumstance."

"Could we set up a house inside your compound here?" Mr. Johnson suggests. "That way our family could work here and we could stay with them. We'd … well, maybe I should say: I'd be willing to pay to live here to be with my family."

She nods. "That sounds like a good idea to me. I'll run it by my supervisors and check on the availability of vacant houses."

"Thanks, Mrs. Schwartz. Now let me ask another question. I hope I'm not getting too personal with this, but none of us has paid any attention to the slave trade so we're at a loss as to what goes on. How many of your family have you found?"

"Most of my family is dead, so I'm not typical. I found my cousin's two children two years ago. I'm still looking for my cousin and her husband. Other than that, I'm looking for my in-laws but only the few whose names I can remember; if I ever get one, they'll give me the names of the others. Let's see: that's a total of around twenty, and I've found two. For some people though, I've found most of their close family."

He squints with one eye. "Other than death, what prevents you from finding someone? Do you know?"

"I know some of the reasons. Some people are being protected by someone and aren't slaves. We won't ever find them through the slave trade. Some may have been able to evade capture. There's also the possibility that some have joined the lawless gangs. Actually, there could be many reasons why someone wouldn't be on any slave registry. It is possible that there are areas of the country where there's no slavery."

"Can you find them, if they're on the slave registry but not for sale?"

"We're working on a search engine that can do that, but there are too many different databases being used. My tech guy told me he has to hack into systems and get a copy of their program and write code so that he can search it. And don't ask me what he means by write code; I don't know, but he's always saying that. He's also started selling our database program and touting it as universal, but each time he comes across a new database, he has to update his program so they can transfer their data to it. So you see, we're already working on the snags. It takes a lot of time. There's nothing you could want that we haven't already thought of. We've been doing this for over two years. Maybe someday we can set up a website to search for people and establish communications with family, but for now we're stuck with this inefficient system."

"Well," Mr. Johnson drawls. "I didn't understand several of those words, but I can see that you're working on it. We'll just see what happens." He leans back with a smile on his face and waits his turn to talk to one of the two 'MRI technicians' who will enter his family into Mrs. Schwartz's database.

Lily looks around the room and hopes Mr. Finke does not get wind of their new assault upon the perverse system of slavery.

THIRTY THREE

John Thorne dashes to catch up with Lily as she walks toward the old wooden barn which they use for exercise and training. She looks up, "Hi, John."

"Hi, Jackie. We have the final report on fresh graves. They didn't find any unexplained ones and neither did Lawrence find any missing persons on the databases of the other barons, so it looks like they hid any murders Mr. Finke might have done to intimidate them or he's merely threatened."

"I'd guess that the barons are easily intimidated and that he merely threatened. I think most of them aren't wily enough to figure out that they'd need to hide a death. If they were wily, they'd be plotting against him instead of capitulating to his terrorism."

"Or it could be that they don't care enough about their slaves for it to be a threat."

She raises one eyebrow. "It didn't even occur to me that they wouldn't care."

"I ran across it all the time. When they did care, it was merely the financial cost to replace them," John states.

"It's hard to respect anyone who buys into such a despicable practice as slavery. I also don't have much respect for anyone without backbone, and most of the barons around here are a pretty spineless lot. Well, that's when dealing with their peers; many of them are brutal with their slaves."

She guides their conversation to the reason she asked him to practice with her. "Brett's a pretty deplorable guy, but he does have backbone. Usually I can take down an untrained man easily without injuring them but not Brett. He's a determined scraper."

"It really surprised me at the number of broken bones he had."

"That's not the first time I broke his bones," Lily admits.

"Really?"

"Yeah."

John knits his brow. "Tell me about the others?"

"It was just his first interview. He's been on pretty good behavior until recently. I think that's why the committee let him off so easy. And I just cracked a couple of his ribs the first time and only because he fell against the corner of a table."

"How long ago was that?"

"Let's see, it was the February before you arrived which was last September, so that's … hum … eighteen months ago. He's been on good behavior for a long time. I didn't realize it'd been so long. It seems like yesterday that you got here and that was eleven months ago. Well, almost a year now; next week is September."

He allows Lily to precede him into the barn then steps inside. "I'm glad you've trained some other men to be orderlies and escort the vendors to those MRIs. Gary's having a blast since he gets to work with Serena all day, but I was getting tired of spending all day in the hospital."

"We only did that for three days."

"Yeah, but I was getting really bored."

She contends, "You were more than bored. You were anxious and not very communicative."

He lets out a long, slow breath. "Sorry, but I'm still thinking about Brett attacking you. I didn't hear anything, and I was sitting right outside the door!"

"It's a soundproof room. We did that to have a place for private conversations back when Mr. Barton was doing all that eavesdropping."

"What are we doing today?" He puts his foot on a wooden crate and unties his shoe.

She slips her canvas shoes off and puts her keys, phone, and web-link device in them. "We're going to practice together, so you can leave the anxiety behind."

He unties his other shoe. "I'll be all right."

"No you're not. You're acting like an old mother hen, and you're going to make a mistake."

She backs onto the mat. The other men note her sly grin, cease practicing, and gather around the mats.

John follows her. "I don't see the point. I can pin you in minutes."

Her grin turns into a smirk. "Our practices are organized, designed to teach specific moves. Today—other than using constrained blows and backing off when receiving a constrained blow—this is no holes barred, including illegal moves a desperate combatant would use."

"Do you attack me or I attack you?"

"You come after me."

John observes her smug expression and relaxed demeanor for a moment before making his carefully considered move.

After thirty minutes the cheering crowd has swollen to fifty. It would be more, but most residents cannot leave their assignments. They will have to be content with secondhand accounts. Wayne Brashear dashes through the barn door and pushes his way to the front of the excited audience, panting from his dash across the compound. He is ruing his expanding belly due to the excellent food served in the dining hall and resolving to pay more attention to the amount he consumes and return to his neglected exercise routine.

With his hands on his knees, John warily eyes the petite fireball. Lily has used every dirty trick in the book to deflect his attack. He is beginning to tire; he put his greatest effort into his first moves fully convinced that this 'practice session' would last only a few minutes. Her mouth is still closed; she is under no distress. Nolan Graves pushes his way back to the front of the crowd, casually hiding a loaded water pistol behind him.

John sighs. "You're not really a brown belt, are you?"

"My dad couldn't get me to concentrate on belt testing. I called it superficial; he called it getting along with others."

With a grin of amusement, John lifts his eyebrows. "Getting along with others is a concept you had trouble understanding."

"I could see it in gymnastics but had trouble applying it in life. I was much more interested in the training than in honors. Dad had to threaten me to get me to do it."

"What'd he threaten you with?"

"Quitting the training."

"Why were you so interested in training without the accomplishment of earning belts?"

"I wanted to be able to take down my brothers as easily as Dad did."

With an astonished expression, John exclaims, "Your dad fought with your brothers!"

Lily shakes her head. "It was a game like in that ancient movie where the police detective gets attacked in his own home. Turns out it was his houseboy and all for honing his skills. Dad put a stop to it when my brothers got too big."

"But you kept your interest even after leaving home," he observes.

She nods.

"Still with no interest in belts?" he queries.

"No. After I left home, I dabbled in everything I came across."

"I bet your teachers didn't like that very much."

"They sure didn't. One finally confronted me. He said that despite seeming very serious about training, I didn't seem to be interested in advancing. He asked what I was doing. I explained and he took me on the mats, same as I did you today."

"How'd you do?"

"Only took me about two minutes to pin him."

"He was a black belt?"

She nods.

"How many degrees?"

"I think it was four, but I could be confusing him with one of the others."

John inquires, "I don't see how you became good enough to best him, without specifically working on anything past a brown belt."

Lily smiles, "I had my dad to practice with, and we had my first black belt testing scheduled when he died. After that, he wasn't there to push me. Combine that with jumping from place to place because I moved or had a baby, and no one ever pushed me. After my third child, I became known as someone willing to practice outside of class and it soon became apparent that anyone who could beat me would easily pass their testing. After a few years, I had to flub it so that I didn't discourage anyone and that's when he challenged me."

"What'd he do after you pinned him?"

Lily replies, "He recommended another style: close-quarters fighting. I didn't stick with it very long. I found it too gruesome."

Since Lily appears distracted by John's questions, Nolan dashes to John, thrusts the loaded water pistol into his hand, and quickly backs away. John's quick shot misses. She is already upon him, holding his wrist firmly.

Within seconds, he has lost the weapon. He eyes her warily as they circle. He can no longer attack unless he is close enough to grab the weapon. Over the next several minutes, he tries various moves but is unsuccessful at getting close. She easily stays out of his reach. Since she has shown no inclination to shoot, he makes two quick feints then leaps toward her. Water splashes across his forehead and runs down his face. He stops in surprise. Regaining his composure, he sits down and lies back. With his arms and legs spread wide, he turns his head to one side and closes his eyes. "I'm dead."

She tosses the gun to Jack and walks over. With her fists on her hips, she grins. "After a thirty minute break, we'll go to the next lesson."

He opens his eyes. "There's a second lesson? This looks sufficient to me."

She looks at the crowd. "I need four volunteers."

Every former Seal in the crowd grins and raises his hand.

"No military men."

She points. "Branson."

Her young cousin, Branson Parker, leaps onto the mat and prances around making the vee-for-victory sign with both hands.

Brian Ladd, Josie Vaughn's young fiancé, leaps up and down doing jumping jacks to draw her attention. "Brian."

She looks at Henry Davis, Frank and Darla Smith's son-in-law; he grins in anticipation. "Henry and …."

She looks around. Eric Anderson, youngest son of Charles and Denise, is flexing his muscles to edge out the competition of several young men who have followed Brian's lead and are leaping around wildly. Their movements are erratic, yet surprisingly homogeneous in effect, highlighting Eric's tactics for setting himself apart. "Eric."

"Okay," John says without rising from the floor. "After thirty minutes, what exercise are we going to do?"

She leans over him and grins. "We'll fend off four attackers. You will fight beside me. You will not try to defend me or protect me."

John wipes his bare chest with his sweat-soaked shirt. Lily runs her fingers through her wet hair then pulls her damp, clinging blouse away from her body. The August sun blazes upon them as they walk away from the barn. A gentle breeze facilitates the cooling evaporation of their sweat. He uses his shirt to wipe beads of sweat from his brow then looks down at the top of the petite woman's head. "How young were you when you started martial arts training?"

"Three."

"That figures. Have you been taking them ever since?"

"No. Granddad punished me when I was thirteen and made me quit. I started again when Daddy and I moved out but that didn't last long. In college, I took it up again since Granddad didn't have any say about it then. I had to take a few breaks along the way for things like having three babies, but I always went back as soon as I could."

"Ralph made a pretty good bodyguard for you, didn't he?"

"Yes."

"I assume that's because he knew."

She laughs, obviously at an amusing memory. He grins in anticipation; her colorful past always provides an amusing anecdote.

"Several years before the terrorists' attacks, some really dumb guy tried to hold up the dojo."

He laughs. His surreal mental image is a disheveled, desperate addict facing trim, athletic ninjas dressed in black.

"I was leaving so was dressed in jeans, and he apparently thought I wasn't a student. He chose me to gather the loot. I don't know why he'd think anybody on the mats would have anything worth stealing on them. Anyway, I calmly walked over while he held out a bag. Within seconds, I had his gun and he was face down on the floor. Ralph was one of the policemen who answered the call." She takes a deep breath. "I still get scared just thinking about that day. It was the first time anything like that had happened. I started shaking. I knew Ralph, so he tried to comfort me. I could tell he was pretty uncomfortable, so I tried to put him at ease."

"He's a pretty reserved guy isn't he?"

"Yeah, he is. I started talking to him about guns to get my mind off being scared. That's when I started taking lessons from Ralph. I'd realized as soon as I took the guy's gun that I didn't know the first thing about handling it. That was the scary part for me. It wasn't the guy. He was a piece of cake. It was holding his gun and not knowing what to do with it. I was relieved that I didn't shoot anybody by accident, like my instructor who dashed over to assist me."

John states, "I think I have the picture now. We've been trained to protect innocent bystanders, but you don't need that."

"Yeah. I'm not an innocent bystander, and I have an advantage— those who don't know me are taken completely unaware. I don't want you distracted by trying to protect me. And I don't want you blocking my moves."

"You'd have been filled with anxiety if we'd gone after Mr. Finke while I was still trying to be your super bodyguard, wouldn't you?"

"I'd have taken someone else," Lily informs her extremely capable and unyieldingly loyal bodyguard.

"That'd have disappointed m …." He stops in his tracks as a group of young children run out of the schoolhouse and toward the closely cropped grass of the athletic field.

She notices Lucas Thorne in the excited group and looks up at John's rapt expression. "Johnny told me you're going to have another one."

"Uh-huh," he mutters in a decidedly distracted fashion.

She waits a moment then pries into John's thoughts. She does not want him distracted when they meet with Mr. Finke. "What're you thinking?"

"I was just looking at Lucas."

"What about him?"

"I'm still wondering why he looks just like Johnny did at that age."

"We can probably find out. Do you really want to know?"

He nods. She whips out her phone. "Jeff, where are you? … Break away and come over to the ball field by the school."

Jeff Clark walks up and plops beside Lily as she sits, ankles crossed, on the grass beside John Thorne. A ball bounces toward them. John reaches up and bats it back toward the children.

Jeff grins and leans back on his hands. "Well, I popped the question. Jenny said yes. I asked Tommy for her hand, and Mary's planning the wedding."

Lily looks at Jeff and grins. "Well, get in line."

He laughs. "We've had a slue of them, haven't we?"

She nods and looks over at John. "Not going to speak to your cousin?"

"Hi, Jeff."

"Hi, John. What's up? You're kind of quiet."

With a sober expression, he turns to Jeff. "Jackie seems to think you know why Lucas doesn't look the least bit like Mr. Barton."

"Well," Jeff intones with obvious anxiety. "That's because he … ah … had problems with … ah … in that area."

"Oh? … So what was going on over there?" John asks.

"Stephanie's never told you?"

John looks back toward Lucas and shakes his head. "I don't think she even wants to think about it."

"Well … it was bad. I'd prefer not to think about it either. Let me be very brief. Soon after the terrorists' attacks Mr. Barton raided some pharmacies and then his wife split. Then there were … other problems, so we destroyed his stash. After that we 'helped' him raid the pharmacies and for 'some strange reason' never found any more of the various medications for ED; I mean we hid them behind other medications on the shelves and we told him we didn't find any and he bought it.

"After he found Cisco somewhere, he used his wiles and threats and the unsettled and dangerous conditions to get us under his control and … things got worse. He killed … I mean he had Cisco kill or beat anyone who didn't … ah … do as they were asked. The multitude was now outnumbered—by two men—and we had to go into survival mode. We quickly discovered that some decided to survive by becoming informants. Most decided to survive by becoming isolated. Only a few of us continued to trust our own little clique."

Jeff turns and looks at John, who is still focused on Lucas, his blank expression not betraying the turmoil in his gut. "Understand that we were protecting your girls. No one touched your girls."

"Who?"

"Who?" Jeff queries in puzzlement.

"You said *we* not *I.*"

"Stephanie, Johnny, Mike and I."

John jerks his head toward his cousin. "Mike's here?"

Jeff shakes his head. John's face falls.

Lily takes advantage of the pause. "Tell me more about Mike. I keep hearing him mentioned, but don't know much about him."

Jeff replies, "He was my brother."

With trepidation, John leans toward Jeff and guesses, "Mr. Barton killed him?"

Jeff nods. John reaches past Lily and puts his hand on Jeff's shoulder. "It's all right, man. Thanks for protecting them. Where's Mike buried? I'd like to go see him since he gave his life for my family."

Jeff tries to wipe his teary eyes without it being noticeable. "I'll take you over there sometime, maybe tomorrow if you don't have to work."

"I'll let him off tomorrow," Lily states. "After all, it's Saturday. In fact, I'll let him off Saturday and Sunday."

"Thanks."

Jeff looks over at John. "We knew Stephanie was your wife, but she didn't recognize us so we didn't tell her. We didn't want it to get to Mr. Barton. He'd have used the knowledge to really grind us down under his thumb even more. She needed to think of us as kind strangers, so she wouldn't endanger herself for us."

John nods. "I understand. It's too bad one of you didn't decide to take him out."

"We were trying," Jeff admits. "But we had to be very subtle. We couldn't even talk to each other and lay out a plot. We knew others were thinking along the same line, but Cisco or later Ricky would have tortured and killed anyone just for talking about it."

"What were you doing?" John asks.

"We'd made our own stash of drugs and experimented with slipping them into his food. Unfortunately we're engineers, not pharmacists, and never managed a lethal dose before using them all. Since we weren't communicating, one of us could have been giving him something that counteracted someone else's attempt. The cook was doing her best too. His food was heavy on fat, sugar, salt, and any other thing bad for you. She was succeeding better than we were. He loved her cooking … except when one of us slipped in too much of something that altered the taste. She really got in trouble when he threw food against the wall, but she still turned a blind eye when we came into the kitchen. We couldn't communicate, but we all knew and never interfered with another's efforts … never knowingly interfered, that is.

"We also pitted Cisco and Ricky against each other. We assumed we'd fare better if they were adversaries. We managed to sabotage any new man who looked like he'd become a competent guard, and we also covered for the incompetent so Mr. Barton wouldn't sell them. We even thwarted his attempt to establish a cell phone system; we didn't want to lose our warning system."

Lily interrupts, "What warning system?"

"We used texting to warn each other when Ricky was coming around."

"Clever," Lily states.

Jeff continues, "I'm not sure what some of the others were doing, but we managed to make life tolerable with our multipronged and uncoordinated sabotage."

Jeff slowly shakes his index finger. "I had one big success. I managed to dose his wine with something available from the local drug dealer. It made him suggestible, and that's how I got him to decrease his demand for Lucas."

Surprise flashes onto Lily's face. "You did that. I thought Frank did it. He took credit for it."

Jeff raises his eyebrows. "I wanted him to! He was saving my life. I just happened to run into him when I went out the back with Lucas. I thrust Lucas at him and told him to go home immediately. That's the only time I've ever seen Frank speechless. He stood there with his mouth hanging open while I slammed the door in his face."

"Jeff, are you sure you want to be confessing stuff like this to me?" Lily raises her eyebrows, obviously teasing but with a nugget of disapproval. "After all you've mentioned dealing with the local drug dealer."

"I was dealing with him only to bribe one of the drug-addicted guards, so I could get out the door with Lucas. I eventually ratted, and Commander Williams shut him down."

"You make me wish that I'd won the bid for Ricky," Lily mutters.

"We saw Ricky as a great opportunity."

Lily turns to look at Jeff.

Jeff continues, "Pitting Cisco and Ricky against each other had a great deal to do with Cisco's disappearance. We'll never know whether he just absconded or Ricky came out and killed him, but at least, he never came back."

"Which was worse: Cisco or Ricky?" Lily asks.

Jeff shrugs. "As to having a conscience, both were without one. Cisco was not too bright, so he was unpredictable. Ricky was crafty and that made him more predictable; he didn't go off half baked like Cisco."

"So you preferred Ricky?"

Jeff replies, "It had definite advantages, especially since he never had any competent help."

Without pausing, Jeff suddenly blurts, "Say, Jackie … I hear you grew up with Mr. Barton. What was he like then? Was he as bad back then?"

"I wouldn't say I grew up with him. I got him banned from our house when I was four. I found him to be a real terror. Oh!" She plops back on the grass and covers her face.

With concern, John leans toward her. "Jackie, what's wrong?"

She takes a deep breath. "A long-hidden memory suddenly resurfaced."

"With what I've heard of your childhood, I'm not surprised."

Jeff closes his eyes, chastising himself for stirring up bad memories. "Sorry."

"It's all right." She sits up and takes a deep breath.

Jeff and John look at her. She is staring at the children. They glance at each other. Jeff breaks the silence. "Are you going to tell us what dastardly deed Mr. Barton did as a child?"

She takes a deep breath. "To start with: I was three when Granddaddy insisted that I stay home instead of staying at the drug store with Daddy. I think I was getting in the way, so Daddy agreed. But that didn't work either. Some of my earliest memories—other than being at the drugstore— are of screaming and running and grabbing my grandmother around the legs when my brothers bothered me. One day Clarence and one of his brothers were there too. When I ran into the kitchen, my grandmother put down the knife she was using and started wiping her hands so she could pick me up. I grabbed the knife and ran after Clarence."

She props her elbow on her flexed knee, leans her mouth against her fist, and gnaws her knuckles.

Jeff glances at John then back to Lily. "What was his dastardly deed?"

"He was just pestering me, nothing really bad. It was things like if I said *don't touch me,* he'd creep up behind me and touch me with the tip of his finger. I had no peace, so I got really mad."

The two men look at her as she stares unseeingly at the children. John breaks the silence. "Did you get punished?"

She grins. They chuckle in anticipation of a funny anecdote. She takes a deep breath. "Even after they sent all five boys outside, they couldn't get me to give up the knife and I had no qualms about running with it in my hand. Daddy came home and got me. He took me straight to the dojo and signed me up for lessons."

John flops back on the grass. Laughter shakes his entire body. Jeff wipes tears of laughter on his sleeve.

After a few moments, she sighs. "It's funny now, but it sure wasn't back then. It's also scary to merely recall my childhood, especially after what they found in a secret room in the basement of the Grande Hotel. It included some photo albums which explained some unsolved murders from my childhood. So to really answer your question: yes, he's always been .... How should I state it? Hum ... shall we say without a conscience, not even a ... twinge."

Jeff stands. "I'd better be getting back."

She turns to face him. "One more question before you go. I don't look anything like my cousin, so why do you two look like brothers?"

"We're double cousins. My mother and John's father are twins. My father and his mother are brother and sister."

John's expression turns somber. "Jeff, would you mind telling me what happened over there? I know there were beatings and stuff, but Stephanie can't talk about it."

Jeff plops down, plucks a blade of grass, and twirls it between his fingers. "Johnny's beating was because he wouldn't tell his sisters to unlock the door and come out of the closet. Mike had put a sliding bolt inside the closet door so the kids could hide when Stephanie wasn't there. Stephanie was furious about Mr. Barton beating Johnny. She railed at him and broke his cane, so we put a big bolt on the outer door too. Cisco broke the door and got in, but we had reinforced the closet door and he couldn't break it down.

"Mr. Barton's next step was to sell Johnny and threaten to sell the girls if Stephanie wouldn't hand them over. Of course, she wouldn't. We reinforced her bedroom door and put on two large sliding bolts.

"He sent Mike and me on assignments to get us out of the way. We were almost beside ourselves. James and Pete volunteered to go with Mike, so he could return as soon as possible. Stanley went with me. All three of these guys were risking their lives for us. I guess Mr. Barton didn't find out and that's the only reason Cisco didn't kill them.

"When Mike got back, Cisco was beating Stephanie. Mike struck him in the back of the head with his tool box and knocked him out cold. I don't see how he could swing that heavy box that high. I guess he was furious. He then took Stephanie and the girls to the clinic.

"Stanley and I had one setback after another so didn't return as soon as we had hoped. We found Cisco beating Mike. I took the largest tool in my kit and whacked Cisco from behind.

"Mike was barely conscious and muttered that he'd done the same thing. Stanley and I scooped him up and put him in a truck. As we raced to the clinic, Mike roused enough to tell me what had happened."

Lily guesses, "You didn't make to the clinic."

"It was late. You'd already left. We saw your van on the road to the hills and gave chase but Mike died. We buried him in the hills."

Pointing in the general direction of northeast, Lily mutters, "That cairn of rocks just over the hill?"

Jeff nods and stands up. "I really have to go. Jenny and I have a premarital counseling session scheduled."

As Jeff strides away, Lily calls, "Do you want to move him to the cemetery here?"

Jeff looks back at John. They both nod then turn to Lily. She nods, indicating that she has noted their decision.

Jeff turns and walks away.

Lily turns back to John. He is staring unseeingly at the children as they form a single line in front of one of the teachers. She turns toward the schoolhouse. The other teacher takes her place at the rear as the children reluctantly leave their playground.

Lily grimaces because John still seems depressed. "Say, John."

He looks at her.

"Something's still bothering you isn't it?"

He puts his forehead on his knees. "Uh-hum."

"Want to share?"

He shakes his head.

"How about you share anyway?"

He looks up with sadness in his eyes. "It's just that I know Mr. Barton was making videos, and now I know for sure that Stephanie was in them. I guess that's one reason I haven't talked to Stephanie about what happened over there. I didn't want to know. It's better to merely suspect and hope you're wrong. Now I know I'm not wrong."

"I don't know when he started making the videos. I assume it took him a while to get that set up after he got here. She was there just a few months. The migration was in late fall, October and November. I got her the first week in March."

He sighs. "It's still distressing, even if there's just one photo of her."

"I know. We're all in agreement about that, and they're doing something about it."

He looks at her with hope etched on his stressed features. "Who?"

"Lawrence and his assistants."

"What could they possibly be doing about it? I know everything Mr. Barton stored on those hard drives in the wind tower was destroyed, but they were all over the web."

"Lawrence told me in computer speak. I didn't understand it all. He used words like Trojan and worm and things."

"What are they doing, erasing them on the web or something?"

"Something like that."

"Can a good hacker trace it back here?"

"No. Security is his forte. He has those two computer geeks from Mr. Barton's set up with five computers that are totally separate from all of the others. After something is sent out on its delayed mission, the computer is completely reformatted. It's as if the computer it came from no longer exists. Lawrence assured me that it's totally untraceable."

John smiles with relief. "That makes me feel better. How long is it going to take?"

"He says we'll probably be working on this forever. When they first put the bidding system on the web, it was one hundred percent pornography. At least, he couldn't find any legitimate sites."

"So they're going after it all?" John inquires.

"There's no way to merely search out Mr. Barton's contributions to the filth. They did sign everything they put on the web. That's how Mr. Barton got paid royalties for the videos, but they used so many different digital signatures that they don't even remember many of them."

Relieved, he puts his hands on the grass behind him and leans back. Seeking more detailed assurance, he asks, "Are they erasing, corrupting, or destroying?"

"It depends upon the percentage on a computer. I've forgotten the exact numbers but Lawrence said that if it's most of the files then the hard drive crashes and is destroyed. It goes down in steps to a process of manually checking sites that might be legitimate like medical databases or crime lab files."

"Looks like someone would begin selling virus software."

"Lawrence does. There are a lot of computer viruses and worms and things going around without any unified law enforcement efforts focused on the web."

He laughs and uses his soggy shirt to wipe the sweat from his brow. "I'll bet it doesn't filter out this one."

"It gets the earlier versions, but they're always sending out slightly altered versions."

"How much are we making on this, enough to pay for all their time?"

"It's becoming a very lucrative enterprise." She pulls out her web-link device, taps several times then smiles. "We've had three hundred thousand monthly customers so far this month."

"How much is that?"

"That's three hundred thousand on update fees plus almost a hundred thousand new customers is another two million. That's a new record. Plus Lawrence allows one specialized update a day. So that's ... wow!"

"What?"

"He ups his price anytime he gets too many requests for personal service. So far this month, we've made one and a quarter million on specialized updates and that's not counting the database program he sells."

He whistles. "I'd say Lawrence and his staff are earning their keep. That's more than three and a half million. So what's a specialized update?"

"Lawrence is always adding new viruses to the list that the software blocks. If someone is infected with one we don't block, they can opt to allow access to their site so Lawrence can add it and clean up their computer."

"What does he do if they have porn on their site?"

"He checks to make sure it's not a legitimate site. If not, he waits until the worm has destroyed their site then notifies them that it's their turn."

"That seems like gouging, to infect their computer then charge them to clean it up."

"He only charges the high fee on obviously perverse sites. On legitimate sites, he discounts the fee and since it isn't our virus causing the legitimate site the damage, we're doing them a legitimate service. Also he can quickly determine if someone doesn't have viruses and charges them a minimal fee since that's an automated first check of anyone who signs up."

"Has anybody got mad about losing data?"

"He includes the recommendation to make regular backups in all communications and warns them that he can't retrieve destroyed data."

He rubs his chin. "It still seems unethical. Now, don't take me wrong; I'm glad they're eradicating the filth, but it just seems underhanded."

"I know." She wipes the sweat from her brow. "But there is no law right now. No government or industry is policing the web. Remember how you felt just a few minutes ago and how you've been feeling since you got here and how it's been detrimental to your relationship with Stephanie and how she won't talk about it?"

"That's why I said don't take me wrong. I like that you're doing something about it. It's just the ethics of the method."

Lily expands her argument, "We have several dozen people here who have admitted they have the same problem, so we probably have several hundred altogether. Mr. Barton wasn't the only baron making his living off the internet. The counselors approached the security committee several months ago. Depression is a huge problem among survivors of abuse. They warned that several were suicidal and requested that we consider policing the internet, at least until law is restored and we have a government willing and able to police the web."

He smiles. "Lawrence will probably work for the government, when that time comes."

"He's been working with our local government from the beginning. We have official authorization for this but only from our local government, so this must remain confidential. The web is as lawless as society was during those riots after the attacks."

"And you understand the feeling of regret too, don't you?"

She nods. "Yeah, you took notice of what my brother ... ah ... step-brother said, didn't you?"

"Yeah."

"I definitely have some things I'd like to forget."

"And other people don't forget them, do they?"

She shakes her head.

"I'm surprised your dad didn't tell you about your mom?"

She looks at him with a puzzled frown then brightens. "Oh, you mean my mother. Mom was my step-mom."

She focuses her gaze on the grass between her feet. "I think he did tell me, but I didn't realize it. He'd tell me stories about my mother. I was fascinated, but it didn't jive with Mom's personality. Of course she was sick for several years, so I just thought that was it. He'd always end with *your mom doesn't want to talk about this.* I just didn't realize that when he said, *your mother,* he wasn't talking about Mom."

"But those clippings brought it all into focus?" he rhetorically asks, to confirm his assumption.

She nods then in an effort to get her mind off her painful memories and turn John's thoughts away from his pain, she asks, "Are your girls enjoying their new tea set?"

He smiles and Lily is delighted with the serenity displayed on his face.

"We have a tea party every night just before bed. They're having a blast, but I'm at a loss to come up with the wisdom that Ralph apparently imparted to his daughter."

"That'll come in time," Lily assures him.

A scowl furrows his brow. "Johnny's looking a bit left out. He's not about to join the tea party, but he seems to be missing the camaraderie."

"He needs some father, son time, something that's not so feminine."

John looks over at Lily. "Any suggestions?"

She shrugs. "He's been running with the other boys."

"Would you suggest that I join them or should we have a separate time?"

"Let Johnny choose, but I can tell you that all of the boys would be delighted to join the Seals."

"That's a very good idea. We'll have to have a shortened stint with the boys; they wouldn't be able to complete our workout."

Her phone rings. "Hey, Brad. What's up? ... Oh. ... Hold just a moment."

She turns to John. "Spencer Blakely escaped the work detail. They're chasing him through the hills near here, taking advantage of the opportunity to train the officers and test out the equipment we ordered for use with Mr. Finke. Do you want another exercise of working beside me, especially since you'll be with me at Mr. Finke's?"

He grins. "I like any kind of excitement."

THIRTY FOUR

It is eleven p.m. A large crowd has gathered around Al's bank of computer monitors. Their attention is focused on the central monitor. They pay no heed to the increasing warmth of the densely populated room on the unusually hot September evening. Several jostle for a better view. Al's fingers fly across the keyboard. "Okay, it's on the monitors on both ends too."

With a better view, the crowd settles. The grainy, infrared satellite image on the three screens is easy to interpret. A dozen forms slowly approach the rear of a large house in an isolated area northeast of town. Al runs his pointer across an image. A box appears. *ID #SLJM0000138 – Official - authorized.* He runs his pointer across each image. Only the numeric portion of the ID number varies. SLJM stands for: Schwartz, Lily Jacqueline; military.

Al slides the pointer across an image moving within the house. A photo and a text box appear. *Glenn Corbett – Matthew Finke - authorized.*

Randall Laird had gladly informed them that Glenn is a creature of habit. As soon as the last resident of the main house retires for the night, he begins his nightly rounds of checking windows and doors. Soon the indoor ritual is complete. He opens a cold beer, goes out the back door, and steps onto the patio. After a quick scan of the area, he walks over and sits on a rock fence surrounding the untended garden. It is his practice to make his outside rounds after several minutes of quiet solitude. Al has been watching the repetitious scenario every night for a month. Only the time varies, being the most erratic on weekends. Monday through Thursday are the most predictable.

But tonight, unbeknown to Glenn, three former U.S. Navy Seals are hidden in the shadows on the other side of the low fence. The trio of forms quickly merges with Glenn's. Remaining close together, the four forms retreat into the surrounding area, followed by the other nine. It is obvious that nothing has alarmed the other residents of the house. Al takes a quick glance at satellite images on other monitors. Neither have any of the residents in Mr. Finke's other houses become alarmed. Glenn Corbett has silently disappeared into the darkness of an otherwise quiet Monday night.

Mr. Brashear smiles with satisfaction. "It is a go for tomorrow. Mrs. Schwartz, it certainly took you a long time to set up the meeting, but at least, that gave us time to thoroughly check out and train with the equipment."

"Yeah," she replies, "he was resistant. We were hoping to set up the school in town this month, but I guess it'll have to wait until October. I'm hoping tomorrow goes well, so we'll feel safe enough to go ahead."

"It is obvious that all your prep work the last two months has paid off. Not being anxious to set up a meeting with Mr. Finke—at least, not any more anxious to meet with him than any of the other barons—did not alert him that this is more than a discussion. Mr. Corbett found Mr. Laird's bloody clothing and ID card at the rendezvous point. He saw the farce at the emergency room and came out and took note of the dozens of 'fresh graves'. Mr. Finke is apparently satisfied that he has pulled the wool over your eyes, and Mr. Corbett saw no reason to change his nightly routine and now he is out of commission."

Todd injects, "Let's hope Mr. Finke doesn't see any reason to be suspicious now and cancel the meeting."

Mr. Brashear nods. "I think we have done this as unobtrusively as possible. He should not have any reason to be suspicious of us, and we needed to get rid of his henchman. Mr. Laird informed us that he is the only one with the skills to challenge us."

Lily stands. "I'll be showing up anyway. Even if he calls to cancel, I'll still show up to offer him my 'sympathy and support'. After all, I've lost several men who just disappeared at night. I could even offer him some of my men to send out a search party. Let's get some rest. We have a big day tomorrow. Just let me know in the morning if the weapons raid is successful."

Sitting behind Lily in the SUV, John Thorne adjusts his unobtrusive ear piece. "It's too bad Ralph doesn't get to go on this raid with us."

Lily makes sure the transmitter under her blouse is not making a telltale bulge. "I'm just glad that his tea parties are going well."

"I know that delights his daughter," John states. "My girls give me a report every night when we have our tea party: the first tea party the Saturday that he woke up, the next day he could hold the cup, when he sat up, when he sat in a chair, when he first used a walker and they sat at a table, the day he went home, how he gets around the house, and how they walk him across the alley for rehab in the hospital. I get the full report!"

She smiles, delighted with the recovery of the man she considers her mentor, the policeman who taught her gun safety and sharpshooting. Without the expertise Ralph taught her, she would have been ill equipped to handle the crisis after the terrorists' attacks. Mentally he is doing well without any lost of memory due to his concussion or the hypoxia he endured before they could get the first unit of donated blood into his system. It is only the damage to his hip caused by the bullet and the idleness forced upon him during his recovery that are causing him problems, but that is overshadowed by the joy of being reunited with his wife and children.

John inquires, "Now how do I recognize Mr. Finke?"

"He looks like a weasel," Lily replies.

Brad Kraft laughs. "I know exactly who you're talking about. What are our plans once we're inside?"

She turns to look at the three men in the rear seat. "We wing it. We play along with whatever Mr. Finke does until we have something damaging on tape."

Brad looks at the men curled up in the cargo area of the oversized SUV: one Seal and one computer geek. "Wes, are you ready to go?"

"I'm reading everyone loud and clear. So far Marvin is also reading everyone loud and clear. We'll see if he still is once we get there. He and Commander Williams are going to have to stay back at the limit of the range on Lily's mike to stay hidden. It'd be nice to have two copies just in case Mr. Finke manages to get to this one."

"You're going to have three Seals with you, so you should be safe."

"I know. It's comforting that the one back here with me is armed and that all the men in the brush are also armed."

"You're going to be all right, Wes."

Brad turns back toward the front. "Jackie, did you get the report on the weapons raid?"

"Yeah, that was brilliant, breaking Glenn's key in the lock, jamming it. Hopefully they won't be able to open it and discover they have no guns or ammo."

Brad inquires, "Does everybody remember the codes?"

Marvin's reply comes in loud and clear over their earpieces. *"The stone is turned* means Mr. Finke is subdued. That's the one I'm waiting on."

John rattles off all the other codes and their meaning, for the benefit of the untrained participants such as Marvin.

As they approach the last corner before Mr. Finke's isolated compound, Lieutenant Jones pulls his official car to the side of the road. Commander Williams allows the SUV to pass, then gets out and walks into the brush to find a good observation post. Marvin stays in the car with the lieutenant, but the other two officers take their positions as guards in the front and rear of the patrol car.

Lily looks down at the engagement ring on her left hand. She wonders when Max ordered it. Probably before she agreed to 'date' him, she surmises. Her thoughts turn to former senator Howard Wood. A week after meeting him, he began instant messaging her. It soon became clear that he was interested in a relationship. A relationship with Max was long distance enough; she did not want to begin one that required travel to another city, especially with a man she hardly knew. Perhaps that was one reason she so quickly became engaged to Max, not that she hasn't fallen in love with Max. She did, however, want a longer courtship before taking the plunge. Howard took the news well, and she has flashed her ring to a couple of other potential suitors. Since she does not want any distractions when she talks to Mr. Finke, she slips off the ring and slides it into her pocket.

Jack stops the van in front of the main house.

Lily says, "Marvin, can you hear me?"

His clear reply would elicit smiles, if they weren't in a position to be watched from the house.

John hops out and opens the door for Lily. She slides out and walks toward the house followed by John and Brad. Jack and Trevor get out on the driver's side and walk to the front and rear of the vehicle. They nonchalantly lean against it as if they expect their job to be boring.

When she is six feet from the door, a man opens it and steps back allowing them to enter. With a smile, Mr. Finke greets her at the entrance to a large parlor. She takes note of the new carpet and furniture and surmises that he redecorated after killing Officer Hayes.

"Welcome, Mrs. Schwartz. I've arranged entertainment for your men while we meet." He sweeps his hand toward four young women.

John and Brad grin and leer at the women. The women giggle as they flirtatiously pose for the two good-looking and athletic men who appear extremely interested.

Lily smiles at the conniving power baron. "Thank you, Mr. Finke, but my men are on duty and will stay with me while we meet. I started that practice after Reginald Patterson's little debacle. Please send the women away."

John and Brad wipe the grins from their faces, turn away from the women, and step up behind Lily.

"Very well." He motions for the women to leave then indicates the sofa. "Please have a seat."

"Thank you, Mr. Finke." She walks over and sits near the end. John and Brad select positions slightly behind either end of the sofa. They place their hands behind their backs, and their eyes display no emotion.

The baron sits down in an armchair opposite the petite baroness. A heavy mahogany coffee table is between them. It reminds Lily of the table in Commander Tyler's mansion. Noting the scratches on the otherwise pristine tabletop, Lily surmises that it just might be the table belonging to the "Tyrant" who showed no respect for the finely crafted table in his possession.

Mr. Finke's casual demeanor belies his sinister plans. "Please call me Matthew."

"Thank you, Matthew. You may call me Jackie. I'm pleased to be able to meet with you today and delighted that our relationship is comfortable enough to use first names."

"So am I. Jackie, may I offer you something to drink: vodka, scotch, or coffee?"

"Coffee will be fine, thank you."

She takes note of the sole guard standing by the door. It does not appear that Mr. Finke's plans include using force. She is delighted; she will be pleased if she can get damaging statements on tape without having to call in the men hiding in the outlying brush.

"Jackie, what topics have you planned for today's discussion?"

"I haven't planned anything specific. You may guide our discussion, Matthew. What would you like to discuss?"

"I don't want to discuss the co-op other than saying that I'm against it."

"Very well. What concerns you about our situation in town?"

One of the young women walks in with a silver tray laden with a silver coffee service and four china cups. She sets it on the coffee table in front of Mr. Finke then turns and grins at Brad. He retains his impassive expression. She coyly grins at John as she steps toward him. He remains impassive with his eyes apparently locked on Mr. Finke, but he is well aware of the attractive young woman. He holds his breath until she walks out of the room.

Mr. Finke pours coffee into a cup. "Sugar or cream?"

"Both thank you."

He ladles a heaping spoonful of sugar into the cup and then pours in cream. After stirring, he lays the spoon on the saucer and hands it to her.

"Thank you." She sets it before her and stirs while he pours a second cup.

Mr. Finke looks at John. "Sugar or cream?"

She quickly intervenes, "Thank you, but my guards are on duty, Matthew."

"Very well." He puts two heaping spoonfuls of sugar in the coffee and stirs.

She hides her grin. If he won't drink his coffee or spills it, she will know he is trying to poison or dope them. If he does drink his, the poison could still be in the cream.

She lays down the spoon and puts her hand over the steaming cup. "Too hot, I'll have to wait a bit. So Matthew, what's your first topic?"

He lays his spoon down and leans back. "I've been hearing conflicting reports."

"Of what?"

"Some have said that there are antislavery rebels killing masters in other towns, but Commander Williams says he hasn't heard anything about it."

"I can see why the commander hasn't heard about it. The only communication he gets from other areas is from the transport guards. I doubt if they'd know unless they'd been attacked themselves or the rebels had taken down a complete town near here. News of a single raid is hardly going to be spread about. The commanders would probably instruct their men not to talk about it to the transport officers." She picks up her spoon and stirs her untouched coffee.

"So what have you heard?"

She hides her displeasure at using the abominable term slaves. "My slaves come from all over, including the east and west coasts. They've seen it happen, and I'm getting that report more frequently now than I did last year."

With a tilt of his head, Mr. Finke inquires, "Do you have any idea how close any of these attacks have been?"

"It's difficult to determine distance without accurate maps or familiar names of cities, but I'd guess about two hundred miles."

"You're saying that it's coming this way?"

Lily replies, "The first report was the closest, so I don't know that there's any indication of a direction of a movement. That the first report was closest is more the result of expanding communications. The raids appear to be multiple, unorganized attacks. One could pop up anywhere, anytime."

"What are your suggestions for meeting this possible attack on our comfortable way of life?" he states with emphasis on the word possible to indicated his assumption that she is creating the rumors for her own self-interest.

She cradles her cup in her hands and looks up at him. His coffee sits on the table, untouched. She smiles. "I'd rather find a nonviolent solution."

"Such as the co-op?"

She shrugs. "After all, it's just a name on the system."

"But a co-op implies that all members are owners."

"We could use corporations. A single individual can own a corporation, or two could run a partnership."

"Do you think these criminals are using the web to find masters and take them down?"

She shrugs and sets her coffee cup down, dissatisfied with the benign nature of their conversation.

He smiles. "Jackie, I can see how you've charmed the other masters here."

"Charming beats what I hear some master around here has been doing to exert his will over," she stops herself before saying the commander, especially since she would actually mean former Commander Somerton, "others."

He grins. "What have you heard?"

"I've heard about murder, threats, and such like."

"Who's doing it?"

She looks him straight in the eyes. "People are reluctant to say. Whoever's doing it has great power over his victims."

His mouth doesn't move, but his eyes betray the pride he feels at being called powerful. She keeps her expression neutral, ruing the fact that his dead-giveaway facial expression does not transmit over audio equipment.

"I hear you've had many deaths recently."

She skirts the issue to avoid a boldfaced lie. "The engineer who set up our water system is gone. Makes one wonder doesn't it?"

He smiles and pulls a knife from a crevice of the chair. Two men walk in from the hall and the guard by the door takes a step toward John. John and Brad, unobtrusively, heighten their alertness.

She leans forward with a look of concentration on her face, hiding her glee and pretending to be oblivious to the danger. She makes a carefully calculated reply. "Are you implying that you know something about an attack on us?"

He smiles. "How many of your slaves did I kill?"

Lily forces herself to frown. "I'm not going to give you the pleasure."

"Doesn't matter; this whole town is under my control. Commander Somerton is out of the picture thanks to Reggie, and Commander Williams is in the dark. He's all caught up in his efforts to rid the badlands of bandits. He thinks he can make travel safe; naïve neophyte!"

It is obvious to her that he has no plans to let her survive. She is certain he will confess anything now and craftily guides the conversation. "How many have you had to kill to establish your domination?"

He laughs. "Not many. Most of the barons are cowards. Mere threats have worked with all of them. How they became barons, I don't know. Let's see: I killed one officer to put the heebie-jeebies in Commander Somerton. Commander Blakely and Commander Tyler were both fellow thugs so no threats were necessary back then, just an occasional bribe. They both liked my girls. So add one to all your deaths."

She lifts her chin. "You're calling yourself a thug?"

He laughs then glares at her. "My best thug is missing."

"Your best one huh?"

"Yeah."

"What happened to him?" she asks.

"I don't know. We got up this morning and couldn't find him."

"I've lost quite a few like that. I suppose most of them ran away, except for those Mr. Barton kidnapped."

He admits, "I lost my mechanic too."

"Sorry. Having a mechanic is a necessity."

"I assume you killed both of these men?"

She looks him straight in the eyes. "I can assure you, we didn't kill any of your men."

"I know you've killed others."

She looks at him with wide eyes. "Who?"

"Reggie Patterson."

"It was an officer who shot him ... after he shot Commander Somerton and my bodyguard," she emphasizes.

John does not correct her. In the confusion of that day, apparently he and Lieutenant Jones are the only ones who know the truth. Even Linda appears to believe her husband is the hero, a crack shot, which is far better than the young lieutenant has ever done on the rifle range.

Mr. Finke chuckles. "Like I believe that! I was there! There's not an officer in the bunch who could've made that shot!"

He glares at her for a brief moment then states, "You also killed two officers during Commander Somerton's coup."

"That's true but—and this is a big but—one was a sniper, tasked with killing one of my men."

"Why'd they want to kill him?"

She rues having to confess on tape but perseveres, hoping for more damaging confessions from the ruthless baron. "They had no intention of taking him into custody, like they had been instructed to do."

"If you're such a law-abiding person, why didn't you turn over your errant man?"

"At the time, I didn't know he was errant. We were merely using him as bait to take down an abusive commander. I was merely assisting Commander Somerton at his request."

"What about the other officer?"

LYNN VADNEY

Lily replies, "He attacked one of our young women. I personally shot him when he took a shot at me. He missed my head by a mere inch."

"I'm not going to miss." He leaps up.

She leaps onto the coffee table. He swings the knife. She easily wrests it from his hand. John takes down the guard who lunges at him. Brad easily fells his two attackers with swift kicks. Four men rush in. The first two are easily dispatched by John and Brad.

Mr. Finke makes two feint moves then lunges at Lily. She collapses in his arms. He takes the knife from her limp hand and lets her slide to the floor, too startled to react.

John quickly knocks his third opponent unconscious then immediately kicks Mr. Finke in the hip and grabs the knife. "Mayday! Mayday! Call the helicopter!" He tosses the knife to Brad who has felled his fourth attacker, scoops up Lily, and rushes out the front door as the camouflaged men rush in the back to take custody of Mr. Finke and his personnel.

Dr. Martin Maxton releases the rear corner of the gurney and slows to a stop. The entourage of medical personnel disappears into the surgical suite with unconscious Lily. He watches the swinging doors until their gyrations come to a halt. He morosely steps over to the wall, leans his back against it, and slumps onto the floor. In sorrow, he lays his arms across his knees and presses his forehead on his arms.

John paces the hall, going no more than twenty feet in either direction. After six laps, he mutters, "I blew it. I let him kill her."

Max looks at Lily's bodyguard. "No, you didn't."

John stops and glares at him. "I know she's not dead, but I failed!" He jabs his chest with his thumb. "I don't know what he did, but I let him do it."

Max shakes his head. "Something else is going on."

John throws himself on the floor beside Max and leans against the wall. "What do you mean?"

"It's not an injury."

"Oh?"

Max remains silent, so John asks, "Then what is it?"

"Acute intracranial hemorrhaging."

358

"That could have happened in her sleep, couldn't it?"

"Maybe," Max replies then heaves a deep sigh. "I shouldn't have been on the helicopter."

"Why not? You're a good doc."

"She and I have been seeing each other."

"I know. But what's that got to do with it?"

"There's a reason why doctors shouldn't treat their families. We're emotionally involved."

John leans his head against the wall and stares at the blank wall across from them.

Max groans. "I should've checked her out before she went today."

"She looked and acted normal to me. What would you expect to find?"

"Nothing pointing toward an intracranial bleed, but maybe ... something ... something that would have concerned me enough to nix the plan."

"Here you go second guessing yourself. You've convinced me to quit kicking myself. Now you need to quit kicking yourself."

"But you're not the one who wanted to marry her," Max grumbles and lays his head on his arms.

THIRTY FIVE

Darla Smith sits in the media office in a newly refurbished building just off the town square. She is filled with apprehension as she watches a satellite image on her monitor. Two large vans are approaching the northwest checkpoint. She enlarges the image from the security camera at the checkpoint.

Three officers at the checkpoint are also watching the satellite image. Only the presence of several military men hidden in the brush dampens their apprehension. As the vans approach the last curve before the checkpoint, an officer minimizes the image, exposing the view from the security camera outside. Two officers draw their pistols and crawl under the counter beneath the window. The third adjusts his earpieces and turns up the volume on his music. He begins dancing within the confines of the small guardhouse, while inconspicuously watching the approaching vans.

Frank Smith's face is clearly visible on the monitor as he leans out the driver's window to read the sign instructing all drivers to pick up visitor passes. His blond hair is shaggy but clean and his handsome face is ruddy from exposure to the sun. The dancing officer picks up a handful of cards, leans over the counter, and begins counting the men in the first van.

Frank hopes the officer can hear him over the music. "Fifteen."

The officer nods, counts out fifteen passes, and hands them over. "Thanks."

The officer nods and pushes the button which opens the gate. After disbursing passes to the driver of the second van, he returns to his dancing until the two vans are out of sight. He then plops onto the floor and leans against the wall.

One of the other guards stands up, holsters his weapon, and teasingly but truthfully states, "Hard job huh?"

Frank slowly drives toward the town square, taking note that there are no cars or pedestrians on the streets. If it weren't for the guard at the checkpoint and cars parked at the clinic, he would think the whole town was deserted.

He slams on the brakes at the first note of loud music. The second van almost rear ends him. He hears tubas, trombones, drums, and trumpets playing a march—not particularly well—so he assumes it is a high school band, perhaps playing for some special occasion, which would explain the deserted streets. As the rebels listen to the approaching band, two young drum majorettes come into view from a side street. Frank then assumes it is an elementary school band but wonders why no one is lining the streets to watch the parade. When the first musicians appear, he realizes it is a high school band. He sets the brake and slides out of the van. He leans his slender, six-foot frame against the van to maintain a position of cover beside the van.

The majorettes stop fifty feet away. The band marches in place until the final chord. The smallest majorette grins. "Hi, Mr. Frank."

"Hello, Brianna. How are you?"

"I'm fine. You're going to have to put down your guns."

"Oh sorry, I don't think I want to do that."

"Do it anyway!"

Startled at John Thorne's loud demand from a nearby rooftop, Frank looks up. John is aiming a scoped rifle at his head.

"John, you wouldn't want to hit the children would you?"

"There's no chance that any of us will hit the children. Neither will any of you be able to get off a shot." John grimaces, thinking about the children walking closer than instructed. In fact, four hundred feet closer than instructed! That they allowed the children to participate at all is based on knowledge of Frank's character, that he will react with more restraint with children present. It was a gamble that several argued against, but the pleas of the girls won out.

"How many rifles are aimed at us?" Frank calmly inquires.

John replies, "How many passes do you have?"

"Oh," Frank mutters with sudden understanding of their new system of requiring the passes.

"Frank." He looks back at Brianna Pruett. "Kiowa and I want you to put down your guns."

Frank clears his throat. "Guys, it looks like we're going to have to comply. These girls can be trusted, and I'm sure John and his cohorts can shoot the buttons off your shirts." He gingerly removes his pistol with his left hand, lays it on the ground, and puts his hands on his head.

Brianna points at the media building. "Go halfway to that building."

As soon as the last man joins the line in front of the building, armed troops from nearby alleys swarm the two vans. Within seconds all weapons have been removed, and the rebels have been frisked and declared unarmed.

John lowers his weapon. "Okay, Frank. You can all put down your hands."

He grins, "Thanks." His grin disappears when Darla steps out the door and onto the steps.

She pulls her jacket together in the cool December breeze and despite her anxiety, pastes on a smile. "Hi, Frank."

"Hi, Darla. How are you?"

"I'm fine. Welcome to Somertonville."

"Why Somertonville? What happened to the name of Somerton?"

"When communications expanded, there was another Somerton and they'd had their name since the eighteen hundreds so we changed our name."

"What's going on around here now?"

"I'm the editor. I prepare the news broadcasts for the radio, and we're planning a TV station in the future."

"Where do you get your news?"

"We have secure communications worldwide through several reliable sources."

His eyebrows shoot up in surprise. "You have international news?"

She nods. "But we're very selective with what local news we air. Security is still a major issue in spite of our recent advances."

Henry Davis opens the door.

"Hi, Henry."

"Hi, Frank."

Robert Somerton rolls his wheelchair onto the wide top step and halts beside Darla. Henry goes back inside and shuts the door.

"Hello, Commander."

"Mayor."

"Mayor?"

"Yes, Frank. I'm the elected mayor of Somertonville."

Mayor Somerton turns to the band. "You kids can go back to school."

With obvious disappointment, Brianna Pruett and Kiowa Steele yell, "Bye, Mr. Frank."

Frank turns and smiles. "Bye, girls."

Before she turns away, Kiowa grins and adds, with great emphasis, "I'm just like Miss Lily!"

Frank watches as they lead the band away but quickly turns his attention back to Mayor Somerton and asks, "What happened to put you in a wheelchair?"

"Reginald Patterson didn't like his father's will and tried to take out the executors."

Frank asks, "What happened to Mr. Patterson?"

"We're not sure. It looked like a natural death, but we received a tip that Reginald could have done his old man in."

"I suppose he denied it?"

"He was already dead, so we didn't get a chance to ask."

"Did you grill the informant?"

"He's dead. He was one of the pirates on the northwest road, and they wouldn't surrender. We took them out over three months ago."

"You said executors. Did Reggie take out the other one?" Frank inquires.

"No, just winged her bodyguard."

Ralph Merrell hobbles out the door, stops beside Mayor Somerton, and leans on his cane.

"Hi, Ralph."

"Hi, Frank."

"What do you do now?"

"I'm police commissioner."

"I gather there's no commander anymore?"

Mayor Somerton answers. "Bruce Williams succeeded me as commander. He's now the police chief, and Brad Kraft is in charge of the military."

"Oh, so ...." Frank lapses into silence as his daughter walks out with an infant.

He beams with pleasure and pride. "Hi, Alex. Is that my grandchild?"

"No, Daddy; this isn't Daryl Ann. I'll bring her out after her nap."

Alex turns to her mother. "I fed her, but she's still fussy."

Darla takes the baby. Alex watches her mother soothe the infant snuggled against her neck then dashes inside.

Frank grins at Darla. "Did I get you pregnant?"

"Yes."

"I thought you said you couldn't?"

Darla's face flushes bright red at such a personal question in the presence of others. She clears her throat and softly mutters. "That's what I thought menopause was all about."

"What'd you name her?"

"This is Melissa."

"Melissa!" Frank exclaims. "Why'd you name our baby that?"

"Frank, our son is Frank Leroy Smith, Jr. This is Missy's daughter. You got her pregnant too."

He tilts up one eyebrow. "Why are you taking care of her?"

"Missy died in childbirth."

"Oh." He smiles.

"Frank! How can you smile?"

He grimaces. "I never did like that b …. Say, is Posse still around?"

She welcomes his leap to a less personal topic. "He died—of old age, I think."

"Sorry. I kind of liked that old coot. He had some odd ideas but was obviously very intelligent. Who succeeded him as president of the council?"

"Steve Williams."

"One of the whistling Williams brothers. I bet he makes a good one."

She nods as she thinks of the white-haired and extremely diplomatic gentleman with the ever-ready smile which frequently cuts across his black face.

Frank asks, "Are you mad at me?"

Warily, she looks at her husband while wondering which of his many nefarious activities he is thinking about. "For what?"

"For getting her pregnant." He lifts his palms up. "It was all her idea."

Darla frowns. "I know. She told me. It was always her idea, from high school on. Boy! What she told me about your high school days."

He mutters, "It probably wasn't all true," and looks down as if nervously searching the ground, apparently for his self-respect.

He looks up. "I guess it doesn't matter now that I'm going to be taken into custody, but I would like for you to visit me once in a while. You're the only one I ever loved, and I didn't intentionally destroy our relationship."

"You're not going to prison," Mayor Somerton interjects.

Frank looks at him with one eyebrow skeptically cocked.

Mayor Somerton forces a smile onto his face. "About three months ago, Jackie and her men took down the last depraved power baron who was oppressively exerting brutal power over the other barons. Since then we've established—"

Frank interrupts, "Who was that?"

"Mr. Finke who operated the water utility. Since then we've established a rule of law which includes democracy, and business enterprises have replaced the barbaric slave system."

Frank grins and exclaims with surprise, "Lily delivered on her promise!"

"There may still be some isolated incidents of brutality, but we're trying to root them out," Mayor Somerton admits.

Frank contorts his face into a scowl as he looks askance at Mayor Somerton. "Okay. You have democracy, but that doesn't explain why I'm not going to prison."

"The agreement we made to establish our new system included total amnesty for everyone for every prior act." Their heated debate flashes through Mayor Somerton's mind. It lasted three long, grueling days and was only resolved because two unfortunate incidents settled the worst of the sticking points. They found Matt Finke dead in his cell of an apparent suicide, and another especially brutal baron felt his life was in danger and voluntarily accepted a life sentence in prison instead of a precarious freedom amidst the freed slaves he had treated so inhumanly. "With one exception," he quickly appends.

"Murder?" Frank guesses.

Mayor Somerton shakes his head. "One person was exempted and is now in prison."

Frank grins. "So I'm not in trouble for ensuring Mr. Barton's eventual demise?"

Mayor Somerton shakes his head. "The more we found out about him, the more … the more … ah … well, you'd of had a strong defense in our new, fair judicial system. That arrogant man kept evidence of his crimes. We found it when we razed the hotel."

Frank tilts his head to the side. "When did this amnesty start?"

"Two weeks ago, when we wrote up the new laws."

"So I'm off the hook for Ricky too?"

Mayor Somerton raises his eyebrows. "You killed him?"

Frank nods. "He came after me and would've killed me. He was unarmed and pretty beat up but was still overpowering me, and I couldn't get the upper hand. I know you may not believe this, but some Asian dude, well skilled in martial arts, appeared out of nowhere and took him down. It took him three seconds flat. I checked Ricky's pulse and told the guy that Ricky was dead and to get out of there and I'd take care of it. He disappeared as fast as he appeared then I broke Ricky's neck and carried him up and threw him down the cliff."

"We didn't see your footprints."

"I wore Ricky's shoes. They were a little small but I managed it without permanently injuring my feet. Coming down barefoot was a bit painful, but what I was actually referring to was that with Ricky's past surely I'd of had a good defense for taking him out too."

Mayor Somerton shakes his head. "We couldn't prove any of his crimes; he couldn't be identified in any of Mr. Barton's videos. He was one wily man."

Frank puts his hands on his hips and grins. "But he was *il Drago* and had about twenty known hits up his sleeve."

Ralph abruptly slams the tip of his cane on the steps. "So that's where I knew him from: the Dragon, a suspected hit man for one of those mobs back east. I knew he looked familiar. Now I remember. We received an APB on him when he disappeared several years ago."

John calls out, "How about that officer?"

Frank looks up at John. "I gather that you found him."

"Yeah, nametag and bullet hole in the back of the head."

Ralph scowls at Frank. "I assume you have an explanation."

"I hope it's more than just that the road pirates prevented traveling to another town," Mayor Somerton adds.

"He was Commander Tyrant's assassin," Frank replies, using their nickname for brutal Commander Tyler. "He was sent to take all of us out, but he underestimated Lily. He begged me to shoot him; he said the other commanders would return him to Commander Tyler and that he would be tortured. The commanders apparently always returned escaped officers to each other."

Ralph sighs. "So you accommodated him?"

"No, I didn't," Frank asserts.

"Then who did?" John demands.

"I made him do it." Frank looks at the unbelief on their faces and grins. "I gave him one bullet, and stood there aiming at him, so he couldn't shoot me."

With his voice infused with a tone of interrogation and a hint of disbelief, John queries, "How could he shoot himself in the back of his head?"

"He used his thumb. I hope you noticed the entrance and exit holes. If I'd done it, the angles would have been different."

Frank's claim is unbelievable, but knowing that an argument would be futile, Ralph states, "I can accept that." He also knows that Frank is wily enough to think ahead and set up a scenario that vindicates him. He apparently did that when he was in high school. Melissa suspected that he killed two classmates who had hurt her and apparently felt enough guilt herself that she needed to clear her own conscience by talking about it. Lily tried to get her to talk only to her counselor, but when Melissa mentioned her suspicions, Lily checked with Frank's mother and determined that the known facts confirmed Melissa's basic story. Both boys died; one died in a car crash with Frank driving, and they found the bones of the other many years later when the lake dried up during a severe drought. However they will never be able to prove that Frank is guilty of the officer's death and amnesty applies anyway.

Frank politely inquires, "Are we free to go?"

"Frank." He turns his attention back to Darla. "We'd like you to stay. Brianna, Kiowa, Thai, Lizzie, and the others all pleaded with us to give you a chance. We fixed up that hotel just past the square for your guys."

"What about me? Do I get to stay with you? Or are you too mad at me?"

She tilts her head to one side. "We'll see."

He holds his palms up. "I promise to be faithful from now on."

Mayor Somerton interjects, "Frank, you have amnesty here but if any other jurisdiction asks, we'll have to extradite you. Understand?"

Frank nods.

"We'd also like to place each of you somewhere, all of the ones who want to stay in this area anyway. Frank, you can work with the engineers, and we'll have to find out what each of your men can do. We'd like to place each one in a job he'll like. The reason we insist upon this is that when we let Spencer Blakely and his men out of prison on the amnesty program, they refused. Within days most of them were back in prison on new charges and their victims were pretty disgusted, so now we have some people here who are fed up with the amnesty program. Please let us place you. We don't want any more debacles sowing dissent."

Frank looks at his men. They nod. One man speaks for the group. "We'd really like that. We'd like to see our wives again. Frank said he sent them to this area. We're tired of this fruitless rebellion, and we appreciate the amnesty. We'll try our best to be law-abiding citizens from now on. We were all law-abiding citizens before the civil unrest."

Frank turns back to the Mayor Somerton. "Okay, we're all agreeable. Do we get a week of rest before we have to start to work?"

"Sure."

"I have another question before this meeting breaks up," Frank requests. "I noticed on our way in that the town appears vacant. In fact we haven't seen anybody for about the last hundred miles."

"We didn't want your little band of rebels to hurt anyone before you got here. That would've destroyed your chances for amnesty and disappointed the girls. We used our new security system to clear all civilians from your route. We use it to warn us of the roving road bandits and trap them, and you are a roving band of bandits. You just haven't been working in this area, so we're not going to imprison you."

"You're not lying to me, are you? You really have a free and democratic and open society around here?"

"Yes, Frank. People wouldn't trust the authorities if they're allowed to lie, so we put it in our law that all officials are not allowed to purposefully and deceitfully lie."

Frank cocks his head to one side. "You're kind of nitpicking with those terms, aren't you?"

Mayor Somerton clears his throat. "No one wanted to be prosecuted for making a mistake."

"Another question," Frank states. "I noticed a scaffold on one of the churches on my way into town. I suppose you have freedom of religion too?"

Ralph chuckles in amusement. Frank looks at him then at the amused expression on Mayor Somerton's face.

"Yes, Frank. We do have freedom of religion and several groups have begun repairing the buildings. It'll be a while before any of them are ready for occupancy." Mayor Somerton looks at the ground then back at Frank. "Did you know Lieutenant Littlefield was a priest?"

"I didn't even know he was a lieutenant. So he's Father Littlefield now?"

John laughs. Frank looks up.

"They call him Father Abraham. The kids even have a song. It really amuses him," John states.

Uncomfortable with the topic of religion, Frank teases, "Hey, Navy guy. Are you missing the sea? Do you think you'll be going back soon?"

"I'll have to stay here even if all the other Navy guys go to sea." John grins. "My wife has a thriving political career."

"Is she on the town council?"

"Regional council."

Frank raises his eyebrows.

Mayor Somerton chuckles. "Yeah, Frank. The entire region has stabilized from Perkins up north, where Senator Wood has been elected to the regional council, all the way to the port."

With his eyes still on John, Frank inquires, "I guess you at least get to work in your field?"

"Yeah, we've had an exciting time the last few months."

"I guess you enjoy target practice too?"

John grins and nods.

Frank asks, "Who's the best shot?"

"None of us has ever beat Jackie."

Frank laughs. "I could beat her. If you guys will let me handle a gun, I'll challenge her."

Ralph states, "Frank, I never saw your pattern of bulls'-eyes as tight as hers. Not even that guy from out of town, who beat you at the last skeet shoot, had such a tight pattern."

"Okay, where is she? I'll challenge her."

"They laminated her target. It's their benchmark for everyone to try to attain. No one's done it yet," Ralph says.

"It was probably a fluke," Frank asserts. "She probably couldn't do it again."

Ralph sighs. "I saw her do it almost every time. I used to practice against her, hoping I could beat you in the skeet shoot."

"I've had plenty of practice this last year. I challenge her," Frank repeats since no one appears to be taking his challenge seriously.

With a very soft voice, Darla says, "Frank."

He turns toward her.

"Lily's dead."

Surprise flushes his face. "Who got her?"

"The doctors said it was natural causes."

"What happened to all her enterprises?"

Darla replies, "She wrote a will. They're all set up as autonomous entities with every person being given a proportionate share of ownership depending upon how long they'd been here. Alex, your mom, and I were each given one-third of the shares for your service. She even counted the thirty gallons of gas you contributed. She paid close attention to that Scripture[1] about masters treating their slaves justly and fairly, so left quite a legacy in more ways than one."

Frank tilts his head. He appears at a loss for words.

Darla fills the silence. "That's what a good leader—"

"What I was thinking is that I have a wealthy family?"

Darla keeps her smile subdued. "Everybody that she rescued is wealthy. All of her businesses are booming. Well ... there were a few who sold their shares for a pittance before the market had time to stabilized and we knew what our shares were really worth. Others, like Susie, invested wisely."

"I'm going to miss her."

Darla scowls. "But you were always at odds with her."

Frank grins. "I like a challenge; she was always a challenge, but she did a great job."

"You called her incompetent," John interjects.

Frank looks up at John. "She was an incompetent secretary. That doesn't mean incompetent in other areas. Part of her problem as my secretary was her defiant attitude, but that trait was what enabled her to defy the brutal society. She was a leader who irritated, but she was a leader who kept focused on her goal and that carried all the way to a plan for succession. Too many businesses and even governments fall

---

1 Colossians 4:1

immediately upon the leader's death. It is impressive, let me emphasize: *very* impressive, that she set in motion a viable system."

SINKING SAND; Grab the Pole

Book one of the Compound Series: The Story of U.S. Navy Seal John Thorne

"**First Novel:** Author Lynn Vadney has written a Christian fiction thriller, *Sinking Sand; Grab the Pole,* the first book in the Compound Series. The story features Navy Seal John Thorne in a world thrown into chaos by terrorism." —Glenn Dromgoole, author, book columnist

"Thanks for the great book. As a former soldier, I had complete insight into a story about a U.S. Navy Seal. Thank you for such a great read. I'm looking forward to the next book in the series." —Matthew Estrada

"Sinking Sand; Grab the Pole is set in a future America, torn apart by terrorism, and it hits close to home with chilling accuracy. I would classify the unique genre combination as a Christian Fiction/ Mystery/ Dystopian/ Espionage novel. The author has managed to seamlessly merge Christian Fiction with genre fiction.

"The book follows former U. S. Navy Seal John Thorne who, after the collapse of the United States, has been bounced between prisons and slavery. He has planned escape after escape to search for his family. Fighting bouts of PTSD, he has to decide if the compound is safe or if it is the cover of a far more dangerous and sinister brainwashing cult.

"With the cliffhanger ending you'll be glad that the sequel is already out!" —Marianne S. Parker

"The two strong points in *Sinking Sand; Garb the Pole* are the strong, intriguing plot and the well-developed characters. This great adventure story is worth reading.

"Worldwide terrorism attacks toppled the world governments, followed by a few months of total chaos in which greedy, ruthless men would stop at nothing to gain power. Over time, a new society was born: a society built on a ruthless slave trade.

"When U.S. Navy Seal John Thorne, is turned over to baroness Jackie Schwartz, his first thoughts are only of escape. He must decide if the compound really is safe as everyone says or if he and everyone else are being brainwashed into a cult." —John Black

Comments: "A real thriller, a grabber from page one." "I'm enjoying your book, and I'm impressed with John's love for his wife." "Kept me interested, but I kept wanting to tell your protagonist to 'open his eyes'." "Really enjoyed it and hated to put it down. I can't wait until the next one." "The ending was a complete surprise; I didn't see that coming."

NOT *the least bit* SORRY
Book two of the Compound Series: The Crisis Ignited by Frank Smith

"**Christian fiction:** Novelist Lynn Vadney has published her second Christian novel in The Compound Series — *Not the least Bit Sorry.* The story is set a couple of years after terrorist attacks have disrupted society around the world. Frank Smith, an engineer in Texas, hasn't seen his wife and daughter since the chaos began. He hopes they are still alive and that he will have a chance to rescue them."

—Glenn Dromgoole, author, book columnist

"Espionage, intrigue, and nail-biting action make *NOT the least bit SORRY* a fun read.

"It follows the compound's top engineer Frank Smith. He's been doing the best he can to get by while his family is missing but then his wife turns up and she has the worst news possible. Their teen daughter has been enslaved by one of the most morally abhorrent slave barons in the area, Barton. Frank knows it is only a matter of time before she is abused, and he must rescue her at all cost.

"The leader of the compound has her hands full between near-miss assassinations and continuing her quest to bring families back together in this new lawless America. There are corrupt slavers everywhere and what's worse, even the slice of law that governs this part of our post-terrorist country is corrupt. Lily, 'aka' Jackie, has her hands full trying to put right the world that has so much wrong in it.

"I felt my heart stop for a moment when Frank attempts a daring rescue. I don't want to give too much away, but if you loved the first book, you will not want to miss out on this new thrilling chapter."

—Marianne S. Parker

Comments: "I've already read it; I couldn't wait. Book one left me wanting to know what was going to happen." "Your novels are good books for Christians. There are no bad words or anything offensive and a great story. They even include Scriptures." "wow! good book, how do you think of all of it? I had to wait until I knew I had time to devote to reading because I wouldn't be able to put it down and I was right—looking forward to book 3 now." "What great plots. Where do you get your ideas?"

The FULL WEIGHT of THEIR SURVIVAL

Book three of the Compound Series: The Trials of Lily Schwartz

"**New Novels:** Novelist Lynn Vadney has published the third novel in her Compound Series. *The Full Weight of Their Survival* focuses on the efforts of Lily Schwartz to protect a small group of exiles after worldwide terrorist attacks have created chaos everywhere."

—Glenn Dromgoole, author, book columnist

"*The Full Weight of Their Survival* is book three, but it is not necessary to start with the first two books in the series. The books follow a theme with sometimes overlapping time periods but from a different point of view. When a later book covers an event which has been covered in a prior book, the later book adds to it by telling it from a different prospective. However, I believe the character development from the earlier books would be missed if the books were read out of order; it is the large variety of strong characters which drive the plot.

"The books are imaginative, well written, intriguing, and easy to follow. They are fast paced and full of action. At times good luck seems a little too good, but it does bring the story more quickly to the more intriguing parts.

"This book explains how Lily became a slave master and leader of the compound and gained her official status in the society."

—John Black

"*The Full Weight of Their Survival* was an excellent book. Once I started reading, it was hard to put down."

—Anita Love

Comments: "I'm enjoying this book. Lily is my favorite character, and it's great to have a book about her." "That's good writing. I enjoyed all three." "I'm amazed at the plots you come up with. Don't see how you do it, but it makes great reading. I enjoy your novels."

STEPHANIE'S ANGUISH
Book four of the Compound Series: The Tragedy of Baby Lucas

"Series Continues: Author Lynn Vadney continues her post-apocalyptic novel series with the fourth book, *Stephanie's Anguish: The Tragedy of Baby Lucas,* dedicated to kidnapping victims and their families."
— Glenn Dromgoole, author, book columnist

"If you enjoy books with a strong theme of intrigue and suspense, I am sure you will not be disappointed with this book or any book in the series. Also the main characters continue to develop throughout the series.

"On the overall timeline this book covers a few months which took place just prior to *Sinking Sand; Grab the Pole.* It starts with the kidnapping of Lucas Thorne and follows the details of how the residents of the compound handled it. This book gives some additional insight into Mr. Barton and his compound. However, it also covers many minor events which were happening during this time period, often leaving the kidnapping as 'the eight hundred pound' gorilla looming in the background. This is one reason the books are so interesting; there is a lot going on, not just one topic at a time.

"Knowing generally how the kidnapping turns out is not a problem. The intrigue and suspense are still present as the story works toward that ultimate ending, plus the overall intrigue and suspense inherent in the new society carries throughout the series."
— John Black

"The author has a talent with words! I get involved in the story and just don't want to quit reading. I have to wait until I have time to read the whole book because they are so hard to put down. Looking forward to book 5!!!

"The timetable at the front of the book tied the books together in the series."
— Sheri Watson

Comments: "The characters in this series seem so real; I am going to miss them when the series ends. They are like family. I know them so well, I almost expect them to walk in. The story is like real life with sorrow mixed with the good times."

Reviews used by permission. Some have been edited for length and typographical errors and approved by the reviewer. Comments are from personal communications. Those recalled from memory may be paraphrased.

INFORMATION

Check the author's Facebook page or LinkedIn page for updates on the expected publication date of Lynn's next novel, as well as e-book and i-book editions of the Compound Series and updates on the availability of the novels at bookstores and on websites. The Desert Willow website has ordering information for the Compound Series and other publications of Desert Willow Publishing.

BOOK REVIEWS FOR CHRISTIAN READERS

Do you find it difficult to search out good books to read in the plethora of novels available? Check out some of the book review websites and Facebook Fan pages.

Cowgirl Book Reviews on Facebook was created by an avid reader. It is a forum for sharing readers' opinions on both books that are jewels worth considering or fiascoes to avoid. The fan page is geared toward Christian readers or any avid reader of fiction. Nonfiction titles may also be reviewed. Feel free to post your own opinion of any book you have read for the benefit of others. No specific format is required; just state, in your own words, your opinion of the book.

www.desertwillowpublishingonline.com

www.facebook.com/LynnVadneybooks

www.facebook.com/CowgirlBookReviews

www.linkedin.com
[search for Lynn Vadney]

For more information or comments, email Lynn at:
lynnvadney@gmail.com

CPSIA information can be obtained
at www.ICGtesting.com
Printed in the USA
FSOW01n0243170615
7953FS